# SABBATICAL

*A Romance*

# John Barth

PENGUIN BOOKS

Penguin Books Ltd, Harmondsworth,
Middlesex, England
Penguin Books, 625 Madison Avenue,
New York, New York 10022, U.S.A.
Penguin Books Australia Ltd, Ringwood,
Victoria, Australia
Penguin Books Canada Limited, 2801 John Street,
Markham, Ontario, Canada L3R 1B4
Penguin Books (N.Z.) Ltd, 182–190 Wairau Road,
Auckland 10, New Zealand

First published in the United States of America by
G. P. Putnam's Sons 1982
First published in Canada by
General Publishing Company Limited 1982
Published in Penguin Books 1983

LIBRARY OF CONGRESS CATALOGING IN PUBLICATION DATA
Barth, John.
Sabbatical.
I. Title.
PS3552.A75S2   1983   813'.54   82-22309
ISBN 0 14 00.6619 5

Printed in the United States of America by
R. R. Donnelley & Sons Company, Harrisonburg, Virginia
Set in Baskerville

The author gratefully acknowledges permission from Warner Bros., Inc., to quote
lyrics from "Sailing Down the Chesapeake Bay" by Havez & Botsford. Copyright
1913 by Warner Bros., Inc.; copyright © Warner Bros., Inc., 1971. All rights
reserved.

*for Shelly*

# I

*The Cove*

# KEY

There was a story that began,
Said Fenwick Turner: *Susie and Fenn—*

Oh, tell that story! Tell it again!
Wept Susan Seckler. . . .

Graybeard Fenn would be happy to give it another go; we* have fiddled with our tale through this whole sabbatical voyage: down the Intracoastal in the fall in our cruising sailboat, *Pokey, Wye I.,* from Chesapeake Bay to the Gulf of Mexico and across to Yucatán; all about the Caribbean, island-hopping through the mild winter of 1980; and in May through our first long open-ocean passage, from St. John in the U.S. Virgins direct for the Virginia Capes, Chesapeake Bay, Wye Island, the closing of the circle, sabbatical's end. But before he can invoke his dark-eyed muse, sole auditor, editor, partner, wife, best friend, Fenwick is interrupted for two nights and a day by

*A STORM AT SEA,*
*in which we lose an important navigational chart*
*and very nearly our boat and lives.*

Though we do not court it, we are no strangers to foul weather. Grizzled Fenwick—bald, brown, bearded, barrel-

---

*This *we,* those verses, Susan's tears, these notes at the feet of certain pages—all shall be made clear, in time.

chested—is a sailor since childhood; sunburnt Susan, sharp and shapely, since our marriage seven years ago. In our shallow Chesapeake, where the chop is steep and sea-room tight, we stay in port when the forecast threatens. But even your fair-weather sailor will now and then get caught out and must batten down, plot position, reef or furl, aim for open water, and cross fingers. We have weathered squalls enough, especially in the Gulf and the inky-blue Caribbean, to be reasonably confident of stout *Pokey* and ourselves; we have been prepared for heavy weather in the long haul home.

But ours has proved till now a disarmingly easy passage: fast reaching across the tradewinds watch after watch, riding the Antilles Current through sapphire days and diamond nights; a bumpy brisk beat across the Gulf Stream, where current and breeze lock horns; then reaches and beats and runs by turn as the Temperate winds swing around their highs and lows. Some clouds, some showers, some sun—we have sailed bare-assed and turtlenecked by turns—but no storms, even as we give wide berth to the Place That Sank Two Thousand Ships: Cape Hatteras and environs. Now we are, by our best reckoning, one day from landfall: after five days of northing up the 70th meridian, we have turned the corner and are slipping west along the 37th parallel toward Hank and Chuck,* close-hauled on a light southwesterly and in no rush. We want daylight upon our transit of the large-ship lanes that converge at the Bay's mouth; what's more, the barometer has dropped since morning, and the forecasters are changing their tune: frontal winds from the north, gusty at times.

After sundown we see against broken clouds the reflected glow of city lights from below the horizon ahead: Virginia Beach, Fenn reckons, and hopes we're far enough offshore. The name catches Susan's breath; brings tears to her eyes.

---

*Susan's nicknames for Capes Henry and Charles, at the entrance to Chesapeake Bay.

Fenwick knows why.* The wind dies; stars blink out; *Pokey* slats and wallows in the swell. We see the running lights of distant freighters.

To cheer his saddened friend, Fenn hugs her hard and speaks his opening verses into her hair; Susan sniffs back tears and responds with hers into his jersey. She's off watch, but has lingered in the cockpit to see what's what, weather-wise, and to avoid the seasick-making cabin of a wayless boat in ocean swells. Cut in the diesel, Fenn considers, to bring our bow into the seas and check the roll? Drop the main and furl the big genoa till the breeze returns, to spare their chafing against the shrouds? Okay, he decides, and consults the compass over Susan's shoulder, wondering the while what words best follow Once upon a time.

*Blam! Blooey!*

### A DIALOGUE ON DICTION,
*three days later, safely at anchor in Poe Cove, Key Island, Virginia†*

SUSAN: *Blam!? Blooey!?*

FENWICK: Damn straight. That storm blew up like a sawed-off simile.

S: Like . . . ?

F: Like nothing I never saw before, Suse. Had my effing finger on the starter-button, I did, and the next thing I know I'm arse over tincup down the companionway. Thought I'd blown the effing lid off somehow. I remember wondering, Did we leave the effing valve open on the propane tanks after dinner? I never *saw* a gale blow up out of a calm like that, a dry gale to boot. No lightning, reader; no thunder; no rain; stars out—then *blam!* Unprecedented, in my not inconsiderable experience.

S: Blam.

---

*As shall the reader, presently.

†And reconstructed here from Fenwick's notebook for our story, where Susan sounds sometimes more pedantic than she ever ever is.

F: Blooey.

S: In the *Poetics*, Aristotle distinguishes between lexis and melos—"speech" and "song"—and discusses them separately, since in Attic drama there really were both spoken dialogue and choral songs. In my sophomore Elements of Fiction course we use Aristotle as our textbook, but I combine lexis and melos into the general heading of Language. Under that heading we consider all questions of tone, style, diction, the effective management of dialogue, the strategic deployment of metaphor, and what have you.

F: That seems sensible to me, Dudu.*

S: Most critics would agree, I believe, that a certain range and variety of diction—not only as between the speech of various characters in a story, to help differentiate and characterize them, but also within the prevailing narrative voice itself—can be both refreshing and strategic: a change of rhetorical pace; a humanizing shift of perspective. I think of old King Lear, one moment railing in grand style against the world's hypocrisy, the next mumbling "Pull off my boots: harder, harder: so." As Edgar puts it, "Matter and impertinency mixed."

F: Edgar Poe?

S: Edgar the Earl of Gloucester's son, in Shakespeare's play.

F: What a teacher you are, Suse. No wonder your students fall in love with you.

S: Thank you.

F: Count me in with you and Aristotle on that diction business.

S: But *Blam! Blooey!* You're turning our story into a comic book!

F: That wind nearly turned it into a one-liner. Even without the effing Coast Guard's almost running us down. Oy oy oy: now we know why they're called Coast Guard cutters.

---

*A Creole term of affection, picked up recently by the speaker in Guadeloupe, French West Indies.

S: So: after a splendid four-thousand-year tradition of sea-voyage fiction, from the Egyptian papyrus of the Shipwrecked Sailor, said to be the oldest story in the world, through Homer and Virgil and the Arabian Nights and Defoe and Melville and even Edgar Poe to Crane and Conrad, all with their big set-pieces of tempest and shipwreck—what has suggestively been called the Overwhelming of the Vessel—*we* proudly enter the narrative lists with Blam and Blooey.

F: Damn straight we do. Those chaps all had *warning:* Odysseus, Aeneas, old Sinbad there. Robinson Crusoe. And Whatsisname, that windbag of Conrad's.

S: Marlow.

F: Right. And that pirate fellow in the *Decameron*; you left him out. Landolfo Ruffolo, his name was. Piled up his carrack on a sandbar in a gale off Cephalonia.

S: Fenwick Turner, you amaze me.

F: I used to read books in college days. Those blokes all had a little warning, for Christ's sake; an effing foreshadow or two, you know? But us: *Blam! Blooey!*

S: And all these effing thises and effing thats: I won't have it, Fenn. This is our story, that I love; it's our love-and-adventure story, that ought to speak and sing and soar and make us laugh and cry and catch our breaths et cetera, and you're X-rating it before we even get to the sexy parts.

F: I'm mucking up the melos, you think.

S: Damn straight.

F: Hum. Did you know that it's a generally accepted fact about twins that we tend characteristically to regressiveness, one manifestation of which is a readier slipping into turpiloquence than is the case with other people?

S: Turpiloquence.

F: Effing dirty language. We tend that way.

S: One may acknowledge the tendency without accepting the regression. Do I* turpilocute? No.

---

*Susan too is a twin.

F: You weren't knocked arse over tincup into the bilge.

S: You're evading the issue, Fenwick. Anyhow, if I remember correctly, and I do, that tendency you invoke applies more to opposite-sex than to same-sex dizygotics. I won't have it, honey. Between ourselves I've gotten used to it, but there'll be no effing effings in our story.

F: You insist. In the face of verisimilitude.

S: Eff verisimilitude.

F: I'll make you a deal: I'll take out every effing in the script except the ones in this passage, and those I'll soften to "effing."

S: I can live with that.

F: But blam and blooey stay.

S: Must they?

*F: My finger was on the effing starter-button! I was wondering what to say to you after *Susie and Fenn.* Then *Blam! Blooey!*

S: Take that, Joe Conrad.

F: Meanwhile, Professor, we've blown our suspense. Who knew till now we would survive that gale?

S: On with the story.

*Blam! Blooey!* From calm to half-gale in so sudden a wallop that Fenn is pitched down the companionway, mightily bruising arms, ribs, and legs, but luckily breaking none, only lacerating his scalp a bit. For a stunned second he wonders what exploded: our engine fuel is diesel, but we cook with propane, whose vapors have been known to sink like gasoline's into bilges and turn pleasure boats into bombs. Then he feels *Pokey* roll almost to his* beam-ends, sees Susan clutching a stanchion for dear life, hears her shriek his† name, and realizes as he yells back that what has blown up is the weather. He struggles up into the cockpit and

---

*Our vessel is 33′4″ long, cutter rigged, tiller steered, diesel auxiliary powered, and male.

†Fenwick Scott Key Turner, age 50, son of "Chief" Herman Turner and Virginia Scott Key of Wye Island, Md.: former United States Central Intelligence Agency officer, more recently (until 1978) a consultant to that agency; author of *KUDOVE*, an exposé of the CIA's Clandestine Services

roller-furls the genoa while Susan at the helm sheets in the main just enough to bring the bow a bit to windward. We are five minutes into the storm, and already steep seas are building. Fenwick scrambles below, where all is chaos, to don life-vest and safety harness, never mind foul-weather gear yet; then scrambles back to the dangerous work of going forward to reef the main. Though he is clipped to a lifeline, Sue's relieved when the job is done; she angles *Pokey*'s bow into the seas with the club jib staysail while the main luffs. So rapidly does the wind increase, by the time Fenn returns to the cockpit and trims the mainsheet, we are overpowered and must shorten sail again. He delays by luffing until Susan is slickered, jacketed, and safety-harnessed; then he goes forward a second time on the pitching deck, in the howling spray, soaked and chilled, to reef the club jib and double-reef the main. Now we have a measure of control: with Susan safely harnessed at the helm and *Pokey* temporarily holding his own, Fenn goes below to towel himself quickly, suit up in foul-weather gear, and secure loose items in the cabin before rejoining his frightened friend.

We have precarious leisure now to exclaim together at the sudden violence of the gale: *Blam! Blooey!* The anemometer hangs at thirty to forty knots and gusts higher, but stars can still be seen between the scudding clouds. We survey our damage: Fenn's head-cut is bloody but superficial; our self-steering vane seems kaput; we have shipped a bit of water, and discover that our automatic bilge-pump switch has died, though the pump still operates. Everything on deck and aloft appears secure. We begin, if not to relax, at least to breathe more normally.

But the seas are rough and growing; the wind shows no sign of abating; minding the helm is white-knuckled work.

---

division (CS); currently on unpaid "sabbatical leave" between careers. But his wife of seven years, Susan Rachel Allan Seckler, B.A., Ph.D., age 35, associate professor of American literature and creative writing at Washington College, Chestertown, Md., on sabbatical leave at half salary for the academic year 1979/80, shrieks only "Fenn!"

We are both too shaken for either of us to go below and leave everything to the other. For the next thirty-six hours we remain in the cockpit except for short excursions to the head, to the radio direction finder, or to the galley for a quick fix of chocolate, cheese, raisins, water, rum—whatever can be swigged and swallowed in a hurry. We spell each other hourly at the tiller and catnap against the cabin bulkhead, under the spray dodger.

By dawn the bilge-pump motor has gone the way of its automatic switch; fortunately we have a manual backup system. The self-steering linkage is stripped and unusable; the radio direction finder operates only intermittently; the VHF masthead antenna has worked itself loose. Minor nuisances all, since we're near the end of our ocean passage. Of more concern is a certain fitting at the mast spreader, to which a starboard lower shroud is attached: surveying the rig by daylight, sharp-eyed Fenn observes that this fitting has developed a tiny, alarming wobble. On our present tack, no immediate peril; the tension is on the portside shrouds. But the slack that permits the wobble may also work the fitting loose: should it let go, so might the mast on any other point of sail, and this is no weather for going aloft to attempt repairs.

Our other concern is our position. The wind is too northerly, and our last estimated position too close to land, for us to run before the gale without fear of piling up on the Outer Banks. On the other hand, we are too near the big shipping lanes to risk heaving to and going below to ride out the storm. Hence our toiling north-northeast on the port tack under triple-reefed main and double-reefed jib, to preserve our sea-room without being carried too far off-shore, while keeping an eye out for freighters. But during the day, though the sun perversely breaks through from time to time, the wind slightly increases: while the Norfolk weather station reports thirty knots with gusts to forty, our indicator indicates ten and twelve above that. We run the engine slowly to keep our bow from falling off the wind. We are weary, wet, and duly (but not unduly) scared, especially as the long day ends and our second stormy night approaches. We have seen no freighters since mid-afternoon. We daresay we have a proper offing; we wish we knew how far south of the 37th parallel our leeway has carried us.

At dark, Susan straps herself into the pitching galley to make hot thermoses of coffee and bouillon and a supply of peanut-butter sandwiches. Fenwick, at the helm, decides we'd better have Chart 12221, Chesapeake Bay Entrance, at hand in its clear plastic case as well as its southern neighbor and the smaller-scale ocean chart. Since Susan is busy with both the galley stove and the RDF beside it, Fenn breaks a rule* and extracts the chart from between two others in order to replace it on top. He steers with one foot, keeps an eye on the steep black growlers, and holds a penlight between his teeth.

Brava! Sue charms the RDF into confessing a positive, unequivocal bearing on Chesapeake Radio Beacon 290, dot dash dash dot at 300°; she calls it out, then twists the antenna to find a second bearing for plotting a fix. But the gadget dies just as Fenwick, bending to look for that beacon with his purse-mouthed light on the half-secured chart, inadvertently lets *Pokey*'s bow fall ten degrees off: the next sea strikes us more abeam than its forerunners, flings Susan against the galley sink (another green-and-purple hip), obliges Fenn to grab a stanchion with his chart-case hand and the tiller with his right. Chart 12221 flaps off toward Kitty Hawk. Groaning Fenn slaps the chart-case under his left buttock to secure it, returns the bow quickly into position to meet the next wave, removes the penlight from his mouth to shout Shit, there went Twelve Two Twenty-one; you okay, Suse? and hearing she is, to announce loudly over his left shoulder to the black Atlantic, the eye of the wind, the teeth of the gale: You win, Poseidon! We're going to heave our ass to and get some rest!

---

*The rule: do not remove nautical charts from their cases while on deck in rain or breeze, except in greater emergencies than this.

Susan wonders Is it safe? Fenn hopes so. It is *not* safe, anyhow, to wear the both of us into exhaustion: look what happened to Odysseus, in very sight of home. What shall we do for a chart? Fenn hopes he knows the approach well enough to manage without it; we can always follow the freighters in; then we've got the Cruising Guide. We switch on the masthead strobe, upon which, with the radar reflector, we depend to avoid being run down in the shipping lanes: it flashes thrice and dies, perhaps short-circuited somehow by that loose antenna. Fenn complains to Poseidon: Overkill!

Very well, then, we must return to two-hour watches: Fenwick will take the first, to adjust and monitor the heaving-to and look out for ships while Susan sleeps, at least rests, below. No stars tonight; the wild air is filled with spray. We kiss seriously through the companionway, and Sue retires to the leeward settee berth wishing she were religious. Fenn sheets the reefed main in hard, backs the jib, lashes the tiller hard over, and adjusts the engine RPMs for just enough thrust to keep the bow at a safe angle to the seas. Once he gets it right, he sits with his back to the wind, in the lee of the cabin, and judges by the compass whether we're holding our position.

The view astern is terrifying; the view ahead more so. But with occasional fine tuning *Pokey* holds position, and at last the wind begins slowly to abate. By midnight, when Fenwick relieves Susan for his second watch, the anemometer is averaging thirty. We shake out one reef from each sail and cut the engine. The silence is welcome, and the boat tracks better under sail alone. Off-watch at 3 A.M., groggy Fenn is drowsing in his berth and trying to recall the main features of Chart 12221 when Susan shrieks his name again. He piles up the companionway ladder and finds her wrestling to unlash the tiller and free the jibsheet: before she can do either, a fair-size ship thunders across our bows, so close that its wake broaches us. Fenn has just time, before the next wave rolls *Pokey* on his beam-ends like that first blam-blooey blow, to catch sight of the diagonal red-orange slash of a

Coast Guard cutter; by the time we're righted and back on course, the ship has disappeared.

Sue's in tears. Fenn's heart slams; he is too shocked to curse. Unharnessed, he very nearly went over the side in that knockdown. Why did the cutter not veer to starboard and cross our stern? Why did it not now return to determine our safety? For that matter, how did it manage not to remark us on its fancy radar and avoid the near-collision? Hands shaking, Fenwick calls angrily on Channel 16. No reply: perhaps our VHF has joined the list of casualties? The best excuse we can imagine is a poor one: that the cutter was rushing full speed to some rescue so dire that even a near-ramming had to be ignored. More likely, a green watch officer simply missed our blip on his/her radar screen and charged on without ever seeing us.

By dawn our gale has blown itself out and is replaced by a mild breeze from the south-southwest. In time the seas subside. With our last strength we unreef the main and the jib staysail, unfurl the genoa, and settle down for an easy reach across the swells. However spent and shaken, we have much to be thankful for: we are alive and physically intact, as certain people dear to us are not;* the rigging-strain is still safely on the port shrouds, and upon climbing the mast-steps to inspect that wobbly tang, Fenn finds he can simply tighten its bolt; the RDF, with much coaxing, yields another reasonable bearing on that Chesapeake beacon, which we find in the binoculars soon after sunrise and salute with a weary kiss. From there it is a mere fifteen or twenty nautical miles west-northwestward to the threshold of the Bay: the combination bridge and tunnel between Hank and Chuck. At 1000 hours we raise the Capes themselves: Sue's fast asleep. Ninety minutes later we're at the bridge, in a thicket of freighters, tankers, and naval craft from Hampton Roads. Fenn wakes his wife to say hello to the U.S.A. and relieve him at the helm.

Hello, America. It is in fact not unstirring to reenter our

---

*As shall be shown.

republic, in particular our home waters. But beyond the
wring-out of that storm, we have grave matters on our
minds, personal and impersonal. To mention only the
lightest of them: Susan Seckler, while reasonably patriotic—
her field, we remember, is American lit—is no fan of the
Department of Defense in general, a bleeding chancre on
the nation's economy in her opinion, or of the U.S. Navy in
particular, which she regards as a mammoth self-promoting
pork-barrel at least as much concerned with its own per-
quisites as with our national defense. Its gargantuan presence at the mouth of the James River, off to port, chills her
liberal blood. And Fenwick Turner, mild conservative but
ardent conservationist, though he still hears *Victory at Sea*
music at sight of a murderous gray missile-frigate or an
unbelievably looming aircraft carrier, knows enough at
firsthand about governmental waste, incompetence, feather-
bedding, time-serving, and covert skullduggery to regard
those vessels as ruefully as he regards the river they issue
from: the noble James, birthplace of white America, poisoned from head to mouth perhaps forever with insecticide
dumped knowingly and illegally by Allied Chemical.

   We attempt a joke involving the name of that insecticide,*
the name of our boat, and our respective famous alleged
ancestors,† after whom *Pokey*'s name takes its meaning, but
we are too tired.

   Even so, we decide over lunch not to put in at Hampton
Roads, but to press through the muggy afternoon to the
mouth of York River, another twenty-five miles or so to the
northwest, to a familiar anchorage in Sarah Creek. It too has
certain disagreeable associations,‡ but what has not?‖ And it

---

   *Kepone.
   †E. A. Poe and F. S. Key.
   ‡It is not far from ISOLATION (at Camp Peary), a CIA training
ground for both its own recruits and foreign personnel, some of whom
are trained there without ever knowing they're in the United States.
   ‖We have not forgotten Susan's tears at mention of Virginia Beach.

is at once airy and snug enough to ride out a storm in, should another come through. We can reach it by dusk and lay up there to rest and make repairs before moving on.

Susan takes the tiller. Fenwick strips, sponges his body, pins our wet gear onto the lifelines to dry, tidies up belowdecks, opens all hatches to ventilate the cabin, drinks a warm beer (Corona, from Mexico, stocked in Tortola, B.V.I.), and turns in to sleep, instructing Susan to follow the well-marked York River Entrance Channel buoys—a red and black couple every nautical mile—till she reaches the last pair, and then to wake him, unless she needs him earlier.

She does, but, exhausted herself, realizes the fact belatedly. Six nautical miles northwest of the bridge-tunnel, in the middle of the broad Chesapeake, two equally well-buoyed channels diverge in a quickly widening Y: the port arm, York Entrance Channel, leads to York River; the starboard, York Spit Channel, which drowsy Susan mistakes for our chartless course, soon swings northward up the Bay. By the fourth pair of buoys she sees that we are far off course; with the binoculars she finds many markers off to port, where we surely ought to be—red, black, black-and-white—but there is no sorting them out without Chart 12221.

Oh, Fenn, she groans, I've got us lost! Back in the cockpit, bleary-eyed and apprised of the situation, he checks his watch: *We* got us lost. But we have some daylight left. Let's cut over to westward and look for the other channel buoys.

We wonder what that little island is.

The breeze is failing. We'll give it half an hour and then crank up the diesel if we're not doing better than four knots. Somewhere in the crotch of that Y ought to be York Spit itself: a drowned peninsula with enough water over most of it for all but very deep-draft sailboats. In the distance we see a lighthouse, surely York Spit Light, at the end of that shoal. Here and there on the western horizon are sundry feature-less points of land, and between them the mouths of tidal estuaries. New Point Comfort, Mobjack Bay, the Guinea

Marshes, York River itself—all are over there somewhere.
Once we locate that left-hand aisle of channel buoys, it
should lead us safely where we want to go. But the afternoon
is waning, and what *can* that low-lying island be, just behind
what we're calling the York Spit Light? Neither Fenwick's
memory (only approximate for this part of the Bay) nor the
stylized end-paper maps of our Cruising Guide to the
Chesapeake show an island on York Spit. Can we have got
turned around altogether?

Susan berates her negligence; Fenwick his, for losing that
chart in the first place and for not remembering in the
second to warn her of this Y, which he himself had
forgotten. A large trawler-yacht, crewed by browned and
bearded, salty-looking young men, passes close to port:
*Baratarian II, Key I., Va.* As Fenwick waves, Susan calls on
Channel 16: *Baratarian Two, Baratarian Two:* this is sailing
yacht *Pokey*, sailing yacht *Pokey*, right next door. Come in,
please, *Baratarian Two.* Over? After a few seconds' silence
she repeats the call, adding illegitimately* This is important,
*Baratarian:* we lost our chart in last night's storm, and we
need a fix and a harbor for the night. Over.

This time *Baratarian* crisply and properly directs us to
switch to Channel 68, where before we can ask more specific
questions we are informed by a gruff female voice that the
lighthouse ahead is indeed York Spit Light, with York River
to port and Mobjack Bay to starboard. That the nearest
secure overnight anchorage is Key Island, shoreward behind
the light. On the far side of that island we will find a cove
marked by a lighted stone jetty: entrance is straightforward,
leaving the jetty to port; we can anchor in twelve feet
anywhere inside. Going ashore is not recommended—
snakes, mosquitoes, poison ivy—and as the island is otherwise uninhabited, no supplies are available. But the holding
ground is good, the anchorage secure in all weathers. Over
and out.

---

*Channel 16 is for calling and distress-messages only, not for
conversation.

Key Island? We've never heard of it. And logical Susan
wants to know how an uninhabited island comes to have a
lighted stone jetty and be the home port of *Baratarian II*. It
must be uninhabited, we decide, when our obliging infor-
mants are at sea. That seems to be where they're headed, at a
faster clip now that our conversation's done: the trawler has
opened her throttles and is speeding oceanward.

Well: Key Island it shall be, only an hour away and no
need to use the engine. We are relieved, and mildly charmed
by the coincidence.* The strain slips from us; ice, charts, and
other supplies can wait: let's get the hook down for the first
time since St. John and go to sleep. In lusty baritone Fenn
sings:

> There was a story that began,
> Sang Fenwick Turner: *Susie and Fenn.* . . .

And smiling Sue replies in clear contralto:

> Sing me that tale from beginning to end!
> Cried Black-Eyed Susan to her dearest friend.

He removes his eyeglasses, which hang round his neck on
a lanyard of black marline, and leans out over the cockpit
gunwale to make certain we've cleared the first of a sudden
thicket of crab-pot buoys between the lighthouse and the
island. We have. As he ducks back under the starboard
lifeline, it sweeps the hat from his lotioned and perspiring
pate to the near-calm surface of the Bay; there it floats
bottom-up like a limp black Frisbee beside the bobbing buoy,
already yards astern.

My hat, says stricken Fenn.

Your beret! cries Susan from the helm.

Mi boina, Fenn laments, accent on the bo. Oh, Susannah!

Quickly and calmly Susan orders Get the boat hook. Gybe-
ho. Watch the boom. She puts the tiller hard over, uncleats
the mainsheet, and pays the boom out smoothly once *Pokey*'s

---

*Fenn's parents' place on Wye Island, *Pokey*'s home port, is called Key
Farm, after his mother's maiden name.

stern has crossed the light breeze. Never mind the club jib; thank God the starboard shrouds hold. Steadying the tiller then between her thighs, she sheets in the main, trims the genoa for beating, and threads us back through the pots to where Fenn's hat has settled awash. Specs on, Fenwick leans out from a midships portside stanchion, boathook poised, like a whaler emeritus squinting in the long light.

Got it, he says, harpooning deftly as we slide past. Whoops. The wet felt spins off the hook; his second stab sinks it. Shit.

Stay put, says Susan. Gybing again. She shoves the tiller hard a-starboard and brings us around on a port reach, winching in sheets as the sails flop over in the humid air.

A touch more to port, Fenwick requests from the other side of the deck. Never mind the floats. We overrun two without fouling either: each clunks under our keel and skeg and pops up astern. I see it: starboard, starboard. Let the sheets go now. Perfect. Ah.

He spears again—the black disc floats suspended half a foot under—and succeeds only in pushing it deeper, out of sight, before our leeway sweeps it under the hull.

Another pass? asks Susan, sheets in hand, as we luff.

Nope. Adiós, dear boina: last and most valued of my several head-coverings.

Hasta la vista, hat, Susan murmurs, and puts us back on course for Key Island, around whose edge we now espy the promised jetty. Fenn replaces the boathook, trims the sails, kisses her hair.

Good try, Suse. Perfect handling.

Would you take the helm now, please?

He does, heart full: should she ever need to manage singlehanded . . .

What will you do about keratoses? she wants to know.* I'll make a bandanna, says Fenn; I'll make a burnoose. Susan minds the depth-sounder now as we work in toward the

---

*Fenwick's scalp and forehead are susceptible to these sun-induced lesions. Hence the hats, which he sometimes loses overboard.

jetty. Thirty-eight feet, thirty-one, then suddenly seventeen, sixteen, sixteen. The island, though low-lying, is more woods than marsh, apparently houseless and dockless. The jetty, which we now leave dutifully to port, is a new, expensive looking affair: reinforced concrete protected on both sides by heavy stone riprap, with a sturdy green beacon on the outboard end. The tide is out, but we have at least eight feet of water all the way into the cove—*Pokey* draws five—and twelve to fourteen once inside: generous by Chesapeake standards.

The cove itself is snug but roomy, lined with oaks and pines, unoccupied but for a noisy flock of crows and one quiet blue heron. High wooded banks to the west, the weather side, where those crows say hello and change trees; sandy beach and some marsh grass to the east, where that heron watches impassively. In short, an ideal anchorage and perfectly empty.

We are damned if we have ever heard of a Key Island on York Spit in the lower Chesapeake. We cannot imagine who built so formidable a breakwater to shelter an undeveloped cove: a multimillionaire, we reason, would have a dock or two, and a mansion fronting the open water and backing the cove: we see the ideal site for it as we slide in on the last of the breeze and set the anchor with the last of our headway.

We kiss—our ancient custom upon reaching safe harbor— and look about us, grateful, curious, tired.

It is May's last Friday. The water is warm for spring; the air too, and close. No sea nettles yet in the Chesapeake to sting us, and but few mosquitoes; a bit of daylight still at 2030 hours. Bone-weary as we are, we find ourselves excited to be securely anchored again in the U.S.A., and in so handsome and secluded a spot. We strip for a short swim in the long last light: salty Triton and salt-teared Naiad. It is not our sweet Caribbean; on the other hand, no sharks come into these shallows at night to feed. We call the place Crow Cove, after our welcoming committee; then when Fenwick, floating, wonders whether Key Island is named after his alleged anthemic ancestor, we rename our anchorage Poe Cove after Susan's, and in acknowledgment of its mysteriousness and those birds.

Back aboard, we spray each other's skin with bug repellent—Fenwick busses Susan's bruise—and sip the (warm) champagne reserved to celebrate safe passage. In the brillig cove, the cork-pop echoes like gunshot; the quarter-liter that ejaculates overboard we offer to Poseidon, who without quite doing us in has kindly shown us what he can do. Still naked, we make languid love* and a cold supper, over which we review the storm and enjoy that Dialogue on Diction. After clean-up we settle awhile in the dewy cockpit, to watch the moon and sip Barbados rum with air-temperature tonic. We shall scout the island tomorrow, make what storm repairs we can, and look for a place to reprovision before continuing up the Bay. We are out of ice, low on fuel, and down to two or three daysworth of food and water; we need spare fittings, too, and Chart 12221 to locate Key Island and Poe Cove.

You're my island, sleepy Susan murmurs, kissing her husband's chest. She lays her head there briefly in the salt-and-pepper fuzz, then sits up: to hear his heart beat breaks her heart.

He kisses her lap. You're my cove. Puts an ear to her tidy belly as if to listen for a heartbeat there.

Don't. Let's turn in. We do, in our separate berths: Sue's in the main cabin, Fenn's forward.

Anchored sailors sleep lightly. In the calm small hours we hear splashings near the hull. Bluefish feeding? Otters? Fenwick's watch glows 3 A.M. Are those voices in the distance now? More splashes, heavier but farther off, and a muffled exclamation, female, as if people are scuffling in the shallows.

Fenn? He's already climbing the companionway with the

---

*Lazy Susan lies supine, too tired to pivot on Fenwick's lap. The force of her orgasm therefore takes her by surprise: it feels as if a flock of frightened cohunks liquidly lifts off inside her.

portable spotlight, which he shines around the shore. Sue climbs up behind; hugs him for warmth. Nothing. She shivers in the dew. We retire, but find ourselves restless: those odd noises in this odd place, together with the novelty of riding at anchor, still as a building, and being in bed at the same time, no one on watch.

I miss my Canada geese, Susan says huskily in the dark, recalling how they honked in by the hundreds as we left the Chesapeake last fall. Where are my cohunks?

Where's my boina? Fenn laments from up forward. I miss my boina, and my boina misses me.

Our poor boina. Jesus, I'm tired.

My faithful boina. Me too.

You were wearing that boina when we first remet, on Cacaway Island in Nineteen Aught Seventy-two.

I'd been wearing it by then a dozen years already.

Those years don't count. Where was I?

If I tell you the story of my boina, it will come back to me.

The story? Or where I was?

Mi boina.

How so?

That's another story. First comes

## THE STORY OF FENWICK TURNER'S BOINA.

In the late fall of Nineteen Sixty, when you and Mims\*
were fifteen, and Count† and I were thirty, and Dwight

---

\*Miriam Leah Poe Seckler ("Mim," "Mimi," etc.), Susan's sororal twin, their mother's delight and father's despair: a college dropout and Peace Corps alumna once briefly imprisoned in Tabriz and Teheran by SAVAK, the then Shah's secret police, and by them briefly tortured with not one but two electrical devices—perhaps the only U.S. citizen to have experienced that misfortune. Now freaked out in Fells Point, Baltimore, as shall be seen.

†Manfred Herman Turner ("Count," "Manny," "Fred"), Fenwick's fraternal twin and Susan's common-law stepfather, later her brother-in-law: a senior officer in the CIA's Clandestine Services division (code-named KUDOVE). Missing without a trace since March, 1979, from the cutter *Pokey, Wye I.*

Eisenhower was winding up his presidency, Marilyn Marsh*
and I had been married for a decade already, and Orrin†—
who's as old now as I was then!—was nine.

What a way to start a story.

Try to sleep. Your stepfather had long since gotten over
our rivalry for Marilyn Marsh in college days and had taken
up with your mother.‡ He had also long since joined the
Company and was on his way to becoming the Prince of
Darkness. Count's activities at that time were along some axis
between Washington, Lisbon, and Madrid, though his specialty was still Soviet counterintelligence, and he was often in
Vienna, Helsinki, New York City—

Sometimes he was even with Ma and us in Baltimore,
Susan says. Okay, I'll be quiet. What do you suppose those
noises were, hon?

Damned if I know, Suse. Damned if I know. So: I had
taken my little B.A. in political science and my little M.F.A.
in creative writing, and I'd tried for seven disagreeable years
to make a go of it in D.C. as a free-lance journalist and night-
school teacher, all the while privately still aspiring to be a
capital-W Writer. I had placed, as they say, half a dozen
artsy stories in little magazines, but my M.F.A.-thesis-novel,
much rewritten over the years, had not as they say found a
publisher.

*Marilyn Marsh Turner (no known nicknames, but always called, by
her first husband, by her complete maiden name), 49, Fenwick's wife from
1950 until their divorce in 1970. Subsequently remarried, redivorced, re-
remarried, re-redivorced, she has re-reassumed, to Fenwick's and Susan's
mild chagrin, her first married name. Cf. p. 311.

†Orrin Marsh Turner ("Oroonoko"), 30, son of Fenwick and Marilyn
Marsh, currently doing post-doctoral research in molecular biology in
Boston (where his mother has also settled) and, with his wife, expecting
Fenwick's—and Marilyn Marsh's—first grandchild.

‡Carmen B. Seckler (middle name unknown; Carmen says it's Buzz
off, buddy), age circa 55: part Jewish, part Gypsy; girlhood survivor of the
earliest Nazi concentration camps, in which the rest of the B.'s were
murdered; widow since 1949 of a movie-theater-chain owner, Jack
Seckler, by whom Susan and Miriam; common-law wife since 1951, and
now presumably common-law widow, of Manfred Turner, by whom Gus
(see note pp. 32–33). Currently kerflooey in Fells Point, Baltimore.

I think I hate this part.

Bear with it. My official careers weren't doing particularly well, either: no newspaper syndications, no job offers from either the good magazines or the good colleges. The shine, as they say, was off my marriage; MM had secretaried all those years to help pay the bills, but she was bored with her job. She wished she had either trained to be something more interesting or married somebody more successful. Genug.

As they say.

Nineteen Sixty we declared our Wanderjahr: one might even say our sabbatical. It was also a test. We sold our car, withdrew our savings, subleased our apartment, took Oroonoko out of school, and went off to spend the winter in the south of Spain, where I was to get a *real* novel written at last. Neither of us had been out of the country before; the plan was to live cheaply till spring somewhere along the Costa del Sol, which hadn't yet been turned into Miami Beach; then to make a camping reconnaissance of western Europe, whereof I would keep a useful writerly notebook for future reference. Then I'd either come home to a new career as a capital-W et cetera or else give up that ambition for good and take a full-time newspaper job.

One observes, Susan can't help observing, that you were as innocent in some respects as you were poor.

Yup. No wonder I wasn't making it in political journalism. But my hat.

Your hat.

In Nineteen Sixty, one still went to Europe as often by ship as by plane. We crossed to Le Havre on the Holland-America Line's *Nieuw Amsterdam*, three very green Americans, very excited, very impressed, and not a little nervous about going to live under no auspices whatever in a country we'd never seen and knew not one inhabitant of. A few nights out, the crew put on an international cabaret: after the Dutch and the English and the French and Germans and Italians had done their things, three Spaniards from the galley played guitars and sang Spanish songs. In that

Holland-America Line context, they sounded more exotic and, um, impassioned than they'd have seemed aboard the S.S. *United States* or in a D.C. restaurant; I found myself overwhelmed by the realization that Spain was not just a state of mind but a *place*, for Christ's sake; not just a backdrop for Don Quixote and Don Juan and bullfighters and flamencos, but a real place with trains and taxicabs and plumbers and schoolteachers, and I was taking my family there blind, on a shoestring budget, to find a town to hole up in while I tried to write a fucking novel, excuse me—and what in the world were Marilyn Marsh and Oroonoko going to do with themselves while I did that, and why in hell hadn't I gone into law or medicine or something real and profitable instead of for Christ's sake *writing?*

In short, a blue funk. The North Atlantic was real, Spain was real, Generalissimo Franco and the Guardia Civil were real, and they all made *me* feel awfully imaginary. MM's nerves were on edge too, it turned out: that night we had a terrible, exhausting row.

Your boina.

Mi boina. In Le Havre we picked up the VW Beetle we'd ordered in the States and loaded our gear; then we drove down through France and across the Pyrenees as quickly as possible, staying where Mister Frommer told us to in *Europe on Five Dollars a Day* and actually managing, the three of us, on ten or twelve, including car expenses. The weather was too raw and cold for camping; our idea was to get south and set up housekeeping as soon as possible, to beat the hotel and restaurant bills; sightseeing would have to wait till spring and summer. Our chief activity in Paris, for example—first visit for both of us—was shopping for a small camp-stove. We weren't sure the Spanish *had* camp-stoves, and we would need one later. . . .

All fairly depressing to recall; but the fact is, once we were on the road our morale improved, though I went on being somewhat dazed by all that foreign reality. Nothing like being behind the wheel to perk an American boy up.

Marilyn Marsh, I should say here, had neither French nor Spanish; I could read both imperfectly and speak neither well; I was too busy coping with customs officers and currencies and road maps and traffic and concierges and restaurant waiters to make writerly entries in my famous notebook.

Not till Madrid did we take a breather. Manfred was there for a few weeks doing the Devil's work under embassy cover, and we'd agreed to let him show us the city for three days. More exactly, Marilyn Marsh and Orrin and I did the *Guide Michelin* stuff during the day, with advice from Manfred on priorities, while he did whatever dark deeds he was over there to do—in fact, I believe he was surveilling a certain KGBer who was surveilling our Air Force's secret training exercises to help put down hypothetical left-wing anti-Franco uprisings in order to protect our air bases in Spain. At the end of each afternoon we'd meet him at our hotel—the Europa, just off the Puerta del Sol, a good tip from Frommer—and then spend the evening together in town.

We were as impressed with my brother as we were with the Prado and the Retiro park. Count was so *easy* in that city, and knowledgeable about it; he dealt so quietly and efficiently with Madrileño cabbies and maître-d's and shop-keepers, bargaining and joking with them, keeping Oroonoko entertained with Siege-of-Madrid stories while he pointed out Hemingway locales to me and steered MM away from the tourist traps to where the real shopping bargains were. Handsome Manfred: my worldly twin! Already at thirty he could've done the same in half a dozen European capitals and every major city in North America. Oh, Count!

Marilyn Marsh was wowed. She'd chosen me over Manfred in part because she'd understood that he was more of an adventurer than a husband. But my career had not moved along, whereas if you forgot what Count was really doing—Marilyn Marsh was fairly good at that—he looked like a rising young foreign-service officer. And since she *had* a husband now, Manfred's adventurer aspect was a plus instead of a minus. He could have had her for the asking there in Madrid; she told me as much, about half seriously. Count didn't ask.

On our last day there, we bought my boina, in a shop that sold nothing but Basque boinas. The most practical hat in the world: windproof, weatherproof; you can wear it every season of the year with any outfit from black tie to bathing suit, and you can carry it in your pocket when you're not wearing it. Count said the Basque boinas last longer than French berets or boinas from elsewhere in Spain. Mine is, in fact, immortal. I put it on there in the store; I wore it to the restaurant that night; I wore it for the next twenty years until this afternoon. And I'll wear it again when it floats back to me, or I to it.

That last evening in Madrid we ate at the Commodore, on the Serrano at the Plaza Argentina: five forks in the *Michelin*. It was the most splendid meal we'd ever eaten in our lives by a factor of several, for about six dollars a head. Unbelievable: I wish I had a piece of Roast Suckling Pig Commodore in my mouth right now, as I tell the story of my boina. I was proud and envious of Count, even more because he shrugged off MM's flirtation without hurting either her feelings or mine. Exactly half seriously, over the last brandy of the meal, he invited me to think about joining the Company if things didn't work out with the Muse. There were plenty of interesting desks besides DDP,* which he knew I disapproved of. I might be interested to know that a couple of his fellow officers published spy novels—it was not a bad cover—and that a couple of minor U.S. writers were on the Company's tab as sometime agents. But he hoped everything would click for us down in Andalusia. He himself was impatient to finish his work in Madrid and get back to Carmen and Gus† and you girls.

---

* Deputy Director, Plans: a.k.a Clandestine Services (CS), cryptonym KUDOVE.

† Gus Seckler-Turner ("Mundungus"), son of Manfred Turner and Carmen B. Seckler; younger half-brother to Susan and Miriam; radicalized in the late 1960s by that latter semi-sibling, not then freaked out, and by

Well: the only thing that clicked that winter in Andalusia was my portable Olympia, and it to no avail. We found a cheap little villa to rent near the beach between Torremolinos and Fuengirola: comfortable enough by local standards, but designed for Spanish summers. Tile roof, tile floors, stucco walls, no heat except a tiny fireplace where we burned olive wood, which is a bit like burning rocks. The temperature hung in the low fifties, indoors and out; raw winds blew off the Mediterranean; our floors and walls sweated. The other villas in the little compound were vacant. We tried to be excited about being in Europe, but what we were in was a sarcophagus, and a bind. Orrin wished he were back in school; Marilyn Marsh wished she were back in her office; I wished I were back in my study at home. I was too distracted by the foreign reality of everything to concentrate; anyhow my novel wouldn't come together. It was supposed to be about the politics of political journalism—I knew something about that subject—but it had taken an autobiographical turn and was more and more about a frustrated writer and a marriage strained by its first reciprocal adulteries.

But never mind that. My problem—other than insufficient imagination, weak dramaturgy, and the amateur's typical lack of a real handle on the medium of prose fiction—was how to tell any sort of American suburban middle-class story in a country that rubs your nose in your basic moral principles every day, as our life in the U.S. of A. didn't do from one year to the next.

Exempli gratia: Caravans of Gypsies used to pass along the road behind our villa, and the women would rummage through our trashcans in the rain. If they saw us working in the kitchen, one of them would rap on the windowpane and

---

his mother, not then as confirmed in her kerflooeyhood, in Carmen's own opinion, as she has become since Gus's disappearance—and presumable torture and death, in Chile, in 1978, where he had gone covertly in 1977 with a group of anti-Pinochet exiles in Washington, D.C., followers of the late President Salvador Allende Gossens—and his father's more recent disappearance from or into Chesapeake Bay.

point to her mouth and her baby—they all had babies. We'd open the window and give her an orange, or some bread. Then the other Gypsy women would come running with *their* babies, and bingo! It was either give all your goods to the poor, as Jesus orders, or start saying no to presumably hungry people. We decided to say no to presumably hungry people. But sunny Spain, romantic Andalusia, doesn't let you off that easily. The first gitana we said no to—I mean shook our heads at, through the window—promptly fished an old moldy orange-rind out of our garbage, spat on our windowpane, and stuck the rotten rind first into her own mouth and then into her baby's. When we drew the curtains, she laughed at us—a brassy tenor laugh that I can still hear—and then discussed us in Gypsy Spanish with her baby for several minutes afterward, standing in the raw rain, of course. Poor Oroonoko was especially upset; none of us had seen or done such things before, but he'd never *heard* of such things. After that we kept the curtains closed whenever we were preparing food. ¡Buen provecho!

So. If we'd been art historians on a grant to count the gargoyles on every village church in Spain, at least we'd've got our gargoyles counted. But to go to another country under no auspices and with no contacts, not to vacation but to write a novel about life back home, and to say to that country, in effect: Be interesting and inspiring; redeem this wretched weather, our financial sacrifice, the disruption of our normal lives—that would be an unreasonable demand to make of Eden itself. Orrin and Marilyn Marsh huddled around the olive fire in the mornings and read books from the English lending library in Torremolinos while I shivered at the typewriter in our bedroom. In the afternoons we did the marketing and looked around a bit, but it was the wrong season for exploration. Most evenings it was back to the old olive fire again. Not surprisingly, the Turners began to quarrel—always mutedly, for Orrin's sake, since there was no real privacy in that cottage.

The hat. Along with the fish-and-garbanzo chowders that

MM stewed on our Parisian camp-stove when the kitchen stove died, as it often did, my favorite thing about España was my boina. Because of the chill, I wore it indoors as well as out; I doffed it only to take our ninety-second showers and to sleep in our damp and narrow and noisy bed. Thus December, January, and most of February. We were impatient for spring to come, so that we could get out of the Villa Dolorosa, as we called it, and on the road: camping, we knew from experience, would be one hell of a lot more comfortable and interesting. But the wet winter dragged on and on. Then, one Saturday late in February, I first lost and recovered mi boina, as follows:

High up in the Sierra Bermeja, which rises behind the Costa del Sol west of Málaga, is the ancient town of Ronda, dear to Cervantes, Goya, Hemingway, and Joyce's Molly Bloom, who mentions it in her famous soliloquy. Ronda's chief attraction, other than picturesque streets and the oldest bullring in Spain, is a spectacular sheer gorge called the Tajo—Spanish for "cleft"—which in fact cleaves the town as if Paul Bunyan had split it with his ax. I remind you of Pilar's story in *For Whom the Bell Tolls*, of the Republicans' capturing her village from the Loyalists during the Civil War and forcing all the local "fascists" to run a gauntlet leading to a certain cliff: they were clubbed en route and then pitched over the edge. Pilar describes their individual deaths—some were pounded to jelly; some were ushered untouched to the cliff and forced to jump—and then she remarks that that was the most dreadful thing she'd witnessed in her life—until three days later, when Franco's soldiers retook the town. Hemingway doesn't name the place, but Count had told us in Madrid that that town was Ronda, and that cliff the famous Tajo, which we shouldn't miss.

So we piled into the VW and drove down the coast past Marbella—all high-rise hotels now, but still a quiet little resort in Nineteen Sixty—and then turned inland for the long climb into the sierra. It was a fine cold morning; Marilyn Marsh was menstruating and edgy, but we were all happy to be going somewhere, and much warmer in the car than we ever were in La Villa Dolorosa.

On the far side of Marbella we were stopped by a Guardia Civil. We'd seen those chaps everywhere, of course, standing guard on empty headlands with their olive uniforms and Napoleonic hats and automatic rifles, as if a new Moorish invasion were expected any minute, and the sight was always more or less unnerving. One remembered their bad press from Hemingway and George Orwell, and it was plain enough that twenty-five years after the Civil War, they were still there to remind the survivors which side had won. It was not agreeable to be halted by a Guardia Civil, weapon in hand, in the middle of an empty Spanish street.

This one was a moonfaced fellow with a thin mustache and five o'clock shadow at nine A.M. He asked us, sternly, where we were going. Ronda. ¿Americanos? Sí. ¿Turistas? While Marilyn Marsh fished for our passports, I told the chap as levelly as I could that we would be turistas in Ronda, sí, but in Spain generally we were visitadores. I had some trouble with the "would be," but the distinction seemed important to our dignidad. The Guardia waved away our passports and pointed his automatic rifle at an old man standing on the curb nearby: his father, he explained, who lived in Ronda and was waiting for the next bus, an hour yet. Would we mind delivering him there.

His manner was, uh, courteous but unsmiling. I said sure—much relieved, though there was little enough room in the car. Marilyn Marsh murmured in English that she hoped the old fellow didn't have bugs. He was in fact shabby but clean, a wizened little man with half a dozen bad teeth and no good ones, wearing an old double-breasted gabardine and a white shirt buttoned to the neck, with no tie. All the way up to Ronda—only two or three dozen miles, I guess, but most of them in second gear and a lot of them in first—he asked Oroonoko questions in Spanish about America, which I translated and answered when more than sí or no was required. The usual: sí, we make a lot more money over there than you-all do here, maybe twenty times more; on the other hand, a loaf of bread costs us twenty times as much; on the third hand, there are undeniably twenty times more of us touring your country than there are of you touring ours, et cetera. Marilyn Marsh, who had about had it with Spain, declared to him in cheerful English that the two occasions on which she'd seen sunny Andalusians laugh were, first, when part of a building under construction in sunny Málaga had collapsed upon a sunny parked automobile unfortunately vacant, or the joke would have been even funnier to the laughing crowd of idle sunny bystanders, and second, when a five-year-old boy snitching a ride in the rain on the tailgate of a donkey-cart in sunny Torremolinos had been pointed out to the carter by the laughing crowd of idle bystanders and by him kicked brutally across the sunny calle to the idle feet of the laughing crowd of sunny et ceteras. No hablo americano, the old man muttered to Orrin. But it redounds to your national credit, the then Missus Turner went on in effect—she'd been reading up on reciprocal atrocities in the Guerra Civil—that the sunny Spanish could never be guilty of an Auschwitz, for example. In the first place, your ovens would have died, like our kitchen stove, instead of your Jews, whom you'd got rid of anyhow in the sunny Fifteenth century, no? And in the second place the whole idea of extermination camps would've been too impersonal for your exquisite Moorish tastes. Much more agradable to push folks off a cliff one at a time into a gorgeous Mediterranean sunset, as you did near Málaga—three hundred, was it, or three thousand? Or to rape and then kill a convent-full of nuns in the manner of the saint of their choice—was that Barcelona or Valencia?

Young Oroonoko, I could see in the mirror, was shocked to the socks. Our old man smiled and shrugged and nodded, embarrassed for MM's sake, I believe, that she persisted in speaking gibberish. He remarked that the mountains hereabouts were rich in water, also pine. All the way up he bummed Marlboro cigarettes from Marilyn Marsh—we all smoked in those days—and flicked the ashes into his left hand. Even the butts he would spit on and save in his left hand: the backseat ashtray, he told Orrin in Spanish, was too clean to use. On the outskirts of Ronda he asked to be let out, offered to pay us the bus fare, thanked Orrin politely when we refused his money, and then casually emptied the contents of his left hand onto the car floor, wiping his palm on the seat-cover as he bid us adiós.

Ronda. Mi boina. It was freezing up there, and a big wind off the Serrania de Ronda made it unpleasant to be outdoors. Nevertheless, in the main square was MM's sunny congregation of idle bystanders: all male, mostly dressed like our old man, faces out of Goya, all staring at us, none smiling. Ours was the only car in motion; it took a certain courage to park and get out; indeed, we decided to have a look at that Eighteenth-century Plaza de Toros first, to collect ourselves. Orrin spat on Kleenex and swabbed the soiled seat-cover: his mother explained, in answer to his direct question, that she had been rude to the viejo because his country appalled her. That what she had said, though admittedly impolite, was not a tenth part of the whole truth. That the old man's business with the cigarettes was almost certainly not retaliation but a very Spanish combination of solicitude and insouciance, such as led to defecating on the stairs of cathedral campaniles, but only on the landings, and always off to one side.

The boy was quiet. I remarked that it had been a long season. The old bullring abutted the Tajo; we learned from the guide, to my discomfiture and Marilyn Marsh's grim gratification, that not only had the Republicans and the Loyalists thrown each other into that gorge, but the Catholics, Moors, Visigoths, Vandals, Romans, Phoenicians, Ligurians, Celts, Iberians—and no doubt the odd Hapsburg, Bourbon, and drunken tourist—had also been Tajo'd, as for that matter had been, routinely for some two hundred years, all the bulls and picadors' horses killed in that Plaza de Toros. Orrin was wide-eyed; MM was freezing. Let's get the hell home, she said, thirty minutes after our arrival. It sounded awfully as if she meant the U.S.A.

I insisted we at least drive through the rest of Ronda and walk out on the Puente Nuevo across the gorge. She consented, for Orrin's sake, but herself remained in the car. Oroonoko and I walked out over the great stone arches of the bridge, looked around at the splendid ring of mountains and down into the amazing, breathtaking Tajo. I held his hand tight: it *had* been a wretched season, and a wretched (though mostly sunny) day. The wind slammed through the gorge. I leaned over the bridge rail, awed as much by the violent history as by the scenery, and tried to remind myself that the voltage between two people, the pressure-cooker of a single human heart, is as fit stuff for literature as are the epic convulsions of history and geography. I had even written in my dumb notebook, sometime in January, *Calliope is not the only muse*. True, true, true. But.

A great buffet of wind from behind took off my boina, and down it sailed; down and away and out of sight. Ah, damn, said I. Just a hat, but I liked it. We went back to the car, where Marilyn Marsh sat coldly doing nothing. I lost my hat, I announced through the windshield. My tone, I well remember twenty years after the fact, was an exploratory mixture of rue, amusement, and irritation, meant as much to sound out her feelings as to express mine. I used that tone often in those days. Too bad, MM replied, and *her* tone was such unmixed contempt for me and disgust with our Spanish project that I found myself saying Let's go look for it: there's a trail to the bottom, where the Roman baths are. Maybe we'll find my boina on top of three thousand yearsworth of corpses.

Was I crazy, she wanted to know. She was freezing, she said through the glass, and didn't give a shit about the trail, the baths, my hat—

I finished the sentence for her: Or its erstwhile owner, no? Suddenly we were outraged with each other. You sit there and freeze in your own ice, I told her: Orrin and I are going to check out this goddamned two-star Tajo. You can jump *into* that two-star Tajo, Marilyn Marsh replied; Orrin's staying here. A spectacular public argument followed, all of it shouted through the closed car windows. Oroonoko was mortified; so was I, especially when a few idle bystanders gravitated our way to see what the Americanos were up to. There even materialized in a nearby doorway the inevitable Guardia Civil. But our buttons were pushed: a wintersworth of adrenaline and more than a wintersworth of resentments fired off.

Never mind.

Finally Marilyn Marsh ordered Orrin into the car. Very dirty pool: I had then either to countermand her order and oblige Orrin to choose between us, or spare him that by letting her have her way. I did the latter, of course; but doing it so angered me that nothing could have kept me then from climbing down into that gorge. As I stormed off to where the downward path starts, MM rolled down her window for the first time, to holler that she and Orrin just might not be there when I got back. All I could think to holler in reply was that I just mightn't *come* back. Not a very devastating riposte. I was obliged to pass the grinning Guardia and a couple of these bystanders, who made way for me, and down I went, feeling as foolish, furious, and futile as ever in my thirty years.

The Tajo de Ronda is about two hundred meters deep. I had expected the descent to be arduous, but it wasn't: only windy and chilly and spectacular. Orrin and Marilyn Marsh could both have managed it without difficulty; among my other feelings was regret that they weren't with me. But it was a relief to be doing something half strenuous alone. Big cumulus clouds turned the sunshine off and on like a ceiling light, sol y sombra. The wind—and my mixed emotions about Spain and my project and my marriage and myself—subsided as I worked down into the cleft. I really had expected to find the bottom littered with the refuse of Ronda, if not with the skeletons of bulls, fascists, and

Phoenicians; but in fact the torrent that had presumably cut the gorge still rushes through it, flushing away its human history and, I assumed, my boina, in the unlikely event that the thing had fallen that far.

The path bottomed out at the ruins of the Roman baths and that rocky stream, swollen by snow-melt from thc Serrania. I rested in the ruins for five minutes, emotionally spent and unhappy. The heavenly ceiling fixture was on sombra. Then I went around the last bend in the path, between pines and free-standing boulders, to get a closer view of the torrent before climbing back to whatever waited for me or didn't, up in town. At the water's edge the sunlight came back on, et voilà! ¡Caramba! Mirabile dictu! Rightside up, at a jaunty angle, on a great round boulder scarfed by rapids like a giant faceless head . . .

What would you say, Suse: a million to one? And floodlit, too, or I might never have seen it on that mottled moon of a boulder, perfectly perched. A sound came out of me, half laugh, half something else; I scrambled carefully out over the rocks to retrieve it before some fluke of wind could undo the first coincidence with a second. ¡Mi boina! I actually kissed the thing; there were tears in my eyes, believe it or not; tears partly of actual feeling for that hat, as I stuck it welcomely and firmly back onto my head and clambered ashore and on up the path to Ronda.

Well, it was a symbol, for sure, an omen. But of what? I kept shaking my head (carefully) as I toiled back up, wondering what I was supposed to do with this extraordinary trifle of a happenstance and my life. Such a happy, tongue-tisking anecdote it would have been, in a better marriage, between better people!

I regained the Puente Nuevo as miserable as when I'd left it. No Volkswagen in sight, no Marilyn Marsh—but there was young Orrin, all alone on the bridge, looking mighty forlornly my way, with a certain familiar typing-paper box at his feet. I had the impression, as I hurried to him, that the idle bystanders looked away.

Dear brave Oroonoko. While I hugged him, he reported soberly that Mom had left as she'd threatened. He didn't think she'd gone far, or for keeps, but he wasn't sure. He had refused to leave with her—unprecedented behavior!— arguing reasonably that he had obeyed her earlier order not to go with me, and that if he was to be Solomoned between us (not Orrin's term), he would try to divide himself equally. What's more—and if I were the storyteller I went to Spain to try to become, I would have established earlier that I had a superstitious fear of losing my manuscript-in-progress, and always carried the thing along in its typing-paper box on our extended outings—what's more, it had occurred to my son that in his mother's anger she might "do something drastic" in the retaliation way: he had taken my manuscript with him when he left the car!

What did I do, Susan, to earn such a principled, reasonable, stubborn son? I was a touch surprised that Marilyn Marsh had actually left; even more that she had left Orrin as well. You can imagine how moved I was by the boy's loyalty, and properly miserable that he'd had to exercise it between his parents. And the sight of that manuscript, my story, on that bridge . . .

Well: there *was* my story, no? Our American domestic misery against the backdrop of España's national misery; the venture intended to renew us, that had only aggravated our differences; the story, bogged down in self-concern, of a story bogged down in self-concern. Now I'm crying, there on the bridge—almost crying here now to retell it, two decades later—and Orrin's saying Come on, Dad; gee whiz, Dad. I want to tell him It's okay, boy, it's okay, but my voice won't come. The I.B.'s are watching us from the end of the bridge. The Guardia Civil ambles out to us, no doubt figuring I'm about to jump, and asks how am I.

I tell him not to worry. Orrin picks up the box; the three of us stroll off the bridge. The Guardia reports offhandedly that mi esposa is parked at the Hotel Victoria, nearby, from where she has slipped back twice already to check that all's well. I thank him for that information. He recommends a good beating, not of course in public, to sweeten her. It works with his wife. I thank him for the recommendation, which I promise to consider. He has heard of our kindness to the father of his colleague in Marbella; he expresses dignified gratitude on behalf of that colleague. Perhaps, I say, he can exercise his influence to find my son and me a cut-rate taxi ride back to La Villa Dolorosa, near Fuengirola. Does he understand? He does, more or less, and knows just the hombre, and will direct us to him.

I make one further request before we leave the bridge. For reasons of honor too personal to set forth, I declare, it would give me great personal satisfaction to pitch this box of worthless paper into the Tajo. Have I his permission?

I rather expected a no: bad example for the citizenry, littering up their chief tourist attraction. I should've known better. He asked me to open it, satisfied himself that there was no bomb inside, and shrugged his shoulders. I thanked Oroonoko for having rescued it, and pitched it over the rail without a glance.

Then as I dickered with our recommended cabbie a block or two from the bridge, Orrin said Here's Mom, and Marilyn Marsh drove up in the Beetle, looking stern and unhappy. I considered going on with my negotiations, which were making progress, but to cut off my nose to spite my face seemed not especially macho. I was in fact touched with pity for all hands—Orrin in particular, but MM as well, and not excluding the Loyalists, Republicans, Phoenicians, bulls, and myself. I wished I had more character, or, lacking that, more talent. I wondered which, where not given, was less beyond acquiring. I wished I were a better father and husband, with a better wife, but supposed myself lucky enough after all to have no worse than I had. I was very tired.

Now I'll come down from Ronda fast. I canceled the cab and directed Orrin into the Beetle. Marilyn Marsh moved over: she didn't like mountain driving, especially in Spain. We went down in high-voltage silence and second gear. By

Marbella I realized that a stage of our life and mine was over; some consequential corner had been turned. By Fuengirola it was clear to me that there would be no novel, no notebook, no camping tour of Europe. That night, in bed in La Villa Dolorosa, MM made it plain that she felt likewise. We packed it in soon after, each blaming the other for spoiling the trip and the marriage, and trying without notable success to spare Orrin our fearful unhappiness. In mid-Atlantic, headed west aboard the *Nieuw Amsterdam* again, I deep-sixed my near-noteless notebook over the taffrail. But I kept the hat. You're asleep, right?

This last in a whisper, in case and in hopes Susan is, in his arms, in his berth, where she joined him in the vicinity of Madrid. Her bare back snugs into his bare front, her behind into his lap; his semicentenarian penis is tucked between her cheeks.

That's the story of your boina? she asks clearly, without turning her head.

You're awake. Well. It's the story of the story that taught me I couldn't write stories. Not that kind, anyhow. Not then, anyhow.

Hm.

It's also the story of the beginning of the end of my first life, though like a healthy oak tree damaged at the roots, it took us another nine or ten years to die.

Jesus, Fenn. Sometimes I wonder.

Me too. Finally, it's the story of how I joined the Company. After we came home with our tails between our legs, I got in touch with Count, who put me in touch with Dugald Taylor and other people. We decided to maintain my cover as a free-lance political journalist. For a while I didn't bother to tell Marilyn Marsh; by that time she didn't care. The household finances were better, and she was establishing her own life. I was four years younger then than you are now, but the new junior officers I trained with called me Pops, as if I were the Pat O'Brien character in a World War Two flick. We trained at ISOLATION, just upriver from here.

The fact is, I'd decided to live a story, since I couldn't write one. Manfred used to talk about operating on history instead of being operated on by it. My private wish, as you know, was to neutralize him, if not convert him. What happened was more the opposite.

So, Susan says: Not only did the Tajo return your hat; it keeps returning the story you threw into it.

But I keep throwing it back. One day I'll tell ours, but not that way.

Two questions, okay? Why does telling me this story—in the seventh year of our own marriage, for Christ's sake, on our own sabbatical—make you believe that your boina will float back to you? No: don't touch me. And get your shlong out of my crack.

No. I'm heartily sorry about the coincidence, Suse; it hadn't occurred to me till I heard myself saying sabbatical. As for the hat: I lost it a second time ten years later, on Company business, late at night on the dock of a certain safe-house across the Bay from here. I told my colleagues this story—just the boina part of it. Next day Count himself found my hat on the beach, washed up by the tide right in front of the safe-house. I had left the place before morning, and Count was on his way to Austria to check with the Vienna station on some Shadrin stuff*—we were working

---

*". . . Captain [Nicholas] Shadrin [of the Soviet navy], who had defected to the West from the Soviet Union in 1959, was approached by KGB operatives, reportedly in 1966, and asked to 'double'—to begin supplying the Russians with intelligence information.

"Captain Shadrin reported the contact to his superior, Adm. Rufus Taylor, of the naval intelligence section of the Defense Intelligence Agency. Admiral Taylor, who died a few weeks before [John Arthur] Paisley's disappearance last year, conferred with James Jesus Angleton, then head of the CIA's Counter-Intelligence Division. Mr. Angleton advised Admiral Taylor to persuade the Russian defector to take the pitch.

"Captain Shadrin did. According to sources, he began feeding the Russians disinformation from a variety of CIA sources. It is believed, however, that one of these sources might have been a 'mole' [a deep-penetration counteragent within the Agency]—and that the disinformation which he was providing might have been [super-]coded, thus
*(Footnote continues overleaf)*

out the disinformation lines. My boina came back to me at Solomons Island by diplomatic pouch from the U.S. embassy in Austria. The question before us now is whether it's the Ronda story that's needed to bring it back this third time or the Choptank River safe-house story, which I haven't told you yet. I'm in no hurry to find out. What's your second question?

My second question is Where was *I* while you were living all this life with the wrong person, being naive and poor together and making babies and going to Spain and learning who you were and weren't? What was I doing getting Bas Mitzvah'd in Pikesville* and graduating from college† and graduate school‡ and writing a dissertation on The Literary Ecology and Ecological Literature of Chesapeake Bay from Ebenezer Cooke‖ to James A. Michener¶ and getting laid by my favorite prof and all the time poor Mimsi working her ass off in the Peace Corps when Johnson and Nixon had made it a nothing and getting herself gang-raped at Virginia

---

*(Footnote continued from previous page)*
reestablishing a link which had been broken by National Security Agency decoders in the early 1970s.

"From 1972 to 1974, a study was done within the CIA on who the mole might be. A report was put on the desk of the then-director of central intelligence, William Colby.

"Soon after the completion of the report . . . Captain Shadrin disappeared while walking through a public square in Vienna. Allegedly, he was in plain view of the CIA station in that city when he disappeared [1975] and has not been heard from since." Baltimore *Sun*, June 10, 1979. See also p. 98.

Of Mr. Paisley, more later.

*A largely Jewish suburb of Baltimore, where Susan's grandmother lives.

†B.A. 1967, Swarthmore College, Swarthmore, Pa.

‡Ph.D. 1972, University of Maryland, College Park, Md.

‖c. 1667–1737?: author of *The Sot-Weed Factor* (1708) and other poems. But Dr. Seckler's subsequently published dissertation (College Park: Maryland University Press, 1974) begins a century earlier, with the Jamestown settlers.

¶1907– : author of *Chesapeake* (1978) and other novels. But Dr. Seckler's dissertation ends earlier, in 1972, the year of its completion. She is either making a joke or succumbing to fatigue.

Beach when she got home and tortured by the Shah's thugs later. . . .

Susan is weeping. The reader now understands, but for one detail, her tears of some pages past, at Fenwick's mention of the lights of Virginia Beach. Well, Fenn says, embracing his wife seriously in the dark, you were doing all that, while I was learning some things at considerable cost to myself and others. Thank heaven you didn't know me this way then! Your Uncle Fenwick! Are you okay?

I'm okay, I'm okay. That little exposition will have to be fleshed out in our story or flushed out from it.

We'll flesh it out later. We'll flesh it out when we reach the Big Fleshbeck.*

I want my sister, Fenn. I want to talk to my Mimi.

You can call her, Suse. We might be able to reach the Solomons marine operator from here.

I'll wait till we know where we are. I can't sleep. Tell me the Second Boina Story.

That would blow the experiment. But I'll do it if you'll go back to your own berth now, so we can sleep.

No.

She falls asleep anyhow now, at once. Spent Fenwick, having strained to hear further noises in the cove and heard none, normal or abnormal, wakes to gray light from sore dreams—of his first wife, of their baby son (in Fenn's dreams, Orrin is always two years old, wearing faded blue Dr. Dentons), of his brother Manfred and the late CIA officer John Arthur Paisley, both of them swimming, swimming vainly—and realizes that he too has slept.

Before breakfast we dive from the gunwales, our morning custom, and splash about Poe Cove to wake ourselves, throwing an old orange tennis ball back and forth. In the fresh wet sunlight we see abandoned apple trees on the high bank among the oaks and pines, but no sign of more recent

---

*In Part II: *Sailing Up the Chesapeake, Sailing Up the Chesapeake, Sailing Up the Chesapeake Bay;* Chapter 2: WYE; pp. 170ff.

human presence other than our own. As he swims to
retrieve a missed high throw, Fenn brushes his foot against
something clammy underwater and reflexively jerks his leg
away. The motion stirs to the surface what looks like a light-
colored rag. Treading water, he touches it gingerly, then
picks it up: a large scarf, kerchief, bandanna; a crimson-
bordered square of white silk or rayon with a light-blue
paisley print; unsoiled, unfaded, intact. He fetches the ball
and swims over to show his find to Susan, who is floating
near shore, bare breasts and belly up. *Pokey*'s stern is
between us. As Fenn pauses at the boarding ladder to toss
the ball into the cockpit, we are startled by lewd catcalls from
among the trees on the high bank: Wash 'em off, baby! Float
it over here! Et cetera. The voice is male, mocking, loud as if
amplified. Susan swirls around, alarmed; sees no one but
Fenn, in the opposite direction; strikes out for the boat.
Lewd whistles follow her. Dig that ass!

Fenn sees no one. Sue splashes up to him, gasping What
the hell. Some asshole with a bullhorn, Fenn supposes,
reaching out to her from where he holds onto the ladder.
Look what I found: a scarf or something. Shall I go up and
throw you down a bathing suit?

Susan wraps the scarf around her bottom instead and goes
up the ladder—there's another loud whistle—and into the
cabin. When bare-assed Fenwick follows, the bullhorn
laughs, and a woman's voice calls Save some for me. We
towel off, shaken, furious. Still naked, Fenn snatches the
binoculars and scans the bank from the cockpit. Nothing but
trees and that indifferent blue heron. Sue joins him, shirted,
shorted. No further comment from shore.

Well, Fenn remarks, we were told to watch out for snakes.
Susan says Now I hate Poe Cove.
Poe Cove is dandy; it's Key I. that's spooky.
Should we leave?
Hell no. Let's dinghy around it after breakfast.
I don't know, Fenn.
But we do it, after eating, launching the dinghy, hanging

the outboard on its transom—and padlocking *Pokey*'s
hatches for the first time since Cruz Bay, St. John, U.S.V.I.
His boina gone, Fenn wraps his bald head pirate-fashion in
the wet scarf; quite dashing, in his wife's opinion. Perhaps it
came from that *Baratarian* boat? We find Key Island to be
small, flat, entirely wooded, its shore by turns sandbeach and
saltmarsh, devoid of coves except ours, and without other
evidence of habitation except the stone breakwater with its
beacon. Half an hour completes the circumnavigation.
Seeing *Pokey* undisturbed where we left him, we go ashore
near the entrance to Poe Cove, on the bank opposite the
breakwater, whence we think last night's noises issued; but
Susan draws the line at exploring the woods. There are no
footprints besides ours. Along with the inevitable Clorox-
bottle float, broken loose from a crab pot and washed ashore
to last forever, we find among the sea-wrack, side by side, a
burst condom and an empty beer bottle.

Aha, says Fenwick: there's a story there.

Susan murmurs Poor girl.

Not a new story, though; neither item looks freshly
discarded; both may have come ashore on the tide. As
ecological Susan scrapes a hole in the sand with her foot and
buries them, she observes that the beer was a Colombian
brand, brewed in Bogotá.

No messages inside? Fenn inquires. Am being raped by
terrorists on the embassy yacht?* He sees his friend stiffen;
regrets the mild joke. But Susan merely and neutrally
replies, Rapists don't use rubbers.

We decide to explore no further: the place is beginning to
get to us. Could there possibly be a Company safe-house on

---

*We have followed with more than routine interest, by newspaper
when possible and radio when not, such Caribbean and near-Caribbean
news stories as the seizure of the Dominican embassy in Bogotá by M-10
guerrillas, the flood of "boat people" from Haiti to Florida, and the
inundation of that state with "boatlifted" Cuban refugees, not to mention
the ongoing nautical traffic in marijuana and cocaine, a certain amount of
it in the least suspicious of vessels: hijacked cruising sailboats.

Key Island? Susan wonders aloud. There could be a Company safe-house anywhere, Fenn admits; no place is safe from safe-houses. But he never heard of Key Island before yesterday, much less a Key Island safe-house. And "tradecraft," during *his* tenure with the Agency, while it included sundry sexual baits and snares, did not include the harassment, by bullhorn, of naked lady swimmers. To be sure, tradecraft may have changed in the restricted climate for covert operations since Viet Nam and Watergate: a short-lived climate of popular disfavor for the Company to which Fenn's own documentary exposé of 1977,* like Agee's and Marchetti's earlier ones,† contributed, and which the present conservative temper of our republic is rapidly reversing. But even so.

En route back to *Pokey* we see a doubler-crab near the surface: a mating pair of blue crabs, embracing, copulating, and swimming sidewise at the same time. As always, the sight rouses Fenwick slightly, despite his tactlessness of a little while ago. It reminds Susan that we've seen no one tending that thicket of early crab pots out by the breakwater. We reboard the cutter and recheck our cruising guide more thoroughly: no mention of Key Island; no indication of it on the chart-inserts of the York River/Mobjack Bay region of the Chesapeake. We spend the forenoon—an airless, sultry one, more summerlike than springlike—making what repairs we can and putting things shipshape after our ocean passage and the storm. Though we remain edgy, we see and hear nothing further unusual ashore. By noon we are ready to weigh anchor, but the Norfolk weather station reports that a cool front will cross the listening area during mid-afternoon, preceded by a line of thunderstorms. By 1400 hours there is a heavy-weather alert for southern Maryland and northern Virginia.

---

*Turner, F.S.K.: *KUDOVE* (N.Y.: Essential Books, 1977).
†Agee, Philip: *Inside the Company: CIA Diary* (N.Y.: Stonehill, 1975). Marchetti, Victor, and John D. Marks: *The CIA and the Cult of Intelligence* (N.Y.: Knopf, 1974). We here acknowledge our debt to these and similar works.

Wise sailors take such warnings seriously. Our anchorage is snug; we've plenty of swinging room even with twice our present scope; in the absence of actual menace from shore, it would be folly to set out before the front has passed. We resign ourselves to a second night in Poe Cove. Fenn rigs a boom-tent over the cockpit behind the dodger and a canvas rainwater-catcher to drain into our freshwater tank. We swim again, without incident—Susan suited, Fenwick not—and watch the black squall-line approach, grateful not to be at sea. Whoever that morning nuisance was, and the noise-makers of the night past, we are pleased to imagine that the heavy weather will curtail their sport. Remembering the doubler, horny Fenn embraces Susan from behind as we float, slips his hand into the front of her bikini bottom, and fingers through the wet fleece to her lips. No.

We hear the first thunder now and feel the first stirrings of northwest breeze. In happy contrast to the blam and blooey of some nights ago, we relax in sweatshirts in the cockpit, savoring the birds' excitement, the sight of the leeward deciduous trees' turning silverside up, *Pokey*'s swinging around on his anchor to point into the squall.

Just before it arrives, a familiar trawler-yacht rumbles in past the breakwater and anchors at the mouth of the cove, a hundred yards distant. We confirm through the binoculars that it is yesterday's helper, *Baratarian II,* and wave greeting to the young man at the anchor windlass, who either does not notice or ignores us. Now the wind picks up seriously; the treetops toss, and sheltered as we are, with no fetch to speak of, we begin to pitch a bit on our anchor rode. The interval between bolt and clap diminishes to a second or so. The standing rigging whistles. The first great raindrops smash into the boom-tent, the deck, the cove. There's the ozone smell. An alarmed bumblebee takes shelter under the dodger with us and will not be induced to leave. The raindrops increase.

At that unlikely moment, *Baratarian* lowers her dinghy—a Boston Whaler slung in davits over the transom—and sends two white men and one black woman ashore: one man and

the woman in yellow foul-weather gear, the other man not.
The storm proper strikes Poe Cove even as they start their
outboard and let go their lines, the two in slickers doing all
the boat-handling. They disappear into blinding rain and
detonating bolts of lightning: weather so suddenly thick that
we cannot see the trawler itself, much less its tender, even
with binoculars; so furious that we cannot imagine putting
out in our own dinghy unless *Pokey* were ablaze or sinking.

For the next quarter-hour, though we catch glimpses of
*Baratarian II* through the downpour, we cannot tell whether
or where its dinghy landed. Then the rain slackens, and we
see the Whaler drawn up on shore, its painter hitched to the
limb of an old fallen pine. The chap without a slicker, we
imagine, must have got himself awfully wet. There is still
much thunder and lightning, but mainly to east of us. The
air is briefly cooler; the wind and rain diminish; the edge of
the front has passed.

Now the black woman in yellow reappears on the bank
alone, climbs down and into the Whaler, and returns to the
yacht. A crewman assists her in securing fore and aft and
hoisting up into the davits. Do they not intend to retrieve the
two still ashore, then? And if not, does the fact not imply a
dwelling of some sort after all, hidden in the woods? What
about those snakes they warned us about; that poison ivy?

It is none of our business; but Fenwick decides to radio
our thanks for the Key Island advice, remark that the place
seems not to be on our admittedly limited charts, perhaps
even request a look at their own 12221 to get our bearings
from Key Island to the margin of the next chart up, which
we have. No response. Well, they're at anchor; no particular
reason why they should be monitoring their radio. But now
Fenn's curiosity must be gratified, the little mysteries shown
to be as innocuous as such things usually are. It is the first
black woman we've ever seen crewing a yacht: heartwarming
sight! The rain has all but stopped (and the still air is muggy
again); he will just pop over in our own dink and say hello.

Be careful, though, Susan frets; it *is* fishy. We have not yet
voiced the other possibility on both our minds: as the U.S.

Coast Guard has attempted to reduce the nautical traffic in illegal narcotics around Florida and the Gulf Coast, that traffic has increased along the coast of New England and in Chesapeake Bay. Close patrol of so much and labyrinthine coastline is impossible, and such are the profits involved that the smugglers have been known to purchase a $100,000 cruising sailboat and scuttle it at sea after a single successful voyage. If Key I. is not a Company operation; perhaps even if it is—oh, dismaying; but we know from the likes of Agee and Turner something of the Company's ties with the Mafia. . . .*

We must shorten scope on both our paranoia and our writerly sense of plot, Fenwick declares, fishing the dinghy in by its painter. But even as he mounts *Pokey*'s transom to climb down in, the vrum *vrum* of big diesels halts him. Exhaust smoke bubbles from *Baratarian*'s stern-ports, and Ms. Yellow Slicker is windlassing the anchor up. Before Fenn can get below to try the VHF again, the trawler is gliding out of Poe Cove toward the open Bay, the distant thunder.

He tries anyhow: Sailing yacht *Pokey* calling motor yacht *Baratarian Two*, et cetera. No reply. It is 1730: plenty of afternoon left for poking into those woods. Absolutely not, Susan decrees: neither the two of us nor you alone. And tired as we both are, I think we should stand watches tonight.

Agreed. Fenwick even considers breaking out his trusty nine-millimeter handgun, until Susan reminds him of Chekhov's dictum that a pistol hung on the wall in Act One must be fired in Act Three.

Then let's holster our imaginations too, Fenn urges. Music. Rum. Love. Dinner. And it's time we let Carmen B. Seckler know we're back. She can call the others.

---

*E.g., not only the Agency's notorious and unsuccessful attempts to use Mafia hitmen to assassinate Premier Fidel Castro (and thereby, presumably, to restore the mob's influence in a derevolutionized Havana), but also the posing of CIA operatives as Mafiosi to make contact with anti-Allende forces in Chile in 1970. See *The New York Times*, Feb. 9, 1981, and F.S.K. Turner's *KUDOVE*, passim.

We do that, first. Susan raises the Solomons Island marine operator, who patches us into Ma Bell; we hear the phone ring in Carmen's Place.* Miriam's scrapey voice says Carmen's, and black-eyed Susan screams with joy Mimi!?

Suse?

We're home!

The sisters shriek some moments back and forth like schoolgirls: We're okay! We're okay! We're okay too! We had this terrific storm a couple nights ago, but we're okay! We were worried about you; it blew the shit out of Baltimore. Where *are* you? Well, we don't exactly know, Mimsi: some place we never heard of: Key Island, on the lower western shore, off the York River. But we're safe, and tomorrow we'll head on up! How's Ma? Is she there? Ma's fine. She's with Grandma † tonight. Nobody here but me and Eastwood Ho ‡ and the boys.∥ And the wimps and the winos.

---

*Susan's mother's bar-restaurant in the salty, boozy Fells Point neighborhood of Baltimore: a small, indecorous, jammed, profitable enterprise, not Carmen B. Seckler's only one. Kerflooey or not, C.B.S. has the late Jack Seckler's Yiddishe kopf on her Gypsy shoulders, in our judgment.

† Havah Seckler, 85, born Havah Moscowitz near Minsk, Russia; exact date of birth unknown, but it was the second night of Rosh Hashanah, 1894, and has therefore been observed since on that occasion, whatever the calendar date. Mother by the late Allan Seckler of the late Jack Seckler and thus mother-in-law, in spirit if no longer in law, to Carmen B. Seckler and grandmother to Susan and Miriam. Now infirm and more or less confined to a private Jewish nursing home in Pikesville.

‡ A.k.a. Can Phung Ho and Ho Ca Dao, 32, of the old university city of Hué, Viet Nam, largely destroyed in the Tet Offensive of February 1968; later of Saigon and Can Phung Island in the lower Mekong. Resident of the U.S. since 1974; Miriam Seckler's lover since 1977, when he appeared in Fells Point, and father by her of her second child (see note below). In Hué and on Can Phung Island, he was a recognized young virtuoso folk-poet-singer in the rich and complex tradition of Vietnamese oral poetry, popular for centuries among the high literati as well as among peasants and children. In Baltimore he prepares steamed mussels and stuffed baby squid, the house specialties of Carmen's Place. More on his American name in note, p. 215.

∥ Miriam's sons Sy (short for Messiah) Seckler, 11—exact sire unknown, but (the reverse of Grandma Havah Seckler's case) date of siring

Eastwood's doing the kitchen; I'm tending bar; Sy's wiping tables. Hold on, Shush;* I gotta water the animals.

She lets the pay phone drop with a clatter; oddly into *Pokey*'s cabin, into hushed Poe Cove, come the sounds of Happy Hour at Carmen's Place. It is very like Miriam not to consider that the clank of the receiver on the metal shelf of the open pay-phone niche might be deafening to the other party, and that patched-in long-distance radiotelephone calls are very expensive. No matter: we listen with smiles and rolls of the eyes to the familiar Fells Point hubbub.

Presently Miriam says Suse? I had to wipe Edgar's ass while I was at it; he shat his Pamper. Say hello to Aunt Shushi, Edgar. Fucking Eastwood won't even tend bar while I talk, 'cause some jerk's reading poetry that Eastwood says sucks. How's Uncle Fenn?

He's wonderful; he's the best. Fenn takes the microphone: I'm wonderful, Mim; I'm the best. You're still letting that Ho character walk all over you?

One day I'll tell *him* to take a walk, Uncle Fenn. It's the situation. He's got poetic license. Do you still love my sister more than God so loved the world? You better fucking had.

I should hope so. Listen, Mims: tell Carmen we're safe in the Chesapeake, and either you or she pass the word on to Grandma and to Chief and Virgie and Orrin and Julie. Don't forget to do it, okay?

I'll write it on the bar in Edgar's shit, Miriam promises.

---

fixed precisely and traumatically—is a hulking, semimoronic, but sweet-natured child, fat and imperturbable as a young Buddha, though all of his possible fathers were Caucasian. Edgar Allan Ho is Miriam's child by her current lover. As Caucasian in appearance as his half-brother is paradoxically Asiatic, the baby was named not alone for its mother's (and Susan's) putative ancestor E. A. Poe, but also after its Vietnamese father's coincidental, extraordinary likeness to that poet. It is Carmen B. Seckler, more than distracted Miriam, who sees to both children's mothering, as well as to their mother's and their mother's grandmother's.

*Another of the sisters' many nicknames for each other. Shush (and Shushi) is short for Shoshana, which is Hebrew for Susannah, Susan, and, for that matter, Rose.

When do you get to Fells Point? Where the fuck did you say you are? Give me my sister, anyhow.

Susan takes over. Mims? Don't forget to make those calls. You forget things.

Yeah. Miriam chuckles. Like getting married.

How's my little Edgar? Are you all right, Mimsi?

No.

Mims!

I'm all right, I'm all right. What's all right? Edgar's all right too. He just shits and shits. Grandma had another operation; I'll let Ma tell you. When can I talk to you, Susele?

Susan consults Fenn with her eyes; he takes the mike. We should reach Solomons Island tomorrow, Mimi. We'll call from there, about this time of day. If we're stuck at Solomons for a while, we'll get together anyhow. Listen, Miriam?

Yeah, Uncle Fenn. Shut your hole, Edgar.

Just say yes or no to this, please: Is there any news about Gus or Manfred?

There is a pause along the line between Key Island and Fells Point. Then Miriam says I can't talk now.

Unsurprised, Fenn quietly insists. Just yes or no, Mim.

No. I gotta go now. Sy's putting beer in the ashtrays, and Eastwood's going to hit him. Be good to my sister, Fenn.

Don't worry about your sister. Somebody should hit that Eastwood Ho.

He's a great artist in a rotten situation, Uncle Fenn, and we did it to him.

Bullshit.

Miriam laughs: It's not bullshit. Anyhow, he *gets* hit. People hit him.

And then he hits you! Susan cries angrily into the microphone.

Miriam laughs again, not merrily. And then I hit Edgar Allan Ho, and then Sy cries, and then Ma gives everybody in the house a free drink.

Good-bye now, Mimsi. I love you.

I love you, Shushi. Come soon. Good-bye. Is it wonderful?

Both sisters' voices are teary. It's too wonderful, Sue says. Over and out, Mims.

After Susan has wept briefly and Fenwick has comforted her, we put together another meal of odds and ends from *Pokey*'s depleted lockers and eat it with warm beer in the cockpit. The evening air is as steamy as if no front had passed; low thunder continues in the east and south. Perspiring, we sit topless, relieved to hear no commentary from shore despite our knowledge that at least two men are on the island somewhere. Only a few no-see-ums bite; repellent messes up their navigation. We tisk our tongues about Miriam's circumstances, Carmen B. Seckler's formidable energy and solicitude. She even takes care of Eastwood Ho, slapping him around or embracing him as the situation warrants and helping to organize a Vietnamese Cultural Center in Baltimore to provide among other things an audience for his art, incomprehensible to her. Once she very probably saved his life by taking a kitchen knife out of his hand before he could assault a former Special Forces officer, drunk at the bar, who boasted of having interrogated Vietnamese peasant women with the muzzle of his service pistol in their vaginas: Carmen knew the chap to be deadlier with his bare hands, drunk, than Eastwood Ho sober with a twelve-inch blade.

Susan will take the first watch. Fenn keeps her company through the forepart of it before turning in. Knowing now that *Baratarian II,* at least, visits Poe Cove, we run our anchor light up the forestay; as the night promises to be muggy, we rig a windscoop on the main forward hatch to drive air into the cabin. Sue muses upon the paradox that we are taking precautions against our helpers: the circumstance reminds her, changes changed, of

## THE STORY OF MIRIAM'S OTHER RAPES,

as does the paisley scarf trouvée, pinned with other wet items on the lifelines to dry, its ciliated teardrop pattern swarming like amoebae or fat sperm.

Her *other* rapes! horrified Fenn exclaims. What other rapes?

The ones after the main ones but before the Iranian one. I guess I hoped you knew from Ma, so I wouldn't have to talk about it ever. But you told me that long sad story about your boina; you owe me one.

Mim's *other* rapes! Jesus, Susan!

We got used to not speaking of it. In the house of the hanged man, et cetera.* But your joke on the beach today reminded me, plus that scarf. In my opinion it's what first drove Ma kerflooey, but Ma disagrees. Grandma says Ma went kerflooey in Forty-nine, when Da died, and that the business with Mimsi just made it worse. Ma disagrees with that, too.

While we're off the awful subject, Fenwick says, may we have your mother's personal opinion of the date and cause of her kerflooeyhood? The reader might be interested. How'd we ever get to calling it kerflooey, anyway?

Grandma. Then Ma herself took to using the word to tease Grandma, and we all picked it up from her. It became a neutral term, like widowhood or divorce. Ma says she was born kerflooey, and that the camps made her even more kerflooey, and that the only time she wasn't kerflooey by ordinary standards was when her straight-assed relatives in Philadelphia got her rescued in Thirty-five when she was only eleven, and made a nice Jewish girl out of her, and she married Da in Forty-one, just in time for the war, and spent the next eight years as a proper fussy wife and mother of us girls in Cheltenham P A, and then took over Da's business when he died in Forty-nine, when she herself was still only twenty-six for Christ's sake, and moved to Baltimore and ran things as well as Da did, et cetera. Ma says that that straight time was her real kerflooeyhood, if you ask her, and that when she started acting strange after Gus's birth in Fifty-

---

*Don't mention rope, the Spanish proverb advises.

three—riding her bicycle and wearing her Gypsy clothes and singing down the street and moving to Fells Point and opening up Carmen's Place and all—that she was just reverting to her natural state, and Miriam's Iranian adventure confirmed it, and then losing Gus and Manfred made it final. Kerflooey.

That makes sense to me.

To me too. Nobody talks more sensibly about kerflooeyhood than Ma does. But from my viewpoint, of course, she seemed to go kerflooey mainly after Miriam's other rapes.

Dear god. Tell on, Suse.

Susan takes a long breath, sighs it out, begins: It was in Nineteen Sixty-eight, same as the main ones. Sixty-eight was a big year for assassins and rapists. It's an ugly story. Mims had always been schizy and nervous and rebellious: just the opposite from me, except the nervous. She wore funny clothes and did grass and coke in junior high school, back when nobody used that stuff except jazz musicians. We were living in Baltimore then, and most of our friends at school dated Jewish boys from Mount Washington or Pikesville, but Mims hung out with a crowd of cool black guys, mainly musicians. She was also the first Flower Child in town. Plus an organic vegetarian, when she wasn't being anorexic, plus anti-alcohol but pro-hashish. She was a real athlete, too; better than me, except she wouldn't stick to training, so she never played varsity and couldn't have cared less anyhow. And her art teachers used to beg her to do painting seriously, she had such a feel for it, but she wouldn't.

That's our Miriam.

So: when I went to Swarthmore, Mimsi went back to Philadelphia, to Temple, where she said the only thing she learned was how to swing both ways. I hardly knew then what lesbianism was, except from reading Sappho in Intermediate Greek. She dropped out after freshman year and joined the Peace Corps to get her head straight, so she said. They sent her to Nigeria, to some little village in the bush, where we were sure she'd get elephantiasis and malaria and be raped and white-slaved or traded for a cow. The Biafran revolt was in full swing; even Ma was worried sick, and Grandma we didn't dare tell. But none of those bad things happened: she taught hygiene to kids and had a major affair with an Iranian public-health person from Johns Hopkins who was doing work there. It was his stories about how the CIA helped overthrow the Mossadegh government to put the Shah in power that turned Mim into a Marxist, and that's how she ended up going to Tabriz later on, in Seventy-one. You know all that.

Never mind what I know. Tell on.

In Nineteen Sixty-eight she was sent home from West Africa to Baltimore on a kind of furlough because of the Biafran trouble. Ma was established in Fells Point by then, and I was into my doctorate at College Park. Mimi seemed— I don't know: *seasoned,* tough, together. I was impressed. She was pro-Palestinian and pro-Viet Cong by this time, but mainly anti-CIA, and having a lot of trouble about Manfred's and your being in the Company. How in the *world* they could've been dumb enough to approach her to work for them under Peace Corps cover on her next tour, when she was convinced they were behind the Kennedy assassinations, and even the Peace Corps was easing her out because of her politics and her instability . . .

She *was* still unstable, despite her seasoned air. She had woozy spells, and sometimes she hallucinated. But she was convinced that the shrinks were either frauds or sexual imperialists or government agents or all three, and refused to see one. I had a good-paying job at Virginia Beach that summer, assistant-managing a motel for one of Ma's cronies down that way, and Mims hitched back and forth a lot between Ma in Baltimore and me in Virginia Beach and her friends in Georgetown.

One of them introduced her to the Company man, in a Georgetown gay bar, and he gave her the cold pitch.\* Mimi

---

\*A solicitation to agentry made without prior cultivation of the "target."

was so outraged that after she finished denouncing him up and down Wisconsin Avenue, she had to stick out her thumb at one A.M. and hitch two-hundred-plus miles to Virginia Beach to tell me about it. I'd been after her about hitchhiking: I did plenty of it myself in Europe, but almost never in this country, except in emergencies. Mim said she didn't give a shit: that America scared her, but not Americans, and one piece of pussy more or less wouldn't change her life, et cetera. That's how she talked, even then. And that's where her craziness comes in: as if our concern didn't go beyond the fuck-or-walk business. In fact, Mims was in a promiscuous period just then because her Iranian medical friend had dropped her. If she was in no hurry and thought her driver was sexy, she'd ball him. Or her. When I'd scold her for hitching and Mims would shrug and say I got here all in one piece, I never knew which she meant.

That particular night she got to Virginia Beach safely in the cab of a seafood truck driven by a Jehovah's Witness and woke me up at six in the morning with a tirade against the CIA: how America was becoming the cancer of human civilization; and she couldn't stand it that her own stepfather and step-uncle, that she loved so much and that she knew cared a lot for her and me and Gus and Ma, were big shots in the Company; and if she thought for a minute that either one of you had set up that little wimp's pitch, she'd write you off for keeps; but she knew you'd never do such a thing to her, whatever terrible stuff you were doing to other people. Et cetera.

I told her the fellow was probably just showing off, or baiting her, and gradually she cooled off. She stayed with me a few days, and we had a good time together. I even got her into playing power-volleyball on the beach! She was a terrific spiker when she was in the mood, even against big guys. It was almost like being back in the Poconos, when Mimi and I were counselors in Camp Laurel. I bought her some acrylics to get her into painting again, and talked my boss into offering her a job, thinking it would be good for both of us to spend the rest of the summer together before she did her next thing. Mim was thinking about going out to Chicago in August to help her friends make trouble at the Democratic national convention. But then she got a sudden craving to talk to Grandma about the Byelorussian pogroms, and so on a bright Sunday afternoon—July fourteenth, Bastille Day, Nineteen Sixty-eight—she packed her backpack, stuck out her thumb, and headed up Route Sixty toward Seashore State Park on the back of a motorcycle driven by a thirtyish black guy with a Wehrmacht helmet and a leather vest that said Richmond Thunderguards on the back. She was wearing her granny-glasses and a granny-gown and a paisley head scarf; that's what reminded me.

The next part you know: how that gang of white Road-Vulture types caught up with the black guy at Fort Story and beat up on him and wrecked his bike and took Mimsi kicking and hollering into the woods and tied her hands with her scarf and wrapped her head in her granny-gown and stole her backpack and broke her glasses, and their girlfriends held her down while the men took turns fucking and buggering her and talked seriously about cutting off her nipples and eating them as some kind of initiation rite, but decided to piss on her instead, all of them, the women squatting over her face, and then they left her tied to a tree with stars fingerpainted on her breasts and the American flag on her belly in the acrylics I'd given her, which she'd never used.

That's right, Susan: you don't have to mention those things.

Well. Shocked and terrified as she was that they'd kill her or mutilate her, Mimsi memorized their voices, and the nicknames they'd let slip every now and then, and little details of information—she would have been a good Company agent! And she kept thinking Thank god they haven't really hurt me yet, except the sodomizing, and even for that they used axle grease from their bike kits. But they didn't beat her or cut her or burn her with their cigarettes or stick

anything into her except their pricks, and some of the
women their fingers. They even told her as they left her not
to worry; that she was near a park trail and somebody would
find her before long.

Very considerate gang-rapists.

She was there four hours—it could just as easily have been
four days or four years—with her head dripping piss and
her legs running semen and her asshole bleeding and the
mosquitoes and flies biting her some, and Mimi actually
thinking she was lucky it was dry weather and not blackfly
season!

Then her rescuer came along.

They never found him. He was a skinny, middle-aged,
redneck-looking fellow in shiny worn chinos, with a gray
crewcut and a leathery face and a gentle gravelly voice. It
seemed to Mimsi he must have known those woods well; he
had no pack or any kind of camping gear, and he told her he
was just out walking. She heard something coming along the
path and groaned as loud as she could through the dress
they'd gagged and wrapped her head with. She remembered
being grateful that there weren't any bears left in that part
of Virginia, and then this easy cracker voice said Lord
amighty, looks like somebody did a job on you, honey.

He undid her head, clucking his tongue at the piss and all
and asking her had she been raped, and was it one fellow or
a gang, and what in the world was the world coming to,
anyhow. And crazy Mim said damned straight she'd been
raped, and buggered and pissed on too, and there were five
of the bastards and three women, a motorcycle gang called
the Dixie Pagans from Newport News, and she'd caught
some of their nicknames and could identify their bikes and
some of their faces. The man chuckled and said Looks like
they're right patriotic, anyhow; but they oughtna put that
Yankee flag on you if they're Dixie Pagans.

She saw what he was talking about—she'd felt them
painting her up, but she didn't know till now what they'd
painted on her. She saw the squeezed tubes of acrylic on the

ground, and some empty beer bottles, and her broken glasses, and the stuff running down her thighs, and she asked the guy if he had a car and would he mind taking her to the nearest police station; the sons of bitches weren't going to get away with it.

Mind you, Fenn, her arms are still tied behind the tree with the scarf; but she doesn't realize what's up even when the guy stops to light a cigarette and says Seems to me you need a hospital more'n you need the po-lice.

Just the police, says Mimi, and Would you mind untying my hands, for Christ's sake?

The man takes a puff, looks her in the eyes and up and down, and fishes out a big pocket knife. It just crosses Mim's mind—but then he goes around behind the tree. The idea had probably just crossed *his* mind, too, and he was trying to decide what he wanted to do. He might even have gone on with the rescue—after all, Mims had seen his face, and she'd made it clear that she meant to identify the Dixie Pagans. But she was getting scared now, and angry at the same time; she started crying and said Come on, already; cut me loose!

He put the blade against her throat to shut her up and undid the scarf and made her lie face down with his knee in her back while he retied her hands behind her. Then he marched her off the path into deeper woods, telling her that if she didn't give him a hard-on he'd cut her up. She asked him what he wanted her to do, and he said You'll probably think of something. He promised to gut her like a deer if she made any noise, and then he stuck his cigarette against her bare ass to show he meant business. With her hands tied, there was nothing Mims could do except suck him off, which she did—he made her ask him to let her do it, and then held her by the hair with the knife blade right across her gullet while she did. Mims told me his cock was long and fat but absolutely flaccid, even when he stuffed the whole thing into her mouth and shot off down her throat. She choked and threw up; then she knew she was in for it.

For the rest of the afternoon he did stuff to her, never

taking his own clothes off, but leaving his fly open and his big limp dick hanging out. He kept her on her knees and burned her some more on the backside, and made little cuts on her when she cried out, and stuck the neck of a beer bottle into her cunt—he'd brought one of those empties from the other place, along with her dress. He cut a willow switch and whipped her with it, and did other things, all perfectly calmly. The worst part was that he kept telling her she was a cheap little tramp who didn't even know how to get a guy excited. Mims had to say stuff like Don't you want to kiss my titties? Don't you want to eat my pussy? Can I please blow your big cock again? She wished she would faint, so he could kill her and she wouldn't know it, but her mind stayed crystal clear. She memorized the pattern of stains on his pants and the label on that beer bottle, and she considered whether to run and scream or bite his penis off, since he was likely to torture her to death anyhow, or hope he'd get just tired and let her go even though she could identify him out of a million.

I haven't told you half the things he made her do and pretend to like it. Mimi said he smelled like sweat and old cracker crumbs. It seemed to her that he actually did want to fuck her instead of torturing her, but he was completely impotent. Every ten minutes or so he'd try to put his penis in, but it wouldn't go, and then it was back to the cigarettes and the knife and the beer bottle and the switch and the blow jobs. Mimi swore that if he'd undo her hands she could stuff it in for him, and play with his balls and finger his asshole while they fucked, wouldn't that be nice? She could see him think it over while she begged him, telling him he could keep his knife right there at her throat the whole time.

Susan, Fenwick says: let's stop this story right now. It's enough to know that your sister was gang-raped, and that the Dixie Pagans all got light sentences because Mim dressed like a hippie and hitched rides with black men on motorcycles, and that they never found this other sadistic bastard. The details are just dreadfulness, even between ourselves.

Susan doesn't agree. Rape and Torture and Terror are just words; the details are what's real. Fenn's a writer of sorts; he must understand that. But it sickens me too, she says. My poor poor Mimsi! Trying to figure out what might save her life, and never once losing her perspective. By this time she was past crying. She thought it was important that the guy hadn't mutilated her yet, or beaten her really brutally, or strangled her. She found herself wishing she had a more erotic imagination. After the first hour he quit burning and cutting her, even though he still smoked a lot and kept the knife in his hand. He wasn't drunk; he never got angry; a lot of the time he just had her stand there while he smoked or played with his limp cock. Eight or nine times he had her suck him off, but he never got hard or even came again after that first time. He seemed edgy and undecided— probably he was out of ideas himself. The scariest times were when he'd go behind her and she couldn't see what he was up to. Then she'd feel his finger in her rectum and have to moan and pretend she loved it. To stall for time, she talked about how much better it would be in a motel room, in a big soft bed.

Then in a different voice he told her to shut up and bend over like before. Mimi thought This is it. She knew she might as well scream and run as far as she could until he caught up with her and slit her open. But she went down on her knees the way he wanted, head down in the dirt with her butt in the air, and waited for the worst. The man spread her cheeks and spit into her crack—and shoved the neck of the beer bottle into her. When she cried out, he twisted it around and laughed and said I'm going to be watching from back here, and if you move one inch in the next ten minutes I'll strangle you in your own guts.

And there he left her, with the bottle sticking out of her ass and raw burns and bleeding cuts all over her belly and behind. But not on her face and breasts, oddly enough; evidently her rescuer was an ass-man. He slipped off into the woods like an experienced hunter, without a sound; and cramped and sore as she was, Mims counted the full ten minutes and then called out to him before she dared to budge.

She told me that her main feeling was enormous relief. She could hardly believe she'd come through two ordeals like that without being butchered. She was able to reach down and pull the bottle out, thinking how a real sadist might have broken the neck off first, or shoved the whole thing into her, or done a lot worse stuff with that knife. Nothing she could do would make the scarf come loose; she tried all that B-movie stuff of scraping it against rocks and tree bark, but she only scratched up her arms instead. So she squatted down and picked up her dress and dragged it behind her through the woods, tearing it and her legs on brambles. She was crying hard then and hurting more every minute, but actually worrying at the same time that she might cut her feet on broken glass or step on a snake or run into that man again. Finally she found a path that led to an empty dirt road, and she walked down that road for an hour without seeing a car or a house. She was naked, bleeding, and dirty, with those painted flags still on her, dried piss in her hair and dried come all over her, trailing her granny-dress from her hands tied behind her, in this stinking hot July late afternoon.

Finally a pickup truck roars up and hits the brakes, and a big burly man jumps out and shouts Where's the sons-abitches did this to you, young lady? Mimi couldn't even answer; she stood there crying and shaking her head. The truck door's open; the motor's running; the guy looks around and trots up to her and turns her around to untie her hands—and the next thing Mimsi knows, he's rushing her across the ditch, back into the woods.

Oh, Susan! Fenn cries.

No threats, no weapons, Sue declares, not even a word. He just threw her into the bushes and choked her with one hand while he unzipped his pants with the other and then choked her some more till she opened her legs for him. No potency problem with this one: he fucked her hard and fast, looking around the whole time to see if anyone was there. As soon as he came he jumped off her, zipped his pants, ran back to his truck, and roared away. The whole rape took less than ten minutes; maybe no more than five. Mimi said it was like getting humped by a locomotive. By the time she got herself up and back to the road, he was too far away for her to read the license plate without her glasses, so they never found *him*, either.

By now it was early evening, and there was very little traffic on that back road. Mim walked along the woods side of the ditch and hid in the bushes when the next couple of cars came by. She'd lost her dress now and was more or less in shock, but still clear-headed enough to worry that it might be a park road that closed at night. She'd had nothing to eat or drink since breakfast, when she never eats much anyhow, and the mosquitoes were getting worse. She decided to walk on the roadside in case she fainted, so that she'd be less likely to die before she was found. Then she decided she'd better try to stop the next car, because if it wasn't a park road she'd be more likely to get raped again after dark than while there was still some light. When she heard a car coming from behind her, she turned her head to face it, but kept her back to it so that they'd see her hands were tied. It was an elderly couple in a dusty Buick, and can you believe it? They slowed down to look and then sped on by! Mimi thinks they were afraid.

After that came another pickup truck with two young white men in it, long hair and jeans, and Mims wondered if she was in for it again. But they were wonderful. They untied her hands and literally gave her the shirts off their backs—it was all they had to put around her—and they asked her did she want the police or a hospital or what, and Mimsi said just please to fetch her to me, and they did, with no questions or anything. One of them knocked on my door and said he had my sister in the car; that she'd been in some trouble and I should bring something to put around her and probably take her to a hospital, which I did as soon as I got control over myself.

That's the end of the story, almost. Mims went to the hospital to prove she'd been raped and tortured, and I stayed with her while the police questioned her. They were good, by the way; not like we expected. Ma came down and was very strong and calm; she urged Mims not to press charges, because if the Dixie Pagans were like some other motorcycle gangs, they'd do even worse stuff to her to get even. But when Mimsi insisted, Ma found her a good lawyer to work with the prosecutor and paid for everything. Then Mims learned she was pregnant—she'd just quit the Pill because of side effects. She decided not to have an abortion, because it might help the prosecution if the jury saw her pregnant, and she was turning into some kind of Right-to-Lifer anyhow. But the Dixie Pagans' lawyer made it seem as if her having Sy was just more evidence of her moral laxity and general spaciness, like her hippie clothes and her hitchhiking. Naturally, Mims wouldn't dress the way the prosecutor wanted her to during the trial. Et cetera. No wonder Ma went kerflooey.

So the Dixie Pagans got light sentences, and the police never found the other two men, and Sy was born, and the other Pagans really did threaten to get even, but Ma put out the word around Fells Point that we had Mafia protection and the Pagans had better stay in Newport News. Not long after that, two of them really did get executed gangster-style, as the papers say, and two more were killed in prison fights, and the group disbanded. But whether it was Ma's friends from Little Italy or Manfred's Company contacts or just coincidence, I don't know.

Neither do I, Suse.

After that, Mims was pure lesbian for a while. When Sy was two she took off for Tabriz, where her Hopkins public-health friend had returned and been arrested by SAVAK for anti-government activity. When they moved her to Evin Prison in Teheran and used the electricity on her, they called the generator by its Spanish slang-name, picana. They'd picked it up from their Latino colleagues while they were all being trained together here in historic Virginia.

Fenwick says Not exactly: foreign nationals were never trained in mixed groups. Not up the river from here at least, and not in my day at least. Our people would've picked up the word from the Latinos and then passed it on themselves to the Iranians and the South Koreans and the rest.

Oh. Anyhow, the SAVAKis didn't really rape her, so that's the end of the rape story. But when they stripped her for questioning they recognized her scars as old cigarette burns and decided she was a seasoned revolutionary who'd been arrested before. So they worked her over with the picana and fucked her once with an electric cattle-prod even though she was American. If she'd been Iranian, they'd have killed her, as indeed they did her public-health friend, who was in fact a revolutionary. When Manfred got her out, I suppose her torturers got theirs. You can still see the picana scars on Mimi's nipples and labia, and the cigarette burns on her ass and her stomach and her thighs. That's why she won't wear a bikini. There, I'm done.

Fenwick apologizes for his thoughtless remarks on the beach vis-à-vis rapists, condoms, and beer bottles, and offers to deep-six the paisley scarf at once if the sight of it bothers his wife. Susan insists he keep it to shade his head until a better substitute can be found for his temporarily lost boina. Our minds are still very much on Miriam and on the Company. There is a bit of thunder yet in the far northeast, not likely to come our way. The exchange of stories has drained us. At Sue's urging, Fenn turns in to sleep for the rest of her watch; at midnight he relieves her. A weak high has cleared the air; a fine white moon, two nights past full, rides over the masthead and lights Poe Cove. There is no dew; the air is delicious. We sit a little while together, comparing notes and savoring the night, before sleepy Susan goes below. Only normal frog and night-bird noises ashore, and the soft sough of the southerly in the trees.

Nevertheless, Fenn decides to continue his watch, though he stretches out on a cockpit cushion and permits himself to doze off from time to time without concern. A few minutes past 2 A.M. he is startled awake by a sharp crack like a gunshot from the woods astern. He bolts up, but decides not to turn on the big flashlight. Susan calls from her berth, then hurries up in her underpants. Damned if Fenn knows.

Not another sound, until the frogs resume. Sue hugs herself in the cooled air. Fenn sets her in his lap and kisses her breasts, mercifully unscarred. We remember that no game is in season; that nighttime hunting is illegal anyhow. Key Island could, we suppose, be someone's private hunting preserve. Or the sound may have been a backfire—but we hear no motor. A tree limb suddenly breaking? But we heard no swish of leaves, no crash. Whatever happened to normal sleep?

For encouragement we speak, not of our recent stories, but of

## OUR STORY.

To Susan's mind, it is appropriate that, in a manner of speaking, we are involved in a nighttime voyage, one common feature of wandering-hero myths. It strikes her as even more fitting that for the last few days, not counting our setback by last Tuesday's storm, our course has been prevailingly westward, that being the traditional direction of adventure. Fenwick thinks she's stretching things a bit, given that the first half of our sabbatical cruise was prevailingly southward and the second half, including what lies ahead, will have been prevailingly northward. But he is not displeased to find our story following, in a general way, the famous tradition: summons, departure, threshold-crossing, initiatory trials, et cetera. He declares it our authorial prerogative, however, to bend the pattern to fit our story, so long as we don't bend the story to fit the pattern.

Susan agrees, and reminds us that it's after the threshold-crossing that things typically get dark and mysterious. Capes

Henry and Charles come late in the day to be our threshold, but Key Island and Poe Cove are on the right track.

Whether or not they're on the chart, adds Fenn.

His wife believes we have a problem there. Tradition calls for the hero's acquiring a guide or helper before crossing the threshold between light and dark, waking reality and dreamlike adventure. But granting that Hank and Chuck were our threshold, not only did we not acquire a guide or helper till after we'd crossed it; we lost one: Chart 12221.

And were almost bisected by the U.S. Coast Guard, grumbles Fenn. And have been made mighty uneasy by old *Baratarian Two*. Some helper. He considers further: Anyhow, there's no particular hero in our story. We're the hero. So we'll be the helper, too. I'll be your helper; you be my helper.

One hand washes the other, Susan says, quoting Grandma. I'm getting cold.

So if our story strays off course from that pattern, too bad for the pattern. Have we decided where to begin it?

Oh, in the middle, says Susan, definitely. In medias fucking res, as my helper would say.

Before his helper edits out his casual vulgarity. Okay: we'll start with the storm at sea, like the big boys, and work in the exposition with our left hands as we go along.

Shivering Susan points out that the reader doesn't know yet for example about her seducing Fenwick on Cacaway Island in 1972, or about Fenn's son Orrin's old crush on her. Our left hands are going to be busy.

Yup. You seduced me?

With a little help from my helper. I'm going back to bed. Good night, Fensele.

Good night, Susele. Good night, Miriam. And Carmen B. Seckler and Havah, and Chief and Virgie, and Orrin and Company. Marilyn Marsh too; the whole cast. Good night all.

Yeah. Good night, Marilyn Marsh. What time is it?

Three. We'll get out of here as soon as it's light.

We forgot Gus and Manfred.

Good night, poor fellows. Rest you easy.

The reader doesn't even know yet about Gus and Manfred, really.

What the reader doesn't know yet would fill a book.

Oy. Who said that?

I did.

# II

*Sailing Up the Chesapeake,*
*Sailing Up the Chesapeake,*
*Sailing Up the Chesapeake Bay*

# 1

# SOLOMONS

Fenwick Scott Key Turner reports in the early morning that although the remainder of his watch was undisturbed, he had worry-dreams all through it about Manfred, Gus, Orrin, Marilyn Marsh, John Arthur Paisley, the U.S. Central Intelligence Agency, themselves. Susan Rachel Allan Seckler, washing her face, reports that *she* had worry-dreams, too, about Miriam, Grandma, Carmen B. Seckler, Chief and Virgie Turner, herself and Fenn. Incidentally, they didn't seem to her to correspond to the Five-Dream Theory.

What's the Five-Dream Theory?

The *Times* carried a story a couple of years ago about a new sleep-research project that concluded that a typical night's dreams follow a sequence like the movements of a symphony. The first dream is a kind of overture, usually short and set in the present. It has to do with some problem that was on our minds before we fell asleep, and it sounds the themes for the four dreams that follow. The next two usually deal with situations from the past, but they incorporate our present feelings. The fourth projects the future and concerns a wish-fulfillment, like not having the problem that occasioned the first dream. The fifth and last one, set in the present again, reorchestrates all the earlier dreams into a grand finale.

Fenwick is in the head, evacuating his bowels, checking the chart inserts in the Cruising Guide, and listening with a certain interest.

*What do you think?* Susan wants to know. *I need to pee when you're done in there.*

*I think that that's the silliest goddamn dream theory I ever did hear of.* He pumps. *I'm a man inclined to pay some mild attention to his dreams, Suse, and I can't remember their ever once following any such sequence. I'll bet even Beethoven's didn't. Prima facie feces. Eighteen, nineteen, twenty. The head's yours.*

Susan declares she's just reporting the news, and we make a bread-and-coffee breakfast, all we have left. The early morning is gray and still, but less muggy; the NOAA* forecast is for a fine hot day, high around ninety, a good southwesterly on the Bay from a big high-pressure cell parked off the coast, and the usual chance of late-afternoon or evening thunderstorms. Rocky as we feel from lack of regular sleep, we are so eager to leave Key Island that we weigh anchor at 0700 without our morning swim and motor out of Poe Cove on what must be nearly the end of our diesel fuel. In jeans, hooded sweatshirt, and leather deck-moccasins, Susan steers *Pokey* out along the breakwater while Fenn—dressed likewise except that his sweatshirt is un-zipped down to his waist, his jeans are cut off short, and his head is wrapped already in that paisley scarf against the rising sun—secures the anchor to its roller chock and swabs the foredeck down.

But he cannot resist bidding her pause for a minute among those crab-pot buoys. Susan thinks he intends to look for his *boina*, the tale of which it depresses her for several reasons to remember. She rolls her eyes and halts the heavy boat with a burst of reverse thrust. The diesel having a left-handed propellor, *Pokey*'s stern kicks a little to starboard as we stop. Our dinghy, still on a shortened painter, bumps the transom.

*What are you doing?* To her surprise, he has fished up one of the markers with the boat hook and is pulling up the line. *Fenwick!*

---

*National Oceanic and Atmospheric Administration.

Just checking, he says. It seems mighty strange that no one has tended these pots for two days.

The mist on the water is already burning off, and the first light breeze springs up, from the predicted quarter. Later Fenwick will explain that, given the commercial crabbers' justly celebrated touchiness about anyone's messing with their pots, it had occurred to him during his watch that waterproof packages in crab pots would be a dandy means of dropping dope. The Key Island Connection. One could even catch crabs in the same operation. But just as he gets the wire trap to the surface—and sees nothing in it but a few disgruntled, autotomic* hardcrabs and one dead perch—an unmistakable rifle shot rings out from shore, and simultaneously a small geyser sprays up half a boatslength abeam.

Get down! Fenn hollers, dropping the pot and throwing himself across the cabin trunk onto the opposite gunwale. Susan is already downward bound as he shouts. From the cockpit sole she shoves forward the gearshift-throttle and barrels off at full speed, never mind the markers, poking her head up just enough to make sure we're aimed Away. Fenn wriggles back to her, snatches the binoculars from their rack in the companionway, and, still keeping a very low profile, scans the shoreline astern, near that jetty.

Okay, he says presently, touching her arm. We're out of range.

His breath comes heavy; Sue's too, as she throttles down. Nothing, he growls, replacing the binoculars. You okay?

Susan nods, eyes closed. We kill the engine and coast for some moments.

Well, says Fenwick: *that* thickens the old plot.

Was it the crabber, onshore, Susan wonders, warning us off his pots? Could be. But he packs a high-powered warner: thirty-thirty at least, and probably with a scope.

Good-bye, Key Island! Good-bye, Poe Cove! When our pulse subsides, we raise the main, unroll the genoa, and run

---

*The blue crab, *Callinectes sapidus*, in extremis tends to detach its own appendages.

northeast wing and wing on the building breeze. Given the
fair forecast and the fact that no marine-supply stores will be
open on Sunday, we decide to spend the day reaching and
running up the Bay, determining our position where possible from the Cruising Guide inserts and from passing vessels
until we're onto Chart 12223: Chesapeake Bay: Wolf Trap
to Smith Point. There will be plenty of yachts out; we shall
watch the sky, check the forecast every two hours, and work
out our go/no-gos as soon as we're back on the map.

It is not long before we see another early riser ahead,
beating our way: a large sloop heeled over and doing nicely
on the starboard tack under main and number one genoa.
We alter course to pass nearby and raise them successfully
on the radio as soon as we can read the name on their
transom. Fenwick explains we've lost our chart in a storm
and requests course and distance to Wolf Trap Light,
halfway between Mobjack Bay and the mouth of Piankatank
River. Hold on, *Pokey*, says a woman on the other end, and a
short while after calls back: Twenty degrees magnetic.
About ten miles. Just follow the line of black-and-white
channel buoys till we see the lighthouse off our port bow.
We're welcome. Over and out.

We want mightily to ask whether there's a Key Island on
their chart; but we'll soon enough have one of our own.
We're making five knots; the black-and-white marks slide by
every nautical mile and a half. By nine we can see the Wolf
Trap Light, fifty-two feet tall; before ten we're abeam of it.
Susan sails while Fenn does his chartwork on 12223 and
12224: from Wolf Trap to Smith Point is about thirty
nautical miles; thirty-three more to Solomons Island. The
breeze, still picking up, has moved a touch more westerly;
our course after Wolf Trap is 000° true, right up the
longitude line of 76°10′ W.—meaning we can broad reach
instead of running, with the wind just enough abeam of our
port quarter to fill the genoa without our dropping the
main: a faster point of sail than dead-running without a
spinnaker. We should reach Smith Point, at the broad
mouth of the Potomac, by half past two if the wind holds;

between us and it along the Western Shore is a string of
snug shelters to run into if we get a storm warning. At Smith
Point we'll make the harder decision to go/no-go to Solomons Island, in the mouth of the Patuxent.

It is a beautiful Sunday, college commencement weather,
stoking up fast ashore but splendid on the Bay. We are ever
calmer and more refreshed as the mileage grows between us
and Key Island. Caribbean music, reggae and calypso, pipes
down from a D.C. public radio station: Rastafarian revolutionary lyrics lilting over the irresistible rhythms. Bob
Marley and the Wailers. Mighty Sparrow's greatest hits.

> Ex-pro-pri-ate de cane fields.
> Geeve um to de pee-pull.

Susan does not resist. While Fenwick, at the helm now,
reflects wincingly upon Company operations in the Caribbean, she peels out of her clothes, lotions herself head to
foot, and dances happily on the windward gunwale, the
cabin trunk, the foredeck. He strips and lotions too, except
for his scarfed head. The air is as sensuous on the
Chesapeake this Sunday forenoon as ever in Jamaica or
Trinidad. Still moving with the rhythm, we do each other's
backs and backsides. The music, the fresh light and sweet
air, the being out of Poe Cove and under way again in
familiar waters—dark-eyed Susan is turned on by these and
by her own exaggeration of sexiness, which now becomes no
exaggeration. Without pausing in her cockpit dance, she
lotions her husband's genitals, continues to handle them,
peeks under the headsails to see that no boats or other
hazards lie near, reaches back to set the self-steering vane,
which Fenn has fixed enough to work in light air. Now she's
kneeling on the cockpit cushion. . . .

Sex at six knots. We are inspired with the joy of being alive
and of our life together; our extraordinary good fortune in
each other and our privilege in the world; the preciousness
of such an hour, such a morning, on such a planet. And
something else.

Fenn holds her a tergo, his heart pumping. Sue's too,

under her breast, under his hand. Done, he is still huge in her. Now he isn't. West Indian political news has replaced the reggae: updates on the new Grenadian revolutionary government, on Florida's deluge of Cuban exiles, on the commemorative T-shirts distributed to wretched Haitian peasants in honor of "Baby Doc" Duvalier's wedding in Port-au-Prince. Fenwick slips out. No change in the situation of U.S. hostages in Iran. Susan wipes us both with paper towels. More kisses. We leave the self-steering set.

Our naked lunch is canned sardines, canned peanuts, canned wheat wafers, and warm canned soda: the larder is truly low. At 1400 hours we're abeam of Smith Point and must make our decision. The forecast is unchanged. If the breeze holds, we can reach Solomons in another five to six hours: i.e., between 7 and 8 P.M. The sun will set about half past eight EDST, and there'll be usable light till nine. On the other hand, should the wind fail, as it often does at the end of a summer afternoon, or should the thunderstorms materialize, of which there is a thirty percent probability, we have little in the way of haven along this next stretch: marshy, shoaly islands to starboard; unbroken cliffs to port—a rarity in the Chesapeake. Moreover, our fuel supply is low enough to make questionable our powering any distance through calm or storm. Prudence inclines to heading in.

What about all these Prohibited Areas? Susan wonders, looking at 12223. Practice-firing ranges. Bombing targets. Not used on weekends, Fenwick assures her. We'll stay out where there are boats. If wind and fuel both run out, she observes, we're in a pickle, storm or no storm. Fenn answers wryly We can always call the Coast Guard. And this *is* the Bay; by ocean standards we aren't liable to get into very serious trouble. No question that the cautious choice would be to run into the first anchorage on the Potomac. But it's only two o'clock; the breeze is forecast to hold, and *Pokey*'s certainly tearing along now.

He is, and that fact tips it. Even after so much and

exhausting sailing, who can say no to such a fine day's sail? There are boats everywhere about now: sloops, yawls, ketches, even a schooner over yonder, bowling along under brilliant spinnakers or big white genoas in the Sunday breeze. It is a perfect day for sailing! We decide to sail, leaving the vane set but standing by to mind the buoys and traffic.

More music, while we make our plans. About sundown we'll radio Carmen B. Seckler. Tonight we'll lie at anchor off Solomons Island; tomorrow we'll rent a marina slip for a few days of rest, repairs, reprovisioning. We could perhaps avail ourselves of the moorings, docks, and houses of several of Fenn's ex-colleagues in the area, but it seems wiser not to. We'll take a motel room nearby, if there is one: hot showers, laundry, air conditioning! Fenwick will bus to Washington to do certain business that needs doing.

Susan wonders whether it's safe for him to be there at all. Fenn thinks so.

So did Mister Paisley.

F.S.K. Turner is not J. A. Paisley.

Your brother wasn't Paisley, either. But he disappeared like Paisley.

I'm neither Count nor Paisley, Suse. On with the story.

You won't mind if Mims and Ma come down while you're in D.C.?

Of course not. Or rent a car, if you want, and drive up there. I'll be gone a day at most: not overnight.

No need, says Susan. We'll be in Baltimore Harbor by next week. They won't mind driving down.

Fenwick considers, then sets forth his private, no doubt whimsical reason for preferring Solomons Island to a mainland harbor. Since the turn of the year, we have been on or between islands. Fenn feels therefore, irrationally but strongly, that tying up at a mainland slip, even anchoring in a mainland cove, is tantamount to ending our sabbatical voyage. It was our hope and intention that by the end of this same voyage we would know better our hearts and minds vis-à-vis several decisions which lie ahead; but by and large we don't, yet. The coincidence of our first Chesapeake anchorage's being yet another island, together with our plan to pause at Wye Island, *Pokey*'s home port, across the Bay, en route to Baltimore, has suggested to Fenwick that we do our Baltimore business not from the city's Inner Harbor but from Gibson Island, at the mouth of the Magothy River, just down the Bay from Baltimore's Patapsco. In short, let's stay with islands, enisled, isolated, until we know better our main landfall. Maybe we'll know after Washington and Baltimore. If not, there's always Long Island. Martha's Vineyard. Nantucket.

Nova Scotia! Susan cries. The British Isles! Then canal through Europe to the Mediterranean! The Aegean islands! Sweet Crete!* Sicily, Corsica, Gibraltar!

Fenwick grins and says The Balearics. The Canaries. Then over to Barbados and back to the Virgins and home again.

No! Through Suez to Ceylon. Micronesia! Polynesia! Hawaii!

Fenn says perfectly seriously We could, you know, Suse. With a bit of refitting. People do such things. Work only as we need to. Screw the world. Sail around it till we're old.

Susan knows, all right, and sees the sense of his whim about Solomons and Gibson. We had allowed for the possibility, if not the likelihood, that our sabbatical cruise might increase rather than decrease certain uncertainties; that is what has come regrettably to pass.

Smith Point—named for Captain John, who first explored our Bay for English settlers in 1608—is now astern; Smith Island, ditto, is off our starboard beam. We are in Maryland waters—another threshold?—and committed to Solomons. Appropriately for a threshold, the Bay here turns a touch westward, permitting us a faster reach north-northwest. There are tankers, containerships, miscellaneous freighters

---

*Sue had a quick hot romance there once, in pre-Fenwick days, in the neighborhood of Heraklion.

among the sailors and sport-fisherfolk. We identify off to starboard Tangier and Smith islands; then uninhabited Bloodsworth, a bombing target; then Hooper, off which Paisley either did it or got it, and, to port, Point No Point, where his abandoned sloop went aground, all sails set.

Isn't it time, Fenwick asks Susan, to give the reader a quick review of the strange true case of John Arthur Paisley? We keep dropping that name; he/she must be wondering. The reader.

In Sue's opinion it would be a breach of verisimilitude for either of us to review that case to the other as we sail along, when both of us know the details painfully well. That particular narrative lapse is called Forced Exposition; Susan's name for it, in the classroom, is Corning the Goose. For as the hapless goose must feel, when to enlarge its liver for pâté de foie gras the French commercial goose farmer rams a hose down its gullet and blows its belly full of corn, so must the reader feel when fictional characters say things to each other that between them should go without saying, just to get the author's exposition done. There'll be none of that, Susan says, in our story.

Fenn ponders, then suggests Suppose the author does it straight out, instead of putting it into the characters' mouths? That's not Corning the Goose, is it? He wonders whether here mayn't be an advantage of novels over plays (he has thought of trying our story as a play): that we can come in as author and give the reader a spot of briefing as needed. Right?

Susan guesses so, if we do it adroitly. Otherwise it's Author Intrusion.

It's always something. Tell you what, Teach: here in the planning stage, let's settle for efficiently; never mind adroitly. Later on, we'll adroit it all up.

Well.

Sure, Suse. We put *Pokey* on the vane, but we stand by to override as necessary. In the same way, we let the author take the helm of our story and brief the reader on

## THE STRANGE TRUE CASE OF JOHN ARTHUR PAISLEY

while we split a warm beer and do some plotting down the road and maybe take turns napping.

Susan Seckler shakes her head and says admiringly Your ship, author.

Thank you. The following account is composed entirely of excerpts from reports published in the Baltimore *Sun* in 1978 and 1979 (except for the last, from January 1980), most of them written by two of that newspaper's investigative reporters, Mr. Tom Nugent and Mr. Steve Parks, with whose kind permission, and that of the *Sun*, we quote:

### CIA LABEL SAID TO BE ON DOCUMENTS ABOARD SLOOP OF DEAD EX-SPY OFFICIAL *

Documents bearing the words "Central Intelligence Agency" were aboard the sloop *Brillig* when it was found aground near Point Lookout the day after John Arthur Paisley, once a high-ranking Central Intelligence Agency official, was reported missing from his boat, a person who was at the scene said yesterday.

Although first reports on the boat were that nothing was amiss, a Coast Guard spokesman yesterday noted that life preservers on the sloop were "scattered about" and "not in their proper place."

Mr. Paisley, 55, of Washington, was found shot to death Sunday night—a week after he had disappeared—in the Chesapeake Bay near the mouth of the Patuxent River. Forty pounds of diving weights were strapped to his chest and waist.

Police officials have leaned toward regarding the case as a possible suicide, but no official determination has been announced, and the State Police investigation of the case continues.

State Police said yesterday they had been unable to determine whether the murder weapon was a 9-mm. handgun, the type Mr. Paisley reportedly carried aboard

---

*Baltimore *Sun*, October 5, 1978.

the ship, or a .38 revolver, a gun type not heretofore associated with the death.

An assistant state medical examiner refused yesterday to answer directly any questions as to whether there were bruises on Mr. Paisley's body. The medical examiner at first noted that the body was badly decomposed, then said he "couldn't recall" and finally referred all questions to the State Police.

Adding to the mystery was a report from a friend yesterday that Michael Yohn, of the Agency for International Development (AID), the last known person to see Mr. Paisley alive, has left the country hurriedly. The friend, who asked not to be named, said he did not know where Mr. Yohn had gone, only that he might be away for as long as six months.

The source who was at the scene, who asked not to be identified, said that an attaché case, which was locked, was in . . . the sloop when it was found. Inside the case were documents which bore the words "Central Intelligence Agency."

Central Intelligence Agency employees were on hand when Maryann Paisley, the victim's estranged wife, went aboard last week. The CIA has officially denied any overt activity in the investigation of the death.

Sources said the operators examined the contents of the case before turning it over to Mrs. Paisley.

One source said that the documents returned concerned an intelligence experiment called "the B Team," which deals with the CIA attracting outside people to evaluate evidence and draw conclusions from the evidence. . . .

CIA officials who all week had contended that Mr. Paisley had left the agency in 1974 when he retired as deputy director of the Office for Strategic Research yesterday acknowledged that he had done consultant work for them since he was officially retired.

"John Paisley worked part-time on a contract basis as a member of the Military Economic Advisory Panel, composed of outside experts, which advises the director of Central Intelligence on the CIA's assessments of Soviet military expenditures and other economic affairs," the CIA announced in a prepared statement.

The Wilmington *News-Journal*, in a copyrighted story yesterday, quoted sources in the Washington intelligence community as saying the CIA is conducting its own investigation because it fears Mr. Paisley may have been murdered by the KGB, the Soviet intelligence agency.

Quoting sources in the Senate Intelligence Committee, the *News-Journal* story said that an investigation is being conducted into the possibility that there was a "high level mole" or double agent, within the agency who was leaking information to the Soviet Union.

The investigation began in August with the arrest of a 23-year-old CIA employee, William P. Kampiles, in Hammond, Ind., on charges of selling information to Soviet representatives on the KH-11 satellite surveillance system. After that arrest, the story said, other classified documents were found to be missing.

Sources said the satellite system, known as "Big Bird," will have the major burden of confirming that the Kremlin is adhering to any agreements reached at the strategic arms limitations talks.

According to the *News-Journal*'s sources, Mr. Paisley, who was an expert on Soviet and Chinese military operations, had helped plan the satellite system.

The *News-Journal*, citing sources, said that the head of the investigation into the leaks had contacted Mr. Paisley on the "remote possibility" that he was a double agent.

The CIA yesterday denied the *News-Journal* story.

A spokesman for the Maryland State Police said, "We do not know if someone got on the boat and did it. We cannot substantiate KGB reports. . . ."

Mr. Paisley disappeared September 24 [*1978*] while on a cruise on the Chesapeake Bay.

Mr. Yohn, the AID man, reportedly went out on a boat to see him about 2 P.M. and after cruising awhile told Mr. Paisley that he was going back to port to watch a football game.

Mr. Paisley was last heard from later that day when he

radioed a friend, Col. Norman Wilson (USAF Ret.), that he was on his way back [*to* Brillig's *mooring at Solomons Island, Md.*], but not to wait for him.

The derelict vessel was found the next day [*aground, with all sails set*] near the mouth of the Potomac River.

Police have quoted friends as saying Mr. Paisley was despondent over his recent separation from his wife. The Washington *Star* reported yesterday that he was also upset because of recent financial reversals and that Mr. Paisley had to take out a loan to pay a back tax debt.

Mrs. Paisley has denied that her husband was upset over the separation.

## SIX MONTHS LATER:
## NEW EVIDENCE CLOUDS
## PAISLEY "SUICIDE" VERDICT*

WASHINGTON— Six months after the body of a former CIA nuclear weapons expert, John Arthur Paisley, was found floating in Chesapeake Bay, new evidence, together with misleading statements about Mr. Paisley's role with the government, tend to cast doubt on the investigation's verdict of "apparent suicide." . . .

The evidence includes a firsthand account by a United States Coast Guardsman who says that he saw an opened package of lunch meat, a container of mustard and a knife smeared with mustard lying on a sink-top counter in the *Brillig*, Mr. Paisley's 34-foot sloop.

In addition to the food, the Coast Guardsman, who requested his identity not to be revealed, said he saw a sailing chart, located near the sloop's wheel, on which a sailing course had been partially mapped out, as well as a life preserver that had been left alongside.

"It looks to me like he had been interrupted in the middle of lunch," said the Coast Guardsman. "It looked like he had filled in part of the chart and then had decided to get something to eat. So he took off his life preserver and went below, down to the galley."

---

*Baltimore *Sun*, April 2, 1979.

. . . In addition to this account, a three-month *Sun* investigation has produced new evidence that indicates a struggle may have taken place aboard the *Brillig* in the hours before Mr. Paisley's disappearance.

The evidence includes a statement by Mr. Paisley's widow, Maryann, who visited the sloop soon after it was found and who said that "a table had been pulled away from the wall. Several screws had been pulled loose, and it was tilted at an angle which would have made it impossible to use." Mr. Paisley, according to several sources, was writing a report during his final sailing excursion, and the table was the only adequate writing surface aboard.

The Maryland State Police, whose investigation concluded that Mr. Paisley's death was an "apparent suicide," earlier said that one witness [*Col. Wilson, aforementioned*]— an intelligence colleague who has since left for Australia— told them the table had been pulled loose from the wall months before the Central Intelligence Agency analyst's disappearance.

But another witness interviewed by the *Sun*—a young woman who was a guest aboard the *Brillig* one week before Mr. Paisley vanished—recalls that meals were served on the same table during her stay aboard.

"The table was working during our sailing trip; we had it up for meals and I also remembered it folded up against the wall," the guest said.

In addition to these accounts, no fewer than six high-level government sources—at least one of whom worked directly with Mr. Paisley on top-secret projects—have told the *Sun* that, at the time of his death, Mr. Paisley—who had been described by the CIA as a "part-time consultant with a very limited access to classified information"— actually was engaged in analyzing extremely sensitive, top-secret documents dealing with American assessments of Soviet nuclear capability.

"I found the initial reports . . . that Paisley had only limited access to classified information shocking," said a former high-level staffer on the President's Foreign Intelligence Advisory Board (PFIAB) who had earlier worked closely with Mr. Paisley on projects involving top-secret

CIA estimates of Soviet weaponry. "In fact, I was surprised that the agency would even try to pander that sort of information.

"There is no question that Paisley, at the time of his death, had access to highly classified intelligence information. . . . And this wasn't academic, outside stuff; it would have been the nitty-gritty."

. . . "The agency is flat-out lying," said one source. "Paisley was never *not* involved in something big."

Mr. Paisley's death was ruled an apparent suicide by the Maryland State Police—the only governmental agency that so far has investigated the case—a few weeks after the badly decomposed body . . . was pulled from the Chesapeake Bay, about 2 miles southeast of the Patuxent River, October 1.

The victim, shot once behind the left ear with a 9-mm. pistol, was found with two belts containing 39 pounds of diving weights attached to his waist.

The State Police . . . identified the body as Mr. Paisley's on the basis of dental records and fingerprints.

But the State Police investigation was marred by several anomalies and inconsistencies of fact.

—Both the FBI and the CIA were unable to locate a set of Mr. Paisley's fingerprints for more than a week after the discovery of the body ("Frankly, that strikes me as incredible," one high-level member of the intelligence community later remarked. ". . . I know for a fact that every time you get a new clearance for classified information, they take your prints again. In fact, it got to be a pain in the neck. . . . They must have a dozen sets of Paisley's prints.")

At the time Paisley's body surfaced, however, both the FBI and the CIA said that his fingerprints had been "lost." The fingerprint identification was not made until about a week after the discovery of the body. The FBI said that the prints had been misfiled: the only available set of prints had been filed under the name of "Jack" Paisley and had been taken when the weapons expert was 17 years old.

—The shooting death took place in the absence of

witnesses, and the body, which was decomposed beyond recognition, was cremated in a CIA-approved funeral home without ever having been observed by anyone who knew Mr. Paisley.

—Both Mr. Paisley's boat and his Washington apartment were searched by CIA repesentatives soon after the discovery of the body. By the time the State Police came on the scene (after the body was found) the original evidence had been contaminated.

—No traces of blood or brain fragments were found aboard the *Brillig*. Thus, the suicide verdict requires one to believe that Mr. Paisley either shot himself [*behind the left ear*] while standing on the edge of the boat (so that the shell casing, the pistol and the blood and brain fragments fell overboard with him), or that he shot himself while in the water . . . wearing 39 pounds of diving weights.

—When the deserted boat was discovered, the wheel was unlocked and the ship-to-shore radio was still playing. Mr. Paisley's widow, who says that she sailed for years with her husband, insists that he was a meticulous sailor who would never have left these chores untended. "Even if he had been under emotional duress, he would have locked that wheel by instinct."

—The first people to be contacted after the discovery of the *Brillig* were officials at the CIA and at the Washington accounting firm of Coopers and Lybrand, where Mr. Paisley had been working as an executive aide for about six months [*in addition to his $200-a-day consultancy to the CIA itself*]. The accounting firm, headed by K. Wayne Smith, a former Defense Department weapons expert who has served on the National Security Council and who has performed weapons-analysis work for both the Pentagon and the Rand Corporation, immediately dispatched one of its employees to Mr. Paisley's apartment.

After being admitted by the landlady, the employee searched the apartment and took away a Rolodex telephone book that contained numbers listed by Mr. Paisley.

The CIA, meanwhile, sent representatives to both the *Brillig* and the apartment. They confiscated a briefcase full of papers that they found aboard the boat and examined other papers located at the apartment.

All of these steps were taken before Mr. Paisley's family—he had two grown children in addition to his estranged wife, Maryann—was notified that the boat had been found. Mrs. Paisley says she was not contacted until about 11 P.M. (the boat was discovered about 11 A.M.). . . .

—Mr. Paisley's wife (the couple had been separated for about two years prior to the disappearance) and several other people who knew him well insist that he was in good spirits just before his disappearance. "He called me up that weekend," said Mrs. Paisley in a later interview. "He said that he was thinking about going sailing—but that if he didn't, we'd have dinner together.

"My feeling is that something very sinister is happening. . . . John was an ethical man—he would never do this . . . to his children. . . ."

Most of the questions about Mr. Paisley's disappearance have focused, in recent months, on his participation in an extremely sensitive and controversial 1978 intelligence project, known as the "Team A–Team B Experiment."

That experiment was launched after White House experts on the President's Foreign Intelligence Advisory Board convinced CIA officials that the agency's yearly evaluations of Soviet military capacity should be tested by comparing them with evaluations made by experts outside the CIA.

After agreeing reluctantly to the proposal, early in 1976, the CIA named Mr. Paisley to serve as coordinator between the agency's A Team—its own, "in-house" weapons analysis group—and the B Team, which was composed of three different groups of outside experts and which was chaired by Richard Pipes, head of Harvard University's Russian Institute.

"It was Paisley who developed the list of people who would serve on the B Team," says a former PFIAB White House staffer. "It was his job to get these guys clearance . . . to discuss their backgrounds. . . ."

## 2 PROBES RESUME ON PAISLEY*

Both the Maryland State Police and the Senate Select Committee on Intelligence have determined that "troubling questions" concerning the death of John Arthur Paisley . . . warrant a resumption of their separate investigations.

. . . Col. Norman Wilson, a former employee of the Defense Intelligence Agency and the last man known to have communicated with Mr. Paisley . . . [*has gone*] to Australia for an "indefinite stay." . . .

. . . Numerous sources have stated that [*Paisley*] was working on sensitive data related to the strategic arms limitation talks (SALT II) with the Soviet Union.

Another source, a former staff member of the President's Foreign Intelligence Advisory Board, earlier speculated that Mr. Paisley might have been killed as part of the U.S.–Soviet Intelligence struggle, in which two Russian spies had been caught.

In October, at the time of Mr. Paisley's death, Vladik A. Enger and Rudolph P. Chernayev were convicted and sentenced to 50 years in prison for attempting to buy antisubmarine secrets from a U.S. naval officer.

The Russians maintained that their agents had been entrapped in the incident. The two Russian spies were traded Friday for Russian dissidents, including Alexander Ginzburg.

The former intelligence board staff member had suggested to the *Sun* that the Russians may have suspected Mr. Paisley was also attempting to entrap Soviet agents at the time of his death.

---

*Baltimore *Sun*, May 2, 1979.

## INSURERS BAR PAISLEY BENEFITS*

Concluding that a body recovered from the Chesapeake Bay last October 1 may not have been that of John Arthur Paisley . . . two life insurance companies have decided to withhold paying off on policies held by him at the time of his disappearance, according to the victim's widow.

Both Mrs. Maryann Paisley and her attorney, Bernard Fensterwald, Jr., confirmed yesterday that they will bring legal action against both companies—the Mutual Life Insurance Company of New York (MONY) and Mutual of Omaha—in an effort to collect $200,000 in outstanding life insurance benefits.

Mrs. Paisley has already collected $35,000 on a CIA life insurance policy.

"We're bringing suit against both companies," Mr. Fensterwald said. "They have informed us that they refuse to pay those claims because they have doubts, one, as to whether or not he's dead, and two, if he is dead, how he died."

. . . Among the anomalies which have cast doubt on both the suicide verdict and the identification of the body are these:

. . . About a week after the request for fingerprints, the FBI announced that . . . the only set it owned had been filed under the name "Jack Arthur Paisley"—and had been taken when Mr. Paisley was 17 years old. These prints, according to the FBI, matched the ones on the hands of the body, which had been amputated and sent on to the FBI by the state medical examiner, Dr. Russell Fisher, during his autopsy. . . .

—Because the body was bloated and badly decomposed, no visual identification of it was ever attempted by anyone who had known Mr. Paisley. Dr. Fisher said he advised the members of the Paisley family that attempts at identification would be useless, but that they could try if they wished; they refused, and the remains later were cremated without having been looked at.

---

*Baltimore *Sun*, May 21, 1979.

Mrs. Paisley . . . later looked at photographs of the corpse supplied to her by the medical examiner's office. "That's not him," she insisted. "I'm positive. That's not his nose."

The body . . . was clad in blue jeans and undershorts several sizes smaller than the ones Mr. Paisley was wearing at the time of his disappearance, according to members of his family.

(Dr. Fisher confirmed during the autopsy that the body recovered from the bay was clad in a pair of size-30 Jockey undershorts; the State Police earlier reported, according to the Paisley family, that the blue jeans also had a size-30 waist. Mr. Paisley's clothing at the time of his disappearance ranged from 34 to 36 in waist size, according to his family.)

—No traces of blood or brain fragments were left on the *Brillig*—even though the dead man pulled from the bay had been shot with an anti-personnel type of bullet which expands on impact, causing extensive damage to body tissue. . . .

—Betty Myers, Mr. Paisley's girlfriend at the time of his disappearance, told investigators that he had sold his 9-mm. pistol—the gun which police allege was used in the death. In addition, State Police so far have been unable to determine where Mr. Paisley obtained the gun.

### TOP-SECRET NUMBERS FOUND
### AMONG PAISLEY'S EFFECTS*

WASHINGTON— A CIA "red-line" telephone notebook—containing top-secret numbers of American spies—was among the effects left behind by John Arthur Paisley, the high-ranking intelligence officer who allegedly committed suicide last September.

Maryland State Police and Mr. Paisley's wife say that the notebook contained numbers and names in his own handwriting. The book bore a strip of red tape along its outside left edge—a CIA marking which indicates that it

---

*Baltimore *Sun*, June 10, 1979.

must never leave agency headquarters and must be kept in a safe.

The notebook contained top-secret telephone numbers which connected American intelligence-gathering operatives, according to Central Intelligence Agency sources who have examined it and Senate Intelligence Committee investigators who also learned that the notebook was found . . . in a briefcase full of papers, recovered from Mr. Paisley's boat.

The Maryland State Police confirmed that they looked at the red-line book, but pointed out that the briefcase . . . already had been handled by several people by the time they arrived on the scene . . . therefore [they] do not dismiss the possibility that it might have been planted there.

The discovery of the red-line phone book, along with several recent statements by officials in the U.S. intelligence community, suggests that Mr. Paisley may have been involved in covert operations at the time of his disappearance—rather than doing routine weapons-analysis work, as the CIA has maintained. . . .

Taking such a notebook, which contains the unlisted numbers of covert intelligence operatives working at the agency, out of headquarters is considered a security breach, according to CIA sources familiar with the agency's communication system.

"You know, for most of us who work here," said one CIA analyst who works in the agency headquarters in Langley, Va., "it's just like any other job. But the people . . . in the red-line books, well, that's certainly the covert side."

Since John Paisley's death eight months ago—officially thought to be a suicide, though coroners refused to fix the blame—the CIA has maintained that John Paisley had no contact with the agency's covert operations and that he never worked in counterintelligence.

But the *Sun*'s six-month investigation of the case has revealed a John Paisley who differs in some respects from the one characterized by the CIA. . . .

—Mr. Paisley regularly interrogated both dissident im-

migrants and political defectors from the Soviet Union—
questioning, among others, a former KGB agent, Yuri
Nosenko, and Capt. Nicholas Shadrin, a defector from the
Soviet navy*—in an effort to locate possible Soviet intelligence operatives within the ranks of dissidents or to sniff
out double agents among the defectors.

According to one counterintelligence source, Mr.
Paisley wrote out questions for Mr. Nosenko—"re-
quirements" to establish the defector's credibility or "bona
fides"—which were presented by professional interrogators, often under hostile circumstances. Mr. Paisley also
analyzed Mr. Nosenko's responses, the source said.

Several other agency sources have confirmed the questioning of both Mr. Nosenko and Captain Shadrin. In
addition, Eva Shadrin, the wife of the Soviet naval officer
(he disappeared while walking through a public square in
Vienna in 1975), said Wednesday that her husband in
recent years [*prior to his disappearance*] had moored his
sailboat at tiny Solomons Island, Md., on the Chesapeake
Bay.

John Paisley also moored his sailboat, the *Brillig*, at
Solomons. It was from this mooring, owned by Col.
Norman Wilson . . . that he set sail September 24 on the
voyage that ended in his disappearance and death.

In addition, Mrs. Paisley and other agency sources have
said that the CIA has operated a "safe house" (a protected
location in which intelligence activities, such as defector
interviews, are carried out) at Solomons for many years.
Mrs. Paisley says her husband often mentioned interrogation sessions that had taken place on the island.

—During the early stages in the second round in the
strategic arms limitation talks, which took place in
Helsinki, Mr. Paisley was approached by agents for the
KGB . . . and was asked to become a double agent . . . on
the subject of the U.S. negotiating position at the talks.
Mr. Paisley immediately reported the contact to his superi-
ors in the CIA, and was advised to "take the pitch,"
according to sources.

---

*See note pp. 45–46.

Mr. Paisley . . . subsequently fed information to the KGB about the United States fallback position in the SALT negotiations and about how the U.S. intended to "cheat" on SALT. It is not known whether Mr. Paisley fed the Russians accurate information or "disinformation." . . .

—Mr. Paisley apparently was involved, about five years ago, in an extraordinarily complicated, agency-wide search for a well-entrenched Soviet double agent, or "mole," who had penetrated the highest levels of the CIA command.

That search, which reportedly culminated in a Byzantine operation called "Kitty Hawk," focused on secret communications in which both the CIA and the KGB regularly contacted Captain Shadrin, Mr. Nosenko, and two other KGB defectors. . . .

While the complicated series of intelligence maneuvers that produced Kitty Hawk has not yet been made clear . . . some agency sources believe that Mr. Paisley—in his role as deputy chief of the CIA Office of Strategic Research— may have been charged with collecting and collating the disinformation which was provided to the Russians . . . during [the] operation. . . . These sources also suggest that Mr. Paisley might have been analyzing the wording of the information provided by the CIA sources—in order to unravel the code, and thus unearth the mole.

"Paisley may have gotten caught in the middle," suggests one intelligence source. "Maybe he learned who the mole was. Or maybe he stumbled across some piece of information which might have led to the mole—and which made him an instant liability."

There is some other evidence to suggest that Mr. Paisley was deeply involved in counterintelligence work—and perhaps in a search for a mole—at the time of his death.

—Mrs. Paisley reports that James Angleton [*former head of CIA counterintelligence; see note, p. 45*] asked her to meet him in a bar a few months after her husband's death. "He came in wearing a black trenchcoat, a hat pulled down low over his eyes, and carrying a newspaper under his arm," she says. "He walked past my table, circled the entire bar, sat down at a table, and beckoned me over.

"He said he had only two questions to ask me. He wanted to know which CIA operatives John had known during his time at the Imperial War College in London, for one thing."

Mrs. Paisley refuses to permit Mr. Angleton's second question to be printed, claiming that it is "too sensitive."


## REPORT SAYS PAISLEY WAS SUSPECT IN LEAKS*

WILMINGTON (AP)— Several members of a secret U.S. intelligence team claim John Paisley was the prime suspect of leaks to newspapers about their project, according to the Wilmington *News-Journal*. . . .

The secret "B Team" of experts on the Soviet Union was set up by the federal government to test CIA assessments of Soviet military strength, according to the newspaper.

The article quoted David Binder, a reporter for the *New York Times*, as saying Mr. Paisley was the prime source for his article about the team's highly classified work.

In that story, Mr. Binder wrote of the B Team's opinion that the CIA had underestimated Soviet military strength. Mr. Binder told the *News-Journal* that while it is highly unusual to reveal a confidential source, he was doing so in this case because he believed Mr. Paisley was dead.

Some members of the team told the *News-Journal* that they felt Mr. Paisley may have leaked the information out of professional loyalty to the agency where he worked for 25 years. During that time he participated in developing some of the assessments the B Team was scrutinizing.

The B Team's role was to see if the CIA—and Mr. Paisley—had done a thorough job in assessing Soviet strength.

Seymour Weiss, a former State Department official, said a Soviet agent would want to discredit the team's conclusion that the CIA was "underestimating Soviet strength." He said such discrediting would "prevent U.S. policymakers from reacting by getting tougher."

---

*Baltimore *Sun*, June 27, 1979.

Mr. Weiss said that anyone connected with leaking secrets from the team could be a double agent.

At the time Mr. Paisley disappeared, he was working on a report for the CIA about the B Team project, the newspaper said. A draft of the report was found on his boat when it was found drifting on the Chesapeake Bay. . . .

Meanwhile, an attorney for Mr. Paisley's estranged wife has called a press conference for today to present evidence that the former official, who was thought to have committed suicide, was murdered.

The press conference was scheduled for Solomons, Md., near where Mr. Paisley's boat, the *Brillig,* was found aground last fall. . . .

## 2 MEN WHO SAW BODY SAID TO BE PAISLEY'S CLAIM THAT NECK WOUNDS RULE OUT SUICIDE*

SOLOMONS— Two men who said they examined the body identified as that of the former CIA weapons expert, John Arthur Paisley, within hours of its discovery last October 1, said here yesterday they saw severe neck wounds indicating that the victim had either been strangled or had his throat cut before he disappeared into the waters of the Chesapeake Bay.

Dr. George Weems, then the deputy medical examiner in Calvert County . . . said he conducted a preliminary autopsy examination of the body at the request of the Maryland State Police, and that:

"I observed what you might call a brush-burn, or bad lesions, stretching from ear to ear. It looked like a rope burn. The skin was red all the way around; it [*the lesion*] was about an inch wide.

"I think probably he was strangled," Dr. Weems said at a news conference here.

The other witness, Harry Lee Langley, Sr., owner of the Langley Point Marina on Solomons Island, said, "The throat had been slashed because a bad gash ran from ear to ear. . . .

*Baltimore *Sun,* June 28, 1979.

. . . "I was there when the body came into the Naval Ordnance Laboratory [*on Solomons*]. I saw the body on the stern of the Coast Guard boat. . . . Put it this way: he either had a bad burn or his throat had been cut."

In Baltimore, meanwhile, Dr. Russell S. Fisher, the state medical examiner who concluded last fall that Mr. Paisley probably died of a self-inflicted bullet wound in the back of the head, dismissed the statements of Dr. Weems and Mr. Langley as "baloney."

"If that's all they [*the widow, Maryann Paisley, and her lawyer*] have, then I'm surprised they even bothered to go public with it. . . .

"I don't give a damn what anybody says. Paisley died of a bullet in the head. Weems did not have time to adequately examine the body. He's under orders to send a case like this straight up to Baltimore, which he did."

. . . A police spokesman who had not attended the press conference questioned the motives of the witnesses produced by Mrs. Paisley's lawyer, Bernard Fensterwald, Jr., asking why they had not come forward with their information in the nine months since Mr. Paisley's alleged suicide.

Mr. Langley said he had been instructed by officials at the Naval Ordnance Laboratory "not to talk. They told me Mr. Paisley was CIA, and they wanted to just . . . put it this way—nobody should know nothing."

But Mr. Langley said he recently decided—after reading newspaper accounts of how insurance companies have refused to pay death benefits on policies on Mr. Paisley—to come forward publicly with his information.

. . . Dr. Weems said . . . that he did not mention the lesion in his preliminary autopsy report, because he was asked only to prepare a gross physical description of the body. . . .

Colonel [*Thomas*] Smith [*head of the Maryland State Police*] volunteered that "If there is any question, I would . . . be inclined to accept Dr. Fisher's examination of the body. He's one of the top men in his . . . field [*forensic medicine*]. . . . Those county medical examiners . . . it's their job just to determine if the guy's dead or not.

"There wasn't much doubt about it in this case," Colonel Smith said.

... "As far as I'm concerned," said Mr. Fensterwald, "[*this new testimony*] clears up any lingering doubts that he committed suicide. These wounds on the neck were serious—and I don't see how he could have inflicted them himself." ...


## BURGLARS HIT PAISLEY HOME
## AS HE SAILED, PAPER SAYS*

WILMINGTON (AP)— Someone broke into John A. Paisley's Washington apartment while the former Central Intelligence Agency official was taking his last sail and removed an assortment of personal memorabilia and secret government documents, the Wilmington *News-Journal* reported . . . today.

. . . Eddie Paisley, 22, the former CIA official's son, was asked by his mother to check on the apartment after she learned of the discovery of the sailboat. . . .

He discovered that papers were strewn about and that a camera, tape recorder and several hours of tape recordings detailing the Paisley family history were missing.

Several 9-millimeter bullets were strewn on the floor of a closet. . . .

[*Kennard Smith, an investigator working for Mrs. Paisley's attorney, said:*] "We knew the building was under surveillance because half a dozen Russians lived on the same floor as her husband. She [*Mrs. Paisley*] didn't know what to do, so she told the CIA. . . .

The newspaper quoted unidentified sources on the Senate Select Committee on Intelligence as saying that Mr. Paisley had some important CIA documents which have never been recovered, including debriefing reports on Arkady Shevchenko, the highest-ranking Soviet official ever to defect to the United States.

Among the items which Mrs. Paisley turned over to the CIA was a note in her husband's handwriting saying: "Now what about Shevchenko?"

An unidentified source in Mr. Paisley's old CIA office was quoted by the newspaper as saying that the former

---

*Baltimore *Sun*, July 1, 1979.

official also had undercover identification documents, detailed inventories of the American nuclear arsenal and a top-secret report of the United States's surveillance capacity. . . .

Mr. Paisley's friends and co-workers . . . speculated that the break-in could have been arranged by a variety of people including the Soviets, the CIA, someone interested in the "B Team," someone interested in his work as an accountant analyzing CIA finances, or his family.

## WIDOW OF CIA OFFICIAL SAYS
## STRANGE BREAK-INS HAVE OCCURRED AT HOME*

The widow of a CIA nuclear weapons expert who died under mysterious circumstances in 1978 yesterday said that her family's home in northern Virginia was broken into last weekend and that scuba-diving gear and radio equipment which once belonged to her husband had been tampered with.

According to Maryann Paisley, her late husband's belongings had been "scattered all over the place. . . . The only explanation I can think of is that someone was trying to frighten me."

. . . In recent months [Mrs. Paisley] has filed several suits against the federal government under the Freedom of Information Act to force the CIA and other intelligence agencies to disclose details about her husband's disappearance.

She said she first noticed the apparent break-in at her McLean (Va.) home Friday evening after walking into the basement and finding her husband's scuba gear scattered about. "I was scared," she said. "It was all spread out—the wet suit, gloves, flippers, tanks, even the weights."

Mrs. Paisley says she did not call the police, however, because there were no evident signs of a break-in, and because nothing had been taken.

On Sunday, she says, she entered the basement again and discovered that several cases of radio equipment—

---

*Baltimore *Sun*, January 24, 1980.

apparatus which had been removed from Mr. Paisley's
sloop in the days immediately following the boat's discovery—had been opened, and their contents also scattered
about.

"It was clear that whoever broke into those boxes
wanted me to see what they had done," she said. "One of
those Atlas tuning things had been taken out of its box—it
was sitting up on a bench with a white belt around it."

Mrs. Paisley also reported that several neighbors had
observed a silver Camaro parked outside her home for
long periods of time on several occasions. . . .

A week after Mr. Paisley's disappearance [*16 months ago*],
the Coast Guard retrieved a body with one wound from a
9-mm. pistol in the head from the waters off Southern
Maryland.

After a brief investigation, the Maryland State Police
concluded that Mr. Paisley's death had been an "apparent
suicide." But this finding was challenged by both Mrs.
Paisley and the U.S. Senate Intelligence Committee, which
conducted a lengthy probe of the circumstances surround-
ing the death.

The Senate committee's findings, which are classified,
were never made public.

On a reasonably stiff sailboat in a good steady breeze, one
spends much time sitting still at a five- to ten-degree angle of
heel, and is naturally inclined to tell, hear, and discuss
stories.

You call that efficient? Susan wonders. We have slipped
into our swimsuit bottoms.

Well, says Fenwick, at least it's reasonably complete, as of
this date. Those insurance companies, we understand, finally paid off. And the author neglected to mention that
early reports spoke of there being a "burst" radio transmitter* aboard the *Brillig*. No cruising sailboat would ever

---

*The sort used to communicate with artificial satellites such as the
KH-11 "Big Bird" (p. 88). They send or receive in a few seconds a great
deal of information stored on tape; the high-speed transmission is an
automatic supercoding.

normally be equipped with one. But there's no follow-up on that detail, even in Missus Paisley's burglary report.

Sue asks what an Atlas tuning thing is. Fenn isn't sure—but it's not a burst transmitter.

I have a lot of questions, Susan says.

Me too. Such as Isn't it curious, in that testy exchange between Doctors Weems and Fisher, that the neck-lesion man, Doctor Weems, either didn't see or didn't mention the bullet wound—even though it was a dum-dum bullet that makes a little hole going in and a big hole coming out? And that Doctor Fisher, the bullet-wound man, neither confirms nor denies the neck lesions?

Yup. And is there really no follow-up on those undersize pants?

Nope. Fenwick's a thirty-four to thirty-six waist himself; he couldn't come near fastening a pair of size-thirty jeans.

If Paisley had a new girlfriend, Susan speculates, maybe he was reducing. But that would've got mentioned. And there'd have been other size-thirties in his wardrobe. Of course, nobody says there weren't. But to take five inches off his waistline—I don't believe it. Something's fishy. Crabby?

Susan.

What about those two friends of Paisley's who left the country right after his death?

Mister Yohn of the two o'clock rendezvous, who sailed back to watch a football game, and Colonel Wilson of the Solomons Island mooring, who got Paisley's evening transmission from off Hooper's Island.

Those reports didn't say Hooper's Island.

Others did. Paisley radioed Wilson that evening from off Hooper's Island to leave the light on at the end of his dock.

Did Yohn and Wilson ever come back?

They did. Colonel Wilson, I understand, visited Perth. A great many U.S. intelligence people have occasion to visit Perth. We have a big satellite tracking station there, for one thing. Count himself went to Perth more than once. In a sense, all roads lead to Perth. It's worth noting, by the way, that as of that evening transmission—if it was really made and if it really was from off Hooper's Island—one had a rough fix on *Brillig*'s position, if one wanted to go out there for any reason. . . .

But Susan points out that neither that alleged transmission nor the alleged 2 P.M. sighting by Mr. Yohn jibes with the Coast Guardsman's interrupted-lunch scenario. Maybe Paisley was making an evening snack when they got him?

Or maybe he sailed all night and next morning, which is bloody unlikely for a casual sail, and died at lunchtime on the twenty-fifth. When was the boat discovered?

Eleven A.M. on the twenty-fifth.

Early lunch? Lunch-meat-and-mustard breakfast?

Susan affirms that anything is possible. There have been moments aboard this vessel of ours when she could have been found wearing Fenwick's boxer shorts and eating peanut butter and oranges at three in the morning. And Fenn once climbed the mast, to free a fouled halyard, wearing nothing but Susan's underpants, on his head. And she can easily imagine a despondent person's being cheerful to her friends, setting out for a sail, plotting her course, making herself a sandwich at whatever hour of the day or night—and then pausing to strap on the old scuba weights and blow her brains out.

So can Fenwick. Catastrophe theory even describes such flip-flops mathematically.

Indeed, Susan persists, it seems to me much harder to account for someone's intercepting *Brillig*, boarding it, shooting Mister Paisley, cleaning up the mess, strapping on the weights, and deep-sixing him. Much less putting the weights on him first, throwing him overboard, and then shooting him behind the left ear while he's in the water.

We are of one mind, Fenwick declares. Such things can be accomplished, but not easily, even in an area like this where military helicopters on training exercises swarm and hover night and day like rackety mosquitoes. And that Paisley could've killed and deep-sixed some size-thirty attacker and then disappeared himself—to Perth or wherever—is even more farfetched. Or that the KGB or the Company has him squirreled away in a safe-house and deep-sixed somebody else in his place. For one thing, my KUDOVE friends would never have used the wrong size Jockey shorts. Poor tradecraft.

Susan remembers that Marchetti* says that psychological breakdowns are considered a virtually normal occupational hazard in Clandestine Services.

And Marchetti is right. As for the mechanics of the suicide: you and I know that a strong swimmer can tread water for a while with forty pounds of weights on, even without flippers. Antonio could've done it for a quarter of an hour with both hands out of the water. . . .

At mention of her plongée bouteille instructor at the Club Méditerranée Caravelle, Guadeloupe, one of *Pokey*'s recent ports of call, Susan sighs Antonio.

For that matter, Fenn continues, Paisley could conceivably hold onto a bilge-pump hole or exhaust port in the transom while he did himself in.

But jumping overboard with those weights on and not getting your pistol wet is a good trick, isn't it? I always go way under before I come up.

A wet pistol, Fenwick says, will fire. You can stick our nine-millimeter under water and fire it. Paisley wouldn't have had to tread water or hold on either. He could shoot himself as he jumped off the transom. He could even shoot himself six feet under.

Susan didn't know that. But of course: those shark-sticks that Antonio showed her use a regular shotgun shell.

So, says Fenn: vis-à-vis Mister Paisley, you and I incline to the least complicated and least melodramatic explanation.

Set it forth, for the reader.

A high-level intelligence analyst who was also much

---

*Victor Marchetti and John D. Marks, *op. cit.*

involved in counterintelligence and who befriended some of
the Soviet defectors whom he helped to debrief, Paisley had
separated from his wife in middlescence. He had found
himself a young new girlfriend. He was up to his neck in the
A-Team/B-Team report and other Company business. He
probably enjoyed his new life a lot of the time and sharply
missed his old life some of the time. He might've had a few
financial problems, but evidently not critical ones. No doubt
he had a couple of security breaches on his record—Count
had scads of them—but not numerous or serious enough to
disqualify him for an all-building entrance pass (there aren't
many of those). No doubt too he had his friends and
enemies in and out of the Company—we all do. Did. And in
midst of this he comes to wonder What the fuck's it all for
and decides to blow his brains out. In order to spare his
family the pain and embarrassment of his suicide, he tries to
make it look as though he fell overboard during a routine
solo sail.

Susan wonders Do we think that the mustard and the
sailing chart and the cheerfulness and the Maybe-we'll-have-
dinner and the Leave-the-light-on and the unlocked wheel
and the radio turned on and the rest were all deliberate? To
make it look like an accidental drowning?

That's what we think, all right; but we're not sure. It could
have been the spur of the moment, as you said—though it
would take more than one moment to get out those weights
and put them on. Incidentally, reader, there was no suicide
clause in his life-insurance policies.

Was there a double-indemnity clause for accidental death
or murder?

Don't know. So we're inclined to believe that John Arthur
Paisley planned his suicide with some care to look like
accidental drowning. Nothing in his Company training
would have taught him what any Eastern Shore waterman
knows: that in warm water especially, the gases of decomposition would eventually float him even with thirty-nine
pounds of lead on. Your classic mobsters, we remember, put

their victims' feet in a whole tub of concrete. In our Caribbean, those scuba weights would've worked: the sharks would recycle him before he bloated. But not in our Chesapeake Bay.

I'll make a note of that.

It's how I'd do it myself, Suse. But with more weight: a hundred pounds at least, for a man my size.

Stop.

I've often fancied recycling myself to the local seafood, of which I am largely constituted.

Please stop. So we don't think that Paisley had discovered the deep mole, or was the mole himself, or was knocked off by the KGB or the Company.

We doubt it—always acknowledging that even stranger things are not impossible. We believe that the fingerprint business and the Company cremation and the break-ins and such are all more or less routine muck-ups, contradictions, blunders, checkouts, and cover-ups for his secret contract work, unrelated to his death.

If that's so, then the only real mysteries, in our opinion, are the broken table, the neck lesions, and the undersize pants.

The table doesn't seem important to Fenwick: How many broken things, aboard *Pokey* and ashore, has he himself repaired, only to have them break again? Stowaway dinette tables with bulkhead brackets are particularly vulnerable: one off-balance bump from a man of Fenn's size—in a seaway, say, or the wake of a passing boat—could lever the thing loose again. The neck lesions, and Missus Paisley's reaction to the autopsy photographs, make us wonder—but the man had been in the water for a week. Those size thirties we can scarcely venture a hypothesis for: somebody else's, perhaps one of his sons', that got mixed in with his stuff at the laundromat and turned up in his seabag, and that he had to put on faute de mieux, holding his stomach in tight as we middle-aged Lotharios sometimes have to do? They remain an undersized mystery. A better question might be whether the man had any motive for suicide beyond the general susceptibility of people no longer young whose lives have turned a major corner. That's where the Company and the KGB might reenter the story. Otherwise, you and I have never found suicide particularly mysterious.

Susan quotes Edward Arlington Robinson:

> And Richard Cory, one calm summer night,
> Went home and put a bullet through his head.

Says Fenwick: Yup.

Poor Captain Shadrin! Do we think the KGB got him?

We do. The yacht brokers in Solomons and Annapolis always have a certain amount of distressed Company merchandise among their listings. Shadrin would have been in Vienna on business, we presume, not on vacation. If I'm not mistaken, the public square that they disappeared him from is Stephansplatz, by the cathedral. Remember it?

Susan remembers that busy junction: two smart streets of shops and sidewalk cafés, converging at the rebuilt Stephansdom. Where Kärntnerstrasse meets the Graben, she says.

And the mome raths outgrabe. It's a long way from the Gulags.

Oh, the poor man. And his wife! Can we change the subject?

Soon. *My* last question is, What do you suppose our Mister James Jesus Angleton's second question to Missus Paisley was, at that Humphrey Bogart rendezvous in the bar? The question that was too sensitive to print?

Susan wouldn't be surprised if the man were propositioning a fresh widow. Her ma has had to put up with a surprising number of such effronteries, from sundry quarters, twice in her life.* But knowing little of Mr. Angleton's character beyond the reported black trenchcoat and dark

---

*I.e., after Jack Seckler's death in 1949 (see note, p. 170), and again after Manfred Turner's disappearance thirty years later.

glasses, she supposes he was questioning her about documents relating to her husband's covert activities.

Fenwick supposes so too—though he doesn't see why a
general phrasing like that would be too sensitive to print.
Now, in the interests of morale and loyalty, the Company
routinely involves its officers' spouses to some degree in its
activities. Estrangements and divorces can therefore be
problematical, for obvious reasons, and an estranged widow
with a real or fancied grievance against the Agency would
seem to be additionally troublesome. At the same time, she
also presents a particular small opportunity. Others with an
interest in her late husband's work are likely to approach
her; Fenn does not mean investigative reporters and oppor-
tunistic ghost-writers merely. If such a woman has not
formerly done or is not currently doing Company work
herself, her present regrettable situation makes it possible
for her to render a service to her country, to herself, even to
the memory of the father of her children—and by recruiting
her, the Company protects itself. *That* proposition would
indeed be too sensitive to print.

Okay. But Sue must speculate why, in that case, Mrs. P.
would bother to mention that there had been two questions.
No doubt because, as a nonprofessional in an extraordinary
situation, struck by the melodramatics of Angleton's rendezvous and manner, she found herself quoting to the
reporter his terse line I have only two questions. Then she
had to hedge on what the second one was.

That's good, Suse.

Thank you. But we're a long way from efficient, Fenn,
which was what this Paisley digression was all about. It's been
no quick surgical strike in the area of narrative exposition.

True. Fenwick maintains, however, that when tacking
upwind, we must use a different measure of efficiency than
when sailing directly for our destination. In his opinion, all
we need do, when we adroit this digression up in the
finished version of our story, is add that if the reader finds
the story of Mr. P.'s disappearance to be rich in discrepan-

cies, unresolved mysteries, and loose ends, he/she will find the story of Fenn's twin Manfred's disappearance from our *Pokey* even richer—it being so to speak a spooky instant replay of our friend John Arthur Paisley's.

We must use quotation marks carefully in the next few lines.

"He wasn't really a friend of yours, was he, Fenn? Susan Seckler asked half-seriously, not for the first time," Susan asked.

"KUDOVE,* Fenwick Turner replied equivocally, was still a fairly small club in my day," Fenn replied, "whose members felt a certain comradely bond, not always unmixed with distrust and other emotions. But, unlike Count, I was never a full-fledged member of that club. Thank heaven."

You're corning the goose, Susan complains. Let me show you how it sounds: I, Susan Rachel Allan Seckler, your wife of going on seven years, your lover of a year before that, and your sort-of niece for twenty-seven years before *that,* certainly don't need to be told such things. They go without saying.

Do they, Shoshana.

"He asked darkly."

Not darkly, Suse. Hopefully.

"For in that shadowy world which he declared and believed he had put behind him, Susan persisted," Susan persists: "the world of information, disinformation, even superdisinformed supercoded disinformation, for all a mere young woman professor of classical American literature could know—in such a world, simple truth and falsehood, fact and fiction, loyalty and disloyalty, may be as difficult to distinguish—indeed, may be as naive a distinction, as . . . uh . . . happiness and unhappiness, or love and less-than-love. . . ."

That is to say, Fenn says sternly, not always difficult at all,

---

*The reader will remember that this cryptonym for Covert Operations was also the title of Fenn's book.

and not always impossible even where difficult. Some things that we can never know, we should nonetheless be *very* disinclined to doubt.

Susan says unsteadily I must be getting my period. When was my last one?

Hold on. Fenn fetches and scans the ship's log, then reports that the last onset of Susan's menses occurred about 1900 hours on 7 May 1980 in Guadeloupe, where people had doubtless taken for a sign of modesty her declining to remove her bikini bottom on the Club Med nudie beach, when in fact it was not her dainty funfunette but her tampon string that she was disinclined to exhibit. Another form of modesty, no doubt—but we don't recall observing any French or German tampon strings, either. Cramps mild. If it's Susan's period, she's a shade early. We note farther on that her last reported ovulation was on 21 May in Little Harbour, Peter Island, B.V.I. Left ovary. Are we advancing the action?

It might seem not—as a tacking sailboat might seem not to be approaching its objective. Yet Susan has a gut feeling that we're getting somewhere.

Fenwick observes that we are in fact getting north-northwest at an average rate of five to six knots, and should raise Solomons Island well before dusk if the breeze holds. He is pleasantly surprised that the self-steering vane is still functioning with his makeshift repair job. There is, however, an increasing likelihood of early evening thundershowers; already one observes the sultry cumulonimbi stacking up to westward, where too—

*Your fucking heart attack, Fenn!*

My FHA? Yes.

On the Ides of March Nineteen Seventy-nine, the day after your forty-ninth birthday!

Got that, reader? This is what's been on her mind for the last two pages.

Well? Susan demands. What was it? We continue to self-steer. A Greek container ship, *KAMEΛΛIA*, slides by to starboard, inbound. Sue is dead serious.

What do you mean What was it? Fenn complains. Did you think it was Diplomatic Flu? It was my FHA! Jesus, Suse!

Calm down, his wife advises. You'll give yourself a heart attack.

I'll calm down when I know what's up.

Susan instructs the reader to remember that line: she's going to use it against her husband later, when *she* needs calming down. In fact, she needs calming down now.

Honey.

Your attack came on the heels of Manfred's disappearance and your joint forty-ninth birthday, at a time when you were still under fire from the Company for publishing your book.

She means *KUDOVE,* reader, Fenn says aside: that critical review, by a former Agency officer, of our covert operations especially in Iran and Chile, publication of which got its author into hot water with his former colleagues, including his twin brother The Prince of Darkness, but won the applause of liberals everywhere, including several whom the author himself is more or less contemptuous of. An exposé published, alas, too late to have the impact of Marchetti's and Agee's books, for example, and too early to capitalize on the Iranian revolution. But that's show business. Please advance the action, Missus Turner.

We are riding together on the high side of the cockpit. Bruised Susan touches bruised Fenwick's thigh. What did Doctor Hunter say *really* caused the attack, honey?

Fenn answers soberly: All the above-mentioned did their bit, no doubt. The stress factor: losing Count after we'd lost Gus, et cetera. The dietary factor: a relatively high sugar and salt and cholesterol intake, now substantially reduced. A moderately high hard-liquor intake, now virtually eliminated. Patient drinks only light wines and beers these days, plus the odd rum and tonic in tropical weather. Has cut down on table salt, eggs, animal fats other than Brie and

Caprice des Dieux. Patient was an erstwhile pack-and-a-halfer, but quit, cold turkey. Is otherwise in perfect health. Do advance the action.

Please, honey. . . . The Agency.

Fenn nods and sighs. Okay. May have developed natural toxins to trigger heart attacks and then vanish without a trace, like our celebrated shellfish toxin for general assassination purposes. Indeed they may have, Susan. And they may have more subtle ways of administering it than that poke of a poisoned umbrella that did for that chap in London a while back. A toxic birthday card, perhaps. A cake, a candle, a kiss. They may even have serious reasons for wanting me dead; reasons that I myself don't know of. Some crazy critic of the Company, for example, inside the Company itself, or inside a rival agency, might want it to appear as though the Company did me in, in order to forestall their being given more license for covert operations in the Nineteen Eighties. In that case, he'd have done better to use a toxin with a telltale residue. But maybe it's not perfected yet, or maybe the hit man bungled the job. I'm still here!

He draws a breath. Or we can reverse the motives, or compound them. Or we can speculate that while the Company was innocent of my maiden cardiac episode, the fact of that episode sets me up for their seeing to my second. Who'd suspect them now?

Susan would. Tell her again that Doctor Hunter's prognosis is correct.

Fenn swears that his report of it is, at least: a fifty percent chance he'll enjoy another episode before fulfilling his normal life expectancy* of seventy-two years plus a few additional on account of his parents' ongoing longevity; a fifty percent chance he'll match or surpass that expectancy, barring accident or cancer, without further tidings from his heart.

---

*For white American males born in 1930 and surviving to age fifty.

Susan wonders: Cancer. Does the Company . . . ?

Fenn doubts it, though he supposes they keep an eye on the possibilities of, e.g., recombinant DNA. Even a galloping carcinoma takes too long for most Agency purposes: the victim could change values and tell all, or supersupercode the superdisinformed supercoded disinformation. Look: there's a Swedish submarine, over by the bombing target buoys.

Sue shudders. Let's get out of here.

We did that already: our sabbatical cruise.

They followed us.

Fenn shrugs. There may have been a chap keeping an eye out. More likely there wasn't.

That barkeep in Cancún.

Your friend Antonio in Guadeloupe. That's why he didn't grab himself a tit at five meters under; it would've blown his cover.

Are you serious? Susan removes her husband's hand from the breast referred to. No, you aren't.

Aren't.

Everything you've told me just now is the truth, Fenn, to the best of your knowledge. I believe that.

Fenwick does too. And if we haven't much advanced the action, we've surely nudged the exposition along.

The action, Susan once again avers, is not standing still: she feels a quantum closer now to her beloved than she did before.

Okay. And neither the Company nor the KGB nor the FBI nor the Mob seriously wants me dead.

How do you know?

For the chilling reason that, not having taken any particular measures to protect himself, he wouldn't likely be here aboard dear *Pokey* with precious her, off Cedar Point at the mouth of the Patuxent, altering course to three hundred degrees, if they wanted him dead. He'd be dead.

For a while we close-reach quietly into the river's wide mouth, between low-lying Cedar Point to port and the fine high headland to starboard from Cove to Drum Points. One tack—the wind has veered westerly—brings us into the river proper and within sight of Solomons Island off its north shore. On its south, even on the Sunday, military training jets, helicopters, and reconnaissance planes take off and land from the Naval Air Station; tomorrow their racket will be incessant. Susan, Fenwick observes, is assimilating his last remarks, not lightly. As she checks the wind vane, her thumb and forefinger pull at her lower lip; her dark eyes squint and unsquint at a nest of fish traps off to starboard and the big aircraft hangars off to port. As in a sound-track orchestration, the first serious thunder rumbles now from ahead: brooding fanfare to

### SUSAN'S OUTBURST!

Suddenly she cries I hate my position!

How's that? The wind at once turns cooler and west-northwesterly; the water darkens; black catspaws dart from the direction of the thunder. This may be a close race.

I'm like one of those dippy women in the Godfather movies, that go on with their normal innocent Italian-American lives, making linguine, raising bambini, while their husbands secretly run all the gambling and prostitution and narcotics in town. I sit here on my essentially virtuous tush with my innocent Ph.D., teaching undergraduates the difference between Transcendentalism and Existentialism, correcting their comma faults, pretending that art and moral values and subject-verb agreement matter, while my husband and my stepfather-brother-in-law and their buddies kill Patrice Lumumba and overthrow Mohammed Mossadegh and Salvador Allende and send agents to Cuba by submarine to make Fidel Castro's beard fall out and get our own president killed in reprisal. . . .

Well, now, Susan—

Be still: this is my outburst!

Okay.

You undermine every government that puts their people's welfare above Exxon's and I T and T's and Anaconda Copper's. You lie and cheat and counterfeit and threaten and bribe and torture and kill, and you train wicked governments to do the same, more efficiently than they did it before. I don't mean you personally, but ¡Jesucristo, Fenn! What right does a man who's ever done such things have to my morally earnest and basically innocent backside, I'd like to know, not to mention the devotion of my heart and mind? Planeloads of beer and whores to supply the Nungs!* Oh, I know; you'll quote me George Alfred Townsend:

. . . the county clerk will prove it by the records on his shelves,
That the fathers of the province were no better than ourselves.†

You'll remind me of Ben Franklin's and Thomas Jefferson's dirty tricks, and the moral warts on Abe Lincoln and Woodrow Wilson and FDR and Martin Luther King, Junior, maybe even on Mahatma Gandhi. You'll invoke the whole Sartrean Dirty Hands business, and the Tragic View of Innocence: No omelets without breaking eggs; If you can't stand the heat, stay out of the kitchen, et cetera. Anyhow, you not only left the Agency yourself exactly because you deplored their covert operations, but wrote a courageous exposé of them insofar as you could without endangering the real and legitimate security of our republic and the lives of decent covert operatives if that's not a contradiction in terms. Let's say at least the lives and welfare of the more or less innocent families of undercover officers. And you did

---

*A Vietnamese-Chinese hill tribe, renowned for their fierceness, employed by the CIA in the 1960s for operations along the Ho Chi Minh trail. The Nungs demanded regular supplies of beer and prostitutes, which were flown in to them at great expense by Air America, one of the Agency's several proprietary airlines. Whiskey, more easily transported, would not do. See Marchetti and Marks, pp. 119, 120.

†From "Upper Marlb'ro," by G. A. Townsend, 1841–1914, in his *Tales of the Chesapeake* (1880. Republished by Tidewater Publishers, Cambridge, Md., 1968). See also note, pp. 214–15.

your best to help restrain the Company's excesses, especially
Manfred's, and later to expose them. And even if you
hadn't; even if you were still in up to your neck, interrogat-
ing KGB people who might or might not be legitimate
defectors, in Company safe-houses on Solomons Island right
over there and our beautiful Choptank River and god knows
where else, maybe even on our precious Cacaway Island—

Not on Cacaway, Susan. Never on Cacaway.

Even then I'd love you to death, because I know that your
heart is good if not a hundred percent pure, and your
character is fine if not unsullied, and you could never under
any circumstances have involved yourself in such ugly
business unless you truly believed that doing so was somehow really necessary to protect our people—not our fucking
corporations and politicians and career civil-service personnel, but our people—against a clear and present danger,
which totalitarianism has sometimes been but socialism
never was. Or unless you were being coerced by threats
against me and/or other members of your family, in which
case by Aristotle's definition your actions wouldn't be truly
voluntary and therefore wouldn't be fully culpable.

Yes. Well.

Excuse me; I'm going to throw up.

She does, salty Susan, or tries to, neatly to leeward. Sad
Fenwick steadies her as she kneels and retches dryly over the
lower gunwale. His friend's outburst, he judges, wants no
verbal response. She goes below, wipes her mouth, returns
with hooded sweatshirt and deck shoes on, takes the tiller so
that Fenn too can prepare for the fast-approaching weather.
NOAA radio has issued another heavy-thunderstorm alert
for most of Maryland. This one, we judge, will not pass to
north of us. It is 1815 hours; thanks in part to a favorable
tide, we have made much better time than we estimated. The
question is whether to anchor at once in the first available
but unattractive shelter—Solomons Harbor itself—or race
the storm to a more secure and quieter overnight anchorage
an hour upriver.

Susan snugs against him, spent. Fenn pats her belly; she presses his hand there. What do you think, he asks her. He considers her face; she considers the approaching storm. Let's press our luck some more, she sighs, and shoot for Mackall.\* Shall we power it?

We decide to try, at near-full throttle, chancing that our fuel will last. Fenn drops and furls all sail and makes ready with the anchor in case we must run alee of the high-banked shore before reaching St. Leonard's Creek. We see the first lightning-bolts as we leave Solomons Island and its causeway to starboard—a far cry from Key, Solomons is packed to the Plimsoll with cottages, marinas, commercial fisheries, and fishing and pleasure craft—and hurry under the tall high-way bridge across the river. The air temperature has been 90° F. all afternoon; the fast-cooling breeze now is nervous relief.

It's going to be a jim dandy! Susan shouts into the teeth of it as Fenn returns to the cockpit. We lose a few precious minutes moving closer to the north shore, which however we can then hug all the way to Mackall. For warmth and safety we don our life vests. In the face of another brilliant bolt, Fenwick says Oh boy. Shivering Susan quotes Eudora Welty:

A whole tree of lightning stood in the sky.

We brace for the thunderclap; it is stunning. We are the only boat on the river; our aluminum mast is the only tall object anywhere about. The sky ahead is black and copper-green and seething: the end of the world. We spot red and green daybeacons, too far away, marking the wide creek-mouth. We shall never make it in time. Like an infantryman leaving his foxhole in mid-barrage, Fenn crouches forward to stand by the anchor. Our hearts are familiarly back in our mouths. Where is the diesel fuel coming from?

---

\*Mackall Cove, at the entrance to splendid St. Leonard's Creek, itself a river-sized tributary of the Patuxent's north shore: a hurricane-hole of a cove, large enough for only two or three boats to anchor in, but sheltered on its three weather sides by sheer banks as high as 130 feet.

We make it, just. Plenty of water in that creek and cove, right up to shore; as if our heavy cutter were a Chevy on a parking lot and Susan a smart-ass veteran attendant, we roar full-throttle past the daybeacons and into snug Mackall immediately to port, the engine already reversed to kill our headway as we sweep in. The cove is empty; the trees on the bank-tops whistle and wave as if applauding Sue's macha driving (now she blasts *Pokey* to a stop as Fenn drops anchor; now she backs down smartly on the rode to set the hook), but in Mackall itself, no air moves. There's another shattering bolt; fat rain strafes us. Fenn cleats the rode at ten fathoms; Susan kills the engine; we pile under the dodger and below, hearts pumping, just as the great wind strikes. Thirty seconds later, having kissed our thanks to Poseidon, we can see nothing but white rain and hail through the cabin windows.

Shit, growls Fenwick, checking the hand-bearing compass: we're backwinded. Oh well.

Indeed, we forgot to allow for the wind's spilling over the high banks like a breaking wave and blowing us stern to shore, 180° on our anchor. Jost Van Dyke and other Virgin Island harbors should have taught us. But so snug is Mackall that while the wind overhead gusts to fifty-plus, and dirt, leaves, twigs, and small branches sail over our masthead, and garbanzo-size hailstones tattoo us stem to stern, we barely roll.

The show lasts for forty-five minutes, during which, weary in body and spirit but immensely relieved and no longer alarmed, we embrace on the main settee, inhale the ozone, and feel each other's pulse return to normal. Virgil knew and Freud confirmed that snug shelter in a storm is aphrodisiac: seven years wed, we are still Dido and Aeneas in their cave. Normal pulses au revoir.

At eight, when all without and within is still again, Fenwick says into Susan's perfect navel if *that* didn't trigger an Episode, we're home free.

From under his ear comes a gurgle of presumable accord.

Already the air is sultry again. The east is black with the storm, sweeping oceanward now across Delmarva peninsula; but Fenn, back in the cockpit, sees the glow of what must be a first-class sunset behind our banks. It won't be airy in Mackall Cove, he calls downstairs. Shall we move out into the creek?

Brown thighs still open and brown eyes* closed, her sweatshirt up around her neck, Susan says from her settee I'm dead beat.

Me too.

She sits up, pulls her shirt the rest of the way off, tosses it across to where her bottoms lie. Sue has a way of sitting Turk-style after sex, lifting her thick hair bemusedly from her nape, that still stirs Fenn as deeply as in 1972, when on that same settee he first observed it. She requests that he please rig the boarding ladder. Never mind if there's Kepone, poop, or oil in the water: she wants a dip before we think about dinner.

Looks clean to Fenwick.

En route over the transom, she kisses his pate, mouth, beard, chest, arms, fingers. What else needs doing on the boat?

Nothing, till we dock tomorrow at Solomons.

Now she's standing half down the ladder, enjoying feeling fucked. Are you sorry we broke our island rule? I just thought of it.

Not in that wind. Anyhow, it was a principle, not a rule.

Wow, though. We break our tails to get to Solomons Island and then break our tails to come here instead.

That's okay. Don't touch bottom or wade ashore, and we'll regard the principle as intact.

Susan lowers her behind into the water, flushes herself, then drops the rest of her in and paddles lazily about. Fenn watches, pleased.

Coming in?

---

*Black-eyed Susan's eyes are a very very dark brown.

Too tired. Shall I call Carmen?

We'll call her in the morning. She won't worry.

So what else needs doing in this chapter, Suse?

Pardon?

Part Two of our story.

Oh. Well. If this is really Part Two, there's a lot to be done yet.

I'm too tired.

Even if we've crossed a threshold and made an almost-night sea-journey, we've still got a brother- or dragon-battle to fight and our middle round of ordeals to undergo, plus a massive Fleshbeck* to manage, where the reader learns our whole past story up to the storm we started with.

Fenn considers. Too bloody tired. Can't we do Part Two in two parts?

Belly-up, floating Susan guesses so, though it occurs to her that if Part One is one scene and Part Two is two scenes, we're committing ourselves to three scenes in Part Three.

Yawning Fenwick suggests we pass under that bridge, like the one at Solomons, when we come to it. Right now he's for calling it a narrative day. We'll tackle part two of Part Two mañana.

Susan's with him. But there's a problem. Our Big Flesh-beck is going to be a *really* big one, it seems to her: a whole scenesworth. If we try to coordinate each major division of our story both with an island landfall (just a suggestion) and with one dream of that allegedly "classical" five-dream sequence of a typical night's dreaming (just a suggestion too, despite Fenn's hooting at that bit of narcology; it has not escaped Doctor Susan that that sequence bears a usable resemblance to the five acts of Renaissance and Neoclassical drama, a division we might easily integrate with the three of most later drama, especially if we follow the one-scene, two-scene, three-scene sequence and regard either the opening scene as an overture to the dreams or the closing scene as an awakening therefrom. Perhaps the Big Fleshbeck ought to

---

*See p. 170.

coincide with our stop at Wye to visit Fenn's parents, or/and at Gibson to visit Ma and Grandma: visits to our past). . . .

For the love of god, Suse.

Undeterred, she bottoms up below him, then declares I'm trying to earn my keep as the innocent academic on this boat. A foil for the world-scarred, rough-and-ready pragmatic hero, but also his complement and sidekick. Watch my sidekick. She sidekicks. Shoot me the soap, would you, Fensie?

He fetches the Ivory and hands it in. The light is going fast; his head is nodding. Susan wonders, scrubbing, why Procter and Gamble don't make an Ivory for skinnydippers that not only floats but shines in the dark.

Fenwick yawns. My eyes are closing. I'm too tired to eat.

So sack in. We'll eat whenever we wake up.

But Fenn lingers, ruminating, and after a while says drowsily Suppose we reserve part two of Part Two for the Big Fleshbeck; does that mean we still have to do the Brother-Battle and the Ordeals before we turn in? I can't hack it.

Sue pops the soapcake over the transom. They belong in this part, but it does seem to be a day for rising above our principles. Anyhow, nobody says that our going to sleep at last has to be the end of part one of Part Two. We can put the rest in asterisks. Or we can let the author take the helm again for a spell while we go off watch.

Come on up here.

She does, dripping, satisfied, and stands before her husband to be toweled. You are resourceful, canny, and wise, Fenn tells her hip, as well as educated, sexual, dainty, tough, morally earnest, and three-quarters Jewish, an advantage even Scheherazade lacked.

Am good cook, Susan prompts him, pleased, and lifts her arms.

Are dynamite cook. Turn around.

Am, while dainty, not little-girl squeamish. Do not blanch or quail at sight of snakes, mice, roaches, blood, sutures, small skished animals.

That's because you're a doctor manquée. Turn around.

Can read hydrographic charts, fold road maps properly, haggle successfully with merchants in countries where haggling is customary. Pick up languages in a hurry. Can figure out any major European city's public transportation system with relative ease, thereby saving cab fares. Am not intimidated by customs officials, bureaucrats, airline clerks.

All true, and more. Around.

Can do a passable imitation, for a middle-class white girl, three-quarters Jewish, of Grinding the Corn.*

Damned passable, Fenwick agrees. You grind the old corn the way I corn the old goose.

Scheherazade *was* a grand vizier's daughter, Susan reflects. That gave her a leg up with the Sultan.

Fenn towels her thighs and calves. You don't wish you were Henry Kissinger's daughter instead of Jack Seckler's. Our business is fiction, not lies.†

---

*A variety of sexual intercourse with the woman atop the man. The movement, first demonstrated to Susan by her sister upon Miriam's return from the Peace Corps, is said by Miriam to be practiced from childhood, under various names, by young African girls of various tribes. We do not vouch for this bit of cultural anthropology.

†This strong remark of Fenwick's is inspired most directly by Dr. Kissinger's statement in a confidential briefing session with Chicago newspeople on September 16, 1970, just after Dr. Salvador Allende's election to the presidency of Chile: "The situation is not one in which our capacity for influence is very great at this particular moment, now that matters have reached this particular point." The statement is not technically a lie, but only the night before, according to an ITT memorandum of September 17, the U.S. Ambassador to Chile, Edward Korry, "finally received a message from the State Department giving him the green light to move in the name of President Nixon. The message gave him maximum authority—short of a Dominican Republic-type action—to keep Allende from taking power." See Uribe Arce, Armando, *The Black Book of American Intervention in Chile* (Boston: Beacon Press, 1975), Chapter 5; also U.S. Congress, Senate, Committee on Foreign Relations, Subcommittee on Multinational Corporations, *Multinational Corporations and United States Foreign Policy: the International Telephone and Telegraph Company and Chile, 1970–71* (Washington: U.S. Government Printing Office, 1973), Part 2, Appendix I, p. 543; Appendix II, pp. 608–615; etc.

She kisses his back and shoulders. I just wonder whether our story wouldn't be the better for it if your advisor and muse and sidekick happened to be Eudora Welty's daughter, or Flannery O'Connor's.

What an idea. We're below now and sacked out in our separate berths. You are a descendant of E. A. Poe via Jack and Carmen B. Seckler, Fenwick declares. That's pedigree enough.

Have we explained that yet? The Poe-Key business?

Damned if I remember. If not, we'll stick it in a footnote when we adroit things up. Or reprise it in the Fleshbeck. Did you get your period?

No. But I'm on the verge, no matter what the log says. Another ovum down the pipes.

Hum.

Better make hay while the sun shines.

Too tired. Maybe once is not enough, but twice is plenty.

For some seconds all's still; yet even as Fenn catches and surfs down the next wave of sleep, he feels his friend's fancy still perking.

Solomons. Can we work in Solomon's judgment? Solomon's temple? Solomon's mines?

\* \* \* \* \*

Let each asterisk represent a night, beginning with that Sunday night the first of June: we emblemize the period both of Susan's menses—which, she reports to the ship's log, commence half an hour later, as if triggered by her earlier grinding of the corn, and cease on the Thursday following—and of *Pokey*'s stop at Solomons Island, whither we move next morning and whence, on that same Thursday, we sail out and up and over the Chesapeake toward Wye I.

Turning our eyes, for the purposes of this episode, from the sustained ordeal of most of Earth's human population, who still in 1980 go to bed hungry when they have bed to go to, and, if they woke, woke hungrier, weaker, damaged five days further in body and mind. And forgetting if we can the

similarly ongoing ordeal of our natural surround, insulted
from the James River to Lake Baikal with five more
daysworth of our dreck and slowly preparing, without
emotion or ideology, to exact its retribution. And leaving
aside whatever ordeals Fenn's vanished brother Manfred
might have undergone in these five days if, as Carmen B.
Seckler still sometimes imagines, he is not dead by either his
own hand or another's, but safe-housed perhaps in Moscow
or Siberia, perhaps but a few hundred yards from *Pokey*'s
slip in Solomons Harbor. And passing over because unspeakable if alas not unthinkable what ordeals young Gus
Seckler-Turner, Manfred's son, Susan's half-brother, may
have survived or failed to survive somewhere in Chile, at the
hands of torturers disposed to their trade by character but
trained to it in Brazil and in nearby pleasant Virginia, or in
situ by experts sent down therefrom: officers and semi-
retired consultants whose yachts swing from neighbor moorings as Paisley's *Brillig* used to swing. What have we by way
of Ordeals to satisfy Susan's pattern for our story?

The fact is, we have among those asterisks not one ordeal
apiece, but two, one of which we each duly report to our
spouse and one which we do not, just then.

After long and solid sleep we wake to a sweaty, overcast
Monday, thank snug Mackall for our shelter, break our fast,
and sail on a small southwesterly back to Solomons, tisking
tongues at the racket of the military. We rent a transient slip
in the harbor, consider a motel room, and decide that *Pokey*
will do for sleeping: the marina has showers and laundry
facilities. Fenwick mails a note to Chief and Virgie at Key
Farm across the Bay, who do not like the telephone: We are
safely home from sea; we shall sail up to your dock before
the week is out. He telephones his son and daughter-in-law
in Boston, to see how goes their pregnancy. No one home.
He supposes jealously they're thick as thieves up there with
Marilyn Marsh, buying baby things together. Susan chides
him: if *she* were ever lucky enough to be a genuine
grandmother-in-the-works, she would damned well be thick

as thieves et cetera. Her eyes mist over. She goes for a Midol.

Now the phone's free for her to call Grandma! Weakly over the wire from Pikesville comes the accented Hello?— the accent that, until she was older, Susan thought of not as Yiddish but as grandparently. Hi Gram! she sings back for the ten thousandth time in the thirty-five years of their particular love affair: We're home!

And now that Grandma has been told, we are.

Havah Moscowitz Seckler says Thenk God. How's Fenn? Grandma had an hour of trouble seven years ago with this marriage: her jewel, her black-eyed Susan, her little mother,* marrying a goyishe divorcé in his forties! Maybe even never having children! But our love soon took care of that.

He's fine, Gram.

Thenk God. Take him around. How's his parents?

Now Susan's laughing. They're fine, Gram, I guess; we haven't talked to them yet. Gram, we just got off the boat! We've been sailing in the ocean, day and night for a week. We just came ashore. Do you understand what I mean, Gram? Susan can feel, through copper cables and micro-wave relays, what her grandmother comprehends and what is beyond her; no phone call but becomes a loving lesson. Do you remember how it was, Gram, when you were seventeen and came across the ocean from Russia, how the boat didn't anchor every night, but had to sail and sail until it reached Philadelphia?

You're in Philadelphia?

No no, Gram. We're in Chesapeake Bay. We're down by Washington. Soon we'll be in Baltimore.

I'm dencing! How is Orrin and Julie?

Gra-am! Listen, Gram. Are you listening?

I'm listening, I'm listening. You been selling.

Teacher to the bone, Susan will not give over until her 85-year-old grandmother, survivor of pogrom and sweatshop,

---

*Susan's Hebrew name, Shoshana, was Havah Seckler's mother's.

who can hardly conceive what a cruising sailboat is, has mastered the distinction between passage-making and hopping between overnight anchorages. This merry lesson learned, Grandma is permitted to play fast and loose with her prepositions: Except I crossed the Etlentic once, now I feel like I crossed it again.

And to ask: How is Miriam? You've talked?

Grandma! How are *you?*

Ask your momma, God bless her; she can tell you better. We call Carmen B. Seckler. Susan first: Hi, Ma! and Fenwick, standing by the pay phone on the marina dock amid the clink of halyards in a forest of extruded aluminum, hears the throaty voice of his remarkable mother-in-law. Thank Christ, it's the Sea Urchins. Where the hell are you? We establish our whereabouts and confirm what Carmen B. Seckler had taken for granted, that we were too busy dealing with yesterday's weather to call as we'd promised. Havah Seckler, we now hear, has had yet another pacemaker operation, her third, during our ocean passage. The gadget will not stay put in her failing musculature: it slips, it infects, it hurts her. She would be dead without it; she is weak and miserable with it—too weak to do much more than listen and acknowledge on the telephone. Another operation may well lie ahead, and Grandma is too weary of pain and weakness to undergo it. Miriam is doing more dope than she should (Well, you *are,* Carmen confirms to Miriam, across some room), but is otherwise okay, for Miriam. Her elder son Sy is a potential problem, but Edgar Allan Ho is a dear baby. His father has taken to "living on tips" (i.e., we learn later, he is a paid police informant on the Fells Point drug traffic, too dangerous a job to explain on the telephone), but since Carmen arranged Kung Fu lessons for Miriam, he no longer strikes her when they quarrel. There is a ton of accumulated mail for us. Business is booming. Carmen has wangled a franchise to open a branch restaurant in Harborplace, Baltimore's fancy new Inner Harbor complex, still under construction, and stands to become either a bankrupt or a wealthy woman. Kerflooeyhood has if anything increased her entrepreneurial acumen; she also consults the Tarot deck. Without Fred,* however, such things bore her. No word about him or Mundungus, but she has an iron or two still in the fire, not for telephone discussion. When will she see us?

Susan proposes the Wednesday: we need two days at Solomons to restore boat and crew. Carmen can't make it— Wednesday is liquor-license-hearing day—but Miriam will drive down; Carmen will send along the first-class mail with her and hold the rest till we reach Baltimore. Are you pregnant yet? she wants to know of Susan.

Ma! Sue gives it three protesting syllables: *Ma-uh-ah!*

Carmen B. Seckler's chuckle is like a growl. Thirty-five isn't too late. What's that sailboat for? Here's Mim.

Susan confirms her sister's Wednesday visit, a two and a half hour drive from Baltimore, and talks for another twenty minutes. Then with a call to Bethesda Fenwick arranges his own Wednesday. A stiff but not incordial voice declares Dugald Taylor here.

And Fenwick Turner here, Doog. Home from the sea.

Fenwick. Are you in town. Dugald Taylor's exclamations and questions are seldom inflected as such.

Solomons Island. We'll be here through Wednesday.

You caught me just in time, Fenwick. I'm about to go traveling. There's a bus to D.C. from the Air Station, I believe.

Fenn finds himself echoing the declarative question: We should talk, then.

We should.

Wednesday noon okay, Doog? I'll stand you to lunch.

Wednesday's fine. On Friday I'm off to Perth.

Ah.

---

*Her nickname, we remember, for Manfred, as is Mundungus for their son.

I'll stand you, says Dugald Taylor. The Cosmos. Noon. Bring Susan.

I think not, Doog.

Quite right. Noon, then; the Cosmos.

This is a friend and ex-senior-colleague of Fenwick's from Agency days, now busily retired. He seems to have, Fenwick reports to Susan, like Carmen B. Seckler, something to say that won't do on the phone. Fenn guesses he'll be going into town on the Wednesday. Susan hugs him quietly: encouragement. She likes courtly Dugald Taylor. Fenwick does not mention Perth.

We stroll the village of Solomons, excited to be ashore again, and begin buying ship's stores and provisions by the totebagful, including a couple of new hats for Fenwick to replace that scarf until his boina returns to him. A weeksworth of fresh goods, a light reserve of canned: enough to see us to Wye and Gibson and the decisions we cannot postpone therebeyond. Time now to clean ship inside and out; refuel, rewater, repair.

In the first marine supply house we see, we buy Chart 12221 and examine it. There is the bridge-tunnel between Capes Henry and Charles. There is the Y of red nuns and black cans where the Chesapeake Channel diverges (going up) into York River Entrance Channel and York Spit Channel, Susan's wrong turn. There is the York Spit Light: Fl 6 sec 37 ft 8 M. There is the York, about whose mouth we find an Allen Island, a Hog Island, a cluster of Goodwin Islands, another of Guinea Marsh Islands.

No Key.

Incredulous, we ask the clerk, the manager, and later the marina operator and our neighboring yachtsfolk. No one knows of a Key Island in Chesapeake Bay. Someone reasonably supposes it might be the local name for one of the small islands in the Goodwin or Guinea cluster: but none shares just the right configuration, elevation, and water depth, not to mention the large breakwater with its flashing beacon, surely charted.

As we work on *Pokey* through that sultry day and the next, and laugh perplexedly with others over the mystery, we find ourselves not mentioning the rifle shots and other alarums; it all smacks too much of paperback gothic with a Hollywood tie-in. *Baratarian* indeed! Some latter-day Lafitte, we suppose, in the marijuana trade, daring the Coast Guard to suspect a wolf in wolf's clothing.

We take showers; shampoo and launder; eat in the local restaurants; sit in barrooms watching television for the first time in more than half a year. Susan trims her husband's hair; her own will wait till Baltimore. By the Tuesday evening we are shipshape: all systems working, all tanks topped up, all lockers supplied, all rigging tuned and gear repaired, all clothing and linens fresh. A strong cool front blows through at dinnertime, bringing with it another severe-thunderstorm alert that escalates quickly into a tornado watch from six till eight. We eat in the marina restaurant, from where we can keep an eye at once upon our boat, the approaching weather, and our fellow sailor Walter Cronkite on the evening news. No tornado comes: just a Chesapeake summer squall like the Sunday night's, terrific for fifteen minutes and then gone. The high moves in behind it, clearing the sky, drying the air; good night for sleeping.

And a good day, the Wednesday, for sailing. We resist personification of our boat; but *Pokey* tugs at his slip-lines in the sparkling A.M. breeze, WNW out of a laundered sky at fifteen plus. What a day for Fenn to struggle into clothing fit for the Cosmos Club, Susan to prepare for company! We should be making sail for Wye and Gibson. Nova Scotia! Portugal!

We kiss good-bye. Sue holds on: it is disagreeable to her for us to be apart even for a day. Unfamiliar in tie and worsteds, Fenn kisses her again and asks how her cramps are doing. Gone, she says; we'll be back in business by tomorrow. She smiles. I'd rather be sailing.

Kiss Mimi for me. I'll try to get back before she leaves.

Be careful, Susan begs him. Kiss Dugald for me. I wish . . .
a couple of things.

So do I. Keep your fingers crossed. Got to go now, or I'll
miss my bus.

Susan will. She reminds him to remove his terrycloth hat
(the best we could find in a hurry) before presenting himself
at the Cosmos Club. Babies, she reminds herself, normally
learn before age one that a parent who disappears from view
will return, almost certainly. But since March of last year she
has never seen her husband leave without fearing sharply
that her next sight of him will be in a hospital emergency
room or morgue, if indeed he does not disappear altogether
like his twin and Gus and Captain Shadrin, whom she
cannot forget. She busies herself planning a luncheon salad
of crab and avocado to serve at the picnic tables near the
dock. Or perhaps Mims and the boys would enjoy a little
daysail. But Miriam will neither refrain from smoking
aboard nor mind her cigarette ashes: two pinholes melted
through the clew of our jib staysail bear witness to her
recklessness. Moreover, she cares only about people and her
mainly verbal interaction with them; to the beauty of St.
Leonard's Creek, say, and the pleasurable activity of sailing,
she would be oblivious. Still, there are the boys, young as
Edgar is and torpid Sy. Susan will see. Already she misses
Fenn.

## FENWICK'S ORDEALS

He catches his bus—strange sensation, to be inland again,
on wheels, out of sight of water!—stuffs his hat into his
inside breast pocket, dons his eyeglasses, and settles down
with notebook and pen for the sixty-mile ride. The reader
has seen that Fenwick Scott Key Turner is a man neither
literary nor unlettered. In Susan's opinion, however—and
she is professionally a literary woman—he thinks about the
medium in a sensible, sometimes original way, unfettered by
ideology, conventional preconceptions, or overmuch sophis-

tication. Between Solomons and Hollywood (Maryland), for example, he makes a notebook note on the Problem of the Literally Marvelous in our story, a problem he means to review with Susan next time we're sailing. Like many of his notes, this one takes the form of an imaginary dialogue with her; its subject is

## THE LITERALLY MARVELOUS.

FENWICK: You and I agree that a story with nothing fantastic in it lacks something essential. But how can we stick the fantastic into the middle of Chesapeake Bay in the May and June of 1980? Ospreys as big as rocs? Giant blue crabs? Sea serpents? Of "Chessie," the sometimes-sighted monster of the lower Bay, we remain skeptical, do we not?

SUSAN: We do. Uncharted islands in familiar waters? But you're right. The Mysterious is one thing: the Paisley case is mysterious; Key Island is mysterious. The Improbable is another thing: Manfred's doing a John Arthur Paisley on the heels of Paisley himself is bloody improbable. But what we're after is the Truly Irreal; the Literally Marvelous.

F: Can't we just do it? Stonewall it?

S: That's your answer to everything.

F: Hey, look: there's a sea monster.

S: There is not.

F: Hm. Suppose you and I reacted with as much incredulity as the reader. Wouldn't that cover our tracks? Show me a sea monster, and see if I'm not incredulous! Yet we won't be able to deny it, even though we can't account for it. The reality of the irreality would be undeniable. We're home free.

S: It won't work. You can have fabulous sea monsters, or sperms and eggs that talk; you can have Fenwick and Susan. But you can't mix the two together. The four.

F: Scheherazade would. Shakespeare would. We can do anything that we can do, Suse. And what we can't do as Fenn and Susan, we can do as Author. I think of those dreams where you understand that you're dreaming: where are they in that five-dream sequence? You're inside the dream and outside it at the same time. Sometimes you can wake yourself up. Sometimes you think you've waked yourself up, when actually you're just another frame out in the dream. Sometimes by sheer willing you can change the scene or the course of the action. Sometimes you think you've changed it, but the thing you're running from still comes after you, maybe in a new shape to fit the new frame. In some dreams I've even been able to test the ontological water: I've called out to you from inside the dream. *Susan!* It comes out *Ooo! Unh!*

S: And I kiss you awake. But let's face it: neither of us has personally experienced one literally supernatural, uncanny moment or event in our entire lifetimes. Ecstatic, sure. Uncanny-*like*, sure. But literally marvelous, no.

F: Yet I won't have our story be unadulterated realism. Reality is wonderful; reality is dreadful; reality is what it is. But realism is a fucking bore.

S: Okay. But we won't stoop to occultism or woozy neogothic.

F: Certainly not.

S: We have a problem.

F: Yup. Odysseus has magic. Scheherazade has magic. Dante has miracles. What do we have?

S: Well: Don Q. has only his delusions, plus that unexplained business in the Cave of Montesinos.* Huck Finn has only his superstitions.

F: The literally marvelous is what we want, with a healthy dose of realism to keep it ballasted. But at this hour of the

---

*Susan's reference is to *Don Quixote,* Part II, Chapters 22 and 23. Quixote's fabulous three-day adventure in the cave is evidently an hour's dream; but of his many encounters with the apparently marvelous, it is the only one unrefuted, and the Knight clings to its reality to the end. Indeed, in II:41 he offers to believe Sancho Panza's lie of flying to Heaven on a wooden horse if Sancho will accept the truth of *his* adventure in the Cave of Montesinos.

world I guess we'll take whatever kind of marvelous we can manage.

S: No compromises, Fenn.

F: Seems to me it's all compromises in this business.

S: Realism is the ballast. I like that.

F: Thank you. Realism is your keel and ballast of your effing Ship of Story, and a good plot is your mast and sails. But magic is your wind, Suse. Your literally marvelous is your mother-effing wind.

S: Now I'm hooked. I want to talk to Edgar Poe in our story! I want Gus and Manfred to come back, and Mim to be okay. Mainly I want us to love each other forever, and never quarrel or get old and die. I want to be a mother without having children. No: I want to have *had* children; to have *been* a mother. No: I want to be a grandmother without having had children. I'd mess up children, worse than Mims. But they have to be *our* grandchildren, not just yours. How did I get on this subject?

F: We'd better consult your mother. Magic is Carmen B. Seckler's department. We'll talk about it when we're sailing again.

S: I don't want to talk about it.

F: I mean the problem of the literally marvelous.

S: So do I.

This note made, Fenn notes that his notes on our story, to which the notebook is principally devoted, have nearly all to do with either such general considerations as the foregoing, or bits of narrative to be incorporated (e.g., Choptank Safe-House Story: 2nd loss of boina), or images (e.g., Is a Y a fork or a confluence? Does the Chesapeake Channel diverge into York River Entrance Channel and York Spit Channel, or do they converge into the Chesapeake Channel? The one inbound, the other outbound; or, in tidewater, the one on floods, the other on ebbs. Analysis versus synthesis; "male" versus "female." Sperm swim up; ova float down. Discuss w. S. next time we're selling.). Almost none, he notes, have to do with description: no bits of scenic detail, no faces, gestures, rendered sensations. He makes a note of this fact: here must be his short suit as an aspiring writer of fiction. Indeed, when somewhere along Maryland 5 two Porsches pass the bus in quick succession, one the color of buttermilk and the other of cured tobacco, Fenn cannot summon better adjectives for them than yellowish-white and brown, though the highway at that moment happens to divide a tobacco from a dairy farm. Perhaps, he remarks to his notebook, a writer with these particular limitations and strengths (he thinks the Y-note not uninteresting) would do better to render our story as a play than to tell it as a novel. D. w. S. n. t. w. s.

The bus makes a stop at Union Station, where Fenn gets off. It is just eleven and a fine bright forenoon for walking. He heads down Delaware Avenue to Constitution, his heart divided—as always at sight of the Capitol, that edifice too familiar, like the face of a parent, to be either handsome or otherwise—between patriotism and dismay. Something he happened to read recently at sea, together with *Pokey*'s present berth, puts him in mind of that summer 166 years ago when a British fleet sailed up the Patuxent from Solomons Island to Benedict, unloaded an army, routed the panicky defenders (among them Fenwick's middle-name-sake), and burned the new capitol and president's house. Francis Scott Key, Fenn has read, had had till then little use for his country, which he thought a vulgar democracy; but the spectacle of its symbolic destruction, followed shortly after in Baltimore by that of its symbolic resurrection,* changed his mind and heart. Fenn's own heart, as always, lifts at sight of the Supreme Court and the Library of Congress off to his left, the complex of museums along the Mall, the memorials to Washington and Jefferson and Lincoln farther on (though his own favorite president is wee

---

*More exactly, its hoped-for symbolic persistence: Key asks the question—O say, does that star-spangled banner et cetera?—but does not presume to answer it.

Jamie Madison); it sinks, not for aesthetic reasons, at sight of almost all the other federal buildings in view, and positively constricts at thought of those ill-chained dragons across the river in Arlington and Langley: the Pentagon and his former employer.*

He moves off the Mall, along Pennsylvania Avenue, and detours up 11th Street to Woodward and Lothrop's department store, to look for something for Susan. Ends up buying a beret for himself instead: Anglobasque, made in England, but 'twill do. According to the 1980 census, the Washington D.C. metropolitan area is home to more than two million people; it is visited by more than fifty thousand tourists on an average day. There are two other customers at Woodward and Lothrop's beret counter: one, a lady, leaves just as Fenn arrives; the other, a gentleman, arrives just as Fenn is leaving. No mathematician, Fenn will nonetheless calculate, once he finds an almanac, that, gender aside, the odds against one of those two's being Dugald Taylor are at least 1,025,000 to 1. Yet the gentleman-arriver-as-Fenn-is-leaving is his old friend and mentor, come to buy a hat for his impending journey to Australia.

Describe Doog Taylor: bald and gray like Fenn, but beardless, smooth, ten years older, unathletic, more plump than husky. From an antique Maryland family of Scottish origin—that's description?—nearly every male member of which since 1830 has been educated at Princeton and read law at Virginia, though fewer than half have practiced that profession more than briefly. Career civil servants, most of them: chargés d'affaires, assistant attorneys general, under-

---

*Not to mention the National Reconnaissance Office, an agency so secret that its very existence was denied until the 1970s (when Marchetti and Marks, among others, disclosed it) and is still officially classified as of our writing this footnote (March 3, 1981); whose 1980 budget was twice that of the CIA—in excess of two billion dollars, concealed in Air Force appropriations; and whose activities have included spying by satellite on U.S. citizens in their own country, such as demonstrators against the Viet Nam war, as well as foreigners in their countries. See e.g., *The New York Times,* March 1, 1981.

secretaries of this and that. A Taylor, Dugald once explained to Fenwick upon declining a presidential request* that he succeed Richard Helms as director of the CIA, may wish to be concertmaster, but has no taste for conducting. Is that description? Twinkly, portly, courtly, immaculate, unmarried, delicately nerved . . .

Doog. Fenn. The men embrace. Susan tells me, Fenwick tells Dugald, that improbable coincidence may start a story, inasmuch as life in fact comprises an occasional gross unlikelihood. But to invoke one to wind up a plot is to invoke the god on wires. You and I must be starting a new story together.

Dugald replies at once Or else our world is run by the god on wires. Where is my Susan.

She kisses you from Solomons Island. You wear boinas now?

Only in the Outback, Doog says softly.

Ah so: Perth. All roads lead to Perth.

Some by design, others by coincidence.

Ours by way of the Cosmos. We're big on coincidence today, Dugald.

Doog buys a navy blue beret and says So is the lower-case cosmos. Don't knock coincidence. He checks his pocket-watch. Let's stroll: the big C won't hold our table long. They stroll, west on G to Lafayette Square and the White House, then take a taxi up Connecticut to Dupont Circle, then stroll again the two blocks out Massachusetts to the Cosmos Club. Did you know, for example, speaking of coincidence, Dugald continues, that one of our senior counterintelligence people in western Europe is a man named Goldfinger. I mean that is his *real* name. Did you know that Arthur Bremer has a sister who once worked in the same establishment as Sirhan Sirhan. You can imagine the FBI's double-

---

*Dugald would prefer the phrase "dodging a presidential wish"; a Taylor does not decline a presidential request unless on the most serious moral grounds.

take at that particular datum. But evidently it's pure coincidence.

It's a wise man, Fenn acknowledges, who knows his Woodward and Lothrop from his Woodward and Bernstein.*

The Cosmos has held Doog's table. Over cold cucumber soup and Sancerre, each man inquires as to the other's heart: Taylor shares with Turner one serious cardiac episode, but, unlike his protégé, has not quit smoking. Both are okay. It is organ day at the Cosmos Club: pink Dugald orders brains, brown Fenwick sweetbreads. They sip the sharp Sancerre. In reply to his friend's next inquiry, Fenn briefly describes our sabbatical cruise and finds himself, uncharacteristically in Dugald's company, rhapsodizing tersely (it can be done) about the Caribbean.

Susan has taught you to be less cool, Doog remarks approvingly. My compliments.

Quite permissible for us ex-officers. Hello: there's Marc Henry.

Fenn smiles and waves across the Cosmos to a sharp-faced, bespectacled, clerky-looking chap in three-piece summer worsteds, their mutual former colleague from Branch 5 (the Southern Cone) of the Western Hemisphere Division at Langley. That fellow, just entering, attaché case in hand, responds with an almost balletlike expression of incredulity and contempt, followed by a reproving glare at Dugald Taylor, then sets his face and stalks into another room.

Goodness, says Fenwick, his own face stinging: I knew which way the wind was blowing, but I didn't imagine it was Force Ten.

Dugald says evenly You know Marcus. In his heart he's

---

*Dugald Taylor's topical allusions, in order: the eponymous villain of an Ian Fleming spy novel; the would-be assassin of then Governor George Wallace of Alabama in Laurel, Maryland, in 1972; the successful assassin of Robert F. Kennedy in Los Angeles, California, in 1968. Fenn's is to the then Washington *Post* investigative reporters instrumental in exposing the Watergate scandals which undid President Nixon.

still OSS, parachuting into occupied France.

With you, Doog. I'm surprised you'll be seen with me. Especially here.

Shame on you, then, Dugald says mildly. The rebuke does double duty, for Fenwick's having published *KUDOVE* and for his imagining that his friend would shun him therefor, howevermuch Doog might deplore the publication. A Taylor may promulgate the most stinging in-house critiques— one of Dugald's ancestors', on corruption in the U.S. Post Office under McKinley, is legendary, and is said to have led Theodore Roosevelt to appoint Charles Joseph Bonaparte to houseclean that bureau. But one does not "go public."

Not so, Fenn insists—to himself at the moment, but to Dugald more than once in time past. Simply one doesn't go public as a first resort. You know how *my* in-house reports fared! You know how the Company tried everything short of actual dirty tricks to stop Marchetti and Agee and Kermit Roosevelt* and me from "going public."

My book didn't get anybody killed, he says aloud. If it crimped a few careers and quashed a few operations, so much the better.

Dugald replies My compliments again on your prose. You do write well. How's the novel coming.

---

*Grandson of the aforementioned Theodore, a former CIA officer, and author of *Countercoup: The Struggle for Control of Iran* (N.Y.: McGraw-Hill, 1980), a review of the roles of the CIA and its British counterpart in overthrowing Prime Minister Mohammed Mossadegh of Iran in 1953 and replacing him with the Shah Mohammed Reza Pahlevi. Susan thinks Fenwick mistaken in his inclusion of Mr. Roosevelt in this catalogue: according to *The New York Times* (November 13, 1979), McGraw-Hill's scrapping of the first edition of *Countercoup* was prompted more by objections from British Petroleum—whom the *Times* reports as owning "a 40 percent interest in the [Iranian] oil consortium," and who the book alleges provided cover, through its predecessor company Anglo-Iranian Oil, for British covert operations in Iran—than by direct objections from the CIA. A better candidate would be the unfortunate Frank Snepp, author of *Decent Interval: an insider's account of Saigon's indecent end, told by the CIA's Chief Strategy Analyst in Vietnam* (N.Y.: Random House, 1977).

Fenn won't have the evasion. It's not the same thing. Can we talk here, Doog?

His friend smiles. That's why I suggested the Cosmos. Safest place in town outside of an embassy code room, once the entrée is served.

It is. The old friends consider a young beaujolais; but the Sancerre is only half gone and will quite do. Dugald Taylor speaks now at length, quietly, over his brains and fresh asparagus. Beyond doubt, Fenn's book and its pre-decessors, along with the general public and congressional reaction against our Vietnamese and Chilean adventures and the Watergate fiasco, contributed to the lowering of Agency* morale and the reining in of its covert operations in the middle and latter 1970s. Resignations and early retirements, Dugald's own included, ran high; recruitment of able trainees—Marcus Henry's job these days—grew increasingly difficult despite the poor national job market for college graduates, especially in the liberal arts. The better Catholic universities such as Notre Dame and Ford-ham, which had long since replaced the Ivy League as prime recruiting ground, and to which by the middle 1960s were added the better state universities, had themselves given way, faute de mieux, more and more to "streetcar-Catholic" colleges—your local Loyolas and Canisiuses; to branch campuses of the state complexes—Ogontz, New Paltz, Yp-silanti; and even to community colleges—Catonsville, Har-risburg Area, West Liberty—where patriotism still runs high among blue-collar children with white-collar aspirations. But economic inflation, the oil squeeze, the lapsing of Soviet-American détente, the convenient bugaboo of the Ayatollah Khomeini, the protracted holding of the American hostages in Iran, and a new, "post-Viet Nam" generation of under-graduates, have effectively reversed that trend, both on the

---

*Dugald has never been known, in any humor, to refer to the Central Intelligence Agency as the Company.

campuses and in Congress. He Dugald does not have to tell Fenwick that all the half-baked novelists in the land, and not a few full-baked ones, are writing spy novels, for example, many of which, like the latest crop of tsk-tsk exposés of the Agency, barely conceal their fascination and envy beneath their knee-jerk moralizing against our skullduggery. Fenn's will not, he trusts, be another CIA novel.

Decidedly not, Fenwick promises. That is almost the only thing he can say for sure about it. But he cannot promise that the likes of certain of his ex-colleagues will not drift through it from time to time on the narrative tide.

Dugald lifts his glass to that metaphor and continues: in short, the lads in Langley—and, more and more, the lasses: an important new area of recruitment, as Fenn might have heard—are prospering again, and gearing up for new covert operations in the 1980s whoever wins the November elections. It is Dugald's understanding that both the CIA and the Pentagon are reviving chemical-biological warfare research, almost dormant since the latter 1960s, on the strength of recent Soviet applications of such weapons in Afghanistan and their infamous anthrax accident in Sverdlovsk in April 1979, which killed more than a thousand people—and which he personally believes as likely to have been a breakdown of their rickety health-care system as a bacteriological-warfare production accident. We are particularly excited (Dugald uses the pronoun with poker-faced irony) about new developments in molecular biology; he understands us to be either funding indirectly or investigating the feasibility of a number of gene-splicing projects, to the end of designing viruses for which there are no antibodies, or for which only we possess the antibodies—but he cannot vouch for this matter firsthand. Legionnaire's Disease, by Fenn's friend's best information, was *not* one of our experiments, serious Soviet contentions to the contrary notwithstanding. Admittedly there would have been a dandy cover: who would have suspected even us—despite the precedents of our spraying San Francisco with a test strain of respiratory bacillus in the late Sixties and of our sundry experiments upon unwitting war veterans in Veterans Administration hospitals—of experimenting upon an American Legion convention in the Cradle of Liberty, the City of Brotherly Love? To be sure, we shall not employ our patent viruses for individual assassination; we have an ample inventory of devices for that purpose, several of them developed since Fenwick's day. But to eliminate a small, cohesive group—an encampment of guerrillas, say—a properly antibodied mole could administer a literal kiss of death. The wonders of science.

The mention of moles brings Fenwick's erstwhile mentor, over coffee and cigar now, to Manfred, who in certain areas had been *his* mentor. He Dugald can tell all he knows on this head without fear of being lip-read, say, from across the room, he declares, for he knows only that there are two schools of thought among his professional acquaintances concerning Manfred's Paisley-like disappearance, and they are the obvious: that Fenn's twin, accidentally or on assignment, had discovered the deep mole still believed to inhabit the Agency despite Operation Kitty Hawk, and had been neutralized by agents either of the KGB or of the mole him/herself; or that Manfred *was* the mole, and had been neutralized by the team who discovered him so to be—whether killed or sequestered constituted two sub-schools of opinion. It is *not* generally felt—though Dugald himself does not dismiss the possibility—that John Arthur Paisley's nautical suicide* simply inspired Manfred Turner to follow suit, for whatever reasons.

I don't dismiss that possibility either, Doog.

You don't. Do you know of any reasons Count might have had for killing himself.

Fenn recognizes his friend's question to be professional. By replying straightforwardly—that he knows of none, but

---

*Taylor's term; he and Fenwick are of the same mind on this matter. It is a pity that he does not indicate whether knowledgeable people in the Agency and on the Senate Select Committee on Intelligence share their opinion.

had been distant from his brother since leaving the Company and writing *KUDOVE*—instead of asking whether Dugald is currently an Agency consultant, he signals his understanding and acceptance of this state of affairs.

Dugald nods and sighs. We don't know of any either.

Thanks, Doog. I can't really imagine that Count would have used *Pokey* to kill himself from. He knew I loved that boat; he knew that Susan and I were planning our sabbatical cruise in it. I'd have sold the thing after his death if it weren't the boat Susan seduced me on.

I see.

Count could hold a grudge; I think he never quite forgave me for divorcing Marilyn Marsh, for example. But he wasn't spiteful, and he loved his family. Either somebody got to him, or he drowned accidentally and happened not to get found like Paisley. Was he the mole, Doog.

No. *A* mole, possibly, though I strongly believe not. But not *the* mole, Fenwick. Before the year is out, another mole of sorts in our midst will be indicted in the Federal Court in Baltimore.* We've got the goods on him. But he too, in our opinion, is not *the* mole.

The reader will have appreciated Fenn's inflecting his question Taylor-fashion. It is to be appreciated further that, Dugald having replied unhesitatingly and unequivocally, it would be improper for Fenn to ask additionally, out of mere curiosity, what his friend appears to know: who "the" mole might be.

Anyone in Count's line of work, he remarks instead, makes serious enemies.

Dugald puffs and nods. Serious and sophisticated enemies. In our house and in others.† As I'm sure you know, Count did not always delegate his work to agents and cutouts, as he should have done.

---

*See note p. 308.

† We believe Dugald Taylor to mean by "others" not the KGB but the various branches of the U.S. Defense Intelligence Agency (DIA), beside the scale of whose budget and operations the CIA's are small potatoes.

I know, Doog.

In certain very sensitive areas your brother was an incorrigible do-it-himselfer, against all policy.

I know that.

He not only preferred it that way, Fenn; he enjoyed it, I'm afraid.

Mm.

Luncheon is finished; their meeting is not. After a few moments' silence, the two men exchange a glance; Dugald says I've signed the chit already. Shall we stroll.

They do, back toward the Mall. Splendid lunch, Fenn says.

Wasn't it. I needn't point out to you, Fenwick, that your public criticism of us, together with your upcoming academic appointment—I forgot to congratulate you on that. . . .

Thanks. I may or may not take it, after all, or Susan hers.

Really.

We might chuck everything and sail around the world.

Oh, well, then. I was going to say, you've got a dandy cover now for doubling, if you were of a mind to double.

Dugald. For one second it occurs to Fenn to wonder whether his friend might be the deep mole. But Dugald goes on to declare, in a particular way he has of speaking of delicate matters with scarcely a motion of his lips, that should Fenwick be approached by foreign agencies, or the American agents of foreign agencies—not the KGB, one would guess, but some less sophisticated outfit such as DINA*—and should he be inclined to take the pitch, he Dugald is authorized to say that their common former employer stands ready to forgive Fenwick his trespasses and assist his presumable search for further information about Manfred and Gus.

---

*Directorio Nacional de Inteligencia, the Chilean secret police responsible, e.g., for the murders in September 1976, a few blocks from where Fenn and Doog are strolling, of the late President Allende's Ambassador to the U.S., Orlando Letelier, and his young American associate Ms. Ronni Moffitt. See *Assassination on Embassy Row*, by John Dinges and Saul Landau (N.Y.: Pantheon, 1980).

Fenn halts on the sunny sidewalk of Dupont Circle. Gus.
Yes.

Clearly there is more to come. Fenn considers the situation for five seconds and then promises to perpend their
former employer's offer. They resume their walk.

I should like to ask, Dugald continues affably after a time,
whether you have, to your knowledge, already been so
approached.

Not to my knowledge, Doog. But as we know, et cetera.

Of course. Mysterious Agency!*

What Fenn really knows is that the conversation in
progress may be the very approach Dugald speaks of, and
his friend the agent, or the agent's agent. They wait for a
traffic light. Fenn says as they cross You mentioned Gus.

I did. It has come to our former employer's knowledge
that among the anti-government prisoners being held on a
certain island off the southern coast of Chile, there are a
number of non-nationals, not all of them from Bolivia,
Argentina, or Cuba.

Dugald.

These non-Chilean desaparecidos have not been termi-
nally Disappeared, not all of them, for the usual reason:
their families might be interested in assisting their repatriation by the customary means. You'll be interested to hear
that your mother-in-law has already been approached by the
agent of a government friendly to Chile—

Carmen!

Carmen.

Jesus Christ, Doog! What government? Fenn points to the
ground. Ours?

Dugald shrugs his eyebrows: the question is improper. It

---

*Dugald Taylor was a student of literature before he went to law
school and gravitated into the CIA by way of wartime duty with the Office
of Strategic Services. His reference here, a standing irony among him,
Fenwick, and their vanished colleague, is to the hero's invocation of the
spirits which opens Lord Byron's choral tragedy *Manfred* (1816): "O
mysterious Agency!"

has been suggested to young Gus Seckler-Turner's mother, he continues, that in exchange for her cooperation, this agent's sponsors will ascertain at least whether her son is among those non-Chilean prisoners. If then a mutually satisfactory further relation is established—and if indeed Gus is still alive—she need not abandon hope for his repatriation. You know how those things go.

Fenwick feels ill. He takes Dugald's arm—almost seizes it—and discerns at once in his friend's eyes that it is not Doog who proposed this familiar extortion. Fenn does know, very well, how these things go: if Carmen B. Seckler's first information turns out to be disinformation, her contact will regretfully report that her son is dead. He is relieved to hear now from Dugald that Carmen's immediate, street-wise reply was exactly what friendly counterintelligence would have advised: Prove to me that my son is alive, and then we'll discuss your proposal further. But what on earth, he wants to know, can anyone hope to learn from Carmen B. Seckler in the way of useful classified information, especially now that Count is out of the picture? Carmen and the neutron bomb? Carmen and the cruise missile?

Now it is Doog who halts, twinkling, at the corner of Farragut Square. How about Carmen and the cruise. Your cruise. You.

You're joking.

No.

There's nothing there, Doog. Listen: Gus and Manfred disappeared; I had a heart attack; Susan had a paid leave; we took a long sail. We had a couple of decisions to make about what we want to do with the next part of our lives. There's the Swarthmore job for her and the Delaware job for me. There's that novel in the oven, or play, or whatever. There's *Pokey* and Portugal and the rest of the globe. There's other business. But there's no information. Some turkey is wasting his time. I'm clean.

Let's stroll, Dugald suggests. They do, down toward Pennsylvania Avenue. I believe you, Fenn, of course. But suppose Carmen were to beg you, for instance, for her son's sake, to mount a serious campaign to persuade *your* son, upon completion of his postdoctoral project, to pursue his researches under Agency auspices.

Oh, Doog.

Stroll, Fenn.

They stroll, but Fenwick is dizzied.

Or if that friendly government happens not to be this one—Dugald gestures toward the White House—you might persuade Orrin to share his expertise in the gene-splicing way with certain private researchers of that government.

Fenn is incredulous. Chile?

I didn't say Chile. I said a government friendly to—

I won't do it, Doog. Gus will have to die, if he isn't dead already.

Dugald nods once. I didn't imagine you would. And I don't know, by the way, whether the poor young man is dead or alive. Better off dead, I imagine, than in Tejas Verdes* or the like. But Carmen might decide to approach your son directly. The two boys were close, I understand.

Orrin won't do it. He'd fucking better not!

Dugald Taylor, who is without profanity or other casual vulgarity, winces slightly and observes that many a scientist has been known to rise above his/her principles.

Not Orrin, Fenn declares grimly. To him, pure science means morally pure, too. Doog, I'm flabbergasted. I'm sick. Sorry.

No no: I'm grateful to you. And it goes without saying that I know you're clean in all this, but I'll say it.

His friend's relief is evident. Thank you, Fenn. I am, in fact, clean. But the pitch to Carmen Seckler was serious, I think. No doubt she'll be perfectly candid about it with you when you see her.

---

*An interrogation camp north of Santiago particularly infamous as a torture center just after the 1973 coup and the establishment of DINA, whose first chief was also commandant of Tejas Verdes. See e.g., the *Amnesty International Report on Torture* (N.Y.: Farrar Straus & Giroux, 1975), p. 208.

Dear god.

Well. The pair have reached the E-Street tangent of the Ellipse and stand at the Zero Milestone. We say good-bye here. I'm off to Perth on Friday. Don't ask.

I shan't, Doog. Friday, is it. Good journey.

Dugald considers. We mentioned our episodes, Fenn. I must tell you that I've heard rumors, which I wish I could refute, that our Research and Development people now have in their bag of tricks a fairly effective inducer of cardiac arrest.

No.

Very possibly it's not so, but something just as nasty likely is. All the same, you may want to confide this rumor to your doctor, as I've done mine—though there's not a thing he can do with the information, medically. The trigger is alleged to be a hundred percent clean, though nowhere near infallible.

Fenwick Scott Key Turner's eyes water. God damn us, Doog.

Yes.

You. Me. Count. All of us.

Well. We are not yet a truly wicked government, in my opinion.

But we are sure as hell not poor in wickedness.

Dugald sighs and nods. We are not poor in wickedness. Wiedersehen, Fenn. Good sailing. Kiss Susan.

Fenwick extends his hand—and then, on a shared if not quite simultaneous impulse, the friends exchange a quick parting kiss themselves. A young black man passing by with a radio the size of a salesman's sample case says Faggots. Fenn grins, says God bless America, and squeezes his friend's smooth hand. Dugald twinkles.

Fenn's second ordeal, the unreported one, occurs two hours later on the bus ride home, somewhere between Charlotte Hall and Mechanicsville in southern Maryland. He is telling his notebook about Dugald Taylor: specifically, along this stretch of highway, he is casting up fictitious names with a properly Scottish ring to them, in case Doog winds up on the payroll of our story, and reflecting, as he casts, upon their post-luncheon talk and longstanding friendship,* when for the second time in half a century a very large hand inside his chest clutches and squeezes his heart as he had squeezed Dugald Taylor's hand. It is a minor seizure, nothing like as painful or consequential as its predecessor of the year before. In ninety seconds it subsides; in five minutes it is gone. He loosens his necktie. His pulse rate continues high, probably from consternation, and he is in a sopping sweat.

The obvious question preoccupies him through the rest of the bus ride, and will again after the distraction of comparing official ordeals with Susan. Likewise some sub- or ancillary questions, perhaps less obvious, such as whether Dugald could have been the *unwitting* transmitter of R and D's (rumored) infernal new toxin, and whether its dosage has been refined to the Warning level; even whether the rules of dramaturgy permit a scene that begins with a dialogue on improbable coincidence to end with an improbable coincidence. Can a pistol hung on the wall in Act One, he asks his notebook, be fired in Act One?

On balance, however, though shaken, he receives this postscript from his heart a good deal more calmly than he received the original message: evidence, he is pleased to infer, that the peace he has made with the prospect of his death is not merely notional. His concern is for Susan—and for Carmen B. Seckler, who has suffered enough bereavement already and whose attempted coercing must be dealt with.

This last reflection is therapeutic: anger displaces calm concern. It cannot be Doog! Well, it could: his friend might be being coerced as well. But with threat of what? Dugald

---

*It was Taylor's example, much more than Manfred's, that persuaded Fenwick to join the Company in 1960 and to move gradually from the Historical Staff, where he worked as a chief editor of the endless memoirs that senior officers are paid to write upon their retirement, to the Directorate of Operations, or Clandestine Services, Doog's and Manfred's bailiwick.

Taylor is at least as moral a man as Fenwick: no threat to himself would likely make him acquiesce in such a business. His ex-wife is happily remarried; he has no children. No doubt there are siblings, nieces, nephews; moreover, people not only change or modify their values over time, but take one by surprise: Marilyn Marsh, for example, since *their* divorce, has manifested both a managerial talent and a capacity for self-righteous deceit which astonish him, so foreign had he imagined either to her character. But Doog! My my.

By the time he disbuses at Solomons, Fenn's sweat is dry, his pulse its normal sixty-to-the-tick. It is good to be back among the banging halyards and kvetching gulls. He removes his necktie, opens his shirt, lets his eyeglasses hang from their lanyard, and ruefully prepares to conceal from his wife as pointless, at least for the present, the tidings of this second episode and its possible cause. He *will* tell her— indeed, he will consult her about—the reported extortion of her mother and what might be done to end or make use of it, short of his resuming work for the Company. Love for Susan floods Fenwick's soul. So full of secrets were his latter Agency years, he hates the least lapse of candor in his marriage. He craves powerfully to talk with her. Much as he cares for poor wrecked Miriam, he hopes that she and her brood are gone.

Apparently they are, or else are in the village and Susan with them. As he reaches the pier, wishing he had found some sort of gift, Fenn is disappointed to see no sign of his friend on the boat. His skipperly eye observes at once that *Pokey* has for some reason been freshly hosed down and scrubbed, though we did that chore only yesterday. Moreover, the water valve has been left on (the hose is dripping at the nozzle), and our deck brush and bucket are on the finger-pier, where they might easily be knocked overboard, instead of in the lazarette where they belong. No great matter. But in the cockpit is a more troubling sign: a green bottle of Moselle, four-fifths empty, on the sole, and one nine-ounce paper cup, also not quite empty, in a gimbaled drink-holder.

Something has gone wrong. Fenn steps aboard, calling Susan without reply. Now he sees her, prone on the starboard settee in work-shorts and T-shirt, her face swollen from crying. As he hurries to her, his heart clutched by concern, she turns her face away. He touches her: she shrinks from him, then draws him to her, holds him desperately, weeps again. In time unfolds the tale of

## SUSAN'S ORDEAL.

Miriam and the boys arrive after noon—she chainsmoking, crazy-haired, leather-sandaled; eleven-year-old Sy wearing hard-soled shoes, black socks, black bermudas on his fat legs, and, unbelievably, smoking a cigarette too; and two-year-old Edgar Allan Ho also wearing leather soles and wielding a vintage 1930 metal toy truck with missing wheels: a sharp-cornered gift from some Fells Point "antique" dealer and patron of Carmen's Place. Horrified Susan makes haste to intercept them: can Mimi really have forgotten that leather soles won't do on wooden decks?

Now Sy spots his Aunt Susie and galumphs toward her, his belly lopping over the belt of his old-man's shorts. Edgar trots after. Thin-faced Miriam halts to light a fresh cigarette with the butt of its predecessor. Don't run! Susan calls. As if she'd cried Hit the deck, both boys at once go sprawling. E. A. Ho has merely lost his balance: fortunately, he loses his toy as well, into the harbor, before it can damage either *Pokey* or himself. He comes up bawling but unhurt except for small splinters in the heels of both hands. Heavy Sy, however, stubs his black-leather toe on a dock plank and goes down hard: both knees and one elbow skinned; a wicked brush-burn on one forearm; the bag of fresh tomatoes—which Carmen has sent down with the inevitable welcome store of rye bread, corned beef, sweet münster—squashed under him, where he'd clutched it to keep it safe.

Splinters, blood, and tomato pulp from shin to chin, he rolls onto his back—as well as onto both his lighted cigarette and more tomatoes—and lets go a heroic caterwaul.

Susan breaks the dock rule herself and runs to help. E. A. Ho, turning to his mother for succor, trips and sprawls again. Miriam surveys the scene impassively, draws on her fresh cigarette, and flicks the old one away without looking to see whether it falls into the water or somebody's cockpit. It is not the moment to invoke the no-hard-soles rule. Hindsight suggests that Susan might have made use of the dock hose as both first aid and preventive medicine, removing the boys' shoes and Sy's pulpy clothing and washing their cuts before anyone came aboard; at the time she is too concerned for their hurts and distracted by their howling to think of it.

And so *Pokey* is boarded by mother and children, and on Sue's subsequent conservative estimate, which Fenn cannot gainsay, the ship sustains more damage in the next ten minutes than in our entire ocean passage from the Virgins, including the storm off Hank and Chuck—and yet more damage before the short visit is done than in those first ten minutes. The bloodstains in the settee fabric are probably permanent, as are the cigarette burns on the holly cabin sole, on the mahogany chart-table fiddle, on the teak washstand counter in the head. The blood and tomato stains in the teak deck planking, like the shoe-leather scratches on the cabin and cockpit soles and the companionway ladder, will yield to laborious refinishing next season; but the custom-made cockpit cushion will have to be replaced (little Edgar discovers the galley knife-rack while his mother holds forth on Susan's moral irresponsibility in choosing a tenured associate professorship in an elitist college over working with deprived inner-city children. Susan, in the head compartment, is washing and bandaging Sy; by the time she sees what's up and shrieks at Miriam to disarm the child before he cuts himself, Edgar has blithely slashed the vinyl cushion-cover. Even then, it is Susan who must dash through the

cabin and up the companionway to snatch the knife.
Miriam—unmoved, unmoving—declares that the little
fuckers have to learn from experience that knives are
dangerous). And Fenwick will have to remove, dismantle,
reassemble, and reinstall the marine toilet itself, half a day's
messy work: What a pain in the ass, Miriam remarks when
Susan, almost in tears now, reminds her how to pump the
thing; but Mim neglects to mention that she too is menstruating, until she has plugged the plumbing with a
discarded tampon and a filter-tip cigarette.

Susan so far has been literally too busy coping even to kiss
her sister hello. By the time she gets the boys desplintered,
washed, disinfected, bandaged, untomatoed, disarmed, and
unshod, she is near hysteria. The blocked toilet—Miriam has
shat in it, too—and the cigarette burns, of which Sue now
discovers the first, on the washbasin counter, while trying in
vain to clear the blockage, do the trick. Nobody wants her
crab-and-avocado salad anyhow: Mim and the boys tanked
up at a Burger King on the drive down. The visit Susan has
so long looked forward to is over in thirty miserable
minutes: she screams at her sister to get off the boat: Off!
Off! Cute Edgar Allan is frightened into bawling again; he
has also shat his diaper. Wide-eyed Sy picks his Buddhic
nose and wipes his finger on the settee. Susan goes clear out
of control: Get off! Go home! Go home.

Jesus, Shushi, Miriam says—laying her cigarette on the
chart-table fiddle—you're tighter-assed than ever. She picks
up Edgar. Come on, Sy. Is Fenn cheating on you or
something? He'd better not.

Go away. Go away. Weeping Susan herds them up the
ladder, out of the cockpit, onto the dock. Unprecedented
behavior for her, who normally shrugs off her sister's
familiar criticisms—the first ten minutes of any reunion—
and minimizes property damage by adroit preventive measures, so that their abiding love and concern for each other
can come through. Now, on the dock at last, she understands that she must henceforward see Miriam only on

Miriam's, or neutral, ground; and even half-hysterical she is saddened by this recognition. She hugs and kisses her sister—whose great dark eyes, her sole unravaged feature, twins to Susan's, at once fill up like Sue's with tears—and springs back onto the boat, down into the cabin, out of sight.

I'm sorry, Susele! Miriam calls after her. Sue is weeping on the stained settee. Sy hoarsely complains Ain't we going sailing, Ma? His mother replies No, asshole: we busted the fucking boat. Sy wails You said! Said shmed, says Miriam: we're going home. E. A. Ho joins his half-brother's bawling; the family exits as noisily as it arrived.

Then I scrubbed everything inside and out, Susan sobs, and I worked and worked on the head and couldn't clear it, and everywhere I looked I saw more gouges and scratches and cigarette burns.

It's all right, Fenwick tells her. It's all right.

So I decided to get drunk, but I just gave myself a cracking headache. Mims and I didn't even get to talk! I even forgot to put Ma's münster and corned beef on ice; I had to throw them out. How's Doog? Hold me. Poor Mimsi. God.

No real news, Fenn says. It'll keep till tomorrow, when we're sailing. I'm hungry.

I'm sick. What shall I make you? She forgot to give me the mail, too, and I forgot to ask.

I'll bring us something from the restaurant. The mail will keep. What can you eat?

Susan sits up and pushes her hair back with both hands. The number three club on wheat toast with mayonnaise and chips. And a medium Coke. I'd better wash up and go with you; I need to pee. Poor poor Mimsi!

The little marina restaurant is almost empty. Navy planes blast in and out of the air station. Returning from the women's room, Susan says her face looks awful.

No it doesn't. How's your period.

Her eyes refill. Mim's wrong, Fenn. Kids aren't unimportant just because they're well off.

Your sister is nuts.

Never mind that. Somebody has to teach the super kids too. They're important. And I'm good at it.

You're the best.

I'm not the best. But I'm good, and what I do for bright kids is important. They're important. If I didn't teach college, I'd look for the most academically elite private high school I could find. Maybe even junior high. Gifted kids are precious.

We have explored these waters together many times before, but Fenwick understands that they must be cruised through again for Susan's solace. It is not that the inner-city deprived don't matter, we reagree, or the rural deprived, or the old, or refugees, or recidivist criminals, or who have you; there is to be found among them the occasional diamond in the rough, and no lack of lesser minerals and honest ore. But the excellent and privileged matter also—diamonds in the smooth, Sue calls them; and if she is less antipopulist than Leonardo da Vinci, who dismissed the mass of humankind as "mere fillers-up of privies," she is unabashedly more so than her sister, who will not acknowledge that a young Mozart is in any consequential way more valuable than a semiretarded and pregnant fourteen-year-old escapee from an institution for wayward girls. Besides, she Susan has her own weaknesses and strengths: she would be wasting her best talents teaching English as a second language to newly arrived Cuban refugees.

Between ourselves, all this is preaching to the converted. But though the sisters had no time to talk this afternoon, we know also that there is another aspect of Miriam's loving criticism of us (like Grandma, she esteems Fenn second only to her sister, for loving her sister so) less easily countered, howevermuch the critic's own current life might fail to exemplify it. For more than half a year now we have not been, and just possibly for a considerable while to come we shall not be, teaching the gifted or exposing the misdeeds of the CIA or doing any other socially useful thing. We have been, in the main, indulging ourselves, amusing ourselves. We have been playing.

Over the third quarter of her club sandwich, Susan lays that term on the table. Fenn knows what it betokens: his wife's dark sometimes feeling that our years together, precious as they've been to both of us, are themselves a kind of playing: not finally serious, as the lives of Susan's child-raising, house-buying contemporaries might be said to be serious. . . .

Fenn won't have this, not tonight. You're wrung out, hon. We haven't been just playing; we've been also playing. We're on a well-earned sabbatical leave: my first since Spain; your first since kindergarten. Things have happened in our lives. We have decisions to make. The idea of sabbaticals is to catch your breath, take stock, get perspective. That's what we've tried to do. We've read a lot; we've thought and talked as we sailed; we've made notes. That reminds me. Never mind. Not everybody has to be D. H. Lawrence or Dostoevsky, thank heaven. You can be morally earnest without being morally afire. You can be serious with a smile. You can even be dreamy and self-indulgent in your personal life— which we aren't, as a rule—and still get terrific things done.

Susan knows all this and more, but appreciates hearing it. And she *is* wrung out. Everything will have to keep till tomorrow, and, unlike the münster and corned beef, it will. Time to end this long chapter. We talk better when we're sailing.

Don't forget to use the head while we're here. Susan climbs out of the booth. Do you have fifteen cents? I want to call Mimsi.

Of course you do.

What about that other ordeal,

## SUSAN'S PRIVATE ONE,

counterpart to Fenwick's cardiac news-report on the bus?

# 2
# WYE

It won't be Wye tonight, Fenwick reckons from *Pokey*'s chart table. Too far.

Susan at the tiller asks What's the forecast?

Partly cloudy, dry, coolish, like now. Light northwest wind. Rain by tomorrow. No thundershowers.

Early Thursday A.M., June 5: we're sailing again and easier in our skins. Sue suggests Poplar Island tonight, Wye I. tomorrow. Fenn was up at dawn and managed to clear our toilet without having to dismantle it altogether; we have left Drum Point to port and are standing out of Patuxent River into the Bay under full sail—main, jib staysail, and #1 genoa—on a nice close reach. Behind us the jets roar in and out; off to starboard, rescue helicopters clatter about their exercises. Our mouths go grim: Viet Nam has given chopper formations a bad image forever. At Little Cove Point, with plenty of sea room, we trim everything in tight and see how high we can point in the easy air, up the Bay, away from Solomons, toward home. Fenn checks knotmeter and compass; walks off the day's projected tacks on the chart with dividers. Poplar or Tilghman, he announces, depending on what the wind does.

We wonder mildly whether this change of destinations will muck up our narrative program, which calls now for a visit to our past. Susan points out that Poplar Island was our first night's anchorage on this sabbatical cruise, nine months ago; returning there now ought to *be* our narrative program. Not the least of sailing's pleasures, in our opinion, is that it refreshes, by literalizing them, many common figures of speech: one is forever and in fact making things shipshape from stem to stern, casting off, getting under way, making headway, giving oneself leeway, taking a different tack, getting the wind knocked out of one's sails, battening down the hatches, making for any port in a storm, getting swamped or pooped, putting an anchor out to windward, enjoying snug harbor. In this instance, Fenn is able to shrug and declare that we set our story's ideal course and then sail the best one we can, correcting and improvising from occasional fixes on our actual position.

Sue says Mm.

Soon Cove Point proper, with its handsome lighthouse and its alarming offshore liquid natural gas terminal, is abeam. A twin-domed tanker is off-loading Algerian gas there, valued for its high BTUs. We give it the prescribed wide berth, tisking tongues: in explosive potential that ship is a floating thermonuclear bomb which could clear this stretch of Bay from western to eastern shore—but it's good to have the gas. The Cove Point LNG terminal is the first of three such sorely mixed blessings spaced along the Calvert Cliffs, which now step sheer out of sight to windward: the second, a few miles farther up, is Baltimore Gas and Electric's Calvert Cliffs nuclear power station, listed with its neighbor in the Cruising Guide among the Major Ecological Trouble Spots on the Chesapeake, though it's good to have the kilowattage. The third—like the Norfolk Navy Yard and noisy PAX* behind us; like the Army's Aberdeen Ordnance Proving Ground and Edgewood Arsenal ahead—is military: the Naval Research Laboratory firing range, marked by a giant parabolic antenna that sweeps Prohibited Area 204.32 on our chart. We suppose it's good to have the security.

---

*The navy's code-misnomer for its Patuxent Air Station.

These grim sisters, visible for miles, will be our principal landmarks for position-fixing through the day. The terminal is now off our port quarter. We lay our first tack almost due north—toward marshy James Island on the Eastern Shore, but tide and leeway will set us east and oblige us to tack again before reaching it. We adjust the self-steering vane. Now we can talk.

Susan and Miriam made long telephonic peace last night, on our credit card. Wasted by her day, Sue reported afterwards no more than that, and we slept. Now, on this six-mile port tack, Fenn hears the particulars. Mim understands and has acknowledged that her general disorderliness drives Susan wild and would so drive many another, if not everyone. While she herself could under no circumstances abide anything so *fragile* as our Goddamn Sailboat, she grants the right of others to feel differently. She apologizes for any harm done and for forgetting to deliver our first-class mail. More generally, she knows very well that she is wrecked, scattered, farchadat; she is distressed by the increasing uselessness and decreasing coherence of her life: hence her ever-growing, urgent wish that Susan's redeem them both.

Fenwick sighs: Miriam.

At Swarthmore, Susan says, Mim says I'll only be giving more to people who have too much already, like giving the best milk to fat babies while others starve. I told her *I* didn't have too much already when I went to Swarthmore: I needed serious terrific professors and hotshot classmates to burn up the library with while Mims and her friends were burning everything *down.*

Fenn applauds.

I granted her that the kids were tearing up the campuses because our government was tearing up the country, and other people's countries. But still. Anyhow, it was babies that were on Mim's mind.

Ah.

If I'm not going to teach blue-collar, and if you and I

don't have kids, the least I could do is adopt a boat-people baby and raise it to be a Freedom Fighter.

A Freedom Fighter.

Yeah. Mainly Mims wanted to know why we don't have children.

Fenn's been taking bearings on the LNG terminal and the nuclear power station, now in view. He puts the hand-bearing compass down on the slashed cockpit cushion. What'd you tell her?

Susan regards their twenty bare brown toes, braced in a row against the leeward seat. I told her most of the truth. We've been over that ground enough already. I compared my feelings about parenthood to Kafka's about marriage: that it's the single most important thing in human life, and that my standards for it are self-defeatingly high.

Mm. Fenwick attends with careful interest: we too have been over this ground—plenty, if not enough. It is near the heart of our sabbatical. He ventures that Miriam will have pointed out that millions and millions of ordinary people manage parenthood.

Right. And I told her ordinary people do it ordinarily. She said I sounded like a bumper sticker. I couldn't go much farther down my Superkid road with her because of Sy and Ho. I just told her again that being an ordinary mediocre parent doesn't interest me. You weren't all that terrific as a father, and Manfred was worse, and Ma's kerflooey, and who knows about Da? I'd fail myself and my children, I told her, even a terrific child, which is the only kind I want, and you would too. Blah blah blah—forget it. But I can't stand it. My life is empty and stupid.

You didn't tell Mim that.

Sure I did. We tell each other everything. Anyhow, she knows that you and she and teaching are the only things that matter to me. Except Ma and Grandma and Chief and Virgie and Sy and Edgar and literature.

Fenwick observes, not for the first time, that that's about

ten things. How many people have ten things that really matter?

And Susan answers, likewise not for the first time, But they're not *ours;* they're no kind of posterity. What keeps Grandma alive? What'll keep Ma going in her old age? Unless you're religious, or some kind of real artist or scientist or statesman, it's kids or nothing.

Fenn reflects, but does not remark, that of Carmen B. Seckler's three offspring, Susan alone could be said to have been more sustenance than expense of spirit, more naches than tsuris. And his own relation to his only child, once warm indeed, has been considerably distanced by his divorce and remarriage.*

Sue concludes her report with a sigh: So now we can't wait to see each other—at Ma's place. I told Mims she wasn't allowed on board again ever. She understands.

We tack. Now it will be five and a half miles westward, back across the Bay toward Calvert Beach, below B G & E's cooling towers, from where we should be able to lay our next port tack straight up to Tilghman or Poplar, depending. Susan kisses Fenn's shoulder. I'm sorry I've hogged the dialogue so much. What did you find out from Doog? Oh, I forgot to tell you: Mims says she thinks Ma's going to do some kind of secret work for the Company. Some secret, when Mim talks about it on the bar pay phone. I told her her paranoia's getting serious. You're not laughing.

Nope.

Fenwick!

The morning's warming up, but it's still shirts on. Fenn checks the knotmeter: four and a half to five. This tack should see his tale told.

He summarizes his conversation with Dugald Taylor, omitting Doog's pitch to him to double, that rumored heart-

---

*Not least because of Orrin Turner's long hopeless childhood crush on Susan Seckler, five unbridgeable years his senior, of which more presently.

attack drug of which he had half-seriously speculated just before his excursion, and his cardiac alarm on the bus ride home, but reporting faithfully the alleged pitch to Carmen B. Seckler, with its awful bait. Susan, beside him, is beside herself; for a moment near mid-channel Fenn imagines she might even attack him.

She shrieks What are we doing here? How could you not have told me this right away? Get me off this fucking toy!

He is shocked. What she means, he soon understands, is that in her opinion we should be laying siege to the State Department's Chilean desk, for example, instead of idling up Chesapeake Bay. He ought not even to have returned to Solomons Island, but to have sent for her instead, and for Carmen. The three of us should be permitting our congressmen not a moment's peace, nor the Chilean ambassador, nor anyone else in position to help, until the rumor that Gus is alive has been verified and his release secured. Jesus, Jesus, she almost screams at him: Get me out of here! *Gus!* At least we should be with Ma! Oh, poor Mundungus!

Her emotion is understandable; her attitude is not quite fair. At the time of Gus Seckler-Turner's disappearance early in '78, well before our cruise was even planned, we mobilized every official governmental resource in his behalf, and Manfred every unofficial one within his considerable reach, in vain. We laid our sieges, did our doorstep-camping, until it was apparent that no headway was thereby to be made, and until Manfred's own disappearance from our boat made new claims upon our exhausted energies. Just this exhaustion, despair, futility, were among the motivations of our cruise—during which, even so, at every opportunity we wrote, radioed, telephoned various authorities, to delay the two cases' going cold. We did everything we could, sweetheart.

But this is new news! Susan protests, less hysterically. She regrets her outburst, especially her denigration of our boat, our cruise, as valuable to her as to her husband, and her imputation to him of irresponsibility—whose exertions in behalf of her half-brother were, with Manfred's vanishment, very likely a cause of his heart attack. She embraces him. But oh, oh, poor Gus!

Now Fenn can remind her that, given the source of the rumor, there is really no one useful to pass it on to who won't already have heard it. The correct reply to such a pitch as that allegedly made to Carmen is the one she has allegedly already given: nothing now to do but wait to hear either from Dugald or from whoever approached her.

But Doog's on his way to Perth!

Fenwick has disclosed this datum; now he remarks that perhaps more's to be learned in Perth than in Washington or Santiago.

Susan's weeping. We ought to be with Ma!

Carmen's okay. And we will be with her, soon. There's every likelihood that this is false bait, Susele.

But it might not be! How can we sit here cruising while Gus is being beaten and starved? Chile's not Iran: *we* wrecked their economy and killed Allende and put those bloody generals in! Pinochet* owes us!

Well. Fenwick guesses it's not that simple, and assures her that nothing can be done faster ashore. These things take a little time. And there's more.

More!

Let's tack.

The cliffs loom ahead, baffling the light breeze. It's past noon; lunch will be delayed. Our new port tack is 005° magnetic; depending on breeze and leeway, in four or five hours it should fetch us the twenty-plus nautical miles either to Poplar Island Harbor, out in the Bay proper, or to Tilghman Island's Dun Cove, just inside the broad mouth of Choptank River. Now Fenwick comes to the bottom line: Dugald Taylor's suggestion that Orrin, of all people, may be the objective of whoever pitched Carmen B. Seckler. He sets forth the reasons why, together with his own speculation

---

*See note, p. 327.

that the somewhat farfetched pitch to Orrin may ultimately be (or be also) a pitch to himself, to draw him back into the Company as either an agent or a double.

More excitement. When the boat settles down, he adds that he needs some time to work out a way to handle all these potential pitches and counterpitches to Gus's best advantage, should that young man prove to be still alive in DINA's custody. Does Susan want him working for the Agency again?

No!

Not even for Mundungus's possible sake? And Oroonoko's?

Oh, god!

Fenn's arm is around her. Painful choices. Clearly, our sabbatical cruise is about over. A difference between Susan and Fenwick—perhaps between Thirty-five and Fifty—is that in that case she'd as leave end it here and now, whereas he is inclined to savor (and is capable of savoring) every last nautical mile before the shit truly and finally hits the fan. My my, he says: are we ever back in the world again. It was sweet being out of it.

Sue's mind is intensely elsewhere. The fun really is over. And it's such an all-right day! Fenn restrains a small self-spiteful impulse to douse sails and kick in the diesel.

Do you think it's possible, his friend now wonders, that Manfred faked a John Paisley as cover for going down there to rescue Gus?

Fenwick doubts it: so cruel a cover! But it is not impossible, particularly if other factors were involved, more important than any damage done to Carmen and Miriam and you and me. I mean really big security stuff; I don't even know what. He keeps to himself a sort of contrary possible unlikelihood, which in fact Susan has considered and kept to herself as well: that radical, tormented Gus Seckler-Turner may have staged *his* disappearance in Chile in order to return secretly to Maryland and revenge himself upon his father for the fall of Chilean democracy and for heaven knows what else—or that (Fenn's version of this dreadful speculation) Gus may have been made use of by anti-Pinochet exiles, "miristas"* or whomever, to set his father up for a hit, and then betrayed by them to the DINA. Not all leftists have hearts of gold. Vis-à-vis Susan's question, he says, we'll probably never know. But for want of real evidence to the contrary, the likeliest hood is that Gus was killed indiscriminately by Chilean right-wing security forces, along with his comrades, while working covertly to undo what his father had covertly worked to do; and that Count was either done in by one or more of his sundry enemies or really did fall overboard accidentally and drown. Not even the placid Wye, though it gives up nearly all its dead, gives up all.

Emotion or not, we're hungry. Sue serves lunch in the cockpit: cold artichokes vinaigrette and the backfin crabmeat salad that didn't get served to Miriam yesterday; canned iced tea with fresh mint that she found growing near the marina dock. We are reminded of the numberless fine meals we've made and eaten together in sweet anchorages aboard this boat; that reminder is pacifying to Susan, whose eyes however still ache with incipient tears for her half-brother. We leave a trail of artichoke petals in our wake: gourmet fare for the Bay's blue crabs.

Of our journey, Susan says I sure liked going down better than coming up.

The female point of view. Fenwick sets forth his note-book-notion about forks and confluences, analysis and synthesis, sperm and ova. This from the man who found farfetched that five-dream theory! Sue's appreciative—but promptly observes that Fenn's note is itself synthetic, not analytical. I'm not *all* male, he reminds her, nor you all female. Just mainly.

His wife stands and stretches. Thank heaven for Mainly.

---

*Members of the far-left Chilean MIR (Movimiento de Izquierda Revolucionario).

Below and above her salt-bleached jeans, cut off at mid-thigh, Fenn enjoys the sight of perfect legs and the strip of brown belly bared by the lift of her arms toward the temperate sun. It is as if, after half a week's menstrual celibacy, her flesh beckons.

Her what?

Flesh beckons.

Fenwick . . .

Odysseus, incognito in the court of the Phaeacians, weeps at the bard Demodocus's song of Troy. Why does the stranger weep? asks King Alcinoüs, and for the next four books O. tells the story of his voyage thus far—so moving his hosts that they wing him home in their sleep-dark, dream-swift ships. Aeneas likewise, astray in Carthage, weeps at sight of Dido's frescoes of the war; is by the Queen received and warmly questioned; tells the assembled (in two long books) how Troy fell and its refugees for seven summers sailed—and Dido's fatal passion is by that tale enflamed. Et cetera. In short, your classic literary "flashbacks," we agree, in addition to being good stories in themselves, are occasioned by some turn in the present action and themselves occasion that action's next advance. If not thus moored Bahamian-style, fore and aft, such retrospective exposition becomes

## A MERE FLOATING FLESHBECK.

The term is Susan's, from childhood memories of her father's accent and his explaining The Movies to her and Miriam in one or another of his chain of small-town theaters in Delaware and Maryland, when the girls were three and four.* Mim used to fidget; today she has slight memory of

---

*Jack Seckler died in 1949 at age 31 when the Cadillac he was driving, alone, back to his and Carmen's then house in Cheltenham, Pa., from a visit to his mother Havah in Pikesville, Md., was struck head-on along Route 40 by a tractor-trailer loaded with live Leghorn chickens, whose driver dozed off at 60 mph east of Elkton, exactly on the Maryland/ Delaware state line.

her father and none of those patient matinee-seminars. But Susan recollects, as clearly as if themselves had been filmed filmwatching and that film many times rerun, the cool empty houses where Jack Seckler previewed upcoming flicks. The Art Deco lights go down at his order; the seat-plush prickles little Susie's thighs and calf-backs as obscure action moves across the screen. Jack shushes Miriam and alerts Susan (already at four the prize student): Comes now a fleshbeck, Susele: you can tell from the fiddles on the soundtreck and how the picture goes woozy and farchadat. Not infrequently the moment would be prompted by a negligeed lady's beckoning seductively to her leading man and reenacting their first encounter—in Jack Seckler's term, their Meet. His daughter used to wonder: Meat? You understand now, Susele: while they're hugging and kissing offscreen in the present time, this fleshbeck shows their Meet.

In our present time Susan objects: We can't float dialect-puns in our story, Fenn. They're just between us. Anyhow, they get lost in translation.

Maybe. Somewhere in Part I, *THE COVE, Key,* Sue proposed that we begin in the middle, here aboard *Pokey,* reentering the Chesapeake, say, on the last leg of our sabbatical cruise, and then fill in with a series of flashbacks what's fetched us here, advancing the present action one step between each flashback until the exposition's done, just before the climax. When she speaks of such matters, Susan likes to affect her late father's accent and what she remembers or imagines to have been his freewheeling fancy. Her heart then brims with frustrated daughterly love, of which Manfred, not to mention Fenwick himself, was the subsequent beneficiary:

It's like we're rollink a big snowball up the hill of risink ection, okay? It gets bigger and heffier with each step from the plot's thickenink. We hef to call beck for more help to push. So each new helper is a fleshbeck; comes the peak, we got the whole team together! We noodge the old snowball over the top in a dynamite climex, and it creshes down the slope of dénouement like a fuckink evelenche.

Jack Seckler never talked like that, Fenn says. My father
remembers him as a cultivated man, related to the Allans of
Virginia.

Hah.

But I think I've got it: Efter the lest turn of the screw
before the climex, no more fleshbecks.

You got it. In Jeck Seckler's opinion, any writer who'd
interrupt a catharsis with a fleshbeck has his head up his ess.

Mm hm. And Fenwick, ready student now as Susan was
then, takes that snowball and runs with it. So instead of a
string of little piddling fleshbecks, why not let's have one big
fleshbeck, as far beck as we can flesh?

Come again, Fenn?

Let's flesh beck pest our own flesh to the spermps and ecks
that made us; beck to the flesh that made them, to the
spermps and ecks that made our encestors' flesh. Let's flesh
beck to Edum and Eef in the Garten: the very first beck of
the flesh of all. There's a Meat for you, Jeck!

Susan observes that Horace advises, in his epistle on the
art of poetry, that to tell the story of Troy's fall one needn't
start ab ovo, from the twin eggs Leda laid. Fenn wants to
know Why not: James A. Michener does it all the time, and
it's earned him millions of readers and dollars. What tex
brecket was this Horace in?

Get out of here with your tex breckets. This is art.

Seriously, Suse: Let's flesh beck to the flesh that all flesh
fleshed from: the Big Benk itself!

The what?

You've told me many a time how Jeck Seckler liked a story
to start off with a benk.

That's not what I meant, Fenwick. I meant we should start
bang in the middle of things, like Homer, and catch up later.

So we'll start with a benk and end with a benk and go benk
in the middle too. We'll benk in the fleshbecks and benk in
the fleshforverts.

Fleshforverts!

Sure, fleshforverts. Part Five, your Dream of the Future. Virgil did it; so can we. Fleshforverts.

Take that, Jim Michener, Susan says.

But comes now our floatink fleshback, while Fenwick and Susan kiss offscreen.

What's our position?

Dealer's choice.

I mean where are we.

Coming up on Red Nun Two, off the mouth of the Little Choptank. Three hours or so from Poplar Island, if the breeze holds. Flesh away, sweet Susele.

Why I?

Because flashbacks, Fenwick mildly asserts, may be said to be "female," following his notion of forks and confluences: rafting down the stream of time, they retrace what, coming up, were dilemmas, choices, channel-forks. E.g., our Meet. But begin, Muse, anywhere you like, and proceed in either direction.

I'll try. The Big Bang banged, a naked singularity. Lots happened in the first three minutes; I forget just what. Then eons passed: galaxies condensed and sprang away from one another like disenchanted lovers, at speeds proportional to the square of their distances, something like that. At least one solar system materialized, a nuclear family with planets nine. Earth's geology transpired; life; biological species evolved; Eocene, Pleistocene—you know. We crawled out of the water, some of us, into the marshes; out of the marshes, some of us, onto dry land, and human history took place. Classical antiquity, Dark and Middle Ages, Renaissance, Reformation, Enlightenment; then Modern Times, now about done. F. S. Key. E. A. Poe. Us. How'm I doing?

I love you.

Havah Moscowitz of Minsk and Baltimore wed Allan Seckler of Richmond and Baltimore and in Nineteen Eighteen begat Jack who wed Carmen B. and begat in Forty-five the dizygotic Miriam and me. Chief Herman Turner of Wye I. wed Virginia Key of lower Dorchester and in Nineteen Twenty-Nine begat the dizygotic Manfred and you. Oh, yeah: and from a line of Cape Cod Marshes sprang in Barnstable the following year Marilyn. That's enough of that.

World War Two ends! In the same year that President Truman establishes the Central Intelligence Agency, Fenwick and Manfred enter Johns Hopkins on scholarship, first of their line to be higher-educated. In their sophomore year, old Marilyn Marsh enrolls at nearby Goucher College, a tradition among Marsh ladies. In their junior year, her sophomore flesh beckons equally to the randy dizygotes. Jack Seckler expires in a cloud of white Leghorn feathers on U.S. Forty, leaving a twenty-five-year-old widow and two four-year-old daughters. Among Carmen B.'s letters of condolence is one from Chief and Virgie: Turner Brothers, the multifarious family business—

Insurance, real estate, accounting, farming—

Has offices next door to Seckler's Acadia Theater in the town of Easton, near Wye I. The two businesspeople have come to know each other over the years, and Turner Bros. does accounting work for Seckler Enterprises. Chief now becomes acquainted with Jack's stunned heir to the Enterprises and is of considerable assistance to her, even managing on a caretaker basis the Acadia and other of her Eastern Shore flickeries. Carmen and her little daughters occasionally visit the Turners' waterfront spread, Key Farm. Time flies; the old plot thickens like béchamel or condensing matter. How'm I doing?

Well. I remember teaching you and Mimi not to be afraid of crabs in the river. You were in kindergarten; I was almost old enough to vote.

Twins and twins, now isn't that cute. On with the fleshbeck. Neither Secklers nor Turners are tacky enough to make bookends of their children. The five-year-old sisters don't dress alike; the twenty-year-old brothers have been friendly rivals all through their youth: athletically, scholastically, socially. They're in the same university only because that's how the scholarship aid fell out. Thumbnail descrips: Dark debonair Count, ladies' man, pre-law, smooth and verbally humorless, yet full of panache and given to undergraduate escapades. Cows in the lecture hall! Whores in the frat house!

Escapades from which, born intrigant, he adroitly extricated his companions and himself.

Fair guileless Fenn, witty and gentle liberal artist, more lovable than his twin if less wildly loved; frequent follower of his brother's lead in small things, staunch goer of his own sweet way in large.

Thank you, Suse. That's very kindly put.

Both play varsity lacrosse on the formidable Hopkins team in their upperclass years: Count attack, Fenn defense. Marilyn Marsh dates both and gives to suave Count one autumn her well preserved virginity; next spring she relieves surprised Fenwick of his. Em Em has a problem: loves 'em both. They have one too: both love her.

Comic opera.

But in the early Nineteen Fifties it is no joke when a condom fails and Marilyn Marsh discovers herself in the family way—almost if not quite certainly by Fenn. Strictly raised, she's in a panic. I'd've been too. Knowledgeable Count proposes abortion and quickly makes the illegal arrangements. Innocent Fenn proposes marriage and is accepted. Where was I?

In first grade and Hebrew school.

The Marshes sternly disapprove, but accept the fait accompli. Chief and Virgie tisk their tongues. In those strange bygone times, marriage ended a young woman's undergraduate career. Tant pis, Missus Turner.

She will come to regret and resent that circumstance in future.

I don't blame her. But this is the past. Orrin Marsh Turner will be born that fall: dear bright Oroonoko. In the summer of his gestation the brothers each assistant-manage,

for Turner Brothers, one of Seckler Enterprises' movie
theaters. Fenwick's is on the Shore, so that Marilyn Marsh
can spend her pregnancy on Wye I. I remember her! It kills
me to remember actually seeing her pregnant by you, a
hundred years ago!

Count's was in Pikesville . . .

Manfred's was in Pikesville, to remove himself as far as
convenient from the scene. Mirabile dictu, he comes to know
better his actual employer, just commencing, in Grandma's
view, kerflooeyhood. Carmen B. Seckler has sold her house
in Cheltenham and moved with her daughters to Baltimore.
She doesn't even live in a Jewish neighborhood, but has
bought three rowhouses on Saint Paul Street, near the
University; two of them she rents as six apartments to
Hopkins students; she lives in all but one apartment of the
third. That apartment she now lets rent-free to Manfred, in
exchange for his superintending all three buildings during
his final undergraduate year. Carmen's twenty-seven now,
six years Manfred's senior; she's a striking woman who has
turned down more than one marriage offer since Jack
Seckler's death, but has discreetly put by, shall we say, the
abstinence of mourning. She knows all about the Turner-
Turner-Marsh triangle and its outcome. She comforts the
loser.

Lucky loser.

Ma also decides that while she has no interest in remarriage, she wants another child. In the spring of Fifty-one,
you guys take your B.A.'s. Fenwick—faute de mieux,
really—decides to try his hand for a year at writing; he has
had no formal training in the art, but at least he has enough
flair to win a fellowship in the University's graduate program. Manfred, whose general objective as a pre-law student
was never law school but quote the foreign service unquote,
has learned of Allen Dulles's new Directorate of Plans* in
the CIA, which is riding high on the Korean war. He now
focuses his ambition. If you don't mind, Ma tells him in

---

*I.e., Clandestine Services.

effect that spring, knock me up before you leave for Washington. No further obligation. Young Count considers, then willingly accommodates her. The fact is, he loves her, though he hasn't got over losing Marilyn Marsh to you.

I don't agree, Suse. Count didn't love MM the way I did; and if he had to lose, he'd have preferred to lose to me. But losing anything to anybody was hard for him. And by this time he'd begun to become the Prince of Darkness, for whatever reasons.

It was Ma who first thought to call him that, since he was already nicknamed Count. Don't ask me how she knew Byron's poem; maybe Manfred read it to her.

Nope. Your mother knows things. The surprising fact is that Count and I got clear through high school and college without discovering that poem ourselves. Our teachers must have assumed we knew it already. When I finally read the thing, I was astonished.

Sibling incest. Byron and his half-sister. It's a nutsy poem, in your present wife's opinion, but never mind. Anyhow, I can't see Marilyn Marsh as Lady Astarte.*

---

*Count Manfred, in Lord Byron's "choral tragedy," has committed incest with his willing sister Astarte, whose guilty conscience has subsequently driven her to suicide prior to Act I. Nutsy or not, the verse-drama moved Schumann to his Manfred Overture (1850) and Tchaikovsky to his Manfred Symphony (1885). What amuses Susan is that Byron's Faust-like "Prince of Darkness" doesn't *do* anything either wicked or virtuous in the play. His much-invoked "evils," after the long-past sibling incest, seem to be no more than his voluntary solitude in the "Higher Alps" and his profane "researches," which enable him to converse with spirits and demons. We see him harm no one, and though he mentions having killed "enemies" in his own defense, these deeds aren't cited, e.g., in the discussion of his character by his attendants in Act III, and so must have been routine incidents of feudal self-defense. Manfred's crime, in Susan's view, is simply egregiousness: his preferring his sister to all others; his making love to her (fully reciprocated, as she reciprocated his interest in nature and "research"); and his increased guilty isolation following her suicide.

Unlike Faust, Byron's hero makes no compact with the Devil. He is as aloof from Satan as from God; his "researches" are not subsidized by either. His "powers" derive from knowledge, including self-knowledge,

*(Footnote continues overleaf)*

Nor can I. Nor was your mother a Mother Figure. She and Count simply had a serious sexual affair that turned into a serious love affair.

How'm I doing?

You are efficiency itself. Let's get back to the present tense.

The arrangement suits both of them, reader. Ma's like Chekhov: she wants a man around much of the time but not all the time.* Manfred has his training to do and later his assignments to carry out, but he likes a home base, especially after Mundungus is born. He and Ma never marry. No

---

*(Footnote continued from previous page)*

and perhaps from the absence of any moral commitment, but not from any quid pro quo with the supernatural, either demonic or holy. He is in fact morally scrupulous in abstaining from Faust's bargain with Mephistopheles, and on the evidence of the play he employs his "powers" to no end more vicious than conjuring the spirit of his beloved sister and asking her forgiveness for his role in their incest. Susan feels that the "ground situation" of the drama is muddled: it would appear to be Count Manfred's impatience with life, together with some unexplained inability to die—but why he doesn't simply fling himself off a Higher Alp is as obscure as is the suggestion that Astarte did.

Liberal Susan smiles at Count Manfred's Byronic dark hints and posturings. On the subject of (sibling) incest, she likes to quote Percy Shelley's straightforward remarks in a letter to Mrs. Gisborne of November 1819: speaking of the theme of Calderón's play *Los Cabellos de Absolón,* Shelley writes:

> Incest is, like many other incorrect things, a very poetical circumstance. It may be the defiance of everything for the sake of another which clothes itself in the glory of the highest heroism, or it may be that cynical rage which, confounding the good and the bad in existing opinions, breaks through them for the purpose of rioting in selfishness and antipathy.

Así Calderón. As for Count Manfred, it would seem that he merely happened to love his sister, and she him. Sexual depredation and exploitation are what Susan hates, whether of young daughters by their fathers, patients by their doctors, students by their teachers, employees by their employers, Miriam by the Dixie Pagans et al. Count Manfred and Lady Astarte being consenting adults both, and apparently of like mind, she shrugs her shoulders.

*Scholarly Susan refers here to a letter of Anton Chekhov's to Alexei Suvorin in which he declares, " . . . give me a wife who, like the moon, does not appear in my sky every day."

doubt each of them has other consolations when they're apart for long intervals; but it's Manfred who insists that Gus take his last name, and neither of them, to my knowledge, ever has another serious affair.

To mine, too.

He was good with Mims and me, and we were crazy about him. Gus was, too. Other kids saw their fathers more often, but when Manfred was with us, he was with us completely.

I wish to Christ he were with us right now. Present tense.

Would you take it for a while, Fenn? Fleshing beck wears a girl out.

Sure. Our footnote on Manfred—Byron's play—should mention that the legend which supposedly inspired it may be to our point: an allegedly actual case of two Higher Alpine brothers who loved the same woman, quote with whom they had passed their infancy close quote. She marries the elder and then seduces the younger. The elder mysteriously disappears; the lady wastes away; the younger brother is found dead in the mountain pass where he used to rendezvous with his sister-in-law. Count was born almost two hours before I was. Oh well.

Are we telling Manfred's story or Manfred-stories? To our point is Count Manfred's line in Scene Two of Act One:

> . . . I have ceased
> To justify my deeds unto myself—
> The last infirmity of evil.

There is your true Prince of Darkness, reader.

We don't know just what Byron's Manfred did, and we don't know most of what my brother did. But we do know that from early on—it's the middle Nineteen Fifties now—our Manfred does what he does apparently for the sake of doing it. Even in those Joe McCarthy days he never once rationalizes his adventures. He is virtually nonpolitical. In Fifty-three John Arthur Paisley joins him in the Company, and I take my piddling M.A. and become one of those innumerable teacher-writers who aren't much of either.

Don't.

You and Miriam reach puberty. You decide you're Jewish and get yourself Bas Mitzvah'd on your own initiative. . . .

You were there, Uncle Fensie.

Yup: with eight-year-old Oroonoko, who already loved you madly. And Count flew in from god knows where—

Perth?

Perth isn't Perth yet in Nineteen Fifty-eight. Vienna, maybe. And Miriam is proud of you, even though she rejects religion herself and is training Gus to be an atheist.

Your wife won't come because she disapproves of our common-law household.

What rows we had over that. Poor Captain Shadrin defects to our side and is both interrogated and befriended by our Prince of Darkness. Then comes my winter in Spain; my boina; my little crisis in Ronda. Don't forget to keep an eye out for that hat.

Sorry: it's Sixty-three: Mims and I are off to college.

Out she drops and joins the Peace Corps, and you get laid by your professor of American lit. Talk about exploitation.

It wasn't. I always had crushes on my best teachers, but now I was nineteen and twenty and had hot pants. I seduced him. He was very nice, at first.

B.A., Ph.D.

Shall I take that job, Fenn? What in the world are we going to do with our lives? What are we all about? Don't answer. And let's not flash Mims back to the Dixie Pagans. Aren't you divorced yet, for Christ's sake?

Don't rush me: the woman and I had loved each other; it took a while. I've given up writing and teaching and free-lance journalism; I've joined the Company as a historian and memoir-editor. We've moved to Bethesda; Marilyn Marsh flourishes in D.C. as our marriage withers. I have a sense now of what Count does, and I'm properly appalled. By this time he's overexposed in Europe and is being pressured to switch to Viet Nam, but he's more interested in Latin America.

Alas for Latin America.

But he still works with certain Soviet defectors and makes the odd junket to Austria or Iran.

Don't mention that place. Poor Mimsi!

Poor Iranians, too. Doog Taylor draws me into Clandestine Services with the bait that I can do White stuff to counteract or compensate for Count's Black stuff. Count doesn't want me in that department; he warns me it will wreck my marriage. I tell him my marriage is wrecked already. MM and I have gone in different directions.

Spare us.

The first time I lost my boina, I realized I was going to leave teaching and join the Company. The second time I lose it, ten years later, I realize I'm going to leave the Company, and Marilyn Marsh and I leave each other.

At last! On to our Meet!

Not yet. First comes my

## CHOPTANK SAFE-HOUSE STORY.

Uh oh.

We *torture* a man, Suse: Doog and Count and I and some future DINA people that Doog is training. Right over there on Ferry Neck in our beautiful Choptank River, in the same safe-house that Francis Gary Powers\* was debriefed in in Sixty-two. The man is a Chilean walk-in who claims to be anti-Marxist. Doog and the visitors don't believe he's legit. It's my first experience of heavy interrogation. Doog and I are getting nowhere, and the situation is embarrassing because Doog is supposed to be showing me and the Latinos that you don't need beatings and electric shocks and yellow submarines† to get reliable stuff: all you need is the right

---

\*For those with short memories or few years: the CIA reconnaissance pilot whose U-2 aircraft was brought down by Soviet surface-to-air missiles on Mayday 1960. The incident caused a scheduled summit meeting between Premier Khrushchev and President Eisenhower to be canceled. Powers was tried in Moscow, convicted of espionage, and exchanged in 1962 for the convicted Soviet spy Rudolf Abel.

†Torture by systematic near-drowning, so called (after the popular Beatles song) because the victim's head is sometimes thrust into a toilet bowl full of urine and feces.

alternation of bribes and threats, laid on in the right way under the right circumstances. Doog calls Count in from Langley by helicopter after midnight, as the acknowledged maestro. When I walk out on the dock to watch his chopper land on the lawn near the beach—it was a beautiful night, moonlit, about this time of year; the air was sweet; the place itself was a fine sprawling brick mansion, well landscaped; we just put it up for sale recently—I'm out there admiring the water and thinking I'd rather be sailing, and the downdraft from Count's chopper blows my old boina into the Choptank.

For the next three hours I watch my brother break our man down without laying a hand on him. We decide he's probably legit after all; the future DINAs put him in their pocket to use against Allende, and Count gives us a postoperative seminar on techniques of nonphysical inter-rogation.

Oh, Fenn.

Yeah. At the time I'm too shocked to realize how shocked I am. Sometime before dawn I tell a version of my Ronda boina story, how I happened to join the Company, and I ask Count jokingly to keep an eye out for the thing. Doog and I ride the chopper back to Langley to do other business. Count himself is about to go to Vienna again to do background work on Shadrin; he'll get sidetracked to Teheran when he hears that SAVAK's got your sister in Evin Prison.

We'll skip that part.

Yes. But that same morning, strolling out onto the dock at Ferry Neck to watch some watermen tending eel pots, Count finds my trusty boina washed up in the marsh grass. He'll return it to me from Austria, claiming he found it in the Danube.

And you'll leave the Agency. Thank heaven.

I realize after that night that I don't *want* to stand the heat; time to get out of the kitchen. Is that a boina off to starboard there?

Nope: sea turtle. We're all pulling against Manfred by this time, Fenn. There's Mim running off to Tabriz with her anti-Shah friends; she'll tell Manfred plainly not to expect her to approve of him just because he rescues her from the SAVAKis. Gus is radicalized already and threatening to disown his father if the Company overthrows Allende. . . .

The only Marxist apprentice plumber in Fells Point.

Gus happened to believe in the dignity of labor, reader. Plus he liked the metaphor: cleaning the pipes for healthy circulation; getting to the homely innards of things. Nixon's people hadn't spoiled the word plumber yet.

If Mundungus hadn't been a good plumber, he'd've been a surgeon.

Even I used to climb Manfred's back about covert operations. He'd smile and say we were beautiful innocents. Only Ma never questioned what he did. Of course, we had only the most general notion of what he did.

Like many refugees, reader, Carmen B. Seckler, though otherwise left of center, is a hawk when it comes to national security.

And she loves him. By this time she's sold the movie-house chain and opened Carmen's Place and gone kerflooey, and we're all crazy about her. Can we please do our Meet now?

With pleasure. June Seventy-two. You're just a year from your doctorate at College Park. Wouldn't Jack Seckler be proud! I'm two years divorced and getting by in Annapolis as a consulting editor for the Company's memoir factory— that's innocent enough work—and an adjunct lecturer on this and that at Saint John's College and the Naval Academy. I've secretly begun my *KUDOVE* notes and am the proud new owner of a secondhand cruising sailboat already named *Pokey* by its former owner, who understood no more than I that name's future significance. To save money, I keep the boat at Chief and Virgie's dock instead of in Annapolis. Here we go. Mim's back from Iran, wrecked, and you've planned to do a bit of canoe-camping with her, as you did when you-all were younger, in hopes it'll calm her down some. You've landed an assistant professorship for the fall at Washington College in Chestertown, and you want to scout the terrain, so you set out to explore the upper Chester River. I'm in midst of my first real cruise on *Pokey,* with twenty-one-year-old Orrin. We've poked around the Wye and the Miles for a few days to get everything shaken down, and then we've done the Choptank, the South, and the Severn. The plan is to drop Oroonoko off in Baltimore so that he can get on up to Boston and start his own graduate work. But first we want to do the stately Chester. Over?

You sail under the Bay Bridge; you round Kent Island; you enter the mouth of Chester River at Love Point. Got your bearings, reader?

Three miles wide there, I believe. There's a northerly blowing; the first leg is a run, but then the river U-turns, and we're beating up against wind and tide. How about you?

Our canoe trip hasn't worked out, and the week we've allowed for it is nearly up. We've left my car in Chestertown and started on the upper river, but the tidal current up there runs more strongly than I expected, and that week it's in the wrong direction from midmorning to midafternoon. So we've come downstream instead, where the river's wider and the current's less strong. But there the water's too open for comfort in any kind of breeze, so we've turned up into beautiful Langford Creek and done some camping on the upper reaches of its East Fork. But Mimi's bored already, and scattered; every night she has nightmares about SAVAK doing things to her. *They* sure didn't hesitate to get physical.

Yet she says the Dixie Pagans were worse.

Only because in Evin they tortured her for something she believed in, and that gave her some courage. I think the reader's been told already that the Pagans' burn-scars on her skin convinced SAVAK she was a hardened revolutionary.

If she'd been Iranian, they'd have destroyed her.

She's losing control. She forgets to paddle; she's too

farchadat\* to be any help with the cooking and camping. She wants to go home to Ma and little Sy, and I'm wondering whether I can get us all the way back to Chestertown by myself or shall I ask somebody for a tow.

*Then,* Susanna mia, on the equinoctial Wednesday, Twenty-one June: a smashing, anti-Aristotelian coincidence . . .

Not anti-Aristotelian: it begins our story. The Secklers and the Turners have seen one another from time to time, but you and I not often in my college years, because I'm seldom home.

I understand you've grown into a bright and capable young beauty. I gather from Carmen B. Seckler you're in midst of a protracted affair with one of your professors, who can't quite get around to leaving his wife and children.

Excuse me: I'm not a home-wrecker. He leaves them before I meet him, but he won't get a divorce. We break it off when I finish my course work.

An ABD† and a professor-to-be! Count's really proud of you. So's Grandma.

Grandma can't hold it in her mind that I'm not a medical doctor. When I tell her I'm a doctor of philosophy, she says she didn't know philosophy was sick. Let's meet.

You and Mims have peeled out of your tops and rigged them on your paddles like squaresails. You're shooting down Langford's East Fork toward Cacaway Island like a pair of whitewater canoeists.

Shirtsailing! We learned it at camp. The bow girl sails and the stern girl steers.

Orrin and I are slogging upstream toward Cacaway. The main body of Langford Creek must be a mile wide there; god knows why it's called a creek instead of a river. The

---

\*We have used this word twice already in our story, but neglected to define it: Yiddish for scattered, distracted.

†All But Dissertation. Susan will receive her degree formally a year later, in June 1973.

waves have a long fetch; there are big whitecaps, and we're banging into the chop, trying to decide which fork to take when we get to the island. What time is it?

Late afternoon. Cacaway's our destination for the day. I'm hoping the wind will blow out overnight, so Mim and I can head up toward Chestertown in the morning. When I see this sailboat beating in our direction against the chop, I know we'd be swamped out there in open water. I'm also hoping you'll anchor behind Cacaway, whoever you are, so we can scrounge some ice.

But *I've* just decided that the wind is northeast enough for us to keep sailing if we take the West Fork, whereas we'd have to power into it up the East Fork. We've spotted a canoe—the only other boat in sight—and as we come about, Orrin checks with the binocs to see whether its occupants are signaling for help. He reports that it's two chicks shirtsailing. Topless?

We have our life vests on.

And it's well you do, because now you hang a hard right toward the Cacaway beach, and Miriam in the bow doesn't douse her shirtsail in time—

Farchadat, farchadat.

When the next wave catches you broadside, over you go into Langford Creek.

Oh, Fenn: thank heaven for that wave, and for Mimsi's being too scattered to get her shirtsail down! It makes me dizzy to think that if SAVAK hadn't tortured her, she'd never have been so absentminded, and we wouldn't have capsized, and you'd have sailed on up the West Fork instead of coming over to make sure we're okay, and when we met later on, it wouldn't have been in the right circumstances, and we wouldn't be us. Am I supposed to thank the Shah of Iran, or the CIA for helping to bring down Mossadegh?

Don't think that way. What a price.

But what a prize. The bloody century is seventy-two percent done, and at last we meet. We meet.

We meet. Oroonoko\* gets the sails down; I start up the diesel; we chug over to see whether we can help. He checks with the glasses and says They're okay; they're swimming their canoe toward the island; they seem to know what they're doing. Then he says Hey Dad, for Christ's sake, it's Susan! It's Suse and Miriam!

Full speed ahead, to the good part. We don't need help getting ashore, but I'm plenty relieved to see Uncle Fenn and Cousin Orrin, as well as happily surprised. I've hardly heard that you've bought a boat, much less that you're cruising in the neighborhood. I guess our two families are less in touch in these years than we've ever been. Have you dropped anchor?

We've seen that you're in no danger; but a swamped canoe isn't easy to swim to shore with in a chop, and all your gear is wet. So you hang on while we get the anchor down behind Cacaway, and then Orrin piles headfirst overboard to help— in such a hurry that he forgets to put a life jacket on. I shake my head at the funny coincidence and at Orrin's old crush; then I row sedately over in the dinghy, as befits a gentleman my age.

You're only forty-two in that dinghy.

---

\*Dr. Seckler is late with this note, drawn from her dissertation: Oroonoko and Mundungus are American Colonial terms for two kinds (sometimes for two grades) of tobacco: bright and dark (or pure leaf and leaves-plus-stems), respectively. The former term is from the great Venezuelan river and was used in this same spelling to denote any tidewater tobacco-planter (cf. Ebenezer Cooke's *Sot-Weed Redivivus* [1729]: ". . . I thus harangu'd the *Planter:/* Rise, *Oroonoko,* rise, said I . . ."), and sometimes to denote displaced Africans as well, after the real-life hero of Mrs. Aphra Behn's novel *Oroonoko, or, the History of the Royal Slave* (1678). Mundungus, in its sense of cheap or foul tobacco, was an uncomplimentary nickname: cf. Laurence Sterne's *A Sentimental Journey* (1768), in which Mundungus and Smelfungus are Sterne's complaining fellow tourists Dr. Samuel Sharpe and Tobias Smollett, respectively. But Orrin and Gus were so nicknamed for their complexions and their fondness, as small boys, for playing Indians.

You're only twenty-seven in that water.

I've always had a crush on my Uncle Fenn, and you've known it. I like it that you've been sort of a professor and sort of a journalist and sort of a writer. Plus handsome, virile, and gentle. Your beard turns me on, too.

Let's get ashore.

We all do, laughing and splashing and hugging, and bail out the canoe. Our packs are soaked through; the breeze is chilly.

Orrin can't get his eyes off you. I can't either. Personal Flotation Devices are sexy.

I'm prepared to make a fire on the beach, dry out our things, and carry on; but you tell us the forecast is for more wind and showers. I'll have a very tough time canoeing back to Chestertown. We all go aboard *Pokey* and review our options while Mims and I change into dry clothes: yours and Orrin's. That was a turn-on, by the way: your jeans and shirt against my skin.

Okay. But my bottom-line feelings are still avuncular. My little twin nieces-of-sorts, all grown up!

It's finally decided that since you-all are headed for Baltimore anyhow to see Orrin off to Boston, Mimi and I will go with you, towing our canoe behind *Pokey*'s dinghy. Then Gus can fetch Oroonoko to the airport, Mim can get back to her kid, and you and I will sail *Pokey* back to Chestertown, where you'd planned to go anyhow before ending your cruise. I'll retrieve my car, and you'll single-hand the boat back to Wye I.

It would make better logistical sense to sail directly up to Chestertown from Cacaway Island, load the canoe on your car, and then the three of you drive back to Baltimore. Do I point that out, or do you?

Don't you remember? It's Oroonoko's suggestion.

Of course it is. Jesus, Suse: that's as scary to think about as your SAVAK idea. Suppose we'd followed Orrin's sensible advice?

I guess I begin to fall in love with you when you say Let's don't be logistically sensible; let's go sailing.

You second the motion immediately, and Miriam and Orrin shrug their shoulders. We have a fine evening then of swimming and making dinner together and catching up on one another's lives around a campfire on the beach. Dear Cacaway.

Precious Cacaway. Orrin's so good with Miriam! She's always liked him, even though he's hopelessly straight by her standards.

There are some constraints on our talk. I want to hear the details of Mim's horror-show in Teheran, and you want to hear about my divorce, neither of which subjects we can get into with Mim and Orrin there. But we have plenty else to talk about. It's as if I'm discovering you for the first time. Is that redundant?

You want to hear about my love life.

The more we talk, the more I hate and envy that professor of yours, especially since it's not clear that the affair is over. Where'd you sleep?

None of your business.

I mean that night. I remember, of course: we all sleep aboard. You and Miriam take the vee-berth forward.

Our first night ever of sleeping at anchor! I love it, even with Mimsi's nightmares.

Those sure alarm Orrin and me. I'm feeling less uncley all the time, and have trouble sleeping. So sharp; so terrific looking! The image of you in your wet cut-offs and life jacket gives me a whopping erection, which I can't do anything about.

Well, you've been without for quite a while, and you're horny. Me too, a little. When you kiss me good night, I shiver.

Orrin's hooked too, I'm sure. But the five years between you and him is larger than the fifteen between you and me; so it seems to your Uncle Fenwick. Next day we have a rough, wet sail over to Baltimore in chilly gray weather, windward all the way. Poor Miriam gets seasick, but you and Orrin love it, and I love the look of you in foul-weather gear.

I don't want it to end. How did I manage to miss sailing all those years? But let's end it. We tie up at Fells Point, and Gus comes down in his plumber's van.

He looks like a good-natured Caliban. Grease under his fingernails and all over his Big Smiths. I remember his wonderful concern for Miriam.

A big family dinner in the back room of Carmen's Place. Even Manfred's there for a change, and you and Gus and Mim put aside your differences with him for the evening.

It's about the last time that'll happen: Count's already busy in Santiago and Valparaiso. That's a happy evening, Susan; I love my brother, and I can't stop looking at you.

I'm comparing my sort-of-stepfather to his twin brother and already thinking I'm glad you're not *really* my uncle, because you're turning me on. You seem so easy in your skin.

The divorce relaxed me, once it was done with. Marilyn Marsh likewise, I'm sure.

Easygoing, witty, but a mensch. Manfred was always like a coiled spring.

Now it's bye-bye, everybody. Have a good year, Oroonoko! For security's sake I'm going to sleep aboard; you'll join me for an early start in the morning.

The family gives its blessing to the project. Manfred and Orrin come down with me to see us off—Gus is at work already, and Ma and Mims always sleep late. Manfred's going to drop Orrin off at the Baltimore airport on his way to Langley.

Did they sense anything about us, Susan?

Not Orrin, certainly. Manfred maybe. I had sex-dreams all night. Did you?

Nope. Masturbated early and slept like a stone, despite the Fells Point winos and the traffic noise. I really do feel like your uncle, especially when Oroonoko's with us, and I try to keep my lust in check. But I can feel our voltage in the air, and I remember Count's saying Fenwick, I envy you.

He says something more interesting than that, in retrospect: Take care of each other.

Yes. Are we under way?

We are. Nobody gets a sailboat under way with less fuss than you do. That impressed me, especially since you had to tell me everything I was supposed to do. There's no shouting, no confusion. We don't even use the engine to leave the dock.

The breeze cooperates: light and in the right direction.

Orrin hands you the stern line, Manfred hands me the bow and spring lines and kisses me good-bye, you sheet in the main, and we glide away without a sound.

Symbolic choreography.

The quiet of it: saying good-bye in normal voices across the water as we move out into the harbor. It all makes me very aware that now it's just the two of us on this boat, and that excites me. In fact, I'm lushing.

You're blushing?

No. I like following your quiet orders. I like taking the helm and watching you raise the headsails. I also happen to love the sailing and the activity in the harbor. But when everything's set and trimmed, and you settle down beside me on this cockpit cushion with your hip touching mine and your arm along the coaming behind my back, I can feel myself lushing in my pants.

Ah. Lushing.

Fort McHenry's astern now, and we can talk. I ask you about your divorce, and you tell me with what seems to me to be just the right combination of candor and reserve. I'm inspired to reply with the tale of my own late ill-starred romance.

Makes me want to throttle the bastard. But I'm overjoyed to hear that he was chickenshit enough to try to have it both ways, and finally lost both his wife and his mistress.

Seymour Berman will always find another mistress in a

hurry. In fact, he already had another mistress. A sexual imperialist and a bad-charactered sonofabitch in several respects, old Seymour. But a formidable fuck withal, and an effective teacher.

So you acknowledge at the time. I'm impressed. My little niece Susie! My Bas Mitzvah girl! I discreetly inquire whether this same Seymour has been succeeded in your affections.

And I inquire how you've been hacking the single life after two decades of marriage. It becomes known that neither of us is seriously engaged at present.

Mm hm. Bit of a lull in the conversation here. For a while we just sail.

It's a dandy day: bright, fresh, warm; a good westerly to spank across the Bay on. I'm loving it, and it's exciting to find that we can talk so closely and easily. I feel right at home already, with you and with the boat. I remember thinking that this set of circumstances couldn't have been better arranged by a screen-writer.

A neat Meet. And now, aha, after I make and serve lunch under way, the breeze obligingly lightens; the air heats up; time to come out of our sweatshirts and long pants. Do I mind if you change into your swimsuit? Be my guest; then I'll do the same.

I *am* your guest.

Voilà: her sweet flesh beckons. Dear heaven, but it is ripe and splendid! Brown! Firm! Clean! Tough! Dainty!

You neither conceal your admiration nor dwell on it: I like that. I take the helm now while you go below to put your swim trunks on. But I sneak a peek down the companion-way.

So did I, before. I saw an absolutely perfect white tush set off by suntan and thought Oh my, if I could have that. But what would Count and Carmen think? What would Susan think? What would *I* think?

And I got just a glimpse of you from the waist down, standing sideways in the cabin. As you pulled up your trunks, the waistband flipped your big loose penis, and I remember thinking two thoughts very clearly: Dear Oroonoko came out of there; and That will be inside me before morning. I'm still lushing.

Now we talk about literature! The *Odyssey, Moby Dick*, Poe's "Narrative of Arthur Gordon Pym," Huck Finn. We talk about teaching and writing. You mention a bunch of new French and Americans that I've never heard of; they sound too fancy for my taste. I tell you that if I were a writer I'd navigate only by first-magnitude stars: Homer and Scheherazade and Shakespeare and Cervantes and Dickens and Mark Twain. I'd let the lesser lights go; wouldn't even read them. Noise in the signal.

And I tell you that Homer and company are fancier than you think, once you get into them. They just don't wear their fanciness on their sleeves.

You tell me I have the makings of a naive postmodernist.

I meant it as a compliment, mostly.

I'm impressed by your love of contact sports: soccer and basketball, which I was never any good at. Hockey. Lacrosse, which I *was* good at. Touch football. Also by your love of teaching. When you tell me you've arranged to postpone your college job for a year in order to teach gifted high-schoolers while you finish your dissertation, I begin to fall in love with you instead of just salivating and—what was your word?

Lushing. I'm doing it right now. Feel.

The light air puts us into Chester River too late to run the twenty-five miles up to Chestertown. The nearest good anchorage is Queenstown Creek, nine miles in; but we decide to push on another six up into Langford, back to Cacaway.

Where It All Started. I remember thinking that phrase, ironically and seriously at the same time. It's clear to me that something *has* started. I want us to sail and talk forever—we haven't even got to the CIA yet!—but I can hardly wait for us to get anchored and get it on. You've touched me a dozen times already as we talk: congratulatory hugs and pats for getting the hang of helmsmanship and sail trim; a sympathetic buss on the ear for something-or-other; a squeeze of the hand when I grieve about Mimsi.

Squeeze of the hand nothing: I get a full-scale Comforting Embrace out of Miriam and SAVAK.

No overt passes, but you're setting me on fire.

And you me. Praise god for sailboat cockpits: cheek by jowl for hours on the windward seat!

I'm already working out how I'll explain it to Ma, and deciding I'll take the initiative with you once we get parked, to override whatever reservations you might have about going to bed with me.

My twin brother's common-law stepdaughter.

We both keep using such terms—Sort-of-Stepfather, Niece-in-Effect, Virtual Uncle—to get it established that in fact there's no consanguinity, either literal or legal. Obviously we both understand what's coming.

You more than I, Suse. Mine's not even a hope; just a wistful wish. Yours is a plan.

It sure is. Don't ask me why I'm assuming already that it's going to be more than a friendly one-nighter. I guess because in a way we're already Family.

There's sweet Cacaway! The East Fork! Our hook's down. Bit of a swim before dinner, Susan? Stretch the old muscles?

It goes so easily, you'd think we've rehearsed it. I know when I dive off the gunwale that the next time we touch, it will be serious, and that dinner is a long way off. We splash around for a few minutes in the deep spot off the northeast end of Cacaway. Now I see you're at the boarding ladder. I swim over; you reach an arm out to me, smiling in your sweet way, and suddenly I'm all over you.

You astonish me: your passion. You're hot as a Gypsy! There is a lot of Carmen B. Seckler in our Susan.

But you're equal to the occasion. You say one word—
Up.

And practically throw me up the ladder. We go off like two firecrackers!

A whole string of firecrackers. Afterwards, you sit Turkfashion on the settee berth, pushing your hair back with both hands and smiling.

I'm assimilating. You.

I'm trying to assimilate. Us. Your first postcoital words are, and I quote: Shipboard Romance.

That's exorcism. Your reply is, and I quote: Let the voyage not end.

Susan. Let it not.

I am in fact a week getting back to Baltimore. Next day, not early, we sail up to Chestertown to make sure my car's okay, and I call home to announce that we'll be sailing for a while. Not to worry. Mim's ecstatic when she realizes what's happening: you can hear her squealing *Shushi!* clear across the wharf from the pay phone. Ma does a one-second delay and then chuckles and asks to speak to you. Then she says Never mind: she'll speak to you by ESP.

If she does, I don't get the message.

It's an easy one. That week you teach me to sail.

And you teach me to fly. I can't believe my good fortune! And I've never been to bed with such a passionate woman.

Chief and Virgie take it well, when the time comes.

They never warmed up to Marilyn Marsh, and they were always partial to you. I worried how your grandma would take the news later, when she had to be told. For Count to live with her daughter-in-law all those years was one thing: Carmen was understood to be kerflooey. But for her prize granddaughter to take up with a divorced goy fifteen years her senior, of no particular profession . . .

Listen: I could bring home a four-foot Hottentot and Grandma would love him, if he and I loved each other madly.

We did. Do. There's Poplar Island ahead. We'll have to flesh faster, the way the years have fleshed since then.

That week afloat was a perfect week. Idyllic weather. Warm water to swim in at night, naked with the noctilucae. Getting to know each other in those days of sailing and talking. Eating each other up.

Perfect. Finally we have to pack it in and check into our separate addresses to catch up on business. But we can't stand being apart. You quit your summer tutoring job in Baltimore; I shuffle my consulting contracts around; and in mid-July, of all times of the year, we run off to the Caribbean, take a bareboat charter out of Tortola, and sail for twelve days more in the British Virgins.

Not a bad way to improve our acquaintance. Paradise is neutral turf; the boat's unfamiliar to both of us, and so are the waters. Along with the snorkeling and sailing and swimming and sex, we get to cope with a few nasty situations together: rain squalls, dragging anchors, sea-urchin spines.

That U.S. Customs woman in Cruz Bay St. John that I wanted to strangle. The drunken asshole that fouled our anchor at two A.M. in the Bight of Norman Island.

I get to see my new man's competence, if not grace, under pressure. His patience, reasonableness, and high flapping-point. His knowledgeability and range of experience, compared to mine. His knack for making almost anything work. His unaffectedness and general amiability. His good humor and spaciousness of heart. Plus, frequently, his penis.

I get to see my new woman's logistical good sense; her cheerfulness in adverse circumstances; her culinary resourcefulness and skill; the way she learns things fast and doesn't forget them; her enjoyment of all kinds of people and situations, and her canny assessment of them; her general pluckiness—I'd even say courage. Her spaciousness of heart. The number and variety of her passions. And lots of her skin.

On the debit side—

Skip the debit side.

Sweet Caribbean. Will you marry me, Fenwick?

I will. And you me, Susan, on New Year's Eve 1972, so that the whole Gregorian world will make whoopee with us?

And we can take the tax advantage. We'll live in your Annapolis place to start with: it's close enough to Madeira School and College Park for me, and you don't need to be in Langley every day. I'll bet I can even commute to my

Chestertown job next academic year. Should we have a wedding?

Why not? A fine Jewish one, for your and Grandma's sake. I want Oroonoko to be best man; but he's still hurting from the divorce, even though it was mutual and without third parties involved. And if his feeling for you was never really serious, it was a real enough crush. My taking you from him won't exactly mollify any unresolved oedipal twinges he may be entertaining.

Ask him anyhow.

I do. Bless his heart, he bursts into tears, to his own surprise—just as I did in my sophomore year when I learned that Count had scored with Marilyn Marsh. Then he starts laughing at his long infatuation; he tells me that when I die at eighty-five, he'll be sixty-five and you'll be seventy. His juniority will look good to you then, and he'll become the stepfather of any half-sisters and -brothers that we turn out for him.

But he did the job. I love him for that. I wish we could love Julie.*

We'd better learn to. Back to the Caribbean for our honeymoon! Smiling, flower-girt Barbados! You leave private high-school teaching for your college job. More money, which we sorely need.

Minor chords: the Chilean generals, with a little help from

---

*Orrin Marsh Turner's wife since 1975. Wellesley College B.S. psychology, 1974. Employment in Boston and environs courtesy of the Title III special-education law, which requires trained teachers for non-normal children in every public school district. Julie Harvey's specialty (she has retained her maiden name legally, in contrast to Susan, who retains hers conversationally) is dyslexia, and no doubt she is routinely competent at her work. But she is such a startling look-alike for the Marilyn Marsh of circa 1950—and to all appearances cold as a mackerel besides, as MM at her age was not, that five minutes of her company spooks Fenwick and Susan out of tranquillity, and a weekend visit leaves us chilled to the entrails. The young woman senses some negative voltage on our encounters; god knows what she attributes it to, but her awareness of it only increases that voltage. The birth of their child seems as likely to compound as to ease the tension.

their friends, depose and kill Salvador Allende Gossens and Chilean democracy. Gus and Manfred have an epic final quarrel over the Company's role in that affair. You begin writing your book.

The tide's low. We'll go straight up Poplar Island Narrows and turn left into Poplar Harbor at Black Can Three. Dead slow then, and watch the depth-sounder. John Arthur Paisley officially retires from the Agency. In Vienna, Captain Shadrin disappears.

Poor Captain Shadrin. I'm promoted to associate professor.

No minor chord that.

Nor is your publishing *KUDOVE*. But Gus leaves his plumbing job and goes to work underground with what's left of the MIR, and Mimi takes up with her Vietnamese poet friend.

Dead slow. I'll get the anchor ready. Mundungus disappears. Count and I do battle over *KUDOVE*. Favor the port side going in, toward Coaches Island; then swing up to starboard. We'll anchor between Poplar and Jefferson.*

The chart says no.

We can do it, though. Mister Paisley disappears and resurfaces. Count disappears and doesn't resurface; nor does Gus.

Mimsi has her second child. You have your heart attack. We just touched bottom.

The sounder says zero, but we're still moving. A bit more

---

*Poplar Island, off Tilghman Island on the east side of Chesapeake Bay, is in fact three small wooded islands—Poplar, Coaches, and Jefferson—enclosing a shallow natural harbor. Presently uninhabited by humans except for a small marine research facility operated by the Smithsonian Institution (so says the Cruising Guide), the islands are rapidly eroding into the Bay. In the period of the War of 1812, deep-draft British naval vessels anchored in Poplar Harbor for repairs; current charts show a maximum mean-low-water depth of three feet at the entrance and six inside. However, drafts of five feet may be carried in with local knowledge and good luck, of both of which we have some portion.

to port, maybe. There. Orrin and Julie get pregnant.

Is Manfred dead, Fenn?

Oh, I hope not. I wish not. I'd rather battle my brother than mourn him. But I think he's dead.

Six years gone with a whoosh. We're old married folks! Six years of teaching and writing and reading and sailing and traveling and fucking and cooking and occasionally fighting but not very often. Once a semester?

Thrice per academic year and once per summer.

Once per lifetime is too often for us. Hey, I'm due for a sabbatical leave in Seventy-nine–Eighty!

You can't hear me now from up here over the sound of the engine. Let's take that leave, dear Susan. We're at a fork in our channel. We've got to settle the question of having children. I've got to decide whether to try teaching and writing fiction again. You've got to think hard about moving up to Swarthmore and being a serious scholar as well as a good undergraduate teacher. Okay, back down on the anchor. Back, back. That does it. Cut the engine. Cut.

I couldn't hear anything you said up there. Isn't this place spooky? I love it.

I love you, Susan R. A. Seckler. I was saying that we have to choose between taking *Pokey* down the Intracoastal, cruising the Caribbean, and making an ocean passage home, or devoting our sabbatical to trying to find out what happened to Gus and Count.

Doog says we'll be breaking our hearts for nothing.

But the alternative, Susan: *playing*.

Taking stock isn't playing. Plotting our course for the years ahead. I love my brother and I love your brother, but mainly I love you.

Us.

I say let's do it. We'll devote the summer to detective work and planning. If we've turned up nothing by the September equinox, it's anchors aweigh.

Done and done. Here we are.

Snug.

· · ·

If life is like a voyage, reader, a voyage may be like life. If good stories partake of dreams, some dreams may be like stories. After this day of quiet, full-sail sailing, we are indeed snugly anchored at afternoon's end, though with less than a foot of water between our keel and the hard sand bottom of Poplar Harbor. The light wind has died; the air's dry and cool and bugless; the water's clean, but we're not tempted to swim. Though it's far from sunset, a light burns at the dock of the lone cottage on nearby Jefferson Island. No other signs of occupancy over there. It's an ordinary-looking white clapboard bungalow, not unattractive; only the somewhat massive dock distinguishes it from an isolated summer cottage. Fenn wonders idly whether it might be a Company safe-house under Smithsonian cover: the location's ideal.

We dinghy ashore on Poplar proper, wearing long pants, long sleeves, and boat-moccasins against the cool air, and stroll the beach hand in hand for exercise, wary of the snakes we've heard the place is full of. None in sight: only crows, gulls, herons, the occasional osprey, and small fish jumping in the harbor to escape larger ones. Freighters slide past out in the Bay. Clouds bank up to westward, obscuring the low sun now; jet trails score an otherwise clear sky overhead. It feels like late September, when we last stopped here.

We have the islands quite to ourselves, and they are, as Sue has said, spooky. That they were once much larger and populated, and now are not. That they sit off a lonely shore in an expanse of water, now glassy calm. That the harbor they enclose contains a number of mini-islets, some eroded down to grassy hummocks a yard in breadth: cartoon desert islands, upon which Fenwick once stood bare-assed to declare his love for Susan to the birds while ships slipped by from Iceland, Crete, Japan. Finally that, unlike your typical secluded Chesapeake cove, Poplar Harbor is as visually open to the Bay as a coral-reefed lagoon.

We pretend to look for Fenn's boina. Toward dusk we return, pleasantly spooked by the circumambulation and cozied by the day's recall. We sip St. Estèphe and make a splendid dinner from our fresh provisions: loin lamb chops charcoal-grilled off the stern pulpit, spinach salad, Brie and grapes. Then we make light love in the cool cabin, retire to our separate berths, and read ourselves to sleep, as relaxed perhaps as at any time since our leaving these home waters nine months ago. Susan's got her *New York Review of Books,* picked up improbably at Solomons; Fenn, Shakespeare's *Tempest* for the hundredth time. We are reasonably healthy, reasonably successful, reasonably well off, well fed, well fucked, unpersecuted, unoppressed, and still in love after seven years of marriage: the favored of the earth. What is that light on for, at the end of that dock?

Good night, good night.

## THE BIG BANG

A bang, big, startles us at dawn's earliest light. We both jump, but neither rouses up at once, for a remarkable reason that shortly comes clear:

Susan mutters from her berth That fit my dream, exactly! That noise worked right into my dream!

Groggy Fenn sits up. Mine too.

It fit yours too?

Exactly. Hey! I was just coming to a big bang in my dream, and bang! I thought it *was* the dream.

So did I. What was it?

We both wonder: Key Island again? But this bang was more like a distant explosion than a nearby shot. Awake now, Fenn thinks it came from northwestwards, Baywards, rather than from shore. Aberdeen Proving Ground? Too far away, and too early in the morning. Thunder? He goes up to check: it's drizzly out, chilly, but still dead still. Perhaps an isolated thundersquall at the head of the Bay; but he sees no lightning, hears no further booms. That electric light still burns at that dock, to east of us; all quiet over there. Fenwick returns below, still rapt in his extraordinary dream, and closes the companionway slide to reduce the cool draft.

What a dream I was having, Susan says across the dim cabin.

Me too. No sign of anything. Come visit.

She does; we return to fitful sleep, she prone atop him. More dreams and half-dreams: restless now, anticlimactic, scattered like our sleep.

We rise at 0830, late for us, heads rocky. Still still out, cool, close, intermittently drizzling, gray. Both engaged yet in our earlier dreams, we eat a silent breakfast: fresh honeydew, Maryland beaten biscuits. As is her wont in all but foulest weather, Susan finishes her coffee up in the cockpit, wrapped in light foul-weather gear, while Fenn at the chart-table sighs at Miriam's cigarette burn there and says good morning to *Pokey*'s log. He remarks presently up the ladder Looks as if we'll be motoring to Wye I. Two, two and a half hours.

Susan murmurs *Everything* was in my dream.

In mine too.

I've almost got it straight in my head now. I'm afraid to talk: might lose it.

Me too.

Maybe you can write yours down before it goes.

Writing takes too long. While you're putting the front end into words, the back end evaporates.

Susan groans Mine's going! Oh, I'm losing it! Francis Scott Key . . .

Her husband is astonished. In yours too?

Sssh! Oh shit: it's gone. She puts her cup down into its gimbaled holder, covers her face with her hands. *Gus* was in it! I talked to Mundungus!

Fenn gets up from the chart-table. I saw Gus too! Not to talk to, but I saw him. With Count!

He leans against the ladder, his chin resting on his forearms on the companionway sill. Susan touches his head and says, subdued, stricken: Gus is dead, Fenn.

Yeah. Count, too.

She moans They were together! Manfred and Mundungus!

In *his* dream, Fenwick replies quietly, father and son were both drowned. More exactly, they were drowned swimmers of some sort, not sunken sailors, for example, or aquatic suicides. They wore swim-togs—wet-suits, something; it kept changing—anyhow, not street clothes. And that's odd, inasmuch as neither Gus nor Manfred cared for swimming. Count liked to sail and fish occasionally; Mundungus had no use for the water. But they seemed to have made up their quarrel.

Yes! Susan swings her legs off the unslashed cockpit cushion. They were holding each other. Soaking wet!

Fenn takes her hand and, to spare her feelings, does not ask whether in her dream, as in his, her brother bore the awful marks of torture, his the ravages of crabs and other marine scavengers.

Now we wonder: Can two people really dream the same dream? Susan reports that she and Miriam claim to have done so once, when they were six or seven: but she acknowledges that one or the other of them might have stretched or misremembered things to make the dreams fit, so appealing to both was the idea of twins having identical dreams. In any case, they shared the same *sort* of dream one night, about the same general subject, now forgotten. As, she concludes, apparently did we.

Apparently. That big bang—

Right. And the swimming . . .

That big bang was the Big Bang! We really did flash back to it!

Susan squeezes his forearm. *Daddy* was in my dream! We were in his old Choptank Theatre, down in Cambridge— even the R E in Theatre was like that in my dream, on the marquee—and Da was saying Comes now the big fleshbeck, Susele.

Her eyes are teary, but we're excited, engrossed. Fenwick tentatively observes that his dream started off in a fairly realistic way—

So did mine!

Doog Taylor was explaining to me in the Cosmos Club

that R and D had come up with a potent new memory drug for interrogation. It was still experimental: its effects varied unpredictably with dosage and from subject to subject; also from dose to dose with the same subject. But the virtue of it was that the subject could wander about in his own memory like in a landscape; he could guide himself, within limits, and be guided by friendly interrogators. Mine were Doog himself and Count (we were suddenly inside my dream, on the drug, instead of in the Cosmos). I could even interrogate my dream-memory myself, like Dante strolling through Hell with Virgil. I could ask a scene or a character: Where are *you* from? I could talk with myself in Spain at age thirty! It was very realistic hallucination: as if I were dreaming on the drug and knew it, instead of dreaming of a drug-dream. And I could check with Count: Am I doing all right? Who's that over there? Et cetera.

Susan's was the first dream she's ever heard of that began with a syllogism, albeit a skewed, equivocating one. Opposite-sex twins incline to regression, its major premise voicelessly declared. You and Fenwick are twins, the minor premise slyly added, and are of opposite sexes. Ergo, they concluded in unison . . . and let the rest hang suspended as an enthymeme. The logic, Susan remarks, and the talking premises as well, belong in Lewis Carroll.

Brillig! Fenwick cries. 'Twas brillig, and the slithy toves . . . *Brillig* was in my dream, and James Jesus Angleton was a slithy tove. Wait a second. He claps his forehead. Gone.

Bemused, we pump the bilge and head, start up the diesel, prepare to weigh anchor. Our light foul-weather suits are clammy in the humid cool. As Fenn uncleats the anchor rode, Sue emerges from the cabin to take the helm and ease us forward. Instead of a hat or the hood of her slicker, she's wearing that scarf Fenn plucked from Poe Cove. He glances back to signal slow ahead, catches sight of the scarf . . . signals neutral instead, recleats the rode, returns to the cockpit, shuts down the engine, and in an awed voice says to wondering Susan It just came together. You said once that those paisley things looked like fat spermatozoa. That's what the slithy toves were, in my dream. Not just Angleton: John Arthur Paisley, Doog, Count, me too—we were all swimming along together, upstream, like giant sperm. *With* sperm! *As* sperm! It was late evening, or early nighttime: brillig. We were slogging along upstream in the dim light.

Fenwick. . . . Susan is amused, but wonderstruck. Mims and I were *floating!* No: we were like some kind of white-water canoers, but not in a canoe. More like an inflatable dinghy. It was something we were wearing, as if each of us were built into an inflatable white-water raft. And we didn't just coast along: we were busy steering, navigating, radioing back to the . . . what? She puts her fingertips to her cheeks. We were these big, elastic, floating *eggs!*

Now we're laughing, but Fenn says soberly You and Miriam were ova. And we-all were sperm.

Our dreams, then, began differently but came remarkably together: shared memories of the paisley scarf, no doubt, and of other recently mentioned matters. *Flowed* together would describe it better, Susan believes, like Rhine and Moselle at the Deutsches Eck, Allegheny and Monongahela at Pittsburgh, Ohio and Mississippi at Cairo, East and West Forks of Langford Creek at Cacaway Island. In both dreams, it appears—though details of roles and costume differed—Susan was making her way downstream with the current, Fenwick his upstream against it, and there followed, as in 1972, our Meet. We dreamed the same dream from different points of view.

Uh oh. Susan's expression darkens. Were the Dixie Pagans in yours? Or Mim's Rescuers afterwards?

Nope. Was Paco in yours?

Who's Paco?

Fenn shakes his head. Paco was the old man from Marbella that he and Marilyn Marsh drove up to Ronda in 1960, when Fenn first lost his boina. We never knew his name, by the way. Fenwick learned it just now, in the dream, and he's sure it's correct. Paco.

Frank Mann was in Susan's! And Junior Parsons!

Who?

Frank Mann, believe it or not, was the driver of that chicken truck that killed Daddy on Highway Forty in Nineteen Forty-nine. He made a pest of himself afterwards, begging Ma to forgive him for dozing off at the wheel. Ma had to get a peace order. Frank Mann! I was five, Fenn, and I can see him now plain as day: a wizened old guy in dark green pants, hitching up his belt! In my dream he had white Leghorn feathers on him still.

Who's Junior Parsons?

Junior Parsons was a motorcyclist—a *nice* motorcyclist, before Mims and the Dixie Pagans. He gave me a lift once when I was hitching home from Swarthmore, before I quit doing that. His name was stenciled on his crash helmet, which I borrowed from him later in the white-water part of my dream: Junior Parsons, G.G.A.N.R.F. That was in my dream, too.

What's it stand for?

Susan grins. That's what I asked Junior Parsons. You're *supposed* to ask.

Okay, Fenn decides: we're not moving from Poplar Harbor until we get these dreams coordinated. Different viewpoints, different minor characters, different openings, but the same materials. The same general conceit and mise-en-scène. Neither of us has ever heard of such a thing. Where are those dream researchers of yours when we need them? He croons to her:

> Come, sweetheart, tell me;
>   Now is the time:
> You tell me your-oor-oor dream,
>    And I-I . . . will tell . . . you mine.*

Practical Susan says I say leave it to the author. Let's get on up the road to Wye I.

Hum. Well. Okay. Done.

•    •    •

---

*Fenwick is remembering a song his mother used to sing: *You Had a Dream, Dear,* by Albert Brown, Seymour Rice, and Charles N. Daniels.

Done? Okay? Well! Hum! Why, that's some tall order, Susan, Fenn! Probably impossible; certainly improbable; unlikely as our having shared a dream in the first place, in which—let's take a deep swimmer's breath—in which the flashback of our life together and our earlier lives apart, rehearsed all day as *Pokey* tacked, flashed farther back to our conceptions. There's Jack Seckler's sperm romancing Carmen's eggs in Philadelphia, as Maryland's 29th Division hits the Normandy beaches on D-Day: the eggs that will hatch into Miriam and Susan before we atomize Hiroshima and Nagasaki. There's a brace of Virginia Key's bridal ova aswarm with Herman Turner's stout kraut swimmers, just before the sky falls in '29: two are taken in to help make Manfred and our Fenn, the others sloughed away like shipwrecked sailors in the dark. Back, back, we flashed, through the serial confluences of our separate lines—Shalom, little Havah Moscowitz: hide here, not there, or those pogromniks will do unto you as they've done already unto your neighbor.

No no no, Edgar Poe:
Don't go back to Baltimo'.
You'll get mickey-finned for sure. . . .
Quoth the raven: Balti*more*.

And say, do we see Mister Francis Scott Key floating out past the FSK Bridge? Are we dreaming? Whose pinstripes and screen stars? Through the tenderless night Scott Fitzgerald has drunk; Zelda's violently screaming Back, back, from the times of our lives through the space of our place: Can this be our Manfred sailing down the Chespeake, sailing down the Chesapeake, sailing down the Chesapeake Bay* and dropping anchor for his life's last time here in Poplar Harbor? Look again: it's *Byron's* Manfred! No: it's Byron's *cousin*,

---

*From the song *Sailing Down the Chesapeake Bay*, by Jean Havez and George Botsford (New York: Remick Music Corp., 1913).

Captain Sir Peter Parker of His Majesty's Ship *Menelaus,* en route not to Troy but to diversionary action on the upper Chesapeake, while his comrades make a most remarkable commando raid: the burning of D.C. Alas, the Yanks now nail him: Peter Parker's pickled in a cask of navy rum, to be elegized by Byron ere his *Manfred* is begun. Good-bye Washington, hello George, sailing up the Chesapeake from Mount Vernon to Chestertown and on to Philadelphia. Stand on Poplar long enough, the world will float by as the ground floats away. Watch for Chessie the shoal-draft sea monster; watch for Fenn's boina. Here comes Colonel Tench Tilghman, our ferry-borne Paul Revere, carrying the news of Cornwallis's surrender up from York River to the Continental Congress. Ebb, flow, ebb, flow: the languid tidal respiration accelerates like passion's breath. Back, back, some hundred thousand highs and lows: there go the Lords Baltimore, chasing Claiborne off Kent Island, back, back to Virginia. 20,000 tide-turns more: Ahoy there, John Smith! It is not your Northwest Passage, but 'tis brillig, brillig, aye? Now the warlike Susquehannocks paddle down to raid the Choptanks. Occahannock, Annamessex, Nassawaddox, Mattawoman: now the Spaniard, now the Viking, tries to translate Hiawathan, tom-tom-tomming Hiawathan. Too late now to dream of Harriet Tubman and Frederick Douglass, experts when necessary in the Tomming line: here comes and goes the Ice Age. Susquehanna's drowned mouth rises like J. A. Paisley: no more Chesapeake. Plate tectonics spin on Rewind: the continents raft up like week-end boaters back of Cacaway. *Whump:* Pangaea! *Whoosh:* Panthalassa! There goes Mother Ocean, sizzled off like water from a wok. *Whoof:* no planets! *Wham:* no sun! Henny Penny was right: hold your ears; here it comes. . . .

Wow, says Susan, and it woke both of us, and that light still burned on that dock, and I felt— She halts in mid-memory: what she felt in fact was impregnated, by our dream. I don't know what, she says.

Fenwick declares that if our dream left a few things out, like the Underground Railway and Joseph Whaland's Loyalist Picaroons and Susan's ex-lover Seymour Berman, the author's recap left a few things out too, that were in the dream. Little Oroonoko, for example, age two or four or five as he always is in his father's dreams.

We were teaching him how to swim, off Chief and Virgie's dock. Orrin was complaining that the water's too cold; he always chilled easily. We were teasing him about that—gently, because Orrin never could take teasing.

Fenwick stops: that we is not us. It's Marilyn Marsh beside him in that cool Wye water in that part of the dream: trim, pretty, cheerful, twenty-five, no problems between them yet. The young family is ashine with an innocent Eisenhowerian light. He draws his breath. That spooky trawler-yacht *Baratarian* was in my dream, too, he says.

It sailed through Susan's as well, bristling with female pirates! Fenn flushes with dismay at another, unspeakable image from our dream: among hosts and hosts of drowned night-swimmers, going down like polluted alewives on the tide, chilling as a premonition: along with Manfred, Gus, John Paisley, and that hapless interrogatee from the Choptank River safe-house—Dugald Taylor, blue-faced, dead!

I think the author did okay, Susan says. That was some fleshbeck. My hat is off to us. Well done, us. She does indeed remove our scarf trouvée. It is late in the forenoon; cool drizzle persists, but while the flashback flashed we motored up Poplar Island Narrows, into Eastern Bay, around Tilghman Point, down into the mouth of the Miles, up again into the stem of the Wye. Just ahead, defined by the Y of that manicured river, is Wye I. Far cry from Poplar, Solomons, Key: only the map, or a flight above or a trip around it, shows Wye to be an island. Broad, cultivated, set not in open water but among further fields and woods, it is a body of land completely surrounded by land, but moated irregularly by the tines of the forked river and by Wye Narrows, which yokes them like a crooked oarlock pin. We'll be taking the Front Wye: the east, the starboard fork. Key Farm is around a few bends not far ahead. Our story's half told. Susan goes down to fix her hair.

# III

*The Fork*

# 1
# WYE TO GIBSON
## *Under the Bridge*

Three days later, when we leave Key Farm, Wye I., the Wye, the Miles, and Eastern Bay, round Bloody Point into the Chesapeake proper, and set our course north again, up the Bay, under the twin suspension bridges linking Baltimore and Washington to Maryland's Eastern Shore, toward Gibson Island, our next stop—the first prime anchorage on the Bay's west side above the bridge—from where we mean to do our business in Baltimore, Susan sighs Onwards and upwards.

It has been, for her especially, a stressful period, our weekend. We are even more than usually relieved to be under way. Sue doesn't want to talk about it, yet, directly.

### *YOUR 19th IS SUSAN'S CENTURY, YOUR 18th FENN'S,*
#### *or,*
#### *Was Edgar Allan Poe Jewish?*

Says Fenn Mm. After a very windy Sunday—forty-five northwest knots of blue Canadian high—Monday June 9 is fine and dry and cool, with a crisp light westerly for close-reaching in jerseys and nylon shells. Rain likely by evening from a small low-pressure cell drifting like a hawk up the Appalachian ridge, but no storms expected. He turns off the weather, trims in the sails, and takes the helm: it is agreeable at times to steer oneself instead of being self-steered.

Susan stretches out against the cockpit bulkhead and

glumly surveys our wake. Her mind obviously elsewhere—
back at Key Farm, Fenn would bet—she supposes that we
haven't really explained yet to the reader, who must be
wondering, what all this Poe-Key/*Pokey*/Kepone business is
about, beyond our putative ancestries, the name of our boat,
and Allied Chemical Corporation's deliberate, criminal, and
perhaps irremediable poisoning of the noble James River, site
of the first permanent English settlement in America.

Fenwick encourages her: Keep on.

Aye yi. Well. Ma says Da believed that E. A. Poe was as
Jewish as I am and that the Secklers are related to him
through the Allans of Virginia, who were only Poe's adop-
tive bloodline anyhow, but the connection's lost because
Grandma never understood it when Grandpa Allan used to
explain it, and Ma never believed it. John Allan, who
adopted Poe, was a Richmond merchant; does that make
him Jewish, I ask you?

Keep on.

There's an Uncle Artie Golderman back in the line—
Grandpa Allan Seckler's great-uncle, I think—that Jack
Seckler claimed was the model for Poe's Arthur Gordon
Pym. Never mind that Edgar Allan Poe sounds more like
Arthur Gordon Pym than Artie Golder Man does: Great-
Uncle Artie was in corset stays and whale oil in Boston
before the bottom fell out of the business when petroleum
was discovered in Titusville P A in Eighteen Fifty-nine. . . .

Susan.

I need to talk. Anyhow, the world *is* a seamless web.

Onwards, then. Upwards.

Yeah. Be all the foregoing as may—and there's more to
it,* but who cares?—your irrational, romantic, overreaching
Nineteenth is my fucking century, and Crazy Edgar is my
alma pater, Jewish or not. Nervous. Unstable. Frenetic.

------

*There is indeed, and some of us care. In a less low humor Sue might
have repeated, e.g., Jack Seckler's conviction—as reported and doubtless
improved by heedless Carmen—that the merchant Artie Golderman's son
Isaac, who was either shanghaied by or ran off with Nantucket whalers

Brilliant, Fenwick hastens to add. Energetic. Intuitive.

Susan's eyes are wet again. Fatherless. Childless. Self-tormented. Half hysterical. And doomed to an early, unquiet grave.

Susele . . .

She quotes unsmiling from our fleshbeck dream: Quoth the raven: Baltimore.

Enough, honey.

She's still slouched on the cut cushion (which Fenn has patched for the nonce with duct-tape), looking where we've been. Eastwood Ho* is a Vietnamese Poe, she says levelly. He'll get it too, like Edgar and me. Her eyes close. The Overwhelming of the Vessel. I'm going to crap out early and leave nothing behind. I don't want to talk about it. Do Francis Scott Key for the reader, please.

---

circa 1850 and later became a moderately prosperous shellfish dealer in Chincoteague, on the Eastern Shore of Virginia, was the original of Issachar, the renegade Jewish "King of Chincoteague" in George Alfred Townsend's curious tale of that name (1880). If so, either Jack Seckler or G. A. Townsend has altered dates: "Issachar" is in the prime of life on Christmas Eve 1840, when Townsend's tale begins; that is, he is a fictional contemporary of Edgar Poe and Artie Golderman, not of Golderman's errant son. But Susan is distraught. The reader will remember having met George Alfred Townsend on p. 119.

*Okay: we do not know the original name of that Vietnamese folk-poet introduced on p. 54, Miriam Leah Poe Seckler's common-law husband and father of her second child. In Saigon in the early 1970s, after the destruction of Hué, he went variously by the names Can Phung Ho—after Can Phung Island ("Phoenix Island") in the lower Mekong, which he then called home—and Ho Ca Dao, after the intricate, once-popular genre of traditional Vietnamese folk lyric in which he specializes, and which now thrives like a rare, endangered bird mainly on Can Phung Island. In the belief that a westernized name might assist his immigration to the United States, he whimsically assumed the surname of the one American he'd ever met both fluent enough and literate enough to appreciate ca dao: a conscientious objector from Harvard named James Eastwood, who was working for a civilian medical relief agency out of Hué and studying Vietnamese oral poetry on the side. Ho Eastwood was not blind to the ironies of his "western" name; on the contrary, he so savored them, especially when U.S. immigration officials reversed surname and given name, that he clung to it even though its irregularity delayed perilously his eastward flight to the West. In 1977, soon after reaching Baltimore, Eastwood Ho became Miriam Seckler's lover.

I'm too unnerved to do Francis Scott Key for the reader.

Sue presses on. Spring's about over, you know. It'll be fall any minute. What're we going to do?

Fenwick protests that there is a whole summer yet between. But he knows this humor of his friend, and feels equal measures of distress, solicitude, and self-concern. What would he do without her?

Now she taunts: Key wasn't even Eighteenth century.

Familiar waters. Sure he was. Your Nineteenth doesn't start till after the Eighteen Twelve War or Waterloo, take your choice. Just as your Twentieth begins with World War One and your Nineteen Seventies begin with your Yom Kippur War of Seventy-three.

Susan points out, her custom, that nobody much knows what the composer of the U.S. national anthem was like. Not impossibly he was as demon-driven as Poe, or as his namesake, F. Scott Fitz.

Nope. Fenwick's Key was your Eighteenth-century man: enlightened, rational, cool, optimistic, unecstatic, self-controlled. Apollonian, to Sue's Dionysiac Mister Poe. Jack of sundry trades: lawyer, gentleman, amateur poet and musician, prisoner-exchange negotiator, amateur military advisor at the Bladensburg Races. . . .

Susan's languages run together as her spirits sink. Oy vay: give me Beethoven. Sturm und Drang. Donner und Blitzen. Iron and shmaltz.

Give Fenn Mozart: a crisp close reach in sparkling weather.

Tinkle tinkle, Susan gibes.

Boom boom, her unruffled friend replies. I'm no romantic.

Your view of the Eighteenth century is romantic, in your wife's opinion. Your view of rationalism is romantic.

Well: her husband's not anti-romantic, any more than he's anti-her. Says he's got some Manfred in him; even a touch of Poe. And a little Sue Seckler, thank god.

This last invites a certain obvious, loving reply. But Susan's not having it. Hmp.

Hmp nothing. Compared to Miriam and Carmen B. Seckler, you've got a lot of F.S.K. in you. What exactly's eating you so badly, Suse?

Now the real tears come. I need Fenwick Scott Key Turner in me right now, to calm me down. Could we please for Christ's sake park and fuck?

Well, reader: hence the significance of our sturdy craft's name: a union of contraries prevailingly harmonious indeed but sometimes tense, like the physics of *Pokey* himself. More on naval architecture p. 287. But there are no parking places handy on this stretch of water: the Kent Island shore, to starboard and leeward, is beach unbroken but for a couple of very exposed marinas-cum-harbors-of-refuge; and by the time we tripped to windward across the Bay to the Rhode, South, or Severn rivers, the moment would be lost. For such occasions were wind-vanes made: the stretch ahead is clear of boats this sunny Monday morn, and, well, it is agreeable at times to be self-steered instead of steering oneself.

Anon the Bay Bridge begins to materialize ahead. We are back on our separate cockpit cushions, rezipped and (Fenn) feeling well expended. A hundred million of his sperm, give or take ten million, are doing their upstream best in Susan's plumbing, aided by a good head start. But from the helm he says That didn't seem to do it.

I guess not. Thanks anyhow.

Not every day can be Fourth of July. Fenwick would say we managed not badly, considering we had to keep an eye out for crab pots the whole time.

Not your fault. Susan sighs. I'm a crazy lady. I don't know what's bothering me. Yes I do, but never mind. Jesus. Sometimes I think I ought to have an affair.

Fenn feigns perplexity, dismay. I beg your pardon?

### SUSAN WANTS A DYNAMITE CLANDESTINE ADULTEROUS PASSIONATE AFFAIR.

Yeah, she exclaims unenthusiastically. Gimme one of those: a dynamite clandestine adulterous passionate affair.

Susan Rachel.

You had yours. Plenty.

A couple, a couple. And I don't want any more. Everybody gets bruised.

Love-bruises.

Bruise-bruises. You had yours, too, before me.

Licit. On my part, anyhow. I want illicit. Adulterous passion. Deceit, desire; the worm in the apple of the bourgeois Eden. I'm thirty-five already. Pretty soon I'll have to settle for Der Rosenkavalier instead of Count Vronsky. Like that scuba teacher in Martinique, I mean Guadeloupe, the sexy cute one.

Antonio again.

Had me at his mercy, ten meters under with a hose in my mouth, and he didn't even grab a tit. Boy oh boy. Time's running out like air from a tank.

Or like sexual self-esteem from a crestfallen husband.

Right. I got to get cracking.

Susan Rachel Allan Seckler Turner, says pained Fenwick. Carefully raised nice Jewish girl. Assistant professor about to become associate and tenured.

I want it! Trysts! Rendezvouses! Near-discoveries! Stolen hours! Passion!

Does she wish him to play the complaisant husband? Fenn inquires. He is not by temperament cut out for that role, but perhaps with a clenched-jaw effort he might bring it off. Open marriage? That sort of thing?

That's all crap.

I'm relieved to hear you say so.

Complaisant spouses in Susan's opinion are as disgusting as swingers. She wants clandestine servicing. Anna K.! Emma B.! Jealous suspicions! Dressing for Him! Not wearing her underpants because He forbids it! Guilty conscience because she loves Fenwick so much and doesn't want to hurt or dishonor him even the tiniest bit ever, but still! All that shit, you know?

Mm. So you want a tyrannical clandestine adulterous lover. I'm astonished.

Sue looks at him sidelong, almost merrily. Tyrannical in a nice way. I'm not marrying the bastard; I'm just fucking him.

He'd better not slap you around, Fenn warns.

Let him try! I'll Mace him and walk out flat. What I mean is passion stuff. Love-bites that hurt, some. Making me swallow his spunk even though I gag. I'll do the same to him.

Your patient husband can scarcely wait to hear what you'll do to him.

You know what. Like make him keep my cunt-smell on his mustache when he goes home to that juiceless wife of his.

Mustache! Fenn dons his eyeglasses. Juiceless wife! How long has this been going on?

I want it. On the other hand, I wouldn't hurt you for anything.

Well, Suse. You have a problem.

Yeah. Can't I have it both ways?

Fenwick doesn't see how: not in real life. He might try to work out something for her in our story. . . .

Bugger the story. I want the real thing. Passion.

Our sex life isn't passionate?

Sue smiles for the first time today, and Fenn finds himself truly a bit stung now. I told you and told you: I'm not talking about love. I love you more than anybody ever loved anybody. But passion! Clandestine adulterous passion. Hot dog.

What can a chap say?

Nothing.

Hum. He sees her brief animation fade. Does this go into the story or not?

She's staring at our wake again. Oh, in. Sure, in. Give me a dynamite house in there, dynamite kids named Drew and Lexie, and a dynamite clandestine adulterous passionate affair. All the stuff I'll never have, plus loads of money. Plus you, that I would never in this world be unfaithful to. On with the story. But wow: passion.

She goes downstairs to use the head and fix an antipasto lunch with Perrier and lime. Fenn is to call her when we reach the Bridge, if she's not back upstairs by then.

None of the dialogue so far in this chapter means what it said. Life-choices are trade-offs, reader, and loving your bargain doesn't make it painless to pay the bill. Does it, Susan. Does it, Fenn. You've seen some of what the woman wishes, and may have guessed more: that we were of an age, starting out together, instead of the man's having done most married-life things already. That regardless of that, he'd be, would have been seven years ago already, so crazy to have another child or two with her that her own apprehensions and reservations in that quarter would have been, would be, overruled, swept away. That we were living in the sophisticated thick of things in New York City or Paris or both with our dynamite kids and our dynamite friends, or even had a house in Georgetown and a summer place on Martha's Vineyard with our ditto, plus dynamite careers as famous writer him and brilliant professor her, with a circle of friends comprising the celebrated and formidable yet simpático in each of our fields plus people in the other arts and the sciences as well and a few civilized State Department types or senators if there are any instead of futzing around on a sailboat, just the two of us, much as we love each other and sailing, between careers, without fixed address or mutual descendants, with ever fewer friends since *KUDOVE* and almost no social life since Gus's and Manfred's disappearance/death and our sabbatical cruise, our furniture stored in a Baltimore warehouse, our clothing and library and artwork and wines and mss.-in-progress and personal effects stored at Key Farm, where we'll store ourselves for the summer while we look for an apartment somewhere between Swarthmore, Pa., and Newark, Del., maybe in the Brandywine Valley above Wilmington, Andrew Wyeth country, and Susan's beloved old Impala convertible sold to help float our cruise, and Fenn's old station wagon up on blocks in Chief's and Virgie's garage against our return, plus certain medical matters on the horizon or closer, and each of our nose's being yearly more rubbed in her/his own limitations as well as those of his/her spouse—each feeling what William James called the pinch of one's personal destiny as it spins itself out upon the wheel, not to mention the pinches of our common destiny, of vague threats from Fenwick's past, of large choices that must be made within this division of our story, Part III, *The Fork*, however many subdivisions we postpone those choices with. Whereas Fenwick—with one two-decade marriage under his belt, his ambitions tempered, his early economic and career struggles behind him, together with a raised child, fifteen more years than Susan of this and that including in the dying semesters of Life #1 a couple of clandestine adulterous passionate affairs, notice he doesn't say dynamite—would be content to sail on till the end of our story, just the two of us and occasional relatives and acquaintances, if we could afford to and if Susan weren't increasingly and understandably unhappy with things as they are and seem to be going, though the chapter is not done, much less the story, yet.

We had just got our docklines out and ready, see, approaching Key Farm in last Friday's drizzle, when there came out onto the front-porch steps from the white clapboard familiar house not only Chief, waving his cane hello and grinning above his uniform three-piece suit, but—surprise!—Orrin (Fenn's heart stung as always with pride, love, and guilt at the sight of his son smiling too and waving softly like a lean and schooled and gentle Viking); and not only Orrin, but

Oh Jesus Christ, groaned Susan from the bow.

Orrin's Julie: mighty pregnant, mighty blond, mighty pixie-cut, hard-jawed, lean-faced—

Tight-assed.

With a gleaming smile—

Like a goyishe barracuda.

Stop it, Suse.

I know, I'm sorry, I'm jealous as hell, Julie's fine, I hate her.

Her maternity dress was a flowered cotton print—

A shmatta from Filene's Basement.

Oroonoko's wheat-gold hair was cut short as always—even short sideburns, Nineteen-Fifties style, and shiny straightleg chinos—

Long in the crotch and full in the seat, like an old man's. Dear Orrin.

Old-fashioned eyeglasses with heavy black plastic frames. Short-sleeved shirt with button-down collarpoints and a fruit-loop between the shoulders. White socks. Black shoes.

They both have such godawful taste.

I used to dress that way too, a quarter-century ago. Except for the black shoes.

Don't remind me. Can you imagine how they'll dress their kid? Oh man, if I had a kid . . .

Then there came Virgie in her housedress: chain-smoking, permanent-limping from year-before-last's fall and the whole-hip surgery that didn't work on her softened bones, osteoporosis. The air was chill and damp, not good for her, but the drizzle chivalrously paused. Chief waited. She took his arm, won't use a cane, and they started down their lawn to the dock. Orrin guided Julie protectively, one hand at her elbow; they came grinning usward.

Susan muttered I can't take it.

You can, I hope.

Eagerly but almost shyly, as ever, Oroonoko called Hi, Dad. Hi, Susan.

And sang out Julie: Hi, everybody!

We threw them lines to mistie in their separate ways— Orrin's attempted clove hitch around a dock piling turned into a girth hitch, which he then made fast with attempted half hitches that did likewise; Julie cinched enough round turns and figure eights on her cleat to secure an aircraft carrier—and the circuit of our near-nine-month voyage was closed. In *Pokey*'s icebox was Dom Perignon for this occasion, a better vintage than we popped in Poe Cove in Part I; but the time of day was wrong, high noon; ditto the voltage. Sigh.

Chief and Virgie reached the inboard end of the dock and began their careful way out, talking to each other, smiling, nodding. A rare event now, for Fenwick's mother to walk so far, who once—

Home from the sea, Fenn said dryly, and stepped off to embrace his daughter-in-law and son. Susan twinged with unreasonable disappointment that he hadn't handed herself ashore first, though she certainly needed no assistance, who could dock and undock us singlehanded. It was only that Julie and Virgie were being taken such careful care of by their men. Oroonoko of course came over now and offered his hand with mock formality, saying something like Welcome to Wye Island, milady, and Susan took it in the same spirit, wondering perversely why in the world members of this family had to be so goddamn *stiff* with one another—as folks sure were not chez Seckler—and why she permitted herself to fall into the same stiffness. Oh, well, nonsense: Orrin's hug was as genuine as hers; but look at him then (she looked at him then, over Julie's shoulder, even as she embraced her stepdaughter-in-law and oohed politely, aflame with envy and other emotions, over the younger woman's blossomed belly); look at father and son both, embracing so *nervously*, like bashful lovers.

We *are* bashful lovers, Fenwick says now, as we approach the Bridge. We *are* nervous with each other, some. Partly our temperament; partly a side effect of the divorce hassle.

Seven happy years ago! Susan cries up from the galley. Eight!

Fenn shrugs. And of course, not seeing each other as often any more . . .

It would be the same if you were neighbors. It's so false! No it isn't. Just a little tense.

They hugged and kissed—stalwart Fenn, stringy Orrin (his mother's build, whose lucky metabolism does her weight-watching for her)—and said dumb things. *Not* dumb things. Well, like (Fenwick to Orrin) What brings *you* here? Let the reader judge for him/herself.

Fenn protests: What are people supposed to say?

I don't know. Forget it, please. I'm sorry, honey.

Little vacation time, Orrin replied. We thought we'd teach your grandson how to swim while he's still afloat.

Tisk tisk, said Susan, feeling idiotic and piqued by that *your*: it just might be a girl.

Orrin grinned at Julie, who brimmingly pronounced We had a sound-scan!

And you'd better hope it's a grandson, Orrin declared to both of us, because if it isn't, your granddaughter has a scrotum.

Hello there, Skipper! Chief called, settling Virgie on the dockbench. Susan moved quickly to them, away from Julie and from (Fenn's and Marilyn Marsh's, not her) incipient grandson, sure, but she also happens to have a particular affection for old folks, most especially happy old folks. She has taught Fenwick to prize his parents even more than he always did.

He *did* always did—Turner fashion. To many, perhaps, it might seem a fairly flaccid feeling, better described as benign indifference or passive goodwill than as love. Turner parents do not go the extra kilometer for their children, nor Turner children for their parents. Chief and Virgie themselves—the one schooled only through eighth grade, the other pleased to have finished rural high school—worked hard out of lean childhoods and through the Great Depression; they bought Key Farm cheap in a moment of World War II prosperity and can just afford now to pay the taxes on it. Fenwick and Manfred as children were never pressed to achieve, though there was no want of mild encouragement and of pride in their small accomplishments. Chiefs and Virgies do not have heart-to-heart talks with their children; indeed, they do not have very personal conversation with them. They are not disciplinarians; acceptable conduct is taken for granted. They do not go to PTA meetings, meet their children's teachers, discuss their educations, wish certain careers and social positions for them rather than others. Never unsupportive, and accustomed to making small sacrifices for their children from their modest means, they do not make large ones; neither do they expect, much less demand, large reciprocation. They do not "do things" with their children: anything Fenn and Manfred ever learned about fishing, sailing, athletics, clothes, women, civilization, history, life in general—even politics and business, from investing money to reconciling a personal checking account—they learned outside the house. Virgies and Chiefs do not make trips to visit their children or dote on their grandchildren. They are not thoughtful or imaginative, e.g., in the way of gifts or loving gestures. They are affectionate but undemonstrative.

Then what on earth is there in them to prize? Oh, well: Chiefs and Virgies do not quarrel, either between themselves or with others. They do not criticize, carp, complain, belittle, boast, bluff, bully, fret, cheat, exaggerate, ostentate, chase after vanities, or spend more than they earn. They are neither prudish nor abstemious on the one hand nor on the other intemperate. They are unfailingly good-humored: Fenn can almost not imagine them not smiling! That either of them should do a thing dishonest or otherwise disgraceful is unthinkable, at least in less-than-desperate America.* Their life's radius is small—except for Chief's stint in World War I and a short honeymoon not long after, both in guess where Langley Virginia, an Army Air Force base in those days, they have seldom left Maryland's Eastern Shore—but its roots are deep in the loamy life of the place. And after fifty-five years of marriage, they love each other still—Turner fashion.

Fifty-five years! Susan laments. Why can't *we* have fifty-five years together?

Fenwick thanks god we'll have what we'll have; Sue's unconsoled. A hundred and fifty-five years wouldn't be

---

*Who knows what Chiefs and Virgies did in the siege of Leningrad, not to mention in the Gulags or the German extermination camps? Fenwick and Susan believe that they quickly and without fuss succumbed.

enough. Mortality: Jesus! And then to disappear without a
trace! In effect like Manfred; even more like Gus. . . .
Sometimes she thinks we'd might as well end it now. She's
sinking, sinking.

Chief figured we'd see you coming round the bend 'fore
long, Virgie said, returning Susan's hug as Fenwick and his
father embraced, Turner fashion. Daffy as the woman has
become in her last age, Virgie knows enough to prefer
Susan's ready demonstrations of affection to Marilyn
Marsh's reserve, and will tactlessly, obliviously say so in
Orrin's presence. In Carmen B. Seckler, even—of whom
Virgie has never known what to make, so foreign is Carmen
to anything in her small and homogeneous experience—she
has always felt an active goodwill; she never fails, upon
seeing Susan, to "ask after" her mother, as she did now,
characteristically forgetting that we're on our way to, not
from, Baltimore.

Fenn's parents are both deaf, their hearing-aids not much
help. We speak, spoke, loudly to them: Fine! We're just fine!
Carmen's just fine! Miriam, Grandma Seckler, tout le
monde, just fine! Nope, not a word about Gus! Nothing new
about Manfred, either!

I swear, sighed Virgie, firing up a fresh Winston king-size:
it don't make sense. Does it to you? Fenn kissed his mother's
weary, whiskered, fallen face. She would have sighed much
that same sigh over the vagaries of the weather. Does that
mean that she feels her son's loss no more keenly? Of course
not: the defect is in her repertory of expression more than
in her range of feeling. On the other hand, she is undeniably
numb by nature as well as stoical by temper; the range of her
feelings is not to be compared to Carmen's, say, or Susan's.

All hands hugged and kissed, we stood about shouting
four-way pleasantries awhile longer on the tee of the dock.
Then the drizzle resumed. Sue went up to the house with
Virgie and Chief and Julie while Fenwick and Orrin put out
extra slip-lines to berth *Pokey* for the weekend. Later we'd
fetch in our seabags and Caribbean gifts for the company.

Father and son chatted as they secured the boat: pregnancy, molecular biology, the cruise. To spend nine days, not to mention nine months, away from his laboratory would be inconceivable to Oroonoko; his tone, respectful but bemused, made clear that he regards his father as retired, sort of. But from what? As if *he* were the affectionate but uneasy parent and his father the unlaunched child, Orrin wanted to know whether we'll be taking those academic posts we mentioned last fall, or free-lancing for a while yet, or what. When Fenn replied that we might just go on sailing till we run out of wind or money, the young man chuckled nervously, shook his head, and said Terrific!

Pulling on a spring-line to make sure there was enough slack to accommodate the tide but not enough to let the hull bump anything, Fenn asked neutrally So how's your mother, Oroonoko?

Fine. Fine.

That was that, re that. In the house, Julie was busy being pregnant: the talk was of Lamaze exercises, the recentest cautions from the Food and Drug Administration, her obstetrician's sensible middle ground on the episiotomy and local-anesthesia questions. And why not? God help them if they aren't full of the experience! And wouldn't it be too bloody much if they felt they had to curb their enthusiasm with us? All the same it stung, it stings, especially for Susan to hear of arrangements already made for Julie's mother to fly in from Chicago and Orrin's to drop in from practically next door, or up from Washington where she spends some time these days, to help out with the first postpartum weeks.

Chief and Virgie looked on benignly, hearing nothing, interrupting with cordial non sequiturs. In midst of Orrin's talk of RNA and Escherichia coli, Chief wanted to know how Fenn thought the Iranian hostage situation, specifically the failed U.S. rescue attempt, would affect Jimmy Carter's chances for reelection. Virgie declared there was enough chicken to go around for dinner, but warned that she's not the cook she used to be. We conducted at least three simultaneous conversations aloud, at least two more unspoken. Before long, Chief was back to his daily newspapers, Virgie to her ever-present coffee and crossword puzzles, both of them relieved that we have one another to talk to instead of just themselves.

They couldn't have cared less about *our* goddamn nine-month adventure, Susan complains from the companionway. She means Orrin and Julie, not Virgie and Chief, to whom the thing we've done is only barely more conceivable than to Grandma Seckler. And why the hell should they care? she goes on. They're doing real things, not play things. Here's lunch.

We are about to beam-reach under the great twin spans. We have done so half a hundred times in our seven years—setting out, returning, passing by—never without a happy small frisson. Fenn lifts his Perrier in salute: Hello, Bridge.

Hello, Bridge, Sue echoes, and busses his cheek. What a kvetch I am today.

Welcome back.

Sometime on the Sunday, briefly and obliquely, just before Orrin and Julie drove off Bostonward, Fenn spoke to his son about possible pitches from undercover agents. His old friend Dugald Taylor, he declared, had happened to mention that possibility in a general way, vis-à-vis the regrettable likelihood that an election-year Congress on the defensive about the state of our military preparedness would reopen the Pandora's box of germ-warfare research. Assuming they did, Fenn reported Taylor as having opined, any front-edge worker in the field of molecular biology might be of at least hypothetical interest to unfriendly governments, our own included. What did Orrin think?

To his father's pleasure, the young man dismissed the idea as most unlikely, even paranoid. Research in his field was unclassified; indeed, the problem was the reverse of secrecy: researchers rushing to "go public" for fame's sake with less than meticulously tested findings. Moreover, his particular expertise would be of interest only to very high-scientific cultures, of which the only officially unfriendly one had more people in germ- and chemical-warfare research than we. His own projects were such basic science as to be of no direct interest even to the medical profession, much less the military; nor had he information of any use to governments friendly or unfriendly, nor access to such information. He laughed: Even if he were kidnapped, his captors would have to send him back to graduate school to catch up with their own nasty-germ people; that sort of thing was out of his line. Finally, it might reassure Fenwick and Dugald Taylor to hear that as far as he and his colleagues could judge, neither the U.S. nor the U.S.S.R. was very interested these days in germ warfare. The delivery technology was too unreliable; the bacteria were as dangerous to their users as those wild animals Lucretius talks about in that crazy passage in De Rerum Natura.* Chemicals were another thing.

Fenn smiled. I'll tell Doog not to worry. But what would you say if you *were* pitched by our side? To work up at Edgewood Arsenal or wherever. And if not on germs, then on chemicals.

Orrin smiled too. You pitching me, Dad? And he added at once (clear and gratifying evidence that the possibility was not startling news to him): If the pitch was an invitation, I'd say Bugger off. If it was a threat—against anybody except Julie and the kid—I'd blow the whistle. If it was a threat to Julie and the kid . . . He kissed his father's brown brow. I'd discuss it with my dad.

He's a grown-up, Fenn says, beaming. How did I come to have a thirty-year-old grown-up scientist kid? And Julie's okay. More than okay.

They're good for each other, Susan acknowledges.

---

*Book V, wherein, having described in grisly detail how the wild boars, bulls, and lions deployed by early armies turned against and savaged their deployers, the poet doubts whether even military men wouldn't foresee such a backfiring, and concludes that wild-animal warfare must have happened elsewhere in the universe than on Earth.

They're a good couple. They'll be good parents. I wish I were dead.

We are under the bridges, abeam of Sandy Point Light. We close-haul and beat as northwesterly as possible toward Baltimore Light and Gibson Island.

The rest of that weekend never mind. Our sleeping in Fenn's and Manfred's adolescent bedroom. The two younger women's taking over from Virgie (glad now to relinquish any responsibility) the preparation of our meals, assisted by their husbands, and exchanging recipes for squash soups and cold borschts. Fenn's tending bar; Orrin's barbecuing; the younger couples' throwing Frisbee on the lawn and, all but Julie, swimming off the dock in the still cool but not yet nettled Wye. The three generations of men's inspecting the premises together so that Fenn can schedule the necessary maintenance during our summer there, and Fenwick's realizing—for the first time, really—that, given Manfred's death, within the decade Key Farm will be his and Susan's.

And a few decades later, Sue says now, Orrin's and Julie's, and then your grandson's. I envy them. It's killing me.

That's not quite a foregone conclusion, Fenn objects.

Who wants that house anyhow, Susan says perversely. It's a grandmother house. And by the end of June you can't swim in the goddamn water.*

---

*Give or take a week, depending on rainfall and the consequent degree of estuarine salinity. By July, in a normal Chesapeake summer, the stinging medusa jellyfish, Chrysaora quinquecirrha, infests all but the topmost (freshwater) reaches of the Bay and its tributaries, except for certain rare and privileged creeks and coves. The sea nettle occurs in such numbers that by Independence Day no square meter of brackish Chesapeake can be assumed to be sting-free; yet the creature has no significant ecological value: not even, like the formidable Dorchester County saltmarsh mosquito, the reduction of human population pressures on the tidewater environment. Most waterfront-owners seem to prefer boating and fishing—or swimming-pool swimming—to bathing in the natural element. Not so us, enemies of air-conditioning except in extremis and of swimming-pools except for rinsing sea-salt off our skins, and to whom an airless, humid, 90° Chesapeake Saturday afloat is corporal punishment if we cannot hourly strip and dunk. We have a problem here,

Let's cross that bridge when et cetera, says Fenn; we'll be too busy this summer to do much swimming anyhow. He's done with lunch. *Pokey*'s steering himself. At sea, in all but roughest weather, we read a lot: indeed, like any proper sabbatical, our long cruise has been among other things an immersion, beneficial but not nettle-free, in the sea of print. Fenwick has now a clearer idea than he did last fall of what's happened in the world of occidental fiction since circa 1960, when he ceased to pay close attention to it: the Beat Generation has degenerated, the Existentialists no longer exist, the French New Novelists have grown old, the Angry Young Men are middle-aged and petulant, the Black Humorists are serious and tenured, the Jews are assimilated, the Latinos are lively and expatriated, the blacks and redskins pale by comparison, the homosexuals are still clearing their throats, the new feminists aren't impressive though numerous women writers are, Master Nabokov is dead, Master Beckett is silent, Master Borges has turned into Rudyard Kipling, the Nobel prize is being awarded like Swedish foreign aid to obscure authors whom even smart Susan has scarcely heard of and who evidently lose everything but their kroners in translation, there's something called Postmodernism, and, so it seems to our Fenn, lots of room at the top in the decade ahead. Susan has waded with a chip on her shoulder but an essentially open mind through the literary-critical structuralists, deconstructionists, semioticists, and neo-Nietzscheans of Paris, New Haven, and Milwaukee, and been disappointed to find her worst hick prejudices confirmed: one third incomprehensible to her not untrained intelligence, one third comprehensible but bullshitful, the third third mostly irrelevant to what in her

---

which, while of no higher rank in the scale of human problems than the medusa itself, has inspired these verses in Fenwick's notebook for our story:

> Chrysaora quinquecirrha!
> Who'd have thought he'd ever hear a
> Name so lovely laid upon dumb
> Pests as ugly as used condoms?

innocence she still takes to be the critical enterprise: shedding light upon literature. Fenwick's sailing forward with pleasure toward Italo Calvino and Gabriel García Márquez; Susan's backwatering to Aristotle by way of galley proofs of Nabokov's posthumous *Lectures on Literature*, which a friend has sent her c/o Chief and Virgie and which—with her love for Fenn, her affection for the old folks, and her bottom-line perspective on herself—has got her through the strainful weekend and back aboard. But in the busy enclosed waters of the Bay, one of us must always be on watch even when we're self-steering: buoys, beacons, freighters, crab and eel pots, fish stakes, clam lines, trotline floats, fishing boats, runabouts, other sailboats, bridges, and, to be sure, the land itself, both under and beside the water.

It's Sue's turn now. Fenn's writing another notebook-note in that pet form of his,

### ON NARRATIVE VIEWPOINT, SELECTIVITY, AND ADVANCEMENT OF THE ACTION.

FENWICK: What are our options? I mean viewpointwise, for our story. Run them by me, would you, hon?

SUSAN: You mean narrative points of view? First person. Second person. Third person.

F: That's it?

S: Oh, well. First person as either observer or protagonist, and singular or plural, and reliable or unreliable. Third person objective, omniscient, or limited-omniscient so to speak. Third person limited-omniscient limited to protagonist or observer. Third person effaced. Et cetera.

F: I'm listening.

S: Any of the above unitized, shiftified, Cuisinarted, farmisht.

F: That's all?

S: I may have left out some weirdos. But our distinguished predecessors in the storytelling trade appear to have found this basic repertory of viewpoints sufficient to their purposes.

F: We'll use 'em all.

S: Unh-unh. You'll make a mishmash.

F: Omniscient, then. Total omniscience, sprit to transom, masthead to keel.

S: That's not done much either, after Tolstoy and his crowd. Roving omniscience—

F: Not roving: galloping omniscience! Nantucket sleighride omniscience! I want our story told from the point of view of you and me, Orrin, Count, Miriam, Carmen B. Seckler, Grandma, Chief and Virgie, Marilyn Marsh, President Carter, the Ayatollah Khomeini, *Pokey*, my boina, your left ovary, Betelgeuse, and the bluefish I think we just snagged on our trolling line.

S: Got away. Nothing would get told, Fenn. Our story would be like those faculty-student meetings in the Sixties, where everybody from the deans to the Maoist cadres and the janitors had to have their say, and no business got done.

F: Let a hundred flowers blossom. Couple dozen, anyhow.

S: I can hear them now: Where do you roses get off, looking down your elitist stems at us sturdy weeds? We're all flowers, really.

F: Right on. All power to the wiregrass. Off the orchids. Aphid rights.

S: We've got to decide. Do we cultivate our garden or let it go to democratic weed?

F: I never promised you a rose garden, Suse.

S: It's not too late to correct that oversight.

F: I promise you a rose garden.

S: Roses only.

F: Couple of petunias, maybe. Geraniums in there for summer. Half a dozen chrysanthemums for fall.

S: Okay. But flowers only.

F: You surprise me, Susan. What will Miriam say? Where's your residual populism?

S: Out there with my gardening shoes, on the muddy threshold of our story. Crabgrass and aphids have their place in nature, but not in our story. Agreed?

F: Fetch me my trowel, my malathion, my shears, my bone meal!

S: We'll begin by weeding out this dialogue.

F: Not all of it. Anything's allowed to stay that contributes to the exposition or the characterization, or advances the action.

S: Like?

F: Like my remarking that you've had trouble lately keeping your breakfasts down.

Sue suddenly squeezes the tiller and lifeline, clenches shut her eyes, and calls Andrew!

Fenn starts up from his writing. What?

Alexis!

He wonders whether his wife has come unhinged. Sits up straight. Honey?

Susan's crying now; her cry subsides into lament. Lexeee! Droo hoo hoo hoo!

Ah.* Fenn rises to her, offers to take the helm. She shrugs him away: You don't have to take over like the big macho man.

Susan teaches her students that the main use of weather in fiction, other than causing shipwrecks and driving potential lovers into romantic shelter, is either reinforcement of or contrast with the prevailing mood. Today is reinforcement day: at her despairing invocation of those dear names and nicknames, Zeus hits the heavenly rheostat: the dry, week-end-clearing sun and breeze give quick way to altocumulus overcast. By anchoring-time there will be light windless rain.

I *am* the big macho man, Fenwick grumbles. But have it your way.

Now it's anchoring-time. Slickered against the easy rain, sails furled and covered, we motor into the still mouth of the Magothy, past Pavilion Peak on the southern tip of Gibson Island; we spiral up clockwise along the high-banked,

---

*Those are the names by which, had we children, we would name them, son and daughter, daughter and son; see page 219.

mansioned shore, through Sillery Bay and Magothy Narrows into Gibson's perfect harbor, full of empty yachts at permanent moorings, and beyond it into snug Redhouse Cove. We lower the plow, back down to set it, shut off the diesel, do not kiss, briefly survey the dripping cove that we have many times enjoyed in better weathers. To supplement the companionway dodger we rig a boom-tent—more secure than an awning should the wind come on to blow—and retire below, where we peel out of our foul-weather gear and sit about in the gray light, saying little. In other spirits we would enjoy this weather: light rain, snug early anchorage, cozy cabin. We would read; we would write letters, chat, spend a long while making and eating dinner while switching the FM between the Eighteenth and Nineteenth centuries. Perhaps make love again, perhaps not; go to bed early; sleep well. But we're out of sorts; our story's hanging fire. We speak desultorily, as if waiting for the plot of our lives to get on with it. E.g.,

## POE AGAIN:

Susan's friend Edgar Poe declares correctly (in "Eureka") that while from the perspective of Earth—say from Baltimore—our galaxy looks like the capital letter Y, "in reality" it is a disc of stars, a flat swirl or Saturn-like ring. Something like the reverse, it seems to Fenwick and he observes to Susan, is true of our story.

She fingers the bloodstain on the settee cushion and says nothing.

What Fenn means is that though tying up at Chief and Virgie's dock, Key Farm, Wye I., completed our irregular circuit, it ended neither our sabbatical nor our cruise. We have business in Baltimore, business in Baltimore, reachable from Gibson Island by a spur of the city's busline principally designed to carry black maids and gardeners from their apartments in the city to their jobs on the estates across the sentried causeway. We're not sure how long our boat will be riding at anchor here: two days? Two weeks? We're not sure where we'll be going when next we raise that anchor. *Pokey*'s in a cove, but Fenwick and Susan are at a Y.

## NAME-LOSS IN THE MYTHS OF WANDERING HEROES

Yeah, says Susan, but her mind is not on Edgar Poe and the galaxy; it's on business in Baltimore. She observes, not to be unfriendly, that the middles of myths of wandering heroes from many cultures share the feature of the hero's losing or concealing his name, just as he may lose his bearings, his companions, his ship, his clothes, his genital organs, and any other ties to the daylit waking reality he has left behind for the twilit zone of his adventure. Okay? But we have of our daughter Alexis and our son Andrew, Drew and Lexie, Lexie and Drew, only their names. Moreover, if we literally don't know where we're going from Gibson Island and Baltimore, it's because figuratively we don't know where we are.

## MINOR CHARACTERS

Right. For that matter, we have of Drew's and Lexie's hypothetical grandmother Carmen B. Seckler little more than her name and some nondramatic exposition and long-distance dialogue. In our present mood, Fenn wonders either aloud or to his notebook whether formidable Carmen has been earning her keep in our story. The artist Robert Rauschenberg once acquired a drawing by the artist Willem de Kooning, erased the drawing, and exhibited what was left under the title Erased de Kooning, Robert Rauschenberg. If Carmen B. Seckler isn't going to do more than she's done so far towards advancing our action or percolating our plot, Fenn thinks maybe we ought to erase even what little we have of her in the story thus far; drop her from the payroll, even though she is Susan's mother,

Manfred's ex-common-law wife, and one of Fenwick's favorite people.

Go ahead, says sullen Sue. This is a zero-base-budget story.

No hitchhikers, agrees dour Fenn. No freeloaders. No featherbedders.

Gas, Grass, or Ass, growls Susan: Nobody Rides Free.

Fenn begs her pardon?

That's what the initials stood for on Junior Parsons's crash helmet when he gave me a lift on his Harley-Davidson from Swarthmore to Baltimore when I was hitching home in Nineteen Sixty-four or -five, my sophomore year.

Fenwick says Pause.

Says Susan He had crapulous skin and smelled like asafetida, but he was kind of cute. Junior Parsons: G.G.A.N.R.F.

Dot dot dot says Fenwick.

I bought him two gallons of regular.

Sigh of relief, says Fenwick. Well: let's give your mother due process before we delete her. I'll call her up and tell her we'll be in town tomorrow and ask her what's new. We introduced her in Act One; if she advances the action here in Act Two, Doctor Seckler's Rule of Thrice for Minor Characters obliges us to bring her on again in the last act.

Let me call Grandma first, says Susan. Why don't you go up on the front porch and get some air and rig the anchor light so Gram and I can talk.


## SMELTS

Fenwick comes back below when he hears Susan over and out on the radiotelephone. So what did you talk about? Despite worrisome half-thoughts of Orrin, Julie, Susan, it has been pleasant sitting on the foredeck in the mild spring evening drizzle watching ground-fog form around Redhouse Cove and listening to what little he can hear of Susan's conversation with Havah Moscowitz Seckler. He is gratified

to see that, as almost always after talking to her grandmother, his friend is in much better humor.

Smelts.

?

Grandma couldn't remember smelts. I was trying to get
her to remember smelts.

Ah.

We haven't made smelts in a hundred years so I thought
while we're doing our business in Baltimore I'd stop by
Lexington Market and buy smelts but I'd forgotten how
Gram used to fix them so I asked her but she couldn't
remember what smelts meant and I couldn't remember the
Yiddish word for them because smelts sounds Yiddish
already and besides the hearing-aid thing on her phone isn't
working too well and there was some noise on the radio
channel and I forgot to twiddle the squelch knob. Poor
Gram: she was so weak and tired.

Pleased Fenn strokes his whiskers. Your second conversation with your grandmother in nine months, and you
talk for ten minutes about smelts to get her to remember the
word.

I don't want Gram to forget things! It was hard getting
through to her: she's so weak it wears her out to pay
attention, and then she starts worrying she's senile. But boy
oh boy did she ever come to life when she realized it was
*smelts* I was asking her about. She calls them shmelts, like
melted shmaltz; no wonder I thought the word was Yiddish.
But then she says Aha, *shmelts*, do I know shmelts, and off
she goes: You take a liddle this, a liddle that, did I remember
Lieberman's on Park Heights Avenue where she used to get
her smoked whitefish and her carp for gefilte fish and her
shmelts before the neighborhood changed? And by Lieberman was Ravitz the tailor where Grandpa Allan had his suits
made, and on and on she goes, every store on the old block,
how much for chicken livers in Nineteen Fifty.

Fenn kisses her forehead. So how do we smelt smelts?

Susan slumps. It doesn't matter.

Suse?

Oh, basically you fry the little fuckers. The point is, Grams has got smelts now to think about till she sees me tomorrow. Call Ma, okay?

## CARMEN B. SECKLER
### STAYS IN THE STORY FOR SURE,
### BUT HAS TROUBLE WITH THE FACTS OF LIFE.

Okay. Do we tell her she's on notice in our story or not? Not.

Fenwick places a call through the Baltimore marine operator to Carmen's Place on Aliceanna Street in Fells Point. The weather's uncertain for barbecuing off our stern pulpit, but Susan has already thawed a small pork tenderloin roast since noon; we'll take the chance. She fits the charcoal grille into its bracket, starts the coals, uncorks a Sonoma Valley cabernet sauvignon, *Pokey*'s house red, for us to sip in lieu of cocktails while her husband and her mother talk. In five or seven gravelly sentences, depending on punctuation, loudspeakered from the VHF, Carmen B. Seckler pays her dues.

Fenwick! Where the hell are you guys?

Gibson Island Harbor, more or less. Over.

Chief and Virgie sort of thought you were headed straight here. I called them. Did you see today's papers?

Nope.

Get a drink. I was trying to reach you. Bad news.

Fenn and Sue, fearing different things, exchange a glance. What's up, Carmen?

Dugald Taylor died of a heart attack in Sydney Australia.

Susan makes a sound. Fenwick closes his eyes.

It happened on the Qantas Airways Seven Forty-seven, actually. No other details. Over.

Save the paper for us, Carmen.

I did already. You coming in tomorrow?

Early. Fenn shakes his head hard, trying to register the news. I haven't checked the buses. Before noon, I hope.

What do you mean the buses. I'll pick you up at ten.
We'll be staying a few days, Carmen. You got room?
What a goyishe question.
What a Yiddishe answer.
Did Doog have a history, Fenn?
Heart stuff? Not really. Yeah, one episode, milder than mine.

Carmen pauses. So, it happens. I'm sorry to bring the bad news. Drink a drink, Fenwick. Let me talk to Susele. Over.

Susan, tears streaming, shakes her head no but takes the microphone Fenn hands her. He sits on the settee, stunned. Susan wipes tears and swallows red wine and talks and listens. Conversation with Carmen B. Seckler takes odd turns. Via life and death and smelts again and the confirmation of some appointments in town, hairdresser, gynecologist, their talk comes to the elementary processes of sexual reproduction. All children, Carmen B. Seckler declares apropos of something or other, are actually grandchildren. All parents are actually grandparents. Over.

Susan blows her nose on a tissue. What?

What's more, in Carmen's opinion, women and men don't actually reproduce sexually. This truth has always given her trouble, she reports; she thinks it insufficiently appreciated, especially by a country that talks about nothing but sex sex sex. Over.

Ma: you sound half smashed.

Dugald was my friend too, you know. I am half smashed. But you listen what I'm saying about sex, Shushi. Human beings are only make-pretend sexual. And like begets like only in alternate generations.

Susan gives it all three syllables: *Ma-uh-ah!* These radio calls are expensive.

So bill me, I'm going to tell you what I mean. I think of it a lot when I'm missing Fred and Mundungus. And when I'm thinking about your father, too, and you and Miriam and Fenn. You listen now; you'll see it has to do.

Susan only half believes in telepathy, extrasensory perception, and the like, by all which her mother swears. Fenwick not even half. But both appreciate, from frequent past experience, an uncanniness in Carmen B. Seckler that might as well be called psychic; and she does not speak irrelevantly ever. What she means in this instance, as reconstructed somewhile after in Fenwick's notebook for our story, is that a woman's true children are not her human daughters and sons but the four hundred or so ova which she launches, involuntarily and without male assistance, in the thirty-odd years from her menarche to her menopause; a man's, the billions of spermatozoa he generates, also asexually, in the sixty-plus years from puberty to death. These are our children, says Carmen B. Seckler, whom we never know and nearly all of whom die without issue: among a man's, in particular, the mortality rate is brutally high, exceeding even that of striped bass.* Given the rare chance, however, these offspring of ours are truly and totally sexual: contraries, they come together, n ɔt in the pseudosexual way of their parents, one little part stuck briefly into another little part and presently withdrawn, but literally and for keeps, never to be their separate selves again, but to become something both and neither: something unlike sperm or egg, but much

---

*The normal mortality rate of striped bass, or rockfish, between the gamete and the fingerling stage, is estimated at 99.99%. Were it a few tenths of a percent lower, the Bay would be overrun with rockfish. Were it a hundredth of a percent higher, as it presently bids to become, there would be none. But if a man produce only 60,000,000 sperm per ejaculation (the middle range of human male fertility), and ejaculate on the average of thrice weekly for sixty years between puberty and death, dysfunction, or disinterest, and if with those 374,400,000,000 sperm he "father" two children, the mortality rate of his spermatozoa is on the order of 99.99999999999%, or 187,200,000,000 dead for each "survivor." Confronted with these calculations, Carmen B. Seckler will remark that by comparison to such odds, the Jews' deportation to the Nazi death-camps looks like a minor hazard, though she alone of her entire neighborhood survived it. Fenwick will ponder the irony that, such is the power of numbers, if a man, despite these odds, decide in normal circumstances to "father" two children, he probably will. Susan will say Let's change the subject.

like the parents of sperm and egg; something that in turn, but asexually, may generate the likes of them. The Aristophanes of Plato's *Symposium*, in Carmen B. Seckler's opinion, was almost but not quite right when he declared that erotic love is our vain search for our missing other half; ditto the "unitary impulse," the mystic's craving to be one with God. What both reflect in fact, insists Carmen B. Seckler, is not our sense of being the sundered fallen half of a primordial whole, but rather our unconscious memory of having been sexually conceived by the absolute union of contraries. We are not fallen, Susele; we are literally transcendent. But our nonhuman "parents" achieved what by mere "sex" we can never, and that is the reason, whether they know it or not, why all animals are sad after coitus. Over.

I'm not sad after coitus, Susan reports, as a rule. Neither's Fenn. We're more often hungry or thirsty or sleepy than sad after we fuck. Over?

Don't change the subject.

Well I've never understood that proverb, Ma. Maybe it applies to one-night stands. But I've enjoyed those, too. Haven't you?

None of your business. And don't change the subject.

What are you quoting Plato's *Symposium*, anyhow?

What are you pulling your rank? Nobody reads a book but you Pee-aitch Dees?

I'm sorry, Ma.

Fred told me all that, but he was talking about being twins: him and Fenwick, you and Miriam. The children stuff is mine. Don't change the subject, over.

What's the subject?

The subject is whether what you just heard on your expensive radio has to do.

It has to do; it has to do. I love you, Ma.

I love you, Susele. See you in the morning.

Okay.

Kiss Fenn.

Don't worry. Poor Doog.

I should say so, poor Doog.

Over and out, Ma.

Fenwick's up under the boom-tent, using up Kleenex. Susan slips her left hand down inside the front of her jeans and underpants and presses her belly, between navel and pubic hair. Pours herself another glass of red. Fetches the last of the bottle upstairs to Fenn. We speak gravely together of Dugald Taylor, heirless; of probable memorial services; of other things. Presently we make dinner.

Subdued Fenwick decides not to tell her now.

Subdued Susan decides not to tell him now.

# 2
# GIBSON TO CACAWAY
## *The Fork*

T 6/10/80. Redhouse Cove. 0800 up anchor. Cldy, cool, lt rain, still. Half tide falling. Head for Gibson I. Yacht Club boathouse to rent a few days' parking.

0810 hard aground at mouth of Redhouse, on shoal off N shore of entrance.

Fenwick stops talking to the log-book—he wrote while steering with tiller between thighs as Susan secured the anchor on its roller chock, and thus we've managed to run aground on an unmarked but clearly charted shoal of whose existence we were quite aware—says Shit, and we get busy, before the falling tide leaves us stuck until suppertime. Just a few hundred yards dead ahead across the harbor is our destination, the club dock; but the shoal projects between the deeper water of Redhouse Cove behind us and the deeper water of Gibson Island Harbor ahead. To go forward, we must go back.

Luckily for us, no wind or wave action drives us harder aground; and in our Chesapeake a piloting error sets us on sand or mud, not rock or reef. It is no emergency. But shit. Had we been port-tacking to windward, we'd merely sheet in hard now and lean over the lee rail, in hopes our heeling would lift the keel clear, and leeway and sternway take us off. As is, Fenn tries first a quick thrust of the diesel in reverse; when it fails to budge us, he idles in neutral lest stirred-up silt foul the engine water-pump, and we run down our familiar order of expedients. Sue takes the helm; Fenn pushes the main boom, supported by its topping lift, far out to starboard and climbs out to the end of it atop the furled and covered sail—clumsy work in foul-weather gear—to heel us over while Susan tries reverse again. No go. Promptly then (our tide will drop two inches an hour: not much by New England or coast-of-Brittany standards, but every fifteen minutes of unsuccess leaves seven tons of sailboat a half-inch higher and drier) Fenn scrambles inboard, leaves the boom as it is, manhandles spare ground tackle from the lazarette and perches it on the starboard gunwale, pops into the dinghy, loads the spare anchor and rode aboard, rows fifty yards astern, lowers the anchor into ten or twelve feet of water, and rows back to *Pokey*, letting the rode pay out from the dinghy en route. Now he hands the rode to Susan in the cockpit, secures the dinghy, and climbs back aboard while Susan leads the rode to the starboard jib-sheet winch, takes three turns around the drum, pulls the line taut and cleats it, then moves to the engine controls. Beside her now, Fenwick claps a handle into the winch, uncleats the line, cranks clockwise (high gear for speed) until he feels the anchor set, then counterclockwise (low gear for power) and says our first word since Shit.

Okay.

He sets up hard on the winch, and harder; the nylon rode stretches and stretches. Susan gives us more throttle in reverse. *Pokey* swings his stern a bit; Fenn cranks in to the lastmost click; Sue ups the RPMs a touch; muddy water swirls about; we worry; the dinghy, on short scope, bumps against the transom. Just as Fenwick stands to go forward and climb out on the boom again, we slide astern. He dives for the winch, snatches up the slack, cranks in hard. Susan eases the throttle. We're off.

With the engine running in neutral not to foul anything, Fenwick retrieves the ground tackle, pulling us hand over hand stern-first back into Redhouse Cove. Our list of tricks for getting off was far from exhausted; the next expedient, unappealing in the chilly rain, would have been for Fenn to strip and go over the side, crouch submerged under *Pokey*'s forefoot, and push up and back while Susan throttled in reverse. Crude but effective, conditions permitting: Fenn stands six feet, *Pokey* draws five; he can rest and breathe between underwater heaves. But once, alone and aground on a mild Tred Avon mudbank, he foolishly neglected to tie a line between himself and the boat, pushed himself knee-deep into the muck in his successful effort to shove *Pokey* free, and had frantically to work himself out by his own bootstraps, so to speak, underwater, while the cutter glided off downtide. It is the nearest he has ever come to drowning, and thus planted firmly in the placid river-bottom (it occurred to him at the time), his dead body might well have stayed put despite the gases of decomposition and gone undiscovered for a long time, perhaps forever, especially if the boat had drifted a fair way on its own before running ashore and thereby misled the eventual search party. We have more than once considered this scenario vis-à-vis Manfred, a less expert and more reckless sailor, who, despite Fenn's cautionary retelling of this tale, might just possibly have gone aground last spring, neglected in his haste to log the circumstance or secure himself with a lifeline, pushed *Pokey* free from underwater, and found himself stuck like a submerged piling, suddenly four feet tall in five feet of water, until blue crabs picked his naked corpse clean and storm-waves dispersed his bones.

But would there not have been hastily-shed clothing in the cockpit? A pair of shorts? Deck shoes? And would Count have tried this last resort first, before attempting to kedge off with the spare anchor? Possible but unlikely: Manfred disappeared early in the season, when the Bay water is too chilly to enter without a wet-suit and as a *very* last resort. It would have made more sense, if he couldn't kedge off, for him to leave an anchor out in deep water and wait for the tide, or hail a passing vessel. Even if foul weather threatened (it didn't), he'd have done better to stay aboard, with the boat, and radio the Coast Guard if he found himself unable to get off when the weather passed and the tide returned: we are speaking, after all, of a hypothetical four-foot shoal somewhere near the mouth of the quiet Wye, not a knife-edged, shark-patrolled coral reef pounded by the open ocean. Yet even the careful—and Manfred in his pleasures was not remarkably careful—can make imprudent, un-characteristic, or merely incorrect decisions.

Fenwick thinks heavily once again of all this as he hauls us backwards into Redhouse Cove, retrieves and stows the heavy Danforth, and makes more cautious headway toward the main harbor and the club dock. He has thought heavily of it many times, especially when *Pokey* happens to bump bottom—not a rare event in Chesapeake waters. But in this matter no amount of going back has yet enabled us to go forward.

We're warm now from exertion; the light rain tapers off; we shed our slickers. Literary Susan speaks of other goings-back-to-go-forward: Odysseus's return to Circe's island to bury his lost shipmate Elpenor before proceeding on toward Ithaca; Aeneas's return,* before sailing on to the promised land, to bury the body of his faithful helmsman Palinurus, whose unquiet spirit chides him in Hades as Manfred's never chides Fenn in dreams. For that matter, all such heroes' descents into the underworld, where the spirits of the great dead enable and advise them on their future course.

Where must we go back to? Fenwick asks, bemused. Key Island, to find my boina? Keep your eye out: it'll come to us.

Says Susan We fleshed beck already to the Big Benk, and it didn't tell us where to go. Time to move on. She puts out portside fenders, makes docklines ready.

We are not ourselves yacht-clubbers; no burgee at our starboard spreader entitles us to reciprocal privileges. Our

---

*Rather, his *requested* return: the efficient Roman poet makes other arrangements to spare his hero any actual backtracking.

GIYC connection is dear dead Dugald Taylor, once a yachtsman himself, whose family have been Gibson Islanders for a century. In a file of like bona fides we carry a letter some years old from Doog to the then commodore, asking that we be extended visitors' courtesies. We tie up at the first convenient empty space; while Susan off-loads our small supply of perishables into a Styrofoam cooler and gets our go-ashore gear together, Fenwick bears off Dugald's letter in search of dockmaster, club manager, or other adequate official.

He finds one in the club boathouse, at the island end of the causeway that links Gibson to the world and divides its harbor from the Chesapeake: a fortyish fellow, Henry, with a heavy Baltimore accent, in annoyed conversation on a telephone. It is *not* okay, he declares to whomever he's speaking with: I don't care if you know her or not; she can't be picking up nobody here because there ain't nobody here to pick. Hold it.

Smiling, pointing to himself, waving Dugald's letter, Fenwick has caught Henry's eye. Yes, we are expecting a lady from Baltimore to meet us by car along about now, if the security chap will please allow her across the causeway. True, the addressee of our letter is no longer club commodore; indeed, Fenn now learns, is no longer among the living. Its author, too, has lately gone to rest. But you, sir, we, and the GIYC sail on for at least another summer; may we hope that the wishes of these dear eminent ex-shipmates will be honored in their absence?

Awright. We are permitted five nights at a vacant mooring whose regular tenant is en route up the Intracoastal from wintering in Florida. The rent is nominal, since we shall be using no dockside facilities; but we must begone by Sunday noon, or our boat will be towed at our expense and risk to the yard across the harbor, to clear the mooring for its owner. Fair enough: Fenn pays in advance and leaves Henry his name and Carmen B. Seckler's telephone number. Is it some kind of nut lady coming to get us? She's giving Freddie a time over there.

That is no nut lady, sir: that is my wife's mother, the well-known Baltimore restaurateuse Carmen B. Seckler. Of Carmen's Place, Aliceanna Street, Fells Point?

Henry's face lights up. He clearly wants to say No shit! But we are in the Gibson Island Yacht Club boathouse, not Carmen's Place. No kidding! The day is carried. Our mooring is pointed out to us, and our slot in the dinghy rack; Fred is instructed by phone to let the lady pass.

Meanwhile, Susan has off-loaded onto the dock our seabags, garment bags, briefcases, and cooler. As we thread back through the anchorage to pick up our assigned mooring among the local fleet, we see a familiar white Mercedes crossing the causeway, a bicycle racked on its trunk. By the time we've secured all lines, closed all sea-cocks, lockers, and hatches, and set out dockwards in the dinghy, Carmen B. Seckler is with the club manager beside our gear, in exuberant, gesticulating conversation. Like everyone in her purview—Susan, already waving and bouncing in the stern-seat; Fenn, nerves glowing even though he faces backwards and catches only the odd glance overshoulder as he rows—Henry is enjoying himself. It is a livelier chapter than it would have been that has Carmen B. Seckler in it.

Her errand has brought out the Bizet in her: Carmen's black hair is pinned into a tight bun; she wears a wide-brimmed Andalusian riding hat of tooled and silver-blazoned leather with a braided lanyard, and low-uppered high-heeled boots to match; a white wraparound skirt slit sportingly up the side opposite the overlap, which she displays by planting one boot on our Styrofoam chest as on a slain bull's; a blouse to match her skirt and car; a black bolero jacket with intricate silver needlework; a bright Mexican woven belt cinched at the hip and tailing to the knee, not unlike the one we've brought her from Cancún; gold Gypsy earrings, several necklaces in her brown décolletage, several rings, several gold and silver bracelets. She smokes and conducts her conversation with a cigarillo in a stubby white holder, by turns brandishing it like a baton and speaking around it through her teeth. Carmen B. Seckler's skin and eyes are rich morena; she has heavy unplucked eyebrows and an unabashed mustache. She's a lean mid-fifty, Carmen, and in fine trim.

Hi, Ma! Sue bounds onto the dock like an excited schoolgirl, almost tipping the dinghy, to embrace her mother. Carmen B. Seckler's lipstick and eye makeup are soon mussed; she happily clucks and growls; Susan's grunts and squeals sound almost sexual; the women cover each other's faces, necks, and hair with kisses. Henry steps back, grins, nods. By the time Fenn's on the dock, Carmen is holding Susan off at arm's length, the better to turn and inspect her from head to foot before the next embrace. Things Fenwick can't follow are exchanged in merry Yiddish.

Now it's his turn. Oy, what a bull, Carmen says as he squeezes her. She smells of tobacco and good perfume. Sailing does things for you, eh?

Your daughter does things for me. He half-turns her, as she had Susan. Somebody's been doing good things for you, Carm.

The way her mother has with every sideglance, tilt of chin, turn of shoulder, Sue often jokingly complains, makes herself at thirty-five feel like a convent virgin.

Wait till you see, says Carmen B. Seckler.

Susan cries, excited, Ma?

But Carmen turns the subject off, asking Henry with a brilliant smile whether we've cleared Gibson Island customs and may go. Soon as I stow the dink, says Fenwick. Charmed Henry helps him carry it to the numbered rack and then—repeating with pleasure the words Carmen of Carmen's Place, huh?—helps fetch our gear into the Mercedes trunk. Pleased to've met you, ma'am, he declares through the driver's window; y'all have a nice day now. I'll keep an eye on your boat there, Mister Turner.

Fenwick says We thank you. Carmen B. Seckler completes her quick conquest with a serious sidelong left-eye wink as she shifts into gear; Freddie-at-the-checkpoint, as she calls

the bald causeway security guard, waves us through with a
grin and gets for his cooperativeness half-lowered eyelids
and a small, quickly-mouthed kiss through the windowglass.
Some Fred* he is, Carmen grumbles, gratified. He should
live so long.

Susan, beside her on the passenger seat, sighs happily I
wish *I* were sexy.

Fenn volunteers from the back seat that there is Sexual
Sexy, which no Seckler woman isn't, and then there is the
Sexy that comes from crossing borders with shaky papers.
Carmen smiles into the rearview mirror around her
cigarillo: You don't think it's just the Habañera drag?

If I wore it, they'd laugh, Susan says. Her mother replies if
I took it off, they'd laugh. Fenn gallantly declares them both
mistaken.

So how's your Caribbean Sea?

Fast losing its innocence, Fenn answers. Susan presses:
Never mind the Caribbean, Ma. Tell us about your new
friend. How come Mimsi didn't mention him?

Because I told Mimsi not to. Carmen B. Seckler gives us
each a full several-second gaze (at 55 mph) before replying
He manages the Fells Point operation so I can do real estate
and get ready for Harborplace. Dumitru. Mostly Romanian.
Accent on the second syllable, but I call him Do-Me-True.
And he does.

Sue moves across the seat to kiss her mother's cheek.
Carmen announces that we'll be the first occupants of the
newly remodeled apartment above the bar-restaurant and
below Miriam's and Eastwood's third-floor quarters. It was
her own apartment until she bought and redid the adjoining
rowhouse for herself and Do-Me-True; she hopes eventually
to persuade Grandma to move into it; meanwhile it's for us
whenever we need it and for other visitors when we don't.
Real estate, she reports, has become her hobby again, as in

---

*Fenwick calls his brother Count; Grandma Seckler calls him Manny;
Carmen B. Seckler calls him Fred.

the 1950s: she's buying up Fells Point rowhouses to convert into townhouses when Baltimore's downtown redevelopment combines with the next big gasoline shortage to make the area fashionable to live and shop in as well as to drink in. But the new Carmen's in Harborplace, the city's showcase on the Inner Harbor, is her special passion. It is scheduled to open before Labor Day; her interminable consultations with architects, decorators, bankers, city officials, and the Tarot deck are what have kept her sane in her double bereavement. By no means poor before, Carmen B. Seckler expects the new decade to make her rich unless the country goes bust altogether, a prospect at which she shrugs. Kerflooeyhood has been good for her. How long will we be staying?

Through the weekend. There must be a mountain of mail and piled-up business. If we need more city time next week, we'll move *Pokey* up to Baltimore on Sunday.

The apartment is ours as long as we need it, Carmen reaffirms. And after our Baltimore business is done?

Susan says quickly Ask us Saturday. Fenn wants to know whether Carmen has heard anything further about Doog. Any memorial service or whatever?

Their eyes meet in the rearview mirror. Carmen has heard nothing. Fenwick decides he'll telephone a few people; maybe even pay a visit to Langley once he's tested the water. Unthinkable that only last week he and Dugald lunched at the Cosmos. He considers the back of Carmen's head as she sighs and shakes it.

Sue wonders whether we've time for quick detours to Fort McHenry and then to Westminster Churchyard when we pass through downtown Baltimore en route to Fells Point. The official reason is to thank the spirits of our alleged respective forebears for a safe return.* But the harbor view from McHenry's star-shaped ramparts was a favorite of

---

*The fort, of course, inspired in September 1814 Francis Scott Key's "Defense of Fort M'Henry," later retitled "The Star-Spangled Banner." Edgar Poe, his young wife Virginia Clemm, and his mother-in-law are buried in Old Westminster Churchyard at Fayette and Greene streets.

Manfred's; the Poe grave a pet haunt of Gus's; in our family, since last year, those shrines have become their cenotaphs.

 Sure. We have other errands, too (Carmen B. Seckler seldom sails the rhumb line): Lexington Market, to buy fresh squid and mussels for the restaurant; Pikesville, to pick up Grandma. We detour off 295 into the Locust Point area, to Key Highway, past marine terminals and out to the Fort. Too gray and wet yet to sit; the great banner lies limp; both arms of the harbor are still but for one large loaded freighter being eased out by tugs from its Clinton Street pier across the way. We stroll three points of the star. Carmen B. Seckler sings, half to herself, in what might be Romanian. Fenwick speaks of strange Key Island, of F. S. Key (whom we thank), of his own portentous name,* and of "flashforwards"—how they might be regarded as "male," "analytical," "upstream": forks in the channels of life and history, rather than confluences.

Carmen listens closely; asks for more.

Well: Here we stand at a fork of the Patapsco, between its Middle and its Northwest Branches. FSK, down there with the British invasion fleet off North Point in 1814, looked upstream, uswards, through the night's bombardment, at a fork in the road of U.S. history, which was then about Susan's age. His anthem queries an unknown national future.

Carmen says Mm hm.

Susan points out that Key takes hope for the Dawn's Early Light from the Twilight's Last Gleaming, reinforced by sporadic Proofs Through the Night: what might be called flashpresents, lit by Congreve rocket-glare and aerial bombburst. Once again, it is harking back that turns the key, that *is* the key, to harking forward.

Hands on hips on the rampart, Carmen B. Seckler now

---

*The Turner is German, not English: i.e., not lathe-operator, but gymnast. The portent, however, is English, and presupposes another: before one can turn a key, one must find it.

inquires what in the name of bleeding Jesus we're talking about.

Susan hugs her. Fleshbecks, Ma!

We ran aground this morning, Fenwick explains, and had to go back to go forward.

Susan to her mother: Remember Daddy and fleshbecks?

I remember everything, says Carmen B. Seckler.

Susan says Fenn says Doog says the Company has these terrific new drugs that let you walk around in your memory like in a room or a movie freeze-frame, looking for things you didn't know you noticed at the time.

Aha.

I only dreamed that, Fenn reminds her. It occurs to him, irrelevantly, that the word isomorphy sounds like frozen Irish dessert. Fingering his beard, he adds navigation by deduced reckoning to the list of pertinent isomorphies to our subject: we project our course by estimating our position by plotting our track; decide where to go by determining where we are by reviewing where we've been.

Carmen B. Seckler says surprisingly, her arms around both of us, Fooey on fleshbecks. Fooey on the Company. They think they've got potions? Any hack can do the past. It takes the White Witch of Fells Point to do the future.

Of Carmen on such matters we never quite know whether or to what extent she jokes. While we've been poking around paradise, she tells us now, she's been having long night arguments with Manfred's ghost, who appears to her usually but not always in dreams.

Ma-uh-ah!

Carmen cocks a cool dark eyebrow at her daughter. You should see him, god forbid. Cold as a carp and stinks of salt water. His skin's blue and puffy; the crabs have been at him. But he's my Fred, and stubborn as ever.

We are stirred: we beg the reader to bear in mind that Carmen B. Seckler is neither mad nor thoughtless on the one hand nor, on the other, one of us bourgeois liberal rational skeptics. Dumitru, she goes on, was on the scene already, but we weren't lovers yet. Fred wanted me to know he was kaput so I could get on with it, but I still had a bone to pick with him before I could think about another man.

She tells us then—what we had certainly surmised, but she had never heretofore quite confirmed—that her relation with Manfred, whom she still much loved, had been much strained by their son's going to Chile in 1977; they had had a terrible, scarifying row in '78 when Manfred brought her the grim news of Gus's disappearance. We'd fought plenty before, Carmen says; we had glorious fights—you remember, Susele. But never like this one. Thank god you and Mims weren't home. I called him a killer; he called me a witch. Both of us were right: Fred did kill people in his work sometimes, and I know a few things they don't teach in college. But we meant it in the awful way this time. What I wanted his ghost to know was that I still loved him even if poor Mundungus was dead; what I needed to know from him was whether that one fight in particular put him over the edge. I couldn't let Do-Me-True do me till I found out.

We are strolling no longer. Susan and Fenwick exchange Jesus-H.-Christ glances across the seat-back of Carmen's car, where we sit now in the Fort McHenry visitors' parking lot. Fenn has taught Sue to restrain her incredulity as he restrains his when her mother speaks in this vein: to try to regard it as a manner of speaking in which serious things sometimes get said. Carmen B. Seckler needs no reminding of our antisupernaturalism; she does not lightly rub our noses in her visions, voices, apparitions, cards. We hold our tongues; she starts the engine and speaks on as she drives.

Fred told me not to flatter myself that anything I ever said or did could make him kill himself. I'm summarizing: this went on night after night last winter. If you thought I was kerflooey before! Finally he persuaded me. He also said he didn't know whether Mundungus was dead or alive, but better off dead than on a Chilean prison-island. Fred checked one out and saw what goes on. After that we talked a lot about Gus, how much he'd meant to us, and about our

younger days and our life together. Fred's worried about
Miriam's going downhill. He told me how proud he is of our
Shushi and how much he loves you, Fenn. He forgives you
for the *KUDOVE* book, but his own opinions haven't
changed an inch. He said to tell you that any serious and
established intelligence outfit will overstep its bounds now
and then and Make Policy—you know how Fred used to use
that phrase. But he thinks we'd better have a strong one
until the Messiah comes.

We listen respectfully but say nothing. Fenwick wonders
whether the Company has learned to do ghosts.

Then he told me how much he'd always loved me and still
did, and I told him the same. You think ghosts can't kiss?
They can slap you around the room and fuck like billygoats,
excuse my French. Then last March, the night of his
Yortzeit,* we kissed good-bye—that took some doing—and
Fred blew out his own candle. In April I told Dumitru he
could move in.

We drive up into downtown Baltimore, past the Inner
Harbor construction. Carmen points with her cigarillo to
where the new Carmen's will be; she'll show us the details
later today. We park in the Lexington Market garage and
walk down a scrappy inner-city block to the beleaguered
churchyard at Fayette and Greene, to say Hi to Poe before
buying seafood. With difficulty Fenn refrains from asking
Carmen whether his brother's ghost in fact acknowledged
suicide while so generously exonerating her of any responsibility therefor, or whether he left the question as ambigu-
ous as Carmen's report. The image of the self-snuffed
Yortzeit candle is certainly suggestive. But ghosts, he supposes, are prone to ambiguity, especially the ghosts of
people as elusive in life as his twin.

Susan is thinking along the same lines. Our eyes all brim.
Well now, Ed, she begins to say lightly to Poe's tomb: Ma's
ghost story is more in your line than in Frank Key's. Her

---
*In Yiddish, the anniversary of someone's death.

voice clogs; the women weep together, holding each other. Fenn embraces both and walks off behind the church to get hold of his tears, voice, heart; he blows his nose beside Poe's wife and mother-in-law as his own blow theirs beside Edgar.

Oh, Mundungus! one of us cries across the brick-walled yard, over the traffic noise. If we could only know, one way or the other!

Two Japanese students or young tourists, a boy and a girl, enter the churchyard to inspect and photograph the writer's grave. We thank him for a voyage fortunately less eventful than Arthur Gordon Pym's and withdraw to busy Lexington Market—a sensory feast for the long-at-sea! Fenwick and Susan revel in that indoor acre of seafood-, meat-, and vegetable-stalls while Carmen negotiates squid and black Atlantic mussels. Fenn loads them, iced down, into a sturdy cooler beside our own in the Mercedes trunk. Carmen scowls at a bumper-sticker on the car next to hers, advertising a Fells Point competitor: EAT BERTHA'S MUSSELS.

Mims says we should print up our own for the new place, she says to Susan. Catch Carmen's Crabs. I say no.

So do we. Let's go get Gram.

We do, from her old folks' home in Pikesville, half an hour northwestward. The place is attractive, comfortable, expensive. The clientele is well off, the staff well trained, the place well run; Havah Moscowitz Seckler feels more her own woman there than she believes she'd feel in the apartment Carmen offers her in Fells Point. She also fears that if she lived next door, her daughter-in-law's energetic solicitude would inconvenience both of them more than it does now; and against the pleasure of seeing Carmen more often— and, officially, Miriam too—Havah balances the loss of her Jewish neighbors and neighborhood, together with the sadness of seeing more frequently Mim's irregular ménage and (this she speaks of only to Susan) Carmen's robust kerflooeyhood.

Gram! Susan will scold her. Ma's in amazing shape! She survived the camps and early widowhood. She managed Da's business and sold it at a profit. She raised the three of us mostly herself on account of Manfred's work, and built up a whole new successful business with her left hand while she was doing it.

I know, I know, Grandma will assure us.

She sent us to college. She takes care of Mim's crazy family without a murmur. She helps take care of you.

Don't I know? Grandma will ask. You think I don't appreciate?

Now on top of that she's lost her second husband and their only child, and she's *still* got more gusto than Mim and I together! If that's kerflooey, give me kerflooey.

You mutta issa wunnaful poison, Grandma will acknowledge.* Susan, laughing, will explain the word gusto until she's satisfied Gram understands it, then go on to pretend that she too, once her academic tenure is confirmed, means to smoke cigars and teach her class in gaucho costume. Soon Grandma's laughing for the first time since their telephone dialogue on smelts.

Havah Seckler is five feet tall and shrinking, silver-haired, and so delicately skinned in her elder age—from hiding in haystacks from Russian soldiers in her girlhood, she likes to declare—that she must use squares of percale instead of terry washcloths in the bath. From the latest of her pacemaker operations she lightly but incessantly bleeds, and the device has once again slipped out of place. Infection threatens, but all hands agree that she will not likely survive further surgery, which will therefore be postponed as long as possible—a season, perhaps two. She is plagued with arthritis as well; cannot exercise; does not sleep; lives on a diet of unseasoned food in small quantities and pills in large. It embarrasses as well as inconveniences Havah Moscowitz Seckler that she never learned to read and write: certain friends of many years' standing have not guessed the fact. Moreover, television bores her, she has no particular interest

---

*But we shall not normally record her speeches in Grandmese.

in recorded music, she is too weak to pursue a hobby, and, owing in part to her illiteracy, she is somewhat shy with people. Her waking day, therefore—all twenty-plus hours of it—is typically spent alone in her rooms, neither reading nor writing nor watching nor listening nor speaking nor working nor playing, but . . . what? Susan cannot imagine. The question brings tears to her eyes, the more because Gram is in constant low- to middle-grade pain and, unlike Fenwick's ever-more-tuned-out Virgie, is in virtually full possession of her mental and sensory faculties.

What on earth does she do?

I remember things, Grandma says. She also, unavoidably, turns and returns in her mind through the eventless hours small (sometimes misconstrued) slights and large real worries, as well as happy anticipations. For nine months, and almost feverishly for the past several days, she has been waiting to see her Susele again at last.

Despite the half-century's difference in their ages, Havah Moscowitz Seckler and Susan Rachel Allan Seckler Turner admire each other's taste in clothes; despite differences in size and shape, they frequently exchange tailored skirts, blouses, dresses. Susan is wearing one of Grandma's dresses now; we are not surprised to find Grandma wearing one of Susan's skirts.

Kisses! Assurances that not only we but Fenwick's parents too are okay! The ritual offering of food from Havah's tiny kitchenette, accompanied by reminiscences of Seder for twenty in better days! We move to a nearby delicatessen for a quick lunch, Grandma's treat. She would have us go someplace finer, maybe the Pimlico Hotel, still doing business back in her and Grandpa's old neighborhood; but our seafood must be got to Carmen's Place, and after months of Caribbean fresh fish and fruit, Susan craves a quick fix of hot corned beef and sweet münster on seeded rye, cole slaw, kosher pickle, washed down with black cherry soda served in a glass without ice. In the car—she and Grandma ride together in the back, Fenn and Carmen up front—she has reminded Grandma what a fleshbeck is and tried out on her the news of our common dream.

Havah is amused but unimpressed. Why shouldn't you dream the same dreams? You and Fenn are one person.

Now, in the delicatessen restaurant, Sue must set forth the Big Bang theory of cosmogony in order to impress upon Grandma the further extraordinary coincidence that our shared dream culminated in a bang that awoke us both: a noise we were unable to account for in uninhabited Poplar Harbor. Better wake with a bang than not sleep, says Grandma. Nobody hurt? Thank G-d.*

Himself no particular hand at either diplomatic logistics or the art of stimulating the elderly, Fenwick is impressed by the easy arrangement whereby our half-whimsical excursions to Key and Poe have been coordinated with Carmen B. Seckler's business errands and the gradual escalation of Grandma's input, as Susan will phrase it, from us-after-all-these-months through Miriam and Company to Dumitru, whom Grandma has met as Carmen's new business associate but not yet as her living-companion. It is for the sake of this gradual pressurizing that we take lunch neither at Grandma's nor at Carmen's Place, but on neutral delicatessen ground. He admires also Susan's intrepidity at moving from astrophysics in the deli to literary history in the car, as we drive past Harborplace (closer inspection will have to wait; our cooler-ice is melting) to the foot of Broadway, into Fells Point, and Havah tisks her tongue at the ubiquitous winos slumped on stoops with their brown-bagged booze. She does not want to deprecate Carmen's neighborhood in Carmen's presence. Neither would she for anything give offense to Fenwick, though we all know very well that the sight of drunks, ipso facto Gentile, inevitably reminds her that her jewel has married out of the faith. The tongue-tisk, however, she cannot repress. Carmen grins; Fenn too; Susan at once

---

*In Grandmese, the word can almost be spoken thus piously: Thenggdt.

reminds her grandmother that her Susan's allegedly Jewish progenitor, the essential Edgar Allan Poe, was a notorious shikker, doubtless more than once bombed out of his gothic mind on these same streets, and first in a long American line of distinguished literary drunks.

Grandma at once withdraws her tisk. We imagine that she thinks to herself—but will not presume to remind even Susan—that whether or not the Poes were Jewish, the Allans were unfortunately not; a boy is bound to pick up habits from who raises him. What she says, tentatively, is Well, they was theater people, Grandpa said; the Poes was.

Sue whoops; Grandma waits, merry-eyed, to be instructed. Gra-yum! You think Poe drank because his parents were theater people? Do all theater people drink?

I'm just an old woman you shouldn't listen, Grandma chuckles happily. But adds Rest their souls, even you pa and you grandpa liked a little glass slivovitz after the movies. You remember, Carmen.

Carmen B. Seckler grins into the rearview and de-ashes her cigarillo. I remember everything, Havah. The fact is, she tells Susan and Fenwick, a few of those derelicts who inspired this conversation are theater people too, in a manner of speaking: the city police department, with a grant from the federal Department of Justice, is investigating the problem of small-time contract murder—the sort committed not by organized crime and/or the Central Intelligence Agency, but by your disgruntled wife or husband who wants a spouse eliminated without the hassle and expense of divorce, and hires some amateur to do the job for a couple thousand down and a few thou more on fulfillment of contract. Such arrangements have more than once been made in Fells Point barrooms, and so a number of plainclothesmen have posed as casual customers who happen to know someone available for such service, while a number of others disguised as derelicts report the movements of suspects through walkie-talkies concealed in brown bags, also alerting the nearest squad-car to any more ordinary street crime they may happen to witness. The experiment has proved newsworthy but not cost-effective: it has revealed that such amateur contracts are indeed made, attempted, or at least discussed, more than rarely, and that they can be thwarted, and their perpetrators arrested, by elaborate set-ups in which the intended victim participates. But barroom gossip has blown the detectives' cover; the judicial question of entrapment has hindered prosecution; the grant is not expected to be renewed or the project continued. The neighborhood winos, who briefly enjoyed a certain tentative respect and a virtual freedom from molestation, are disappointed in the Justice Department. Some have taken to speaking into their brown bags in an undertone.

Here we are. As Fenn perpends her throwaway CIA remark, Carmen B. Seckler turns off Aliceanna into an alley behind her place, tells the automatic garage door to open, and parks the Mercedes beside a pile of old porcelain washbasins and toilets pulled out by her remodelers but not yet fetched next door to the restaurant dumpster. While she takes Grandma into the house and phones Eastwood Ho to come fetch the mussels, we stroll down to pay our quick respects to other Eighteenth-century streets—Lancaster, Shakespeare, Thames, Fell—and to the dock we first set sail from as a couple. Fells Point has been picturesqued a bit by the city—new brick sidewalks, gas lamps, a parking lot nautified by great iron bollards—but its salty scruffiness is unimpaired: a flotilla of tugboats is moored to honest working bollards at the foot of the street, where too a rusty freighter looms, rat-shields on its hawsers. Greek sailors stroll between Greek bars, killing time till evening. There is broken glass, dogshit, and drunk-vomit enough to keep the scene authentic.

Hello, dock, says Susan with a sigh. Fenwick echoes: Hello, dock. Half-tide plus and rising, we note, and think wistfully of *Pokey*, swinging quietly at his mooring with the other empty vessels. By when we drop that mooring and point him once more seaward, how will things have changed?

We walk back to Carmen's, holding hands, saying little, a touch nervous at the prospect of socializing with so many people after months of mainly just ourselves. Her restaurant, into which we peer, looks unchanged and virtually empty: slack time between late lunchers and the early cocktail crowd. A ruddy, unfamiliar fellow, Fenn's age and size, stands behind the bar: thick black curly hair and eyebrows, walrus mustache, white shirt and dark silk vest—but for a gold stud in one earlobe, he looks like a turn-of-the-century barkeep. Dumitru, we bet, smiling. The rest of the block is a dreary line of unreconstructed rowhouses, some boarded up, and storefronts aspiring to but not achieving raffish charm. Sooty painted brick, cement molded and tinted into a meringue-like imitation of stone, peeling woodwork, dirty plate glass. But on her own house, adjoining the restaurant, Carmen has done an impressive job: its brick front has been sandblasted down to rosiness; wood-, iron-, and brasswork have been restored or replaced; black shutters hang on barred white windowframes—the place would not be out of place in Georgetown or Beacon Hill.

At the top of the polished marble steps, a gleaming brass doorbell plate is engraved C. B. Seckler. Skinny Miriam in much-patched jeans and printed T-shirt answers our bell. The sisters embrace before Fenn can read the T-shirt.

This is kerflooey? Susan cries. Some kerflooey!

Ma's gone Better Homes and Gardens, Miriam says, and turns her great shy eyes to her brother-in-law. Hi, Fenn.

Hi, Mims. As always since her day at Virginia Beach, Miriam is stiff in his arms, and takes his kiss on her cheek. After he hugs hello, Fenn holds her by the shoulders at reading distance.

### VACUUM ASPIRATION SUCKS

One of my rejects, Miriam explains. She has found a new

part-time job doing clerical and copywriting work for a local Right-to-Life group. In keeping with the general propaganda tactic of couching one's position in terms hard to deny on the face of them, and expressing it in the vernacular and through the media of the people one wants to influence, she has worked up a number of slogans for the printed-T-shirt crowd as a feature of the organization's summer campaign. Some have been received more enthusiastically than others. But it's a living.

We authors have to have thick skins, Fenn commiserates, releasing her. You've put on pounds, he says. Did you crack a hundred yet?

Ninety-nine five. You guys okay? she asks Susan, who flushes.

Sure! You?

Yeah. Come on in. Did you meet Do-Me-True?

We think we saw him.

It was Ma's secret surprise. He's terrific for her; a real stud. He'll pat your ass, Shush, but it's okay. He's crazy about Ma. The house is for him.

The hell it is, Carmen B. Seckler rasps from the living room. It's to impress your grandmother.

I'm impressed, says Grandma. She brightens immediately at sight of us. You could dance in the bathrooms, so big.

So move in, Gram, Susan says after kissing her. Then Ma won't have to shlep out to Pikesville all the time to check up on you and do your shopping and all.

I know, Grandma acknowledges: she shleps. She shouldn't so much; I could manage without. Susan declares that Fenn has taught her to think not of how much we can do without but rather of how much we can have. It is a principle we occasionally invoke but do not in fact particularly live by; nor did either of us teach it to the other. But in conversation with Grandma, Susan likes to add Fenwick's authority to her remarks.

Have, have, Grandma approves. Enjoy while you're young.

Big Sy and little Edgar come in now to greet Uncle Fenn

and regreet Aunt Susan. A large brown enthusiastic dog of Hungarian origin, Tibor, has been added to the household; he lopes in with the boys, bounds about, sheds a few hairs on Susan's dress, is dismissed from the company before he can impinge upon Grandma.* Susan appropriates Edgar. Sy cadges a cigarette from his mother and lumbers out with the dog, his familial duty done. He is not a disagreeable boy, Sy, only a fat, a coarse-faced, a slow-witted. We all try, less and less successfully as Sy grows older and larger, not to imagine in him the beefy sadist who got him forcibly upon skinny Mims. It was not Sy's fault! We all—no doubt even Miriam now, though she has not said so—wish much she had aborted or, failing that, miscarried or given the child up for adoption: the unlucky lad senses, even in his mother, our want of easy warmth with him. His Vietnamese "stepfather," half Sy's girth, is not cruel, but regards him as one might a large uncertain member of another, exotic, species. Gus, whom Sy adored, was better, though any reminder of his half-sister's rape would bring furious tears to that young man's eyes. In the gruff business of lugging vises and wrenches and lengths of pipe in and out of the van at Gus's orders, Sy was the happiest he has ever been. He sometimes wakes up wailing still, Miriam reports, for his Uncle Gus, since whose disappearance he has attached himself to Carmen B. Seckler.

The only other man in the house, Carmen herself explains, till Dumitru moved in. Did you see Messy's† mustache? It's dark as mine.

Fenn has indeed remarked Sy's small new additional misfortune: an undeniable dark mustache on his eleven-

---

*The animal is a Vishla, a working breed known for intelligence, companionability, and good manners. But even genetic dispositions are subject to Gresham's Law.

†We remember that Sy is short for Messiah. Carmen B. Seckler has used the alternative nickname so long and noncritically with her unfastidious first grandson that it has lost its pejorative sense and become a neutral nickname.

year-old face, which his schoolmates and the bar patrons must surely tease him with. Some of us sense a quick chill in Miriam and realize that she might remember just such a mustache on one of her attackers. Dumitru rescues the situation by joining us just here with the declaration that a mustache on a woman and an earring on a man—he salutes Carmen with a kiss—are signs of a passionate nature. Add a second earring, Carmen says, and you've got a problem. Add a red neckerchief and a little monkey, her friend replies with a shrug, you've got an organ grinder. But one—he puts an unabashed forefinger behind his studded lobe and grins around at us—is okay. Good afternoon, Havah.

Easily, unaffectedly, he kisses Grandma's hand, then her cheek, before shaking hands with Fenn, who has risen to meet him, and kissing Susan (*she* doesn't turn her lips away) and Miriam, who, as always, does. But she's smiling now. We like Dumitru! He turns to Susan again, removes E. A. Ho from her lap in order to take both her hands and inspect her face and figure with clear delight. Brains too, Miriam reminds him. Plus tenure, Susan says, permitting his inspection, and pension benefits. Dumitru puts a swarthy hand on Fenwick's shoulder and says sincerely We are lucky men.

You and I and Eastwood too, says gallant Fenn, warming all four women's hearts. It is a white lie: we believe neither Miriam nor Eastwood Ho—who is minding the restaurant while Dumitru introduces himself—to be particularly blessed in their connection, but on balance we think Miriam to be the better off. She's flakey, he's sullen, each with good cause. Eastwood Ho frets over her near-absence of wife-and-motherly inclinations: Miriam neither cooks nor sews nor cleans nor instructs nor disciplines, except desultorily; she baby-sits their child and moves from one low-paying part-time job to another. Eastwood Ho at least believes that children are to be parented, households tidily kept; he does an oriental husband's share of strict, attentive fathering, instructing Edgar in virtue and Vietnamese, and—since Carmen B. Seckler is his employer as well as his mother-in-common-law—for the most part curbing his complaints about Miriam's irresponsibility and drugs. He is a good worker, a tidy and abstemious fellow except for occasional drinking-and-singing bouts with fellow refugees, and a dependable lover. Considering that he is also an accomplished folk-singer in a tradition whose audience, even in his ravaged homeland, is dwindling and dispersed, and in Baltimore all but nonexistent, small wonder he's sullen, we think, and given to occasional strikings out. Moreover, he wants marriage, for his son's sake; it is Miriam who doesn't. Why did she take up with him, soon after Carmen B. Seckler hired him three years ago? Miriam's own explanation to Susan is that her rape and torture were far enough behind her so that she was ready for male sexual companionship again; but that she has an uncommonly small vagina—even voluntary intercourse with an erect and normally equipped white or black man, back in her days as a sexual activist, caused her discomfort; she could not insert a tampon without ouching; her rapes tore tissue; Sy was delivered by cesarean section—and she had heard somewhere that Asian men were able and considerate lovers with smaller penises, on the average, than blacks and caucasians. In the case of Eastwood Ho, at least, the generalization held, to their mutual satisfaction. Edgar's birth, a normal delivery by Mim's own insistence despite the general obstetric practice of following one cesarean with others, enlarged her vagina towards female caucasian postpartum typicality: no gain for Eastwood, we presume, but no loss for Miriam, three years his senior, who had learned from him how to be an adequate and active sexual partner again. Susan speculates that quasi-connubial sex may be her twin's one remaining talent.

Eastwood joins the family for dinner in the restaurant's private dining room, where business can be kept an eye on while we're served: mussels in sherry sauce español and a Caesar salad, with flutes of a pleasant Basque champagne. We have by now unpacked our seabags, installed ourselves in the guest apartment, reviewed with Carmen and Dumitru the architect's and decorator's impressive plans for Carmen's Harborplace, groaned at the Himalayas of accumulated mail awaiting each of us, and toasted our reunion with champagne cocktails made by Dumitru at the bar. Strange as it is to see another man than Manfred Turner with Carmen B. Seckler, we are more and more pleased with Fenn's brother's successor. Dumitru has no taste for sailing; professes to be mortally afraid of water. On the other hand, he loves horses and knows enough of modern literature to declare with a patriotic twinkle that European avant-gardism is largely the invention of expatriate Romanians: Tzara, Ionesco, Cioran. . . . He is pleasingly physical with Carmen (He is pleasingly physical period, says Susan), now patting her knee, now bussing her ear, now putting his arm about her waist. Carmen clearly enjoys these attentions, and we are gratified that Manfred's ghost does not abash him. Susan complains aside to Miriam *When do we get our asses patted?*

Shy dour Eastwood comes to table, shakes hands with Grandma, Fenn, and Susan, who kisses him—like Miriam, he smiles and turns his cheek—and nods to Carmen and Dumitru. In our absence he has grown stringy black chinwhiskers to go with his mustache: he looks to Fenwick less like Poe now than like an ascetic, vaguely dangerous young jazz musician. Though never quite at ease in his presence— national bad conscience, we suppose, for what our country has done to his, and a sad wish that he would never strike Miriam no matter how exasperating she becomes—both of us are attracted to Eastwood Ho and fascinated by his art, its apparently effortless stanzas generated by rules so extraordinarily complicated that it is difficult for a Westerner even to comprehend them, much less to savor their subtle application. Such relatively complex of our own verse-forms as the villanelle or the Petrarchan sonnet seem anarchically loose by comparison to Eastwood's ca dao—which, alas, lose everything in translation. Over the three years of our acquaintance, we have gathered a rough understanding of the intricacies of Vietnamese oral poetry; it is like learning, too late, to marvel at the ecological subtleties of a system you've irreversibly polluted; the physiological complexities of an animal you've killed. For example:

You have completed your voyage? Eastwood asks us politely. Yes and no, Fenwick replies: we've come back to Wye Island, where we started, and gone on a bit farther, to Gibson Island. Now we may keep on going, or we may stop. Eastwood nods and ventures But the Wye Island you returned to was not exactly the Wye you left. And Gibson is not Wye, although both are islands. He smiles: That is like the lục-bát couplet in ca dao.

As he speaks and we puzzle, Miriam comes back from changing Edgar and says (vulgarizing a Vietnamese proverb) You can bet your ass there's a poem to prove it, too.

Grandma lowers her glance at this vulgarity. Susan puts her hand on Eastwood's. Is there? Looking shrewdly at Miriam, Eastwood chants in his highly tonal native tongue

> Sông dài cá lội biệt tăm.
> Phải duyên chồng vợ ngàn năm cũng chờ.

The whole table smiles, uncomprehendingly. Susan asks him to translate. Eastwood shrugs, sullen again, and tonelessly recites: In the long river, the fish swim off without a trace. If truly wed, a man and woman can wait for each other a thousand years.

I'll drink to that, says Dumitru. Grandma nods approval. Carmen taps her cigarillo and begins to hum.

Of the several things going on in this little exchange, Fenn recognizes one: that Eastwood Ho's second line is simultaneously an ironic reference to his impatient patience with Miriam and an envious compliment to our more solid relationship. He suspects further that the first line, the sense of which he doesn't quite get, alludes somehow to our long sea-journey—perhaps also to Manfred's disappearance. All this assumed, he admires Eastwood's prompt summoning of a presumably traditional couplet to link what we had been speaking of to Miriam's entrance, her deprecating remark, and their domestic situation. But Fenn does not remember what a lục-bát couplet is or understand Eastwood's comparison of it to our voyage thus far.

Smarter Susan sees what Fenn sees and remembers further that lục-bát ("six-eight") is the standard couplet of Vietnamese oral poetry: a six-syllable line followed by an eight-syllable line whose sixth syllable (in this case năm) rhymes with the sixth of the earlier line (tăm), and whose eighth syllable (in this case chò) must be rhymed at the end of the first line of the next couplet, if there is one: Vietnamese poem-songs run from ca dao of one or two lục-báts to epic narratives of more than a thousand linked lục-báts. Thus she also understands, in part, how our voyage might be compared to a lục-bát: we have sailed back to our starting-place and on a bit farther, from where we may or may not proceed.

When she tells Fenwick this, later that night, in bed, he will remember not only that rhyme is not repetition (the place one returns to is never exactly the place one left: the river flows, but the shore changes too, not to mention the traveler), but that the rules of lục-bát couplets require the eighth syllable of the second line to be of the same *class* of tone-inflections as the sixth, yet not the *same* tone-inflection (năm and chò are both "even" tones, but the former is "toneless," the latter "falling"): thus Wye and Gibson are both islands, but Gibson is not Wye. Should we continue our voyage, we shall of necessity return to (a changed, however slightly) Gibson Island to do it—whence we ought to proceed, in the "next couplet" of our voyage and life, to yet another island.

We are not done! In the pile of mail awaiting us, Susan will find tomorrow morning a shy gift to us from Eastwood Ho: an advance copy of a little book entitled *Ca Dao Viêt*

*Nam,* by an American poet-scholar* who, almost alone among non-Vietnamese Americans except for Eastwood's namesake, could have pointed out to us some further subtleties in Eastwood Ho's remark and little song, had he been with us at the mussels and champagne. He might have pointed out, for example, that that "free" lục-bát couplet conforms to yet other rules in the distribution of its tones (e.g., that all rhymes *must* be on one of the two "even" tones rather than on the four "sharp" tones. That the second syllable of line one must also be an even tone, but the fourth syllable of line two must be sharp, etc.). That since both tonality and context govern the sense of Vietnamese words, and a Vietnamese word can have as many as six denotations depending on its tonal inflection, Eastwood can generate kinds of meaning unavailable to Western poets by playing sense against tone (e.g., by saying là in the "high constricted" tone—which makes it mean "insipid"—where the context leads one to expect the "low constricted" lạ—meaning "strange"—he might suggest in one quick syllable that the unfamiliar, such as sex with a spaced-out American woman, is not always ipso facto interesting). That the melodies of ca dao, while not fixed, derive from the sequence of tonal inflections, within which limits the singer may improvise musically as he improvises poetically within the structural rules of lục-bát. That the particular poem Eastwood Ho came up with in this instance belongs to the popular folk category of male-female replies: Eastwood sang only the first, in this case the male, couplet, to which a Vietnamese woman might have replied

---

*Professor John Balaban of the Pennsylvania State University. *Ca Dao Việt Nam: a bilingual anthology of Vietnamese Folk Poetry* (Greensboro, N.C.: Unicorn Press, 1980) includes a brief, lucid essay on the complexities and delights of ca dao—"free songs"—to which we owe what appreciation of Ho's virtuosity we're capable of.

Ruộng ai thì nây đắp bờ.
Duyên ai nây gặp đừng chờ uổng công.*

Which is as much as to say You are quite right that true love can survive separation; but it's also true that whoever pays the rent may wind up sleeping with the lady of the house, so don't be gone long. We recognize here a long-standing tease between Manfred Turner and Carmen B. Seckler, who we now remember tapped her cigarillo—in warning?—at Eastwood's translation of the first couplet. But the poet could point out that, given the rhyme-scheme of lục-bát, the "male" and "female" couplets are coupled like the couple: the poem is a loving, sportive sally between the "truly wed," such as Manfred and Carmen, so often apart, were; such as the singer wishes he and Miriam might be.

When, back aboard *Pokey* some days hence, steering for another altered island of our past in order to decide our altered future, we discover Eastwood's song in that little book of ca dao, review the general explanation of lục-bát couplets, and, so to speak, put two and two together, our hearts will constrict at the thought of such a virtuoso's† scrubbing mussels and stuffing squid in a Fells Point café, where local self-styled "poets" give occasional boozy "readings" of their mindless, formless, artless "verse" to their cultureless, tin-eared peers.

Oy vay, Sue sighs in bed. Poor mysterious Eastwood. Which is worse for a real artist, do you think: to have nobody in the room understand you,‡ or to have such

---

*As translated by Balaban:
*Who tends the paddy, repairs its dike.*
*Whoever has true love will meet. But take care of time.*

†The final irony, perhaps, is that Eastwood Ho would not describe himself as a "poet": that term he would reserve for the literary practitioners of lu-shih—"regulated verse"—beside which his ca dao are child's play.

‡Well: but it should be remembered that Eastwood Ho's obscurity is not, like Ezra Pound's or Wallace Stevens's, in his art: any Mekong Delta rice-farmer who knew our family situation would savor the several aptnesses of Ho's poem.

delicacies mashed under pages of explication?

Better a flower pressed in a book, Fenwick opines, than no flower at all. His remark neither scans nor sings nor glows with the deep burnish of utterances passed through an oral tradition, but it gets him kissed.* As, for that matter, does Eastwood Ho's gift him, when Susan sees him on the Wednesday morning after the Tuesday night of our discovery of it. He smiles, takes the kiss on his cheek, then frowns and goes on chopping scallions, chanting to himself.

That same night, the Tuesday, there in our bedroom, dinner done and Grandma returned to Pikesville, we speak together of Eastwood, Dumitru, Miriam, Carmen, as we split a nightcap of Molson's ale and give our mail its first rough sorting, throwing out the junk, setting aside the packages—books for Susan, mainly—and separating into different piles the bills and checks, business urgent, business unurgent, personal, his, hers. It will take us the Wednesday and the Thursday, we estimate, to deal with the accounting and the more pressing correspondence—lots of Swarthmore and U. Del. letterheads in that business-urgent pile!—and to set up the Friday's errands. Saturday, perhaps, we shall be able to relax with the clan, do a bit of shopping, play with Grandma, maybe take in a movie or a concert—and review our situation? Sunday we shall either move *Pokey* up to Baltimore or set sail for . . . somewhere.

The sorting ceases when we come upon Eastwood's gift, *Ca Dao Viêt Nam,* and lose ourselves in awe of a people whose principal cultural monument, the product of millennia, is not, as Pound says of European culture, ". . . two gross of broken statues . . . a few thousand battered books," but an extraordinarily rich tradition of folk-poetry and song. Susan expresses a craving to spit on several U.S. ex-Presidents dead and alive, their secretaries of state, joint chiefs of staff, and CIA directors. Fenwick—reflecting on his aspiration to

---

*Fenn's later notebook-note will not: that Eastwood Ho's singing ca dao in Carmen's Place is like Diaghilev's staging a ballet in an evergreen forest with only the trees for audience: he swirls his cast before pines. Susan groans.

that least structured, most anarchic, least oral, most impure of literary genres, the fucking *novel*, for pity's sake—feels faintly foolish. We kiss good night.

Next morning Sue says Oh boy, stirring through her mail-pile after breakfast. We must must *must* get cracking. Some of this stuff is two months old! And for the next two days we do, separately and together. The cruise is over, she sighs, when you hit the paperwork. But Fenn allows that, as in Redhouse Cove, we may merely be going back in order et cetera. It is a fine mild June weekday, seventyish and dry, a light northwesterly breathing through Baltimore, everything blossoming even in Fells Point. But we take our mail to separate desks in separate rooms—Fenwick to the guest-apartment living room, Susan to her mother's office next door—and get cracking.

Sue deals first with business involving her former and her presumable new employer, feeling awfully that we are deciding more by default than by clear agreement that she will exchange Washington College for Swarthmore and commit herself to serious professional scholarship as well as teaching. There are textbook-order forms, course-description forms, address forms (we *have* no address yet!), insurance and pension and contract forms. There are bills to be paid, automatic-salary-deposit slips and other receipts to be filed. Money must be moved around among various bank accounts; she'll leave that to Fenn. She confirms her Friday appointments with hairdresser (she wants her hair shortened and "permed" for the summer) and gynecologist. It begins to look as though she can do her main mail today, spend Thursday reviewing old course-materials to see whether what wowed 'em in Chestertown will play Philadelphia's Main Line. Friday she should be able to go fall-clothes-shopping with Mimi between her appointments. But we've got to settle down for the summer if she's to be ready to teach new courses in a new college in September.

Sometime that forenoon, Carmen B. Seckler comes in with tea. She has been bicycling, she reports, on routine errands in the neighborhood. Today too her hair is drawn back in a bun, but less severely than yesterday's Andalusian; she wears a dull smock, little jewelry, no make-up. Susan kisses her and says she looks like Doris Lessing.

And you look like the Virgin Mary, her mother replies. She sits beside the desk, sips her tea, counts off months with her left hand: January, February, March; then April, May, June. By June, the Virgin Mary was three months gone. Or are you just getting fat?

Holding her teacup in both hands, Susan smiles brightly. No place to ride a bike on a boat.

How come you haven't told Fenn?

Sue regards her tea. Do you think he doesn't know?

I didn't say he doesn't know. It's pretty obvious. I don't get it.

Susan pretends to go back to her desk-work. Me neither, Ma. She can feel her mother's eyes on her face, on her belly. But some other things ought to be obvious, too.

I get it, Carmen says.

Sue writes something on a form. So explain it to me.

Damned if I will. You explain to me why in god's name you scheduled your appointment for Friday thirteenth!

Damned if I will, Ma.

Carmen considers; takes her daughter's arm and says softly Shoshana Raisel. . . .

Susan lets herself be hugged; cries a little. She and Fenn have never kept anything from each other! We despise such games! Presently she blows her nose and asks Carmen whether she's working for the Central Intelligence Agency.

Don't change the subject, her mother grumbles. Okay, change the subject. No. Do-Me-True did, under Fred; they've pensioned him off. Eastwood did for a while, in South Viet Nam, towards the end.

Susan is appalled. Eastwood too?

He informed on V.C. operatives in the Saigon bars, where he was working. Not enough for a pension, but enough to get him out and relocated. He was one of the lucky ones. I knew about it when Fred steered him to me, but Eastwood asked me to keep it quiet. We're all pretty clean now, I think, except Woody sells tips to the city cops when he has anything to sell.

Susan smiles. Woody?

I wish he wouldn't. But artists have their own morality. I hope you're having the baby.

The form before her seems to require Susan's whole attention. These goddamn forms, she says.

What a kid it must be, sighs Carmen B. Seckler and then suddenly puts down her cup and embraces her daughter. Would be, could be, might be! she keens. It's nothing yet. Oh poor Shoshana! My Shushi!

Susan breathes the familiar perfumes of her mother— cigarillos, a scented soap from Crabtree & Evelyn, a touch of toilet-water, love—and thinks of Sy Seckler and Edgar Allan Ho. She wants to cry I'm sorry, Ma! but she feels sorrier for herself and doesn't.

Fenn next door puts on his specs and spends some telephone time with a Boston lecture agent who wants to book him on the campus circuit, somewhat more with his New York literary agent discussing translations and reprint editions of *KUDOVE*. How's the novel doing? Margot Scour-by wants to know. You're into a novel, aren't you? It's finished, Fenwick says; all I have to do now is write it. Margot Scourby advises him not to try comedy. But, she adds, the public seems not to tire of spy novels. Never mind the public, says Fenn; *I'm* tired of spy novels. Never mind the public, says Margot Scourby, and the public will never mind you. Fenwick asks Why not the Great American General Services Administration Novel? Or a family saga about seven generations in the Office of Management and Budget? Comedy, Margot Scourby declares, is definitely not your long suit. Then seriously, Margot: what about a play? There is a pause, presumably abashed, in New York City. What do you mean a play? What do you mean What do I mean a play? I mean a play play, is what I mean.

People in costume on a stage, pretending they're somebody else and speaking lines. I got the idea from Aeschylus and Sophocles. Plays aren't my department, Margot Scourby says; shall I transfer you to the Play Department? That's not necessary, Fenn assures her: it won't be a *good* play. If you want to write a bad play, Margot Scourby advises, I advise you to become a novelist: novelists always write bad plays. Ex-spies, Fenn replies, always write bad spy novels. But profitable, says Margot Scourby. May I call you back, Fenn? I've got a paperback auction in twenty minutes, and I want to practice felinity. Fenn grins: You're ready, Margot. Love to Sam. Love to Susan, says Margot Scourby: write what you want; I'll sell what I can. Says Fenn I'll write what I can; you'll sell what they want. Ciao, Fenn, says Margot Scourby: that's C-I-A— Addio, Margot.

Next, having stalled the U. Del. people unconscionably through the winter and perhaps lied to them in early spring, from the Caribbean, by saying yes to an adjunct professorship that he is not certain he'll take, Fenn either compounds the felony or forces his own hand by filling out the same sort of follow-up forms that Susan's been at for Swarthmore. Perhaps a sequel to *KUDOVE* called Guilty Conscience? he muses. But how crucial to anybody's program can an adjunct professor of upper-level elective courses be?

Having thus done his own kind of practice exercises, he now telephones an unlisted office number at yet another agency, this one in Virginia, and speaks briefly with Marcus Henry.

I thought Marcus Henry hated your guts, Susan says at lunch, in the restaurant. We are comparing mornings over prosciutto and melon and iced coffee and kosher pickle and baby-sitting Edgar Allan Ho until Miriam gets home from her half-day stint with the Right-to-Lifers. The boy sits pensively in Susan's lap and sucks her pickle, a faraway look in his bright round eyes.

He does, says Fenn, but he finds my chutzpah piquant. I asked him whether anything's on deck for Doog in the memorial-service way and told him we wanted in on it if there was. I also let him know I'd like to chat with him sometime soon on business.

You what?

I don't know exactly what. Count once told me that what made him a good CI officer was that he'd learned to trust certain intuitions before he knew what they were intuitions of. I'll bet a good novelist has the same sort of sense: which things he has to know clearly before he can begin, and which bridges he can't even conceive of, much less cross, till he gets to them. Does that make sense?

Some.

Edgar's dripping pickle on your blouse.

So he drips. We've spent our sabbatical that way, haven't we?

Dripping pickle?

Putting off crossing bridges till we come to them and then not coming to them.

Our eyes meet, sort of. Susan bites her meat. What's doing for Doog?

They're setting something up for Friday; Marc Henry's going to call back after lunch and let me know if it's open to the public, his very words. Let me explain about intuitions.

Okay. Give Edgar your pickle. Here, Edgar: eat Uncle Fensie's pickle.

Fenwick explains that as we stood on the old Fort McHenry ramparts yesterday morning and thanked Frank Key for a harmless return and spoke of flashbacks and flashforwards, something reminded him of that old fart Marc Henry.

Did you hear that, Edgar? What do you suppose could have reminded Uncle Fenn of Old Fart Marc Henry?

E. A. Ho squirms shyly, rolls his brown eyes, and buries his face, pickle and all, in Susan's bosom. Genius works in mysterious ways, all right, says Fenn. The point of this anecdote is that when McHenry reminded me of Marc Henry, I remembered that the last time I saw Marc Henry was the last time I was with Doog, eating lunch at the Cosmos Club. And remembering this while we were thanking Francis Key and talking to Carmen B. Seckler about going back to go forward, I had a strong feeling that Marcus Henry has the key to something important to us, or *is* the key to something. Don't ask me what.

You're serious.

I am.

Oo, Edgar, that feels good: pickle your Aunt Susie all you want to. She looks at Fenn. If Doog's thing is Friday, I won't be able to go.

Marcus wasn't sure. The point of the story is, I *got* to him, Sue. I don't even know how. I felt as if I could let my voice speak for itself, and the right words would come out in the right tone. I don't even know right for what.

Susan is listening, Susan says.

What's more, I know it worked, but I don't know *what* worked. I'm going down there and talk to Marcus Henry. Either I've got a big fish on the line, or a fish has got me.

Tomorrow?

Or Friday, if that's when Doog's thing is. I know you loved him, Suse, but part of my intuition is that I should do this trip singlehanded. Not because it's dangerous. Something about diplomacy.

That's some intuition you had there on that rampart.

Thinking of his conversation with Margot Scourby, Fenn declares that it's like what spending years writing a novel without any clear idea where it's going, but perfectly confident that you'll know exactly what to say when the time comes, must be like. Susan says that that doesn't strike her as a very exact comparison. I know what you mean, says Fenn. It is, though.

This is the voice of the enlightened Eighteenth century? Jesus, Edgar, let's go back to work. We stroll with him toward our separate desks. Susan reports I sent in all my Swarthmore forms this morning.

Me too Delaware, says Fenn. We'll decide soon.

Hm. We kiss good-bye. Edgar clings to Susan's leg like a bright-eyed mollusk. Ma told me Eastwood Ho used to work for the Company in Saigon and Dumitru used to work for Manfred. Did you know that?

Eastwood yes, Dumitru no. Are they still on the payroll?

Ma thinks not. Dumitru gets a pension, though. How come you never told me about Eastwood? What else do you know that I don't? The phone on your desk is ringing. Are these phones tapped? Good-bye. I missed you this morning. It seemed queer.

Wiedersehen. It did seem queer. I missed you, too. A good officer assumes all phones are tapped. That might be Marc Henry. I don't know anything else. Eastwood was a Company secret. I love you.

I know. She calls after him I hate intuitions! Fenwick's hurrying for the phone, but he hollers back Is that the romantic Nineteenth century I hear?

It's Marcus Henry. Hostile in the forenoon, he is now hearty: clearly he has consulted with his government in the interval. There is to be a small in-house memorial service for Dugald Taylor at Taylor's church in Bethesda at noon on Friday. The man has no surviving close family: his parents are dead, he was long since divorced, the marriage was childless, his ex-wife is remarried and lives in Walla Walla Wash. The evidence is that our friend was nonsexual, at least in recent years, but he had a great many friends, women as well as men: a tidy celibate active in community and social affairs and deeply loyal to the Agency. Some of this Marc Henry declares; some Fenn knows already; some he gathers.

Deeply loyal, Marcus Henry repeats. I heard you the first time, Marc, says Fenn: I'm deeply loyal, too, but not first to the Company.

We've gathered that, Fenwick.

With me, Fenn says on, the Company comes somewhere after the West Fork of Langford Creek.

What are you telling me, Fenn? Marcus Henry's voice threatens to relapse into forenoon hostility. Your first loyalty is to a goddamn creek, above your country?

Fenwick's perverse intuition tells him he can say no wrong. I didn't say that, Marcus. He marvels at his former colleague's equation, not evidently ironic, of the Central Intelligence Agency with the United States of America. My first loyalty is to Susan. Then to, uh, art. Art and Western Civ, yeah. Then Eastern Civ. Then Northern. Southern.

Very funny, Fenwick.

After that comes places: Chesapeake Bay, the Wye River, the Chester. The East Fork of Langford Creek, off the Chester; then the West Fork. Then the rest of America. After that comes governments, starting with the county commissioners of Talbot, Queen Annes, and Kent, and working up to the U.N. Then federal government agencies, beginning with the Environmental Protection Agency and the Food and Drug Administration.

Marcus Henry has been laughing heavily; now he credits Fenn with always having had a keen sense of humor. The memorial service is meant for Dugald's colleagues, but if it's held in the church—the arrangements aren't finalized yet—his friends and former colleagues are of course welcome. Indeed, if Fenwick will let him or his secretary know what train he'll be coming down on, Marcus Henry will be pleased to meet him at Union Station: they can talk en route to church.

Fenn's intuitions fire away. How do you know I'm not driving down, Marc? I haven't thought about that yet myself.

Marcus Henry laughs. Well. I just assumed, since you all have been off sailing and all. Shirley tells me there's a nine thirty-five Metroliner arrives Union Station ten-seventeen. That'll give us plenty of time to get to church by noon.

Fenn points out that he could leave Baltimore by car at eleven and reach any Episcopal church in Bethesda by noon. Things are clicking in his head.

Well, says Marcus, miffed: you let us know.

Fenn asks point-blank Is Carmen B. Seckler reporting to you?

Marcus Henry sounds genuinely insulted. Jesus, Fenwick:

this is Bell Telephone, not a Company quiet room. His tone turns to businesslike candor. We've had a few conversations with Miz Seckler about your brother, naturally. But she doesn't *report* to us. He pauses, then proceeds with what sounds to Fenwick like a prepared recruiting speech: That's not to imply that we don't have top-drawer women officers. We've come a long way in that way since your time, Fenn. These ladies are real pros; you'd be surprised. Now he chuckles—these shifts of manner seem to Fenn at once as unsurprising and as revealing as . . . what? As cards played on the table*—though what they reveal, he would be hard put to say. It is with such a feeling of rehearsal that he hears Marcus Henry say, still chuckling, Your girl looking for a job? that his response is ready by the question mark: We don't call them girls any more, Marc: young women, we call them.

You know, you're right? See you on the ten-seventeen Friday, Fenwick. We'll talk.

Carmen B. Seckler smokes in during the afternoon to get something she needs from her desk, singing a Chesapeake Bay sea-chantey around her cigarillo:

> O a hundred years ain't a very long time
>   On the Eastern Sho',
>   O way-o.

> Look out, gal, I'm a-comin' home
>   To the Eastern Sho',
>   O way-o.

What a dumb-ass song, she says, rummaging around him. 'Scusi, Fenwick.

Fenn asks the back of her head Do you report to Marcus Henry?

Carmen straightens up and looks down at him with

---

*Aha, Sue will say to this simile: not laid but played. Will say Fenn: That's it, exactly.

disdain. I report to no one, gorgio.* Did he say I do?

No.

She hums and rummages on and finds what she's after, a pack of playing cards. He sort of invited me to, after Fred died, but there was nothing to report. Then another turkey made the pitch Doog told you about, and I told her what Doog told you I told her.

Her.

They're getting big on women officers: Marcus Henry's department, I believe. My feeling was they were just being nice to me because of Fred. They thought the pitch was a compliment, you know?

My consciousness is being raised. Do we have some business to settle, Carmen?

They have, to be sure: Carmen's Place's bookkeeper has managed most of our financial affairs in our absence— affairs by no means numerous or complicated except by our distance and very limited reachability. But he won't be in till tomorrow, Carmen reports. Do your business then. If that's what you mean.

What else is there? Fenwick hopes she won't ask him about Susan.

Well, let's see. Do you like Dumitru? Sure. Do you think the Company did for Doog? Maybe. What for? Haven't the faintest. How's your heart, Fenwick?

They regard each other. Fenn removes his glasses, lets them dangle from their lanyard, decides. I had a scare last week, Carmen, coming back on the bus from Washington to Solomons Island after lunch with Doog.

Aiyiyi. Bad?

Not like before, obviously. But it felt as if it could just as easily have gone right on. I'll have Joe Hunter check it out before we do the next thing, but chances are he'll find nothing. Then I'll tell Susan. Unless I tell her sooner.

---

*This term is alleged by Carmen B. Seckler to be Gypsy for non-Gypsies, like goyim for non-Jews. We do not vouch for it.

They regard each other further. Carmen offers Fenwick a cigarillo from her silver case. No thanks. She takes a chair. It wouldn't be a picnic, Fenn, she says: giving CPR with one hand and sailing a sailboat with the other in a storm in the middle of the fucking ocean.

Come on, Carm, Fenn objects. Susan knows what she's risking with me. We didn't set out for the Caribbean blind.

Unruffled Carmen replies Come on Carm my ass. What are *you* risking? What are you putting on the line for her? What have you got to lose in this marriage?

Not as much as Susan, by a long shot. It's called love, Carmen. Suse and I are both good at it, but Susan's better. Her mother's daughter.

That's the truth, you know.

I know. Fenn does not smile. Suse and I have to make some decisions soon that we were supposed to have made by now and didn't. We're at a fork in the road.

Carmen waits.

For example, I may ask her to support us for a year or two while I try to write something; or I may not. And there are some other decisions.

Like what.

The business with Gus and Manfred took a lot out of *us,* too. We thought the cruise would help. I suppose it did, but not as much as we'd hoped.

Carmen grimaces. Good lord, Fenn. What are you two thinking of?

We're thinking of several things and deciding nothing. Fenwick smiles now at his old friend and points to the card-deck in her hand. Maybe you could help us with a flashforward?

His mother-in-law shakes her head, taps the deck on her chair arm, stands. Nope. These are for business.

*AFTER ANOTHER DAY OF ERRANDS AND DESK-WORK,*
*ANOTHER COUPLE OF FAMILY DINNERS,*
*AND TWO MORE EVENINGS SPENT WITH GRANDMA*
*AND THE REST, IN COURSE OF WHICH WE LAUGH A LOT*
*AND COME TO KNOW DUMITRU A TOUCH BETTER*
*AND APPROVE OF HIM MORE AND MORE,*
*SUSAN MAKES A SHORT SPEECH TO FENWICK*
*AT BEDTIME ON THURSDAY, JUNE 12, 1980—*
*BOTH OF US A BIT HIGH ON ANXIETY AND A*
*ROMANIAN CABERNET SAUVIGNON CALLED PREMIAT*
*—ON THE SUBJECT OF THE INCREASING ROLE OF*
*WOMEN IN THE U.S. CENTRAL INTELLIGENCE AGENCY.*

Maybe we should get Grandma a job with them, surveilling the Old Jews' Home. Maybe I'll chuck professoring and take up dirty tricks. Lots of people change careers in middle life: look at you. Whoever wins the November elections, we've got a new cold war in the works, a new arms race, runaway nuclear proliferation outside the Soviet bloc, extortion by the Organization of Petroleum Exporting Countries, mass starvation in Africa, god knows what in Southeast Asia, dreadful governments in Brazil, El Salvador, Argentina, Chile, Guatemala, and damned near everywhere else. The world's regressing like crazy: is it going back to go forward? But all the forward-looking people will be desaparecidos, along with the whales and elephants and giraffes and rhinoceri. Jesus Hache Cristo.

*FENWICK REPLIES, SORT OF.*

That his royalty statements and lecture invitations assure our minimal solvency for the coming academic year if either one of us teaches. That with the year's anticipated royalties from *KUDOVE* but without lecture fees or any academic salary—but also without the shoreside expense of rent,

utilities, automobiles, and the like—we can continue cruising
until this time next year if the summer's work produces a
publisher's advance on our story and if we're unscrupulous
enough to break our teaching contracts at the last minute.
But that he understands that Susan's nonteaching career—
e.g., her own study-in-the-works of Twins, Doubles, and
Schizophrenia in the American Literary Imagination—requires a more stable base than a sailboat under way: she
needs access to research libraries, room to spread out and let
things lie, colleagues to exchange ideas with. Then there's
the grandson-imminent: do we really want to spend his first
year knocking about the world, missing all his ephemeral
changes up to the walking stage? On the other hand, how
much of him are we likely to see anyhow, given the literal
and other kilometrage between us and the Orrin-and-Julies?
Et cetera. Boy oh boy.

The bed in Carmen's guest apartment is king size, with
separate box springs so that the movements of one sleeper
don't disturb the other. On the Tuesday and the Wednesday
nights we slept in it as if comatose despite the street noise of
Fells Point. Tonight, too, at first, anxiety notwithstanding,
we sleep stoned out for a while. Then, from the small hours
until dawn, bad dreams wake us intermittently: we lose and
find and lose each other in that unfamiliar space. One of us
has brute flashes of apocalypse: the thunderous destruction
of great cities by men who have never seen them; to whom
Leningrad, Firenze, San Francisco are mere target-names.
The other of us dreams of the one's death and of sick old
age in a nursing home without the care and comfort of
children, grandchildren. Harrowed by these dreams, we
wake finally to an ugly sucking noise—its source turns out to
be the dog Tibor, whose food bowl Sy and Edgar have
placed before our bedroom door so that Aunt Susan will be
waked without their being blamed for disobeying Carmen's
orders to let us sleep. Half-blindly and with shocking
premonition of loss, we grope across the reaches of that bed.

## SUSAN'S FRIDAY

The thirteenth is still and warm: preview of next week's summer. Fenwick's only suit both funereal and lightweight is stored at Chief and Virgie's: he must choose between a dark too heavy and a light too light. He goes with the dark too heavy. Susan slips into an airy sleeveless cotton print. Presiding at the stove in Carmen's kitchen, Dumitru compliments her brown arms and shoulders but does not yet pat her ass as promised. We breakfast with dog and family: the normalcy of tea and shmaltz-fried matzoh (with pork sausages!) puts last night's dreams at better distance. Edgar Allan Ho wants Susan's lap; Miriam says No, you'll shit up her dress; Susan says Let him. Big Sy, looking like a small mustachioed Central American dictator, asks Fenn about *Pokey*'s rigging, how come the tension of the shrouds and stays neither pushes the mast through the bottom like a toothpick through a pork sausage nor bends the hull fore and aft like a banana. Once the vocabulary is straightened out, the assumption of Sy's inevitable dullness corrected, and his question understood, Fenwick realizes that the boy has in mind the rational principle of "tensegrity": the balance of tension and compression in strong flexible structures such as Kenneth Snelson's strut-and-cable construction *Easy Landing,* at the Inner Harbor. He can then explain to Sy's satisfaction that most sailboat design is less rational than Buckminster Fuller: *Pokey*'s mast *does* want to push through the keelson, his bow and stern to curl up like the horns of a drawn bow; only the strength of his hull, not any artful balancing of forces, resists such deformations, in fact a cause of leaks in wooden ships. Sy listens Buddha-like and blinks; is gratified. We are favorably impressed.

We kiss the family good-bye for the day. Susan's and Miriam's appointments begin at ten; Fenn's train is at nine-thirty; Sy and Eastwood Ho are baby-sitting Edgar for the day. Miriam drives us to Penn Station in her rackety VW and waits in the car while we say good-bye inside. Fenwick breathes Susan's hair, squeezes her upper arms, kisses her ears. Well, he says: good luck.

Yeah, says Susan.

Wisdom. Courage. Et cetera.

Yeah. I miss you already. When will you be home?

I'll call. The last train gets in at twenty-three nineteen.

She fingers his dark lapel. You won't be that late, will you? You look like a regular business executive.

I feel like a mortician. You look like a jeune fille en fleur.

Yeah.

He kisses her again. I shouldn't be late. Depends on what I find down there. Strength, Suse.

Yeah.

The sisters then drive uptown to the Mount Washington neighborhood and their hairdresser. They find it agreeable to be doing something together again, just the two of them, as they did so many thousands of things when younger. New hair-dos! At the last minute Susan loses her nerve about the tight-curled perm and simply has her hair cropped short. Fenn will be disappointed. To compensate, Mim gets hers teased out into a super Afro, which she declares will excite Eastwood Ho. She looks struck by lightning.

They decide to try her out on the folk of nearby Cross Keys, a stylish development of townhouses, condominiums, boutiques, and the rest, where they will have lunch and look at clothes until Susan's two o'clock appointment. Miriam affects disdain: America, she predicts, will one day be a continuous fancy shopping-mall from sea to shining sea. Kraft presliced individually-wrapped American nothing cheese and nothing bread will disappear; there will be only Brie and baguettes. No more Sonny's Surplus sweatshirts; only "designer" clothes. When The Rouse Company* does

---

*The developers responsible for Baltimore's Cross Keys and Harborplace, Boston's Quincy Market, and the entire city of Columbia, Maryland, among other projects—all which Susan rather enjoys and Miriam scorns.

Fells Point, she imagines, they will refurbish it with premier grand cru winos and decorator dogshit.

I hope so, Susan says. At the Cross Keys Inn they order Fromage-Bleu Burgers and minted iced tea; the waitress compliments Miriam's hair and declares she wishes she had nerve enough. Contempt, Susan is pleased to observe, improves her sister's appetite. The burgers are in fact delicious; Miriam goes at hers with more gusto than Susan has seen in her for a long while.

Now they do the fancy clothing shops, mainly to look: for serious buying they'll drive out to Loehmann's discountery on the Beltway after Susan's appointment and find some of the same items, their famous labels removed, at a third the Cross Keys price. Here is the necessary Finnish-fabric-and-European-high-style-stuff store: bright neo-Bauhaus kitchen scales, expensive little rugs, colorful high-impact plastic stacking furniture, food processors. Susan buys a stretched-fabric wall hanging for Edgar Ho's bedroom—primer-style boats, fish, and lighthouses in gaudy colors—and for Sy a serious make-your-own mobile kit: the clumsy boy's fascination with the physics of delicately balanced forces, as evinced at breakfast, much touched her.

He'll fuck it up, says Miriam; Susan says No he won't.

At ten till two they go to Morris Steinfeld's office, also in Cross Keys. Mim reviews the cartoons in back numbers of *The New Yorker* while Susan confirms for the doctor—a curly long-faced fellow her age who reminds her of a boy she dated in her junior year of high school—what she has reported to him earlier by telephone: that she last menstruated in Bridgetown, Barbados, toward the end of March. That her breasts have been engorged since late April. That she has experienced more frequent nausea all spring than she believes can be attributed to seasickness and subtropical food. That she infers herself therefrom to be two months pregnant. That she wants the pregnancy terminated now.

Handsome Morris Steinfeld hears her out and says soberly Hm. Behind his desk are photographs of his two children, a dark-haired little Sabra and a boy almost Bar Mitzvah age. Let's have a look first and see what's what.

So in another room she strips, pees into a beaker, and, at the direction of a nurse named Pearl, lies on the short table and spreads, feet in the stirrups. Morris Steinfeld enters, palpates, peers, pokes, takes cervical smears. His lookalike was the first boy with whom Susan "petted to climax"; he was permitted her clitoris but not her vagina past maybe the first joint of his index finger. Her rectum was off-limits. She remembers such things as Morris simultaneously indexes the one and thumbs the other, to the hilt, checking out her uterine configuration. Goodell's, Chadwick's, and Hegar's signs, he announces evenly, are all present. Your pelvic capacity is adequate for normal delivery. Let's say you conceived in mid-April: that puts your EDC first week in January. January fifth by Nagele's rule. He smiles. Estimated Date of Confinement: with luck you could unload just before New Year's and take the tax exemption for Nineteen Eighty.

Susan reflects that in mid-April we were working up through the Windward Islands—Martinique, Dominica, Guadeloupe—making our delicious way toward the British Virgins. Morris Steinfeld says with clear care Normally we'd do a complete physical now to establish some baselines for later.

Still in the stirrups, Susan lifts her head and says Abort it, Morrie.

Nurse Pearl's routine smile discreetly fades. Serious Steinfeld moves from between Susan's legs to her side. Wouldn't you like to sleep on that, now that you're confirmed?

That's why I notified you ahead. We're here just for the weekend.

He considers her. You're well within the first trimester, Susan; there's no great rush.

I didn't come here for a rap session, Morrie. I came for an abortion.

You did. Where's Fenn?

Sue closes her eyes. In Washington on business.

But you've talked it over thoroughly, and you both agree you don't want a child yet.

Yes. Susan sits up on the table. No. To the nurse: Could you step outside for a minute?

Pearl shakes her head. Not while you're stripped.

Steinfeld smiles. She's my insurance: the pearl of great price, as the Bible says.

Susan sighs. I faked my last two periods, but I know Fenn knows we're pregnant. He'd rather not raise another child, but he wishes I had one. I didn't tell him I was pregnant because I didn't want to tell him I was going to abort because I didn't want to upset him; I was afraid he'd have another heart attack. I think it's really strange not to have children, but it's my decision, and my considered decision is Abort. All right?

Morris Steinfeld is thoughtful for some moments. Finally he shrugs. You're the doctor. He looks at Pearl and at his watch. Come back about four-thirty.

Why can't you do it now?

Before you change your mind? But he explains that in the case of women who have not borne children, mechanical dilation of the cervix can usually be avoided or made painless without paracervical anesthesia by the insertion of a dried Japanese seaweed, Laminaria, into the vagina for several hours before evacuation of the uterus.

Come on, Morrie! I'm supposed to walk around Loehmann's all afternoon with a twat full of Jap seaweed? You're stalling me!

Morris Steinfeld can get excited too. Jesus, Susan! Do you want to read the manual?

Susan would in fact like to, and will when she gets back to Fells Point. She is resolved to be a doctor herself in her next incarnation. But though reserving the right to ask as many questions as she feels need to, she apologizes for doubting Morris Steinfeld's motives and affirms her confidence in his judgment. Mollified, he offers her the option of local anesthesia and mechanical dilation; but if she chooses it, he'll do the abortion in an operating suite when one can be scheduled, next week sometime. Overnight hospitalization should not be necessary.

Stick the seaweed in, Sue says. I guess it's appropriate.

Pearl fetches Laminaria and a surgical release form, which Susan signs. Why'd you get pregnant, Morris Steinfeld wants to know as he applies the seaweed and Susan wonders where Jeff Greenberg is now, whom he finally married, how many children he has these days, if you don't want children? Greenberg, then a freshman premedical student at Penn, taught her to enjoy Verdi, Puccini, and fellatio. She tried vainly to teach him not to spoil an otherwise agreeable evening by pressing always to go beyond the limit she'd decided to put on her adolescent sex life and then pouting when she wouldn't break her own rules. They dated for a year, by the end of which, given an average ejaculate volume of three to five milliliters, Susan calculated she'd swallowed half a pint of the young man's semen. Mass cannibalism, she supposes, from her mother's view of spermatozoa. It did not seem to trouble Sue's complexion. In his second undergraduate year Jeff found a freshman who would fuck; he and Susan parted friends. She still has the recording of Puccini love-duets he gave her the first time she reached orgasm at his hands.

Our minds weren't entirely made up about some things, she tells Morris Steinfeld. We went sailing to clear our heads. I'd gone off the Pill; Fenn and I both hate condoms; he'll get a vasectomy if we ever get around to deciding not to have kids. Meanwhile we made do with a diaphragm, but we weren't as careful as we should have been. Maybe we wanted it to happen so we'd know for sure what we felt. I hate psychology.

And it did, and you do, Morris Steinfeld wants to be reassured.

Yeah. Seaweed applied, Susan sits up and reaches for her

underpants. Morris Steinfeld instructs her to check with Sharon on her way out to make sure four-thirty's okay. You might have to wait.

I'll wait.

Miriam springs up when Susan reappears in the waiting room and confirms the new appointment—five o'clock, as it turns out. But Susan waits until they're in the car to tell her sister what this visit's been about. Miriam wails, can't help herself; weeps spontaneously and for a while uncontrollably; is in fact unable to start the engine and leave the parking lot. You're supposed to be the normal one! she laments. You and Fenn have to give Ma *real* grandchildren, to make up for Gus's death and my mishegoss! Why do you think I'm into this Right-to-Life shit?

Susan hugs her. That's for our benefit?

Of course it is. Oh, Susele! She keens it; she davvens it: Soo-oo-ooselah! She pounds her fists once, softly, on her sister's abdomen, then kisses and kisses it. No-o-o!

The car windows are open; people can hear. Come on, Mims, Sue says. They'll think we're making out in here.

Miriam cries crazily We might as well! What the fuck good are we, if you're not going to have kids?

Let's don't ask the neighborhood.

But Miriam shrieks Nobody gangbanged you! Nobody stuck beer bottles in your cunt and burned your tits with cigarettes! What's the matter with you!

Susan says I'm getting out of here and opens the car door. Her object is to rein in her sister's hysteria, but the general strain is beginning to nauseate her; she means indeed to walk away if necessary in order not to vomit. Miriam quiets herself, but cannot cease weeping. They exchange places; Susan drives out the Jones Falls Expressway to the Baltimore Beltway and east toward the Loehmann's exit. Except for the odd hour behind the wheel of a rented Ford Fiesta on Tobago and a Jeep on Virgin Gorda, it is the first time she has managed a car in more than half a year. Concentrating on doing it is good for her nerves: she becomes cooler and more sure of herself by the mile, and her confidence helps calm Miriam.

They try on summer dresses and fall outfits. Crazy Mims has good taste for other people: she sniffs and wipes her eyes in the fitting-room each time Susan strips (and Susan's nerves twinge as always at the sight of her sister's scars), but gives her good advice on two tailored suits, one tweedy, one not, to teach at Swarthmore in, and a very sexy slit cocktail dress that she can wear to faculty dinner-parties with impunity, in Mim's opinion, now that she'll have tenure. There's time to kill: they find a pizzeria and agree that its product—which they both prefer with double mozzarella but no other extras—doesn't measure up to Ocean-City-boardwalk standards. They drink two schooners apiece of light beer: a lot for both of them. Susan starts to tell about remembering Jeff Greenberg while Morris Steinfeld examined her, but falters in mid-anecdote even as both are laughing; it is not the approach of five o'clock that gives her pause, but the contrast of such innocent sexual casuistries with Mim's ordeals. Miriam, however, is in the spirit of the tale: she reminds Susan how she Mimi discovered masturbation and demonstrated it for her sister; how they experimented with themselves for hours, so it seemed to them at the time, hands cramped and vulvas sore, until Susan finally got there first with a giggly squealing climax, well before the advent of Jeff Greenberg. How Mims unhesitatingly then had gone all the way with Fred Spicer, captain of their high school swimming team and subsequent Olympic freestyler, and had followed that adventure with many another and less notable, while supporting absolutely Sue's own decision not to copulate till college.

Four-thirty. Susan pays and drives them back to Cross Keys, though Miriam declares she's okay now. I'm enjoying it, Sue says. You can drive us home after.

Five. Morris Steinfeld is running a touch late. Susan reads

an amusing story in *The New Yorker* by Donald Barthelme, another by Grace Paley, and wishes she were a writer, to make life make art if not sense. Five thirty-five. Missus Turner? Sharon directs her to Pearl, who directs her to the same room as before; it seems to Susan that today has been mainly dressing and undressing.

Last chance to change your mind and become a Yiddishe momma, Morris Steinfeld tells her. No. He looks a touch disappointed. We'll aspirate; you explain to Fenwick that this is a very low-risk procedure which in no way jeopardizes future pregnancies.

Okay. Susan spreads. With gloved and lubricated finger Morris Steinfeld fishes out the seaweed; then she feels what must be a speculum opening her up and something else, a rod or tube, going in. Discomfort but no pain. Either nurse or doctor clicks an electric motor on. Susan feels and hears suction. It is the little fetus, she supposes, that succumbs to two particularly nasty, almost feral shlups from the machine, which subsequently purrs like a fed cat.

That gets it, Morris Steinfeld now announces. He rises and grins at her. Some women aspire to motherhood; others have lower aspirations.

Oy gevalt, says Pearl. Sue closes her eyes.

Thought I'd inject a little humor. Pearl'll give you a Kotex. If you're still bleeding this time tomorrow, call me at home. You want a pill prescription?

My old one hasn't expired.

Well. Take care now, Susan.

Pearl provides her with a beltless pad and what sounds like the standard office caution against extensive reliance on tampons. While we've been afloat, the Toxic Shock Syndrome has gone to press: the danger is slight, even slighter if one changes tampons every few hours during menstruation; but until the industry comes up with something new, many women have gone back to the old sanitary napkin.

Fuck it, Susan says.

Pearl shrugs. I know what you mean, darling, but we give the spiel. Personally, I'm glad I changed my life before TSS came along.

Sue cheers morose Mimi with that locution en route home. I changed my life! I love it! It puts us in the driver's seat.

Miriam, driving, says she wishes to Christ she could change *her* life.

Susan does too and says so: she loves Fenn hugely but envies every one of her peers who does normal things like flower-gardening and nursery-school car-pooling and attending P.-T.O. meetings as a P. Back at Fells Point Mim kisses her and goes into the bar to relieve Eastwood of Edgar Allan; Sue goes up to the guest apartment to collect herself before dealing with the world. She finds the place full of fresh roses and coreopsis and her mother, who embraces her at once, rocking and swaying, making a low croon.

Presently Carmen B. Seckler says Well: god knows you didn't have the most inspiring examples of modern middle-class parenthood.

Susan protests Not so. Da was good to them; Manfred took loving care of the family even though he was away much of the time; and who could have been more exemplary than Carmen B. Seckler in the ways that matter?

Hah, says Carmen. You're not completely wrong there. So now? She declares it no disaster, all Jewish wisdom to the contrary notwithstanding, to be childless.

Susan wants to know Who says childless? Since when does one little vacuum abortion mean no kids ever?

I know what means what, Carmen says firmly, and I tell you it's no disaster.

Now Susan weeps. It damn well is! They clutch each other. What's left of Susan Seckler Turner when she dies? I'll kill myself, is what. I'll wait a week or two after Fenn dies to put our affairs in order, and then I'll take pills.

Her mother says into her hair You could do that. It's a pity, but it's no crime. Why cross that bridge before you reach it? You're healthy; Fenn's healthy, sort of. You love each other; you both have good jobs. You're not bad off.

Sue Kleenexes and apologizes for her self-pity; she's sure our problems must appear luxurious to her mother. Yeah, well, Carmen B. Seckler replies; the fact is, we had the same worry in the camps: What's left of me when I'm dead? But it was more democratic, since your parents and children and relatives and neighbors were all dying along with you. Want a drink?

What Susan wants is a sleeping pill. Twenty. Wants Fenwick. Wants our baby. No. Has he called?

He'll be a little late. We're not to wait dinner. Do-Me-True's gone for Grandma. Fenn says he found out some things, but not about Gus and Fred.

Let him tell me, Susan says, and blows her nose again.

## FENN'S

He comes into Union Station from the train platform perspiring already, his dark coat folded inside-out over his arm. A plump, thirtyish black woman in a gray linen pants-suit says Mister Turner? Yes. I'm your driver; Mister Henry and all's in the car. She leads him to a blue government car-pool Chevrolet. There's hawk-faced Marcus Henry waving wanly from the front passenger seat. A woman is on the far side in the back; Fenn can't see her head.

Marcus Henry says dryly Greetings, Fenwick. Hello, Marcus. They shake hands lightly through the window; the driver opens the right rear door for him. Fenn fishes his eyeglasses out by their lanyard from his shirt pocket and slides them on as he bends to enter.

Long time no see, says Marilyn Marsh across the seat.

For a moment and for the first time in his fifty years Fenn is struck quite speechless; he will be pleased later to delete delayed surprise from his list of cardiac dangers.

Marilyn Marsh smiles and pats the seat beside her. Come into my parlor.

Fenwick has stopped in mid-entry. His head and shoul-

ders are inside the car; his right hand grasps the front
seatback. The driver waits behind him to close the door.
Marcus Henry does not turn his clerky head; Fenn imagines
him pursing his mouth to suppress a smile. Marilyn Marsh
Turner at forty-nine—Fenn has not seen his ex-wife for five
years, since Orrin and Julie's wedding—is lean-faced and a
shade leathery from too much sun; her figure is still trim;
her brown hair's bobbed severely; she is attractive in a
plucked-eyebrows sort of way.

Fenn is not cool. Still standing in the road, he exclaims
What the fuck are you doing here?

Marilyn Marsh's expression goes firm. Doog Taylor was a
friend of mine.

What do you mean a friend of yours? You hardly knew
him!

Marilyn Marsh reports coldly that she had got to know
Dugald Taylor well in the past seven years. Maybe better
than you. Please stop shouting and get in.

Fenwick does neither. What the fuck is she doing in this
car, Marc? What's going on?

Grinning Marcus Henry says Get in and we'll tell you. We
should get moving.

Even as he does, uncomfortably as if entering a lair, and
the impassive black woman closes the door and goes to the
wheel, Fenn is smitten with a bizarre but clear intimation of
what their crosstown conversation presently confirms. That
since their acrimonious divorce of ten years past, and
especially since his leaving the Agency in '73, his former wife
has cultivated and closened her acquaintance with certain of
his former colleagues: Dugald Taylor, Marcus Henry especially, even Manfred! That in fact, not without precedent
among ex-spouses of Agency ex-officers, in the first half of
the decade past she received a small stipend for occasional
services—indeed, Fenn might be interested to learn that she
did one or two tiny things for the cause even in the latter
years of their marriage! And that, much rarer among ex-
Agency ex-spouses, she has in the second half of the

decade—particularly since her remarriages fizzled and most particularly since *KUDOVE* appeared—become a full-time officer under Marcus Henry!

And a first-class one, Marcus Henry affirms from the front seat. Fenwick is stunned; also mightily depressed. Too much to assimilate! And yet. The car, he notices, is not heading toward Bethesda.

Marilyn Marsh says cheerily You're looking well. I understand you and Susan have been sailing. Fenn doesn't answer; he does not like to hear that name spoken by that voice! Come on, says Marilyn Marsh: don't pout. Let's have lunch after the service and catch up to date.

No.

With a familiar edge she says Look here, Fenwick: let's don't bore these people with our differences. We're about to have our first grandchild. How can you expect to be a proper grandfather if you go on acting like a child yourself?

Fenn leans forward and asks the black lady please to stop the car and let him out; he'll take a taxi to the church. We've moved the service to Langley, Marcus Henry says. Some problem with the minister, the building, something.

The trouble is Dugald's relatives, Marilyn Marsh declares to both men. They vetoed our plan for an open church service and had their own little thing instead without even telling us. We invited them to our service in Langley, but they've decided to be huffy. Hm, Marcus says.

Fenwick attends their voices: the authority of Marilyn Marsh's, to which Marcus Henry's defers as to a knowledgeable aide's. He asks the back of Marcus Henry's head Has Doog's doctor made any statements?

After a tiny pause, his ex-colleague says Not that I know of. What kind of statements? Any kind of statements, Fenn presses. Not that I know of. Marcus turns his head. Do you know of any statements, Marilyn?

No. She asks Fenwick Who's Doog's doctor?

He does not reply. For one thing, he doesn't know; for another, he doesn't want to speak to Marilyn Marsh; finally, he realizes that he may have just jeopardized, at least compromised, Dugald's doctor.

Whoever it is, mildly declares Marcus Henry, they should sue *him* for malpractice, not spotting that aneurysm before it let go.

Fenwick registers the odd emphasis on *him,* as if to imply that Dugald's relatives are suing someone else instead; but he is too disconcerted to pursue it. Why in the world did Doog not let him know about Marilyn Marsh? So, he says to her, you're a fucking spy these days.

As a matter of fact no. But you're fouler-mouthed than you used to be.

The world's fouler than it used to be. What do you do? Do we have a Cape Cod station?

She arranges memorial services, Marcus Henry says, polishing his glasses with a handkerchief. Why don't we think about poor Dugald now and talk business over lunch.

Fenwick growls disgustedly Jesus Christ. They have crossed the Potomac and moved up the Virginia palisades. As they turn into a certain entrance road marked Bureau of Public Roads Research Station, Fenn begins to wonder whether there's to be any service at all. Has that whole business been bait? Is he to be *interrogated,* for Christ's sake? They pass the first security checkpoint; Marilyn Marsh shows the armed female guard a visitor's pass for Fenn, which she then gives him. His spirits sink and sink.

The parking lots beside the familiar building appear to be full; the driver puts them out at an entranceway and goes off to find an empty space.

All we could get was a small lecture theater, Marilyn Marsh informs Marcus Henry, and leads the way through another security point. They both carry attaché cases, hers discreetly slimmer than his. Fenn tries to find something amusing in the woman's extraordinary metamorphosis. But it is no metamorphosis: Marilyn Marsh seems altogether in place as an Agency officer; more herself than ever. He wonders whether she's sleeping with Marcus Henry, whom he has never loved; decides that she is by choice probably not sleeping with anyone. The headquarters building is air-conditioned; Fenwick dons his dark coat.

He is relieved to see that there is in fact to be some sort of memorial service. In a small, unfamiliar auditorium a group has foregathered; a taped brass chamber ensemble is softly playing the saraband from a suite by a minor Seventeenth-century Stadtpfeifer whose name Fenwick forgets, but to whose work he was long ago introduced by Dugald Taylor. The current director of the Agency is not on hand, but Fenn recognizes one former director and a number of counterin-telligence and Clandestine Services people. A few heads turn as the trio enters through a side door; Fenn gets some unsurprising dirty looks for KUDOVE—but not, he thinks he observes, from the senior people. If the occasion is no trap, he now wonders, might it be a set-up for a pitch?

The assembly seems to have been awaiting them. A young black woman hands them programs, which they have not time to read. Marilyn Marsh leads the way to seats uncom-fortably in front and murmurs something to Marcus Henry, who, case in hand, steps at once up onto a dais flanked by stereo loudspeakers and adjusts his eyeglasses, the lectern light, and a page of notes. He glances over his specs at someone in a rear corner; the beautiful saraband subsides, and Fenn hears the first of three eulogies to his old friend. The gist of Marcus Henry's is the pity of Dugald Taylor's not living to see certain of his long-term efforts begin to bear fruit in the critical and no doubt dangerous but nonetheless exciting years ahead. The gist of the former director's, delivered without notes, is that the 1980s will indeed be a critical decade, not impossibly the most important in the history of this organization since its establishment by Presi-dent Harry S. Truman. We shall need half a hundred Dugald Taylors; there was but one, and he is no more.

As befits the grave occasion, the eulogists introduce neither themselves nor one another. To Fenwick's immense surprise, as the ex-director returns to his seat Marilyn Marsh herself goes to the dais! Fenn opens his program: there is her name, Marilyn Marsh Turner, under Marcus's and Bill's, all without further identification. Oy oy and oy. That baroque composer, he reads, is Johann Pezel; the saraband is from his Fünff-stimmigte blasende Musik, Frankfurt/Main 1685. Marilyn Marsh, whom Fenn cannot recall ever having heard address a public gathering in their life together, speaks now with entire self-possession, also without notes. There is a fitness, she declares quietly, in the privacy of this mourning for our dead colleague and friend. She invokes the tradition, which she believes to be Hebrew, that the world's survival depends on twelve just men, unknown even to one another. She does not imagine, she acknowledges with a short smile, that the Hebrews had our Agency in mind—though she *does* rather imagine that Mossad, our formidable Israeli counterpart, bears in mind this ancient Hebrew tradition! But it is tempting to think Dugald Taylor one of those twelve—she hopes the patriarchs will permit her to say just *people* instead of just men—and the world's continuance that much more precarious for his death, until another take his place. She glances confidently about the hall. Private successes, private defeats, private recognitions, private eulogies—they go with our territory, whether an officer be currently active, consulting, or retired. Astonishingly now for one never interested in or moved by literature, she invokes Franz Kafka's hunger artist, "the sole satisfied spectator of his own performance": only Dugald Taylor himself, she ventures to say, knew the whole story of his services. However, he and we are luckier than Kafka's hero by reason of one another: the world may scarcely appreciate what we do for it; we ourselves may never know one another's whole story. But we know enough to mourn the loss of a John Arthur Paisley, a Manfred Turner, a Dugald Taylor.

The word formication, which ought to mean getting fucked by ants but doesn't, occurs to Fenwick as Marilyn Marsh returns to her seat beside him, rosy with her own rhetoric. His skin thrills with discomfort, anger, bereavement and other grief. He misses Susan awfully; he wonders how she's faring. He mourns dear Dugald; Manfred. The company sits still as from the empty dais comes now a transcription for English horn and flute of the soprano aria *"Schafe können sicher weiden"* from Bach's Jagdkantate: Sheep may safely graze where a good shepherd watches, surely as beautiful a melody as ever was written. Too obvious an irony, Fenn reflects, to have been Doog Taylor's own selection for his memorial service, but so moving withal—particularly in this brave, lonely duo version—that he cannot keep back his tears.

The flute falls silent; Fenwick blows his nose into his pocket handkerchief; the gathering disperses. Several people stop to say hello in subdued voices and shake Fenn's hand, as if the service has been for Manfred as well as for Dugald (if there was ever in fact one for Manfred, Fenwick was neither apprised nor invited). If no one is exactly cordial, none is uncivil. As soon as he can, Fenn asks Marcus Henry to arrange transportation back to Union Station.

We really ought to have lunch together first, Marcus Henry says, actually taking him by the elbow in a comradely way and leading him a few confidential paces from the exiting group. Marilyn Marsh is at his other elbow. Fenn spits out lowly No pitch, for god's sake! Of course it's a pitch, Marilyn Marsh says equably, which you're perfectly free to decline. We're always pitching; we have to pitch. Think of it as a follow-up to your talk with Doog last week at the Cosmos. Marcus Henry urges We can eat together and then talk separately, if you prefer. That's one of the reasons we invited you here. I have an evening flight back to Boston, says Marilyn Marsh, and nothing crucial between now and then. Fenwick growls So take an earlier flight. You are sore, aren't you. Sure I'm sore. Well I'm not. You shouldn't be.

Marcus Henry says I'll just excuse myself while you lovebirds talk things over. You're making a mistake not to hear us out, Fenwick. Oh? *I've* got plenty of reasons to be sore, too: your *KUDOVE* hasn't helped my recruiting. But believe it or not, the country comes first.

Bullshit, Marc, says Fenn: the Company comes first.

Believe it or not, Marcus Henry repeats, those two aren't always at odds. We know who you are and what you think of us; yet we're prepared to make you a sweet pitch.

It goes without saying, Marilyn Marsh says, that you can say no.

Fenn says No. They stand alone now in a corner of the hall. Catercornered from them an aide takes reels from a tape player. Marcus Henry says suggestively Manfred? Gus Turner?

With furious deliberation Fenwick says I'm satisfied that my brother and his son are both dead.

Marcus Henry asks Is that the end of your interest in them?

Fenn considers. Yes.

Marilyn Marsh shrugs and says to Marcus Henry that in that case she's going down to Key I. again and wrap a few things up before flight time. Marcus Henry instructs her to have the chopper take her right from BARATARIA to Washington National if time gets short. Lunch first?

Sure. They move off, conferring. Marcus Henry calls back that Ms. Anderson will return Fenn to Union Station and collect his pass. Unless he'll change his mind about lunch?

Bait, bait, bait beyond doubt; but it is good bait. Fenwick demands irascibly What's Key Island? Marilyn Marsh smirks, steps a step himward, extends her hand. Lunch?

In the event, Shirley the secretary brings their lunch orders to Marcus Henry's office, presumably for reasons of confidentiality: Smithfield ham sandwiches and canned iced tea. It is a larger office than Fenn's ex-colleague used to have: like a gracious executive, Marcus Henry sits not behind his desk but at a round coffee table with his visitors. He and Marilyn Marsh do not tell all, but they tell some surprising things: more, Fenn decides, than they would if they were not prepared for him to leak their confidences—

perhaps to interest potential new recruits? Marcus Henry, he learns, as Dugald had mentioned, is now in general charge of Agency recruitment, supervising divisional recruitment officers for clerical, maintenance, and other support staff, for Junior Officer Trainees, and the like. Marilyn Marsh has not one but two responsibilities, both considerable: for some years she has assisted the New England station in the recruitment—as agents, not as officers—of foreign students, especially Middle Eastern ones. Since the Iranian revolution and the militants' seizure of our government's embassy in Teheran, this operation has become both more important and less difficult: few SAVAKis stationed in this country chose to return home when the Shah's government was overthrown.

In this capacity Marilyn Marsh works out of a legitimate intercollegiate foreign-student assistance organization in Cambridge and reports only indirectly to Marcus Henry. But over the past eighteen months she has also spent much time in Langley assisting in the design (for the expected conservative risorgimento of the 1980s) of an ambitious program of women's recruitment and training—no longer as clerical support staff, but as regular Junior Officer Trainees. At a new camp—downriver from ISOLATION, Marcus Henry goes so far as to say, and code-named BARATARIA—and a special training-ground "out in the Bay itself," the women JOTs are taught all the skills of their male counterparts—martial arts, tradecraft, and the rest—plus the tactical use of sex. In male-supremacist countries they will cover as embassy-staff wives and clerks: Teapot Terrorists, they call themselves, or Killers in Crinolines, passing as society-minded do-gooders—bright, civic-spirited, harmless. What we used to get from the Ivy League, Marilyn Marsh says, we get now from the Seven Sisters. This project has kept her lately more in Virginia than in Massachusetts, reporting directly to Marcus Henry—and, with her left hand, rendering him such incidental services as the planning of today's memorial for Dugald Taylor, who had been of immeasurable aid to her as a consultant on BARATARIA.

Fenwick strokes his beard, chews his ham, looks from Marcus Henry to Marilyn Marsh as they confide to him these remarkable matters. Can this formidable woman, so obviously now thriving in her natural element, ever have been his wife? Orrin's mother? A maker of beef stews, changer of diapers, darner of socks? And why is he being so taken into their confidence? Affecting underwhelment as best he can, he asks presently Could we get to the pitch?

Marilyn Marsh glances at Marcus Henry and says Poor Doog already made it for us, I believe. We're just following up.

Marcus Henry declares We're prepared to take a positive view of your book: part of the post-Viet Nam reaction of the Nineteen Seventies, blah blah blah, like Agee and Marchetti and Snepp and the rest. You-all hurt us, sure; but what you meant to be a stab in the back, we're taking as a shot in the arm. A healthy corrective. It's time we stopped killing the messenger that brings bad news.

Fenn says You don't believe a word of what you just said.

Marcus Henry is unfazed. I didn't say I believed it; I said we're prepared to take that view. You've seen that despite *KUDOVE* we've taken you a certain way into our confidence.

Fenn demands directly of Marilyn Marsh Did you pitch Carmen Seckler to pitch my son?

That's perfectly preposterous. Marilyn Marsh seems not even annoyed. Are you sick enough to believe I'd consent to any undue pressure on Orrin?

What about due pressure, Fenn wants to know.

There's nothing immoral about national security, Marilyn Marsh replies firmly. But our son is a grown man who can make his own decisions. Anyhow, she cannot resist adding, what kind of an operative would that woman be? No offense meant, but *really*.

Listen here, Fenwick, Marcus Henry says in another tone. Our friend Doog had his vagaries, bless his heart, especially after his retirement. Marcus raises two fingers of each hand to put retirement in quotes. The truth of the matter is, except for his advice on BARATARIA, Doog's consultancies were mostly our favors to an old hand, to keep him from feeling put out to pasture.

Did you-all have him killed?

Marilyn Marsh says indignantly Of course not. Don't be paranoid.

Wouldn't you be saying that same thing if you had had him killed?

No doubt, Marcus Henry acknowledges, and chuckles: But don't be paranoid. We didn't.

Trust us, Fenn says.* Well, I don't. Let's wind up the pitch.

Marcus Henry says You don't have to like us, god damn it—

I don't.

—nor do we have to like you, you sonofabitch, to do business with you.

And we don't, says Marilyn Marsh, believe me. You were always too softhearted, softheaded, liberal, and literary to be a good officer.

Softhearted, softheaded, liberal, and literary, Fenn repeats appreciatively: there's the woman I knew and loved. What did you think of brother Manfred?

Again those two share a meaning glance: then Marilyn Marsh declares that in fact, while undeniably a first-rate officer to the end, Manfred Turner became ever more eccentrically cloak-and-dagger through the 1970s. The house joke was that he was playing Marlon Brando playing Mister Kurtz in Francis Ford Coppola's film *Apocalypse Now*—and that like both Coppola's Kurtz and Joseph Conrad's before him, Manfred and his ad-lib policy-making had become a liability to the Company in that sensitive period. We all worried, Marcus Henry admits, that Manny would pull off something really embarrassing and set back our

---

*He is quoting ex-CIA Director Richard Helms.

plans for the Eighties. He was practically in business for himself.

So you disappeared him.

We most certainly did not. If we had, would I be saying these things?

Sure you would.

We personally regret his death, Marilyn Marsh declares. You know how much I thought of your brother. But we won't deny it was a break for the Company. There.

We wish he had retired instead, Marcus Henry says, like Dugald.

Another piece of luck for the Company, Fenn supposes. You're a lucky outfit.

Marilyn Marsh asserts that Dugald Taylor's case was different, he being in fact as retired as they could diplomatically retire him.

You fuckers, Fenwick says at last. You're both insects compared to Doog and Count. Gnats. Fleas. Lice.

Marilyn Marsh looks gratifyingly shocked at this vulgarity. Let's wind this up, says Marcus Henry. The mole who's about to be indicted in Baltimore Federal Court is a career officer who sold classified CI stuff to the KGB for ninety-two thousand six hundred bucks while he was working for us. You know him: Barnett.* You can imagine we're not in love with the guy for doing that, especially since he also blew the cover on seven of our people. But did we kill him for doubling? Of course not. We pitched him to triple, and when that didn't pan out, we gave him to Justice for prosecution. Now, then: we don't love you, either, but we don't believe you're on their tab. On the other hand, we

---

*A near neighbor of Dugald Taylor's, David Henry Barnett of Bethesda, Md., will be convicted on January 8, 1981, and sentenced to eighteen years in prison after pleading guilty to one count of espionage. By his own confession, Barnett sold to the KGB information about HABRINK, a covert CIA operation to procure technical data on Soviet weaponry. Marcus Henry is apparently mistaken, however, in referring to Barnett as a mole: court records indicate that he left the CIA in 1970, and that his transactions with the KGB took place in Jakarta, Indonesia, in 1976. See, e.g., The Baltimore *Sun*, January 9, 1981.

know and they know you're between careers. You're disenchanted with us. Maybe you're pinched a bit for money after your boat ride. . . .

Not a bit, Fenn interrupts him, and says to Marilyn Marsh We've got my wife's academic salary and no alimony to pay.

We also know that *KUDOVE* is coming out in paperback . . .

That'll pay for bottom paint and digitalis. What else is there?

Marcus Henry concludes So if they pitch you, you miserable bastard, and you want to take their pitch and bring it here, you'll find the fucking latchstring out and a place at the fucking table and a bed turned fucking down, even though we fucking hate your guts. That's all.

Fenwick grins. Irate Marilyn Marsh rises and declares But not *my* bed, you can rest assured. I was going to invite you to take a chopper ride with me over Key Island and BARATARIA, since you seemed so interested. But forget it. Go back to your little schoolmarm.

With difficulty Fenwick restrains himself from taking *that* bait, even from replying. Marilyn Marsh glances once more at Marcus Henry, who says he'll have Shirley summon Ms. Anderson to return their guest to town. He himself must be off now on other business. Marilyn Marsh is welcome to use his desk till her helicopter is ready. It's ready now, Marilyn Marsh declares: she has just a few papers to look at first. Ten minutes. Miz A will be here in five, Marcus Henry tells Fenwick. He can wait in here, Marilyn Marsh tells Marcus Henry. Well, it's your party, Mare, but keep him out of my desk drawers; have a good flight back. Bye, Marc, she replies, and directly the door closes says to Fenn less angrily than before You astonish me.

You me, says Fenn. Astonish and depress.

She opens her small briefcase and takes out papers. You haven't said one pleasant word about our son or our grandson in the works.

Not to you.

With all your faults, Marilyn Marsh says, I never thought

of you as a grudge-holder.

I hold only one.

Marilyn Marsh looks at her papers. Whatever it's for, you've held it ten years already. Isn't that a bit much?

Fenwick declares that he has not yet begun to hold. Talk about dirty tricks.

She does not look up. You're vindictive.

Just resentful.

I've offered more than once to be friends.

So has the Kremlin.

For the baby's sake, and Orrin's and Julie's, you ought to come off it.

Pay me what you owe me, and I'll give it a try.

This taunt visibly finds its mark, but like a good officer, Marilyn Marsh controls herself. The facts aren't as simple as you make them out to be.

The arithmetic is. You collected four hundred ninety-one dollars and sixty-six cents in illegal alimony payments before Orrin blew the whistle on your secret remarriage. I was able to stop payment on one check for two hundred forty dollars and sixty-four cents; that leaves a balance due of two hundred fifty-one dollars and two cents. In my softheaded liberal literary way, I see that sum as a symbol of all my other grievances against you. At a modest six percent interest compounded annually for five years, and without even correcting for inflation, the bill comes to three hundred thirty-five dollars and ninety-two cents. Call it three fifty at rock bottom: enough to overhaul our diesel and fix up some odds and ends. When you settle up, we can talk about letting bygones be bygones.

Now she puts her papers down. Petty, petty bastard. Even has the numbers memorized.

Fenn's adrenaline's perking. Damn straight I do.

Well sue me, you sonofabitch. There's your driver.

It's not worth the trouble to sue you. But I sure will hold my grudge.

Hold it till your sphincters rot. Get out of here.

Susan asks admiringly that night in bed Did she really say that?

Not exactly, but that was the sentiment. I like your new hair.

I chickened out on the perm. What happened next?

Marilyn Marsh stormed out ahead of me, purse in one hand and briefcase in the other, to catch her chopper, and Miz Anderson fetched me back to Amtrak. There's my day.

Susan wishes he had offered to cancel Marilyn Marsh's debt if the woman would revert to her maiden name or use her second or third married name instead of her first. Marilyn Marsh has explained to Orrin Turner that she was Marilyn Marsh Turner for more years of her life (by one) than she was Marilyn Marsh; moreover, that that name makes her feel closer to her son and to the new Turner in Julie's womb. But Sue thinks it sucks to have the world contain two Mrs. Fenwick Turners.

Fenn likewise. He ponders too the circumstance that, had he played his cards more coolly, he'd have had a chance to see Key Island and BARATARIA.

And if you'd taken their pitch, says Susan, we just might have learned something about Gus. But we doubt it. And we don't want you to take that pitch. We're glad you put it to her.

Yeah.

Fuck Marilyn Marsh. Fuck Key Eye.

Fuck qui voulez, says Fenn—quoting a hit song of the rock group at Club Mediterranée Cancún, Yucatán, when *Pokey* paused there last winter and we went ashore to eat and dance. But the mystery nags.

What's the big deal? Most of what you learned we foreshadowed in the first chapter. The rest is an unsolved riddle for us to respect.*

---

*Susan's quoting from Franz Kafka's enigmatic sketch "A Visit to a Mine." Fenn twinges at the coincidence of both Mrs. Fenwick Turners' having separately, in the space of half a day, quoted to their purpose one of our favorite authors, numerous of whose lines are touchstones of our daily conversation.

Yes, well. As a matter of fact, before I lost my cool, when MM was talking about BARATARIA earlier on, I managed to get said that I doubted even the Agency, with its crazy budget and all its new toys, could build an uncharted island smack in the middle of Chesapeake Bay, with full-grown woods and natural coves and marshes, or disappear a natural island from all charts past and present without anyone's blowing the whistle.

What did Marilyn Marsh say?

Marilyn Marsh said That *is* curious, isn't it. And she said it like that: flat, no question mark at the end, the way Doog Taylor would've said it.

We are holding hands in bed. Do you think they killed Doog?

Fenn says he believes that that's one of the things we'll never know. Ditto Key Island, what's what with it. The list of unsolved riddles for us to respect is getting pretty long. We'll sail down that way again someday.

Did they kill Manfred?

Fenn doesn't know, but finally doubts it. There is the Heart of Darkness thing, to be sure: not inappropriate for the Prince of Darkness. But there is also tripping over a jib-sheet, cracking your head on a gunwale, and drowning in four feet of placid tidewater.

Will they kill Fenwick?

We think they're not into personal-grudge murder yet; at least not on the officer level. At least not in domestic waters.

Hm.

I would've liked your hair permed, Fenn says. But I like it this way too.

Wait till you see Mim's. Let's sleep, okay?

Whoa, now. I told you mine; you tell me yours.

Not now. Susan squeezes his hand. It's nothing amazing. I talk better when we're sailing. We do everything better at ten degrees of heel.

Then let's leave tomorrow.

Sue says We'll see. Gram's supposed to come over, and we

have last-minute stuff to do to get ready to spend the summer at Chief and Virgie's, if that's what we're doing. She's not being evasive, really. There's nothing very surprising to tell. But later.

Fenn considers several things, among them that Susan has come to bed with her nightie-pants on, most unusual. Well. I'll bet we have bad dreams.

### WE DO,

but first Susan says Fuck dreams. Fenn is distressed: Fuck dreams, Suse? What do they know, Susan wants to know. By the way, she adds, did you know that Alain Resnais is credited with the first feature film to use flashforwards? No. La guerre est finie, Nineteen Sixty-six: Yves Montand, Geneviève Bujold—I forget who else. Ingrid Thulin. Mit fleshforverts.

I hate a fleshforvert, Fenn says next morning, Saturday 14 June, Flag Day, hot and still. His was about failure: professional, personal, physical. Sitting next to him yesterday in the Amtrak coach to Baltimore had been a paunchy self-important late-sixtyish man in soiled summer worsteds— string bow tie, loose dentures, florid face, dandruff on his shoulders like shaken salt from his ill-kempt salt-and-pepper hair—who turned out to be a leading figure in the Virginia Poetry Society, a compulsive self-promoter even unto strangers on a short train ride, and the very odor of failure. In Fenn's dream, Fenn was that man, losing obscure battles with the right-wing Poet Laureate of Maryland. Susan was long since gone, god knows where: she'd left him, and with good reason. Every dollar counted. He had no friends. Marilyn Marsh, thriving, prospering, was thick as thieves with Julie and Grandson Marshall Marsh Turner, named in her honor. But Orrin's career was going ill, and even Marshall Marsh was doing poorly in school. Chief and Virgie were dead; Fenn himself was sick and sore; every movement was painful; Key Farm was falling down; there was no money to maintain it. Even Wye Island was disappearing, and that circumstance was somehow Fenn's fault. An aide to the President-elect was on the telephone, but Fenwick could find no other rhyme for inaugural than doggerel. He smelled death: it smelled like the breath of that Virginia Poetry Society man.

I hate a fleshforvert too, Susan says. Boy oh boy. Hers moved from toxic shock to toxic waste to the linked collapses of our marriage, the economy of the Western world, the natural environment, and the social fabric. At about three A.M. the American middle class evaporated; war broke out between the poor and the super-rich. Julie hated her and turned the grandson against her. Now Marilyn Marsh was raping her with an electric cattle-prod, as Miriam had been raped in Evin Prison, while in the background—

She woke herself and went to the toilet. Though she was still uncomfortable, the vaginal bleeding had all but stopped. Fenn half thought he heard sobs in there, but he wasn't sure where he was—his and Count's bedroom at Key Farm? The bedroom of his and Marilyn Marsh's first apartment, in a student warren on St. Paul St. in Baltimore? His tourist-class stateroom on the S.S. *Nieuw Amsterdam* in 1960? A hospice for the indigently terminal?

He waits for Susan to tell him about yesterday. Through the hot morning and hotter afternoon we assemble most of what we'd stored with Carmen—*Pokey* will go down to Wye Island loaded like a container ship—and pick up a few fresh supplies for that short cruise. We see no reason to protract our stay at Fells Point. Over lunch Fenn tells Carmen B. Seckler what Marcus Henry told him about Manfred. Carmen replies that she is developing a powerful curse upon the military-industrial establishment, buoyed by the recent success of the one she laid on Chrysler Corporation two years back when she traded in her lemon Imperial for the Mercedes. She asks whether Marilyn Marsh should be included in or excluded from. Fenn says Dealer's choice. They are in the restaurant; Dumitru comes over to the booth with Susan, who has been telephoning Grandma. She avoids her mother's eyes.

That night we have a good-bye family dinner. Miriam's hair-do is something else, all right, but has not yet had the desired effect on Eastwood Ho. The sight of her moves Susan more than ever since that cattle-prod flashforward. We all get a little high again, Fenwick and Susan especially. Dumitru makes Romanian toasts to our new careers, to Miriam's Afro, to Susan's ass, which he finally pats, to life and art and Carmen B. Seckler and the star-spangled banner. He begins to go on in English about the Kennedy assassinations, but Carmen cuts him off. Fenwick responds with a toast to Romany and joy. Mim gets the giggles; they turn into the weeps; Grandma hugs her. Eastwood Ho sings a teasing ca dao of which he will translate only the last two lines:

A deep sea and a deep river are easily plumbed.
A woman's heart, though shallow, is fathomless.

Sometimes I want to pop him, Carmen says; him and his lục-bát. But she kisses him instead, on the cheek. We even dance, and Susan gets her ass patted some more, by Dumitru and Eastwood too! What's the matter with you? she asks Fenwick. I'll pat, I'll pat, Fenwick assures her: when you've told me yours. Sue says suddenly I want to go now, and even as Fenn says Now? he realizes that he very much does too, want to go, back to Gibson Island Harbor, *Pokey*, now, not tomorrow morning as planned. It will be a nuisance for us and for whoever drives us; it will break up the party. But we must go.

Carmen B. Seckler as always understands. Grandma has tears in her eyes: for so long she has said to herself Susan's coming, Susan's coming, and now so soon Susan's going. Sue kisses her, we all kiss one another, Fenn kisses Eastwood Ho and Dumitru, Edgar Allan Ho, Sy. Both boys cling lugubriously to Susan until she promises them they can ride along. It will take two cars, says Carmen, but what the fuck. Excuse me, Havah.

No it won't. Sue is the practical logistician again, never wrong. Unless we're all going. Our stuff'll fit in the Mercedes trunk and half the back seat. You and Fenn and Edgar can sit up front and me and Sy in the back. Do-Me-True and Eastwood Ho can mind the store, and Mims can take Grandma home. D'you mind, Ma? Mimsi? They don't. Eastwood? Doom?

Doom, Carmen growls. Jesus, Shushi.

We pitch in, lug seabags and cartons and hang-up clothes including Susan's new ones from Loehmann's. More kisses. Miriam promises to bring the boys over to Wye I. as soon as we're settled in. Final ass-pat from Doom; Carmen B. Seckler says That's enough patting asses. We fit exactly as foretold; there's even room for two fifty-pound blocks of ice in a canvas tote bag; but we're in for many dark dinghy-trips between dock and mooring.

Not necessarily, Susan says. We'll store all but the food and one seabag in the club boathouse tonight and bring *Pokey* to the dock after breakfast to load up.

Gibson Island being Gibson Island, Fenwick doubts that. But she's right again. Carmen B. Seckler recharms Fred the customs sentry; Susan charms Henry the boathouse manager. It being a Saturday night and the club in sedate full swing, Henry doesn't want us traipsing our duffel through the boathouse lounge, but we are permitted a rear loading-door and a corner of his office. Only the hanging-locker items cannot be accommodated. We'll just have to take our hang-ups with us, Sue quips. Fenn says admiringly This certainly is your evening.

It is coming on to midnight, but balmy. We all stand a moment on the dock, Edgar Ho bouncing in Susan's arms and chewing placidly on a small American flag. Were it not for our fatigue and the hassle of loading and stowing so much gear in the dark, we should be sorely tempted to set out now on the ghost of a southerly just springing up. But we are a touch drained and nervous, and for that matter have not even heard a weather forecast. Recorded dance

music older than Susan Seckler wafts out from the boathouse to the dock: Glenn Miller's "Sunrise Serenade,"
Tommy Dorsey's "Opus One." Some yachtsfolk are having
nightcaps aboard: we see cigarette-tips and hear social
conversation from the cockpits of boats moored in the black
harbor. Fenn and Sy find and launch our dinghy and tie it
up to the dock. We promise to take Sy sailing overnight
when he comes to visit, if he will quit smoking and leave his
hard shoes home.

So it's Wye Island, Carmen B. Seckler remarks to both of
us.

Susan says It looks that way. Fenwick sighs and says Faute
de mieux. But plans can change.

Love to Chief and Virgie, Carmen says. We stand with our
arms about one another's waists. Everything is so strange,
Susan says to her mother. Life is too strange, Ma!

Carmen B. Seckler acknowledges that it is that. We thank
her for shlepping us and all; we kiss auf wiedersehen.
Susan's still in a good dress: odd sight and charming, her
climb down from dock to dinghy. Sy calls merrily when her
white-pantied crotch flashes in the moth-rich docklight I see
Christmas, Aunt Susan!

Jesus, Messy, she says amiably, you're weird, you know?
Hand me the hangie-ups.

He does. Fenn remarks You're going to mess that dress.
Susan says It's a shmatta. Bye, Ma. Bye, boys.

Bye all, calls Fenwick. As we row off, Carmen B. Seckler
lights a cigarillo and picks up Edgar Allan Ho; the child
waves and waves from her arms. Sy hollers Bon voyage,
pronouncing both words in English and waving his brother's
flag. Carmen sings to Edgar in what might be Croatian.
Away from the lighted dock, our eyes begin to accommodate. It is never unexciting to row across a dark harbor on a
still night. Up over Susan's head Fenwick sees Perseus and
Company; he looks for Algol, the eclipsing binary that in
most renderings of the constellation is Medusa's winking
eye. He thinks he finds her, but isn't sure. There goes

Carmen B. Seckler, probably, back over the causeway. Starboard, Susan says; Fenn pulls harder on his right oar. Only the whitest hulls are discernible, and they barely. Without a flashlight, we have to hunt about a bit for our boat.

To people relaxing in the cockpit of the yawl *Betelgeuse* out of Wilmington Del., under whose transom we slip, Sue says Howdy. Fenn wonders why he doesn't simply ask her Why in the world did we fake two menstruations, honey, but he doesn't. Port, I think, says Susan. Is this us?

It is. Hello, old fellow. We come alongside and secure the painter; Fenwick hefts the ice aboard and climbs up after. Careful, he says; there's dew. Sue waits in the dinghy while he opens the cabin; then she hands up our seabags and hanging things, grabs a stanchion, hikes her dress to her waist, and takes the long step from dinghy-seat to *Pokey*'s gunwale so that Fenn won't have to unship and rig the boarding ladder. The cabin is stuffy; we open all ports and hatches, rig a windscoop forward. But oh my, it is good to be back aboard. We move easily about the familiar cabin in the dark, not to attract insects. Susan turns back the bedsheets. As Fenn stows our clothes, she embraces him from behind; he murmurs, turns, holds her. More familiar to him in the dark than *Pokey*'s layout is hers: the push of her breasts against his chest, the curve of her behind under his right hand. His penis stirs. Sue squeezes him through his pants and murmurs Tomorrow. It's been a hell of a long chapter, and we're not done with it yet.

This chapter, Fenwick says into her hair, would make a novel by itself.

No it wouldn't.

Naked and at ease now in our separate berths, Susan falls asleep in two minutes; Fenn unwinds more gradually. He feels the cooler air moving through the cabin over his skin; listens to his wife's breathing and the faint dance-band music from ashore. Where are things headed for Mr. and Mrs. Turner? For the world? He hopes we'll have no more flashforward dreams.

## BUT WE DO.

Quick, sharp, more or less awful. Why is prescience never good news? Fenwick's begins realistically enough, from what in fact he falls asleep musing upon: prompted no doubt by Susan's rowing directions, he dreams our possible futures as a literal fork in the channel, or a series of such forks, each presenting us with the options of steering astarboard, aport, or astern. For himself, in the dream at least, going "right" implies as plainly as if charted accepting his academic appointment; acknowledging that in the dangerous real world, as in an alley-scrap, it is often necessary for good governments to resort to dirty tricks; committing his main energies therefore not to further exposure of the Agency, but to improvement of his academic credentials and to fathering and parenting a child by Susan. Going "left" he sees just as clearly to mean declining the Delaware appointment, living off his lecture fees and consultancies for the several liberal "watchdog" organizations which have approached him since *KUDOVE;* spending yet more time in Washington pursuing the disappearance of Gus and Manfred until something, somebody, gives, and dedicating himself heart and soul against Marilyn Marsh's employer, at least the clandestine services end of it: that Agency whose motto, graved in marble in its Langley lobby, is the same as Fenn's alma mater's and therefore a perversion of St. John: *And you shall know the truth, and the truth shall make you free.** There are no children down this fork; at the end of it there is no Susan either. And going "back"? He bids farewell to his beloved, who is young enough yet to find a mate her age and begin a normal family life; he takes Marcus Henry's

---

*John 8:32, quoting Jesus teaching in the temple. Awake, Fenn will acknowledge that inasmuch as Jesus meant "the truth of God as I teach it" and not the disinterested secular truth properly pursued by universities, Johns Hopkins's *Veritas vos liberabit* is also a perversion of John's gospel, though a benign one. The word *free,* too, clearly means different things to Jesus, Johns Hopkins, and James Jesus Angleton, but Fenwick's dream does not concern itself with these distinctions.

pitch and, clearer-headed and singler-purposed than he was in the 1960s, recrosses the Potomac to serve the United States Central Intelligence Agency by subverting it as the most patriotic of double agents: one whose truest loyalty is to his country rather than his department. He mends fences with Marilyn Marsh; they retire together, passions cooled, old quarrels mellowed away. This dream, Fenwick reflects even as he dreams it, appalled, will give Susan the howling heaves.

And for her? Going right (in Fenn's dream they do it literally, in the boat, turning to starboard at the head of the Bay into the Chesapeake and Delaware Canal) means Swarthmore, scholarship, resignation to childlessness if not to childless widowhood. Going left means up the Patapsco to Baltimore, perhaps with Fenn; taking Miriam's cue and giving her talents to some inner-city high school or blue-collar community college; helping the disadvantaged instead of writing one more essay on the mysteries of Poe's "Narrative of Arthur Gordon Pym," a silly farrago after all; perhaps conceiving a child, by Fenn or whomever; perhaps adopting one or helping poor Mim raise her guiltless bastards. What do you mean Whomever? Fenn demands in the dream. Who's this Whomever? And going back? Fenwickless, she takes a job at the Madeira School for girls, just north of Washington, where as once before she enhances the excellence of the excellent, the privileges of the privileged. Teaching there is a perfect delight; her colleagues respect her; her students love her. In time she comes to return the love of a teacher of American history slightly younger than herself whose father was a Kennedy cabinet member and international banker. More than anything else, Fred Henry desires children; they will follow the ancestral path through Hotchkiss and Harvard. He asks Susan whether she'd mind changing her first name as well as her last; she invites him to call her by any name he likes. Fenwick resolves to have Carmen B. Seckler lay a curse upon the cockstrings of this Fred Henry. Unhappily he searches the Y for other futures. Susan's cry wakes him: Reynolds! Reynolds!

What? *Her* night's mare has flashed forward from the night before's, and is for the most part impersonal. Our marriage having failed along with the Democratic coalition, the NATO alliance, the U.S. dollar, and Fenwick's heart, to the strains of "The Star-Spangled Banner," Susan witnesses the physical collapse in turn of the continental United States (which splits anticlimactically at the San Andreas fault), of the hemisphere (when that fault connects with others), then of the solar system, the galaxy, the universe—for some reason all because she and Fenn will have no children. From McHenry's ramparts, which are also *Pokey*'s cockpit, Susan sees the West sink into the sun, the sun into the galactic vortex like Odysseus's ship-timbers into Charybdis, or whatever-it-was into Poe's Maelstrom. *Pokey* himself is now become our galaxy, now our universe, rushing headlong into one of its own Black Holes like that legendary bird that flies in ever-diminishing circles until it vanishes into its own fundament; like Pym's canoe rushing into the chasm at the foot of the cataract at the southern Pole: a black hole aspirating, with a cosmic shlup, us, U.S., all.

Sunday is just dawning over Gibson Island when Sue's cry wakes us. Naked Fenwick scrambles aft in its early light; we clutch, grunt, whimper. However we may later smile at their recounting, our nerves still thrill with appall at Fenwick's dream, horror at Susan's. Rocking, holding him, she weeps like one catharsed. I knew, I knew, Fenn hears himself soothing. Sue wails I just didn't want to *say* it! If I'd said it, I couldn't have done it! I understand, Fenn says, and half does. Sue cries Oh god! What's it all about? What are we going to do? It's okay, Fenn says, hoping it will be.

Calmer once the day is definite, we presently put pajamas on for breakfast time. Washing her face, Susan explains that one J. N. Reynolds of Baltimore, author of "Mocha Dick: Or

The White Whale Of The Pacific: A Leaf From A Manuscript Journal,"* was a friend of Poe's. That his writings are
a likely source of Arthur Gordon Pym. That Reynolds!
Reynolds! were Poe's dying words.

I see, says Fenn, and does, sort of. Look here, Suse, he
says then: let's take the shortcut to Wye I.

Susan's digging through the icebox. What?

Instead of going back down under the Bridge, the way we
came up, let's cut straight across to Love Point and go down
the Chester and through Kent Narrows.

Susan doesn't care one way or the other; she wonders why
the man even mentions such a nothing.

Fenwick lights the stove for coffee. It'll cut an hour off the
ride, which makes sense if we might have thundershowers
later on. It'll let us reach across instead of going upwind in
light air.

Yeah, sure, I don't care, Sue says. Want grapefruit?

Okay. And it'll remind us how happy we were the first
time we sailed over there to Love Point and the Chester
River together. To Cacaway.

Mm.

---

*Published in *The Knickerbocker, New York Monthly Journal,* 13 (May
1839).

# 3
# CACAWAY
## *Against the Tide*

Pink grapefruit from Lexington Market, bagels from
Corned Beef Row. Lox, cream cheese, sliced tomato, red
onion, coffee. Over breakfast we speak further, guardedly,
of our dreams. We trust that that is that, flashforwardwise.
We hope that whatever passes for the fifth and final item in
that silly self-fulfilling sequence (which our story, like a folk-
tale maiden given freedom of the palace but warned not to
open one particular door, appears to be following perversely)—the dream that allegedly reorchestrates elements of the
preceding four into a grand finale—will be less lugubrious.
Apropos of Fenwick's vision of Susan's returning—without
him!—to Baltimore, to teach disadvantaged instead of ad-
vantaged children and to help Miriam raise hers, Sue
declares I've thought of that. The teaching part and the Sy-
and-Edgar part, anyhow.

Oh?

Things won't last with Mims and Eastwood. Only the job
keeps him in Fells Point. Mim's no wife and mother. She
knows how to fuck, but so what? Sue sips her coffee, up in
the cockpit. Maybe she and I should both give up men.
Maybe we'll live together as incestuous twin lesbians and
devote ourselves to Messy and E. A. Ho. I wish they were
girls. No I don't; I like boys. Dear little Ho.

Fenn says Let's load our stuff before the dock gets busy.
Once we're under way we have things to get said.

No acknowledgment. We clean up, strip off our PJs, toilet.

Seven years married, we take pleasure still in the sight of each other's dressing. Sue slips into underpants and cut-off jeans, boat moccasins, a denim workshirt unbuttoned and knotted under her breasts. She wears a gold chain necklace from Fenn from Charlotte Amalie that she rarely removes; gold Gypsy earrings from Carmen from last evening. On an impulse she makes a headband of our paisley scarf from Part I. Fenwick wants to handle her and does, some, but our air's not clear; she permits but won't respond. Yet it gives Susan pleasure, too, to watch his bulky male equipment flop into a tight French swimsuit, gold, she bought him in Guadeloupe, over which for dockwork he slips khaki Bermuda shorts. Like her, he puts on his moccasins and, to her surprise, a pukka-shell necklace symbolic in our family more of setting out on cruises than of ending them. Finally, for her amusement he dons a beige T-shirt she bought him in Roadtown, Tortola, B.V.I., with the legend I BORN HERE, and a wide-brimmed canvas sailing hat from Solomons, already stained with suntan lotion. Duly amused, she kisses lightly his chest, his brown hand. With a man like Fenwick it's a pleasure to be a woman; with a woman like Susan, bliss to be a man. When the air is clear.

As we watch and dress, we check the NOAA forecast and speak as aforementioned of the virtuosity of Eastwood Ho, sullen master of ca dao. The prospect of late afternoon or evening thundershowers is confirmed; until their arrival it's to be a fine warm Sunday, though with only a very light southerly to sail by. Fenn declares We should reach Wye I. well before storm time.

Mm.

If that's where we're headed.

Of course it's where we're headed.

I sense, among the crew, small enthusiasm.

Sue wonders aloud, as we secure the cabin and make ready to move from mooring to dock, whether Eastwood Ho has a six-five couplet as well as his standard six-eight: one that heads back toward its starting place but quits before it gets there. Fenn says Hm.

We warm up the diesel, sponge dew off the coamings and cabin trunk, tie up at the dock, and retrieve our copious gear from Henry's office. When all's aboard, there being no boats waiting yet for tie-up space, Susan goes to telephone her mother and grandmother to say good-bye again while Fenwick hoses down *Pokey's* deck and topsides and then goes below to secure the cargo. The job takes a while: he's a touch surprised to find his wife not back yet when it's done. Long good-byes? We are in no particular hurry; yet while he much wonders what waits us at voyage's end, he's more than usually impatient to get under way. When Sue returns, she finds the diesel idling, the after dockline already cast off. Fenn has one hand on the tiller, the other on the dock.

Susan knows well and customarily humors this impatience, but will not be unduly rushed. From the dock, she casts off the forward line, gives the bow pulpit a firm push off—for an awful moment Fenwick thinks She's not stepping aboard!—then steps aboard as the bow swings out. While Fenn threads us through the harbor, she coils and stows the lines, retrieves the fenders, lets the dinghy out to the full length of its painter; then she takes the helm so that he can uncover and raise the main and the club jib. If there's air enough to move us respectably against the last of the incoming tide, we shall tack down Sillery Bay to the mouth of the Magothy, then unroll the big genoa for a leisurely reach due east across the Bay from Mountain Point, at the foot of Gibson Island, to Love Point at the top of Kent Island: the wide mouth of the Chester River.

As soon as we clear the harbor, Fenn cuts the engine. Bliss, bliss, to hear its last chuff and the slide of seawater along the hull; to be quietly sailing together again however slowly. Maybe we'll set the genoa now, nuisance though it is to reset from side to side each time we tack. Distracted Susan shrugs. We kick off our moccasins and spell each other at the tiller so that both can lotion up against the sun.

How's Gram this morning?

Sue smiles. She says we should have good selling and I should take you around.

So do it.

She does, a quick light hug, and goes back to lotioning her legs, other things obviously on her mind.

Carmen?

It's spooky, Fenn. Ma was waiting for my call. She knew absolutely I was going to call.

That's not spooky; it's Jewish.

Sue shakes her head. She even kept the line clear so I wouldn't get a busy signal.

That's not Jewish, Fenn agrees. It's Gypsy. What's new since ten o'clock last night?

Things are bad, Fenn. Mims had an episode on her way back from taking Grandma home. She drove up to a parked police car on Falls Road near Cross Keys and started talking crazy stuff about the rights of the unconceived. They were going to book her, but she passed the breath test, so Dumitru and Eastwood Ho had to go rescue her and the car.

Oh boy.

Eastwood didn't hit her, but when they all got back to the bar some graduate-student poets were reading their things in there, free verse, and Ma guesses that did it: he sort of went berserk. Doom got *him* calmed down while Ma calmed Mimsi down, but he's given notice to all hands that he's found a job in State College P A, don't ask me doing what. Maybe singing lục-bát́s to the Nittany Lions.*

Oh dear.

He's leaving in two weeks and taking Edgar with him. Ma thinks he's found a paisana up there, but he might be just trying to get away from Fells Point. Nobody blames him, least of all Mimi. Do-Me-True says Eastwood's in trouble in Baltimore anyhow, with the cops or the rackets or the Company or somebody, and ought to move along. I don't know. Evidently they were all holding off on some things for our sake, till we were out of the house. Mimsi's way down.

---

*The Pennsylvania State University football team, named after long-gone denizens of a nearby mountain named in turn after a legendary, lovelorn, and longer-gone Indian maiden.

Should we go back? Fenn fears we ought, hopes we needn't, lays us over on the next short tack. *Pokey*'s moving, but not impressively.

I said Yes, Susan says. Ma said No. That it's better if Mims deals with this first and then we bring her over to Key Farm for a while once we're settled.

Fenn thinks Good-bye summer but says nothing.

Sue flips the lotion bottle into the cabin. Ma also had another major visit from Manfred last night, while you and I were busy flashing forward.

Oy oy oy. We thought Count promised not to make any more house calls.

Yeah, well. This one was definitely a dream, not like the others. It turns out Manfred drowned, all right, but not from *Pokey*. He set all that up so people would think he was Paisleying out, and then he skipped the country to rescue Gus from General Pinochet,* just as he'd rescued Mims from the Shah of Iran.

Oyoyoyoyoy. Have I got a bone to pick with my brother.

Deadpan Susan goes on What's more, he *did* rescue him. His cover was so good that he got himself into Chile and clear down to Punta Arenas on the Straits of Magellan, the bottom of the fucking world. There's this big prison island there, Dawson Island, in the middle of the Straits of Magellan, and that's where Mundungus was. Manfred got out there somehow, and he and Gus actually managed to escape, but the little sardine boat from Porvenir that was to ferry them back to Punta Arenas ran into a Chilean patrol boat—it was the night of July Tenth Nineteen Seventy-nine, summertime here but winter down there—and in trying to shake the patrol boat they hit a rock and the sardine boat went down. The fisherman survived: his name is Alejandro Gutmann, he's German-Chilean, and he had the only life-jacket on board. They caught him, and now *he's* in the

---

*Augusto Pinochet, president of Chile since the overthrow and murder of Salvador Allende Gossens in 1973.

Dawson Island prison forever. The patrol boat was named *Esmeralda*.* Gus and Manfred died of hypothermia, Gus first because he was weak from jail.

Jesus, Suse. Coming about. Your mother's kerflooey for real this time.

Susan replies almost angrily It's okay! I hate rationalism! Fenn holds his tongue. Ma says they're all right, says Sue. They were happy to be together at the end, and hypothermia isn't painful.

Fenwick steadies the tiller in the crack of his ass and trims the starboard genoa sheet for the new tack. How come Count didn't tell her this story till now?

Sue finds our sunglasses. People don't always tell things right away.

Well, that's true.

Sometimes they have to wait till they're ready, or until the other person's ready.

Okay.

Their judgment might be wrong, but it's all they've got to work with. Anyhow, Ma's been having misgivings about Dumitru, whether she has another loser on her hands like Mim and Eastwood and Sy. You remember that Kennedy-CIA-FBI business that he started at dinner, when she shut him up. Manfred told her not to worry, that Leonard Bernstein† and plenty of other sensible people agree with

---

*Manfred Turner's ghost or spirit may be mistaken in this identification. The *Esmeralda* is not a coastal patrol vessel but a regular Chilean navy ship which, with the ships *Lebu* and *Maipu*, was anchored off Valparaiso and used extensively for the torture of Allende sympathizers after the military coup of 1973. See, e.g., the *Amnesty International Report on Torture*, pp. 206, 207. There may of course be more than one Chilean vessel named *Esmeralda*: on Chesapeake Bay one will find dozens each of cruising sailboats named *Windsong*, *Dawn Treader*, *Moonraker*, *Sundance*, and the like.

†Although the well-known composer and former conductor of the New York Philharmonic has expressed publicly on several occasions his dissatisfaction with the official investigations into President John Kennedy's assassination, we do not ourselves know that he subscribes to the notion here attributed to him by the apparition of Manfred Turner.

Dumitru about the CIA—Mafia—anti-Castro connection in Kennedy's assassination, and that Dumitru probably *was* harassed by people from the Agency or the Bureau, as he claims, but that he isn't in any particular danger now and she should tell him so so he can quit worrying already. Also, that this really was the last time she'd be hearing from him, but he and Mundungus are waiting for her and they'll all be together again one day but there's no hurry, they can wait, she should enjoy her life with Do-Me-True first.

Susan.

I'm not done yet. Then Gus came on.

Came on?

Ma's dream was like one of those talk shows. Gus came on and teased her about that sperm-and-egg business of hers. How our children are really our grandchildren? He kept calling her Grandma, and Grandma Great-Great-Grandma.

Good old Gus.

The bottom line of this whole dream was that given the way the world's going, there's something to be said for not having any such grandchildren. They cited for example the proliferation of nuclear weapons, how Israel's supplying the stuff for them to South Africa and Taiwan, all the pariahs; and France to Iraq and I forget who to Pakistan et cetera. The deforestation and desertication of the planet. The decline of almost everybody's living standards. The massive cover-up of toxic waste disposal. The acid rain problem.

That's a half-assed argument, Suse.

Half an ass is better than none.

Was it Count's or Gus's argument? I'm ashamed of them. Or was it Carmen B. Seckler's?

Ma said they all agreed. Susan looks up at him. The message was for you and me, of course: to be content with your sperm and my eggs and not to mind not having grandchildren.

Um.

You might also be interested to know that Ronald Reagan is going to win the November election and increase the military budget and cut back on social programs and build the neutron bomb and the MX missile and *lots* of ships for the navy and support the right-wingers in El Salvador and South Korea and everywhere else and get the government off the backs of the oil companies and the air and water polluters. That's the news.

Thank you. Fenwick wants to say that he can't fancy cozying up to his sperm or Susan's ova: teaching them how to handle a boat and kick a soccer ball and love liberty and justice and good bordeaux. He refrains, knowing Susan can't either. One port tack carries us out of Sillery Bay, down into the Magothy, where other sails are now appearing, getting a leg up on the day. The next starboard tack will fetch us to the river's mouth. In the gentle air, *Pokey* stands at an easy seven degrees of heel and tracks unsteered as if on rails: steady, stately, and out of plumb, like the Pisan campanile. Fenn does stretching exercises in the cockpit: our days ashore have left him feeling overfed and logy. Carmen's dream is no doubt correct about a general downturn. Fenwick himself does not expect to live so long as Chief, or, in his latter years, so well. Herman Chief Turner was born with the century; Fenn expects to die with it, if he lives that long. Chief grew taller than his immigrant father; Fenwick and Manfred grew taller than Chief; but Orrin's the same height as Fenn, and Gus was shorter than Manfred. Neck-rolls, waist-pivots, toe-touches, arm- and shoulder-stretchers. A corner has been turned, feels gloomy Fenn: perhaps psychological and actuarial as well as economic. Twenty squats to tighten his reins against constipation; a dozen push-ups on the cabin trunk; then he returns to the helm.

On his mind is that none of the above considerations is sufficient reason not to reproduce oneself, though all may be invoked as consolation for not doing so; but he keeps this opinion to himself. The fact is that Carmen's preposterous child-grandchild conceit has fertilized his imagination. As we glide on, thinking our separate thoughts, Fenn's are of those beautiful time-lapse films of sperm and eggs coming together. He finds something appallingly yet engagingly male about those hordes of urgent swimmers, most of them thrashing upstream—eagerly? obliviously?—as if in a water marathon, a few flailing off in the wrong direction or back toward where they came from, as if they either didn't get the general message or got it, all right, but elected to dissent from its blind imperative. And he sees likewise something far from invidiously female—something womanly, even queenly—in the egg's cool glide to meet her suitors less than half way. Fenn wants to try upon Susan his notion, exactly half serious (but half an ass et cetera), that among the sundry isomorphies of the cycle of mythic-heroic adventure is the career of the rare successful spermatozoon, from its virgin birth, so to speak, through its threshold-crossing; its dark sea-journey; the loss of its companions (and ultimately its own identity and tail); its election, in the deepest chamber of the sacred precinct, to an extraordinary, transcendent union; its—rather, henceforward, *their*—subsequent serial metamorphoses, as ontogeny recaps phylogeny in the gestatory flight; its recrossing of the threshold and rebirth into the light—so transformed by the adventure as to go unrecognized until some Carmen B. Seckler sees through its disguise to its true identity. The story of our lives.

He will, in time, speak to her of this, and sharp Susan, amused, will point out many another usable parallel in that fecund Irish dessert. But he can't well speak of our story before she's told him hers. He peels off I BORN HERE and lotions his back and chest in the warming air as Susan watches, expressionless.

Okay: we tack now for Mountain Point. Not easy to make conversation this A.M. Fenwick tries silence a while longer, then remarks—apropos of what?—that our both being twins (though dizygotic) ought to give us some kind of authorial edge over, e.g., the Dumas père of The Iron Mask, the R. L. Stevenson of Dr. Jekyll and Mr. Hyde, also Mark Twain, Vladimir Nabokov, and other such fanciers of twins, doubles, and Doppelgängers as images of the divided or narcissistic self; even of the schizophrenia that some neo-

Freudians maintain lies near the dark heart of writing. Oh?
We literal twins, he declares, might justly turn the tables and
use schizophrenia as the image of our plural selves, narciss-
ism as the image of our love for another; for *we* know to the
bone the truth of Aristophanes' wonderful fancy*: that we
are each of us the fallen moiety of a once-seamless whole.
But so far from being doomed to seek forever and in vain
our missing half, whether of the same or of opposite sex, *we*
know that half supremely well, perhaps better than anyone
normally knows anyone else; and our habit of wholeness
ought to make us ideal partners, especially for another twin,
compatible as left hand and right—even if, perhaps particularly if, our original half falls by the way.

So the man fancifully spins on as we leave Mountain Point
abeam and ease all sheets. It pleases him, given the circumstances, to be headed neither upstream nor downstream,
upwind nor downwind, but noncommittally across both
breeze and tide. Inasmuch as our course after Love Point—
down into the Chester, through Kent Island Narrows and
down Prospect and Eastern bays to Wye River—will be
southerly, dead to windward, this leg may well be our last
sailing of the day, perhaps our last for some while. He
returns to the cockpit to settle in for a sweet reach to the
Eastern Shore.

And finds his darling at the tiller in entire tears! Fenn's
heart makes a tremendous stir; opens like a lock or flower as
he takes her around.

Susan wails into his chest-hair It was twins! It was Drew
and Lexie! I didn't have an abortion, Fenn. I had *two*
abortions!

Fenwick has no voice. Her face awful with red wet grief,
Susan explains: that double shlup from the vacuum aspira-
tor, as if the dog Tibor had gobbled two baby mice! She

---

*In Plato's *Symposium;* cf. Carmen B. Seckler by radiotelephone
p. 242 *supra.*

vomits completely now over the portside gunwale while
Fenn holds her hips, and then, her womb and stomach
empty, she disgorges the story. Laminaria. Jeff Greenberg.
Miriam, Loehmann's, Carmen B. Seckler. Morris Steinfeld.
The question why she, at least, hadn't acknowledged our
pregnancy straight out, an unprecedented lapse of candor
between us: a matter not merely of our indecision, but—

It was your *heart!* she cries, miserable. I *hated* all that
faking with the Midols and Tampax, but I couldn't accept
that we got ourselves pregnant before we'd decided one way
or the other! Or that we'd decided not to decide, or decided
no but couldn't acknowledge it. I didn't want to have that
baby, much as I wanted it more than anything! I didn't want
to abort it till we got home, and I didn't want to go around
till then being *pregnant.* I didn't want to talk about it or about
aborting it, to spare both of us. You especially: a big
emotional wring-out in mid-Atlantic. I was afraid for your
heart!

Fenwick squeezes her and says I guess I knew, Suse. I
pretty much understood. He takes a long breath. The truth
is, there's been some new justification.

Terrified at what she hears in his voice, Sue pushes free.
His turn now: the episode on the bus that Wednesday en
route from D.C. to Solomons Island. He would have told her
about it that same evening, but she was wiped out already
from coping with Miriam and the boys on board, and so he
put off telling her and put off telling her, just as we put off
acknowledging our pregnancy and, since Black Friday, its
aborting.

Wild-eyed Susan hears him out. *Pokey* slides east, past
Baltimore Light. Agitation, stress, excitement, Fenwick affirms, can no doubt be triggers: he had been with Doog
Taylor and had heard about the pitch to Carmen, possibly to
Orrin; also about the Company's rumored new cardiac-
arrest capability. On the other hand, be it not forgot that our
storm at sea had no ill effects, when Fenn's heart was
marinated in adrenaline for hours; or that seeing Marilyn

Marsh in Marcus Henry's car—a beam-ends knockdown for sure—triggered nothing in the cardiac way. Fenwick supposes his condition to be like a cheap pistol that will misfire nine times out of ten no matter how hard one pulls the trigger—

Cries Susan And then go off in the nightstand drawer while we're sound asleep!

Well. I won't have us walking on eggs with me. I won't have us living under wraps.

Won't shmont! shrieks Sue. Then calms herself. I want children, she weeps, quietly now, and I'm not going to have any. I don't believe Ma's crap: this is the only life we have, and it's running out so fast! Who gives a damn about TDS in the ALI?* Or all those rights and lefts and sternwardses in your dream—who gives a shit which way we go? I want a normal house with kids and dogs and petunias.

Fenwick feels compelled to remind her You hate dogs.

Sue wipes her eyes on the back of her hand. Yeah, all right, no dog. Also, who gives a fuck about Edgar Poe and his nutsy story?

Serious students of American literature?

So let 'em. House! Kids! Petunias!

What about *our* story, Suse?

What about it.

I'm going to write it; that's what about it. Joking aside, we're going to write it.

Susan looks away. Bully for us. Fenwick absorbs the rebuff. I'm not belittling you, Sue says seriously. You'll write something fine, and that'll be enough for you, because you had all the other things in your other life.

Fenn says stiffly, standing at the tiller, Never mind my other life. My life is seven and a half years old. All the rest was B.S.: Before Susan.

Bull Shit. Sue says she's going to vomit again, but there's nothing left in her to come up. Fenn's feelings are hurt; he

---

*Susan's projected project: see p. 286.

lets her steady herself this time. Presently she goes below to
rinse her mouth and fix two iced teas. She brings them
upstairs and kisses Fenwick's beard, shoulder, shoulder
blades, small of back.

Plenty of sailboats out now. He takes his glass. If there was
life Before Susan, there'll be life After Fenn.

Back on her sea-taped cushion—portside, just in case—
Susan levelly opines that that's not how the world works, as a
rule: just as men and women who begin their sexual lives
late tend to end them early and vice versa, so unfair Nature,
she rather imagines, makes it likelier for people who've had
two lives already to have a third, than for a person who's had
but one to have a second. Anticipating his objection, she
adds Those other connections of mine weren't lives. Blowing
Jeff Greenberg a life? Balling Seymour Berman in his
crummy Plymouth Valiant a life? My life starts with you, and
it'll end with you; you're all I want.

Thank you.

But I have this terrible premonition that it's me who's
going to die. Jesus, those dreams! That awful shlup. . . .

Fenwick sees that his friend is neither joking nor, particularly, self-pitying. He waits, dreadful.

Something else besides Lexie and Drew was sucked out of
her last Friday, Susan says. She doesn't mean she's literally
going to die young; but she's going to be some kind of
invalid: mental, emotional, something. I'm going down,
honey.

Susele! You're strong as a horse. Mens sana, corpore sano,
perfect navel—

I'm going down; I can feel it. And I don't want you to
spend your life taking care of a cripple.

Susan, Susan . . .

Promise you'll kill me if that happens.

This is absurd.

But Sue's frantic. I know you won't! You'll let me rot like a
vegetable in some creepy bin, and you'll feel awful, but you'll
get over it, and in one year you'll have somebody else. It's so

easy for a man! One fucking year! I can see it so clearly! I can even imagine your having another child in your old age, if it's the right woman. She'll make you want to. Boy oh boy!

Fenn sighs I hate this dialogue.

I do too!

You're clear out of control.

Damn straight I am!

He proposes we make a deal: You don't be Dido, I won't be Aeneas. Susan says soberly I am Dido, Fenn: it's taking me longer to do the scene, but I'll get it done. She warms to the idea: Oh boy, there it is, I can see it! Never mind Poe; it's Virgil we're in! You're between lives with me, like Aeneas in Carthage, only you've hung around for seven years instead of just one winter.

Fenwick has let the woman run on. Now with dignity he says I hate this whole conversation, and I'm ending it.

Sue swallows tea. Yeah, you end it. Cut your anchor cables. On to Rome. Find your Lavinia.

For Christ's sake take the tiller, Susan. I'll make lunch.

It's only ten-thirty.

You may be sick, but I'm hungry.

Susan grins a crazy-lady grin. That's it, right there! Boy oh boy! She puts her glass in its holder, kisses his forehead. Fenn's not having it. And though Susan enjoys fixing food—it's one of her major pleasures—and he doesn't, particularly, Fenwick will not let her do it now. She thinks, not bitterly, He's punishing me for telling him the truth about us. As for Fenn, he has found her tirade simply shocking. He *is*, perhaps, reproving her a little by making his own Hebrew National All-Beef Salami with münster and mustard *and* mayonnaise on rye bread sandwich—Make me one too, his wife calls down, and he does, with pleasure—but he feels she deserves that small reproach. Wiping the knife, he finds himself more frightened of the future than he can remember having been since that set-to with Marilyn Marsh at the Tajo in Ronda a hundred years ago.

Wrung out, we chew and swallow in blessed silence. What

a day! The Chesapeake is a Dufy watercolor, brilliant with sails. There in mid-Bay is a windsurfer, of all creatures; it's the new rage. Yonder's a bona fide squaresail schooner. Here's a famous high-tech ocean racer out of Annapolis: a huge sleek half-million-dollar machine owned by a man who made his fortune building shopping malls; it's out for spinnaker drill with a crew of twelve in matching T-shirts. Alexander Solzhenitsyn would sneer; D. H. Lawrence likewise, for different reasons. Fenn shakes his head but admires the thing all the same and smiles, recollecting the story that Leo Tolstoy, after the publication of *War and Peace,* woke from a nightmare crying not Reynolds! Reynolds! but A yacht race! A yacht race!—the only thing his novel didn't have in it. We must see to it our story includes a racing yacht if not a yachting race, nor war nor peace.

The forenoon's waning fast; fine midday heat; just air enough to ventilate the day and keep us moving at three-plus knots toward Love Point Light, five miles ahead. But for the chance of those late-afternoon showers, there is no hurry: the running tide will set us down the Bay a bit, but not enough to matter; we'll be in reach of shelter before the action starts. Given Susan's extraordinary mood, one can hardly be eager to re-reach "home"; she is in no humor to humor Virgie and Chief. Fenn considers whether we oughtn't to park overnight somewhere en route (Queenstown Creek, on the Chester, isn't far out of our way); relax at anchor as in less stressful seasons and run down to Wye Island tomorrow morning. What's another day?

We chew, sip, swallow. Fenwick finds himself withal—and no doubt somehow therefor, but to his own surprise— moment by moment enjoying the sail. Cervantes he decides was right: the road is better than the inn. How more satisfying when the voyage, not the port, was our destination. If life's a journey and the grave its goal, getting there is *all* the fun.

Sue too, though still wasted, finds her nerves unclenching. She peels off her denim shirt; lotions up her breasts: a good sign. She's feeling much as Fenn is now, except for a thing she has on her mind: if, as has been written, the key to the treasure may well *be* the treasure, her question is Is her key treasure enough? To be healthy, comfortably off, in love and faithfully loved, competent in a benign, worthwhile profession, and sailing with one's darling on the gracious Chesapeake on a fine June day—nine-tenths of the mortal world was never so fortunate! Our difference is that whereas Fenwick's doubts and apprehensions, not excluding self-doubts, float on a roilable but prevailingly tranquil nature, a sea not of self-satisfaction or even self-confidence but of essential self-acceptance, Susan's peace with herself is increasingly a matter of interludes, fragile armistices, delightsome but ephemeral calms in a prevailingly restless water. There are rare hours when one can safely windsurf around Cape Horn;* even swim it;† on the other hand, our peaceful Chesapeake has been ripped by freak tornadoes that snap pre-Revolutionary oaks like lath and destroy large boats at the snuggest of moorings. By and large, however, your Doldrums are your Doldrums and your Roaring Forties roar. If Sue can't have children, then no paper on Pym will do. If she can't be an artist, say, of the sort whose work vindicates her life; a dedicated doctor; a passionate visionary—and she will not likely at thirty-five metamorphose into any of those . . . She contemplates morosely the breasts she knows are pleasing Fenn.

Half-hours and channel marks slide by. As we approach Love Point, the small breeze drops; Fenn begins to wonder, with how many hundred other helmsfolk between Canal and Capes,‡ whether to ghost it out, even sit becalmed for an hour in hope of new wind, or pack it in and motor along. The crossing is less than half our way: it is sixteen nautical

---

* A Frenchman, Frédéric Beauchêne, did so in 1979—both ways.

† An Englishman, Bill Watson, did so—both ways—having first sailed around it both ways in a collapsible dinghy in 1962.

‡ The Chesapeake and Delaware; the Virginia.

miles yet down and through and down and up and around*
to Key Farm. We drift past Love Point Light on its girdered
frame. Now the afternoon is sweatsy; once we turn south
into the Chester, what air there is will be too slight and
forward to bother tacking in, especially against the tide. It
looks like diesel-and-awning time.

Even so, Fenn goes below to recheck the forecast and use
the head before we call it quits. The failed breeze, he
supposes, is appropriate: how can one who fears the evening
seize the day? NOAA has increased the probability of
afternoon or evening weather from chance of to likely and
has promoted the showers to storms. It's coming on to 1400;
the motor-trip to Wye I. will take nearly three hours even if
we aren't much delayed at the Kent Narrows Bridge, which
opens only on the hour. We have seen in Parts I and II with
what suddenness and force summer storms in these latitudes
can come on. So much for sailing: we'll power on down
without delay, watching for thunderheads to westward and
rechecking the forecast for alerts. He pumps the head, puts
aside his Bermudas, pulls up his swimsuit, tisks his tongue at
Miriam's cigarette-burn on the sole, steps to cut the radio
and relieve broody Susan at the helm.

*Fenwick!* she calls down at that moment, italics in her voice.
*There's something in the water!*

He hurries up. The wide Chester is dish calm now, slick
calm. One can see at a hundred feet things normally
obscured by even the least rippling of the surface: the tiny
wakes of swimming crabs, the flip of minnows fleeing
bluefish. *Pokey*'s aimed south-southeast but sits dead in the
water, all sails limp, as does every other sailboat in sight,
none of them near. Susan's pointing off the port bow:
Something big and dead, she says, and after a pause A
drowned person?

Four or five boatlengths off, something mottled, brown-
black, smooth, and large floats awash: a hummock of bloated

---

*The Chester's mouth, the Kent Island Narrows, Prospect and
Eastern bays, the Wye's mouth, Wye I.

meat. If, as we believe (setting aside Carmen B. Seckler's latest dream), Manfred H. Turner disappeared into this estuarine system some fourteen months ago, then his flesh has long since recycled through the chain and may be part of any Chesapeake crab or fish we eat; his bones are current-scattered and more or less interred by the restless silt and sand. Yet Fenn's first thought will turn out to have been Sue's too: that our craft has come another kind of circle. That that over there is the back and shoulders of a person drowned; a man; Manfred.

The same thrill that volts this supposition volatilizes and dispels it. Absurd: no Manfred there, no man, no body human. The biggest dead fish we've ever come across, then? For if that hummock is but its curled side, as in the absence of fin or feature it must be, the thing entire must weigh hundreds of pounds and be fatter than any drum or shark we've seen in these frightless waters. It has no scales. . . .

Fenn's fetched the seven-by-fifties now and can rule out giant black drumfish, carp, striped bass. Among scaleless possibilities: too fat to be a shark or porpoise, too fleshy to be a sea-turtle, oil drum, tractor tire; too firm-looking and too dark to be a great moon-jelly; too leathery to be a harbor seal. What else does the Bay contain? No whales, walruses, dugongs, giant squid, or manatees that we've heard tell of (the thing is manatee-size and -color). Once upon a time there were sturgeon, some of great size, but they were long since fished to near-extinction in these parts. Susan hope-fully exclaims Cow-nosed ray! What color is a cow-nosed ray?

We decide to have a closer look and then check out cow-nosed ray in our directory of denizens. Fenwick hands the binocs to Susan and cranks up the diesel, saying How now drowned cow. At *Pokey*'s first harrumph Sue cries It's moving! and by god it is.

## A LEGENDARY SEA-MONSTER
## SWIMS THROUGH OUR STORY.

The hummock rolls; a second appears beside it—no, that's more of the same bulking mass, surfaced farther like a small brown sub, stirred from torpor by the sound of our engine as we push closer. Fenn shifts quickly into neutral, not to frighten or for that matter provoke the whatever-it-is. Larger craft than ours have been holed by whales—but such alarms are blue-water, not estuarine.

What we can see now is maybe ten feet long and two broad, a foot or so out of water, sans dorsal ridge or fin or other appendage; clearly there is more of it fore and aft below the surface. We're two boatlengths away and gliding closer. Fenn wishes the engine were off, but wants steerage way: he turns aside, one hand on the throttle-shift lever. Sue gives a proper gasp as water swirls now behind and on either flank of the creature: fins, flukes, or flippers have been flipped; it's pushing usward. Our skins tingle. Have we sailed out of James Michener into Jules Verne?

Fenwick shifts to forward and shoves the tiller hard astarboard to swing us bow on, hoping to catch the blow under *Pokey*'s sturdy forefoot rather than abeam, where the hull's most vulnerable. The impulse is prudent; the maneuver futile: we are too heavy and have insufficient way on to swing in time. But our sea-thing, too, we see now, is simply getting itself under way—perhaps to warn us off and/or to have a closer look. At twenty feet abeam it rolls and turns as if it knows the COLREGS.* Susan steps back. We see a flipper now, we think, tucked tight against a flank, and a yard or more of thick neck tapering forward to a whiskerless

---

*Collision regulations, or maritime rules of the road, by which, as concerns two vessels under power, *Pokey*'s position in this case gives him the right of way. But neither the Inland Rules nor the International Regulations cover confrontations between man-made vessels and monsters of the deep.

head like a monstrous newt's. No bill, beak, or snout, that we can see. Were there nostrils? Gills? Tusks? Teeth? We can't remember: no tusks, certainly. Was there a mouth, even? Susan thinks so: a hard, fish-lipped one. Fenwick couldn't see. Tail? Never saw it clearly, either of us; but the thrust was smooth and powerful.

What we do see, and shall in memory our lives long, is a round, bright, black, and perfectly expressionless eye, the size of, oh, a quarter, make it half a dollar: taking us in, sizing us up, unblinking as the lens of a spacecraft's camera as the thing completes its ninety-degree turn. Now it puts head and neck underwater again—they were never more than half out—and swims steadily but unhurriedly northward like a giant tadpole toward Love Point Light and the open Bay.

Fenn opens the throttle to follow! Sue scrambles downstairs for the camera! In her haste to hand him the binoculars she catches their lanyard on her headband-knot; the paisley pulls off and is lobbed by that lanyard into the air. Fenn, holding the binoculars in his right hand, lets go the tiller to make a left-handed snatch and succeeds only in batting the band to one side. It hits a lifeline and drops outboard of the cockpit coaming, half onto the gunwale, half over the side. The knot happening to fall outside the toe-rail, the whole thing slips overboard before Fenn can set down the glasses and catch it. Adiós, bandanna.

Susan, heading for the companionway, sees none of this three-second business. By when she piles back up with the Nikon, *Pokey*'s on course again and at seven knots is closing on Chessie—whom by now, though no name's been named, we both understand our beast to be. She snaps the case open, takes a quick shot blind to make sure we get something, realizes the lens cap is still on, hisses Shit, squeezes it off, twists the setting to Infinity, takes a moment this time to frame, presses the shutter release, realizes when it won't press that she hasn't advanced the fucking film, advances it, reframes, reshoots, and contributes to the annals of marine biology a passably clear 35 mm. color exposure of a foam-flecked swirl on the calm surface of Chesapeake Bay, where our monster has just submerged.

Did you get it?

I think so. But not much. It was just diving. Is it Chessie?

It has to be. We surge through the widening swirl, watching for another. Fenn eases the throttle; idles in neutral. Nothing. We glide on, losing way. No other boat is near enough to have seen what we saw: an honest to Christ legendary sea-monster!

Is that it over there? He points off to port, toward Love Point itself, and swings that way.

Maybe. Susan checks with the binoculars. No. Somebody's wake, I think.* For some minutes, as we detour over there in vain, we excitedly compare impressions. Fish? Mammal? Reptile? If the navy has trained porpoises on its payroll, Susan ventures, may not Marcus Henry be recruiting sea-monsters to keep an eye on the Company's nautical ex-officers?† Fenn wishes the thing would resurface, and not only for the mere excitement: he feels sharply that beyond this narrative diversion, this ontological warp in our story—a fabulous sea-monster in our real Chesapeake!—lies something hard and hurtful. Your scarf went overboard during the excitement, he says, somewhere back this way. It's so calm, we might just see it. Shall I climb up and have a look?

---

*She may be mistaken. In any case, unless our Bay hosts more than one Monster of the Not Very Deep, Chessie will indeed make its way around Kent Island, to be sighted next in Eastern Bay on 13 September 1980 by Trudy and Coleman Guthrie, sober and sensible middle-class Marylanders aboard *Impasse*, their Grampian 26 sloop. Ms. Guthrie, a marine biologist's daughter and an able draughtsman, will publish convincing drawings of the animal, together with a matter-of-fact account of their close-range sighting, in the November 1980 number of *Chesapeake Bay Magazine*. See also the follow-up reports by Mr. Bill Burton in the January and March 1981 numbers of the same periodical.

†The list of Chessie's sighters generally regarded as sober and responsible includes, in the lower Potomac in 1978, a "retired CIA employee" named Donald Kyker.

Sue says No, let Chessie have it. We found it when we came in; we should lose it now we're leaving. The Bay giveth and the Bay taketh away.

Fenn shrugs and wonders Who's leaving the Bay, except temporarily to enter one of its forty rivers? He furls all sail now and rigs the cockpit awning, his mind busy with three matters: Susan's distressing report of her Friday and her acute distress thereat, under which he feels something even more distressing about to surface; the astonishing thing that has just swum through our story, more suited to its beginning than to . . . well—a chill goes through him—where are we in it? That's Thing Three: What else will our sabbatical's end end?

Sue steering, we motor southeast into the Chester, which, four or five miles in, swings hard aport around Eastern Neck Island, a wildlife refuge, then runs north toward Langford Creek and Cacaway, then northeast to Chestertown. To starboard, as we begin that first swing, is Kent Island Narrows, our shortcut south: once we turn into it, forty-five or so minutes hence, the ebbing tide will be in our favor all the way down to Wye Island.

If that's where we're going. Fenwick has in mind still, but hasn't got around to mentioning, the option of pausing overnight in quiet Queenstown Creek, just up the Chester from Kent Narrows, to swim, recollect ourselves, and let the promised squall blow through before moving on home. He wishes a thunderhead or radio weather alert would serve as prompter; massive cumuli are duly accumulating in the west, but not yet menacingly, and the forecast is unchanged. We motor on. He takes the tiller; Sue props herself listless against the cabin bulkhead, looking astern where Chessie was. From time to time she squeezes shut her eyes, shakes her head, as if fighting back tears. Fenn's heart sinks and sinks.

By 1500 we're in sight of the go/no-go point: a red and black mid-channel buoy at the upper approach to Kent Island Narrows. From that buoy, which may be left to either port or starboard, it's three miles up-Chester to snug

anchorage in Queenstown Creek, or twelve at least down to
Key Farm. He consults his watch, rotates its bezel, makes
some rough time/speed/distance calculations in his head.
Susan says suddenly We should separate.

Fenn's chest clutches. What? Yet he is somehow unsurprised: the thing has surfaced. What are you talking
about?

She looks at him. I think I'm saying good-bye, honey. Not
for keeps, necessarily. I don't know.

Suse! You're talking crazy-lady stuff.

Yeah, I know. No, I'm not. She closes her eyes, fingers her
gold chain. Those dreams of ours.

I hate a dream!

Me too.

Fenn is incensed. That whole five-dream business is
garbage! Flashbacks, flashforwards! The unconscious is an
idiot!

Susan weeps. I don't want to go to Wye Island. I don't
want to go to Swarthmore. I don't want to do anything.

You're upset.

Now she shouts Of course I'm upset! That's what it's
called: upset! Fenn's offended. Less loudly Sue says I can't
take life. I can't take it that there's nothing but you and me,
and soon we'll get old and sick and die. The hell with it.

Desperate Fenwick reminds her that people talk about
Things Larger Than Themselves. Uh, Justice? Art? All that
upper-case stuff.

Not for me, says Susan.

Teaching. Pursuit of Truth.

Sue declares she wishes she were dead. What is she going
on with it for? Twins Doubles and Schizophrenia in the
American Literary Imagination for god's sake! Freshman
comp! Arthur Gordon Pym! Get her out of here!

Fenn puts the question How about us? Aren't we larger
than oneself?

If we separated, Sue says evenly, you'd be miserable for a
while—

I daresay.

—then you'd get your breath. I'm lost, hon.

Scared Fenwick demands to know what in the world she's
talking about: she's healthy; she's competent; good genes in
there; promotion with tenure. Susan says she knows it
sounds crazy but knows just as absolutely certainly that it's
the truth: It's over for her; it's over for us. Turns out she
wasn't cut out for this life; she wasn't lucky; she isn't a
survivor like her mother. She can't stand to watch what's
going to happen, or to watch Fenn watch her go down.
We've got to separate. She'll go on up to Swarthmore, home
to Ma, something. Fenn'll go to Delaware or Wye I. or
wherever and write his book.

Stop this!

I happen to believe, she says gloomily, that you really are a
writer.

Oh, terrific.

We haven't talked much about that seriously, but I
happen to be a professional reader, see, and I've read all
your notebooks and early manuscripts. You don't talk and
behave like people's idea of a capital-A Artist, but that's
people's idea's fault, not yours. You're not publicly intense.
You don't puff a pipe and make literary conversation. You
clown around, very American. But the fact is, you've grown
into something real since Marilyn Marsh days. I happen to
think there's a good chance that more than halfway through
your life you're about to hit the ground running out of
nearly nowhere and take literature by surprise. Critics will
see in retrospect that everything you did for fifty years—
what looked like false starts and wrong tacks and fartings
around—was perfect preparation for your particular work,
which nobody could've anticipated. Some Ph.D. will argue
that MM was necessary for one stage and that I was
necessary for another, and that after this sabbatical it was
time for your Lavinia.

Fenwick waits for her to finish. You're finished?

Yeah.

Well, get out of here with your Lavinia! I'll pop that Pee-aitch Dee upside his head! Does Carmen B. Seckler know how Nineteenth-century nuts her *other* daughter is?

Susan says glumly Maybe Ma's your Lavinia.

Fenn's really getting angry. Shall we call her up and ask, Suse?

No. It's somebody we don't know yet. But it's time for Dido to get off the boat.

### WE HAVE REACHED THAT RED AND BLACK BUOY.

Fenwick finds himself too flabbergasted, excited, annoyed, alarmed, and distraught either to turn into Kent Island Narrows or proceed toward Queenstown Creek, which Susan's outpour has given him no chance to mention. He throttles down. The river's two miles wide here; we circle slowly in mid-channel. Fenn is astonished almost as much by Susan's estimation of his abilities—and the revelation that she has examined, neither at his invitation nor against his prohibition, not only his notebooks but his sundry past literary efforts!—as by her incredible proposal that we separate. Unthinkable just now either to proceed to Wye I. or not to proceed! We can neither go forward nor go back: forward whither? Back where?

There are no boats near. He throttles down to idle, shifts to neutral, finally shuts off the engine altogether and lets *Pokey* drift on the tide toward the Narrows. He puts by the tiller, squats beside his wife, takes her by the shoulders, kisses and kisses her wet face.

### SUSAN, SUSAN, SUSAN!

You can do something fine! I want to get out of your way! I want to get out of *my* way! She draws a breath. I could stand not having kids if it was me by myself, but I can't stand *our* not having them. It sounds crazy, but it isn't. You don't want kids, I don't want kids, and I want kids more than anything. A house and friends! I want us to be normal and do the normal stuff together, both of us for the first time, and that's not possible. Where was I when you needed me? Why didn't we know each other since kindergarten? Oh, Fenn, I'm so sorry we ever fell in love!

Not in the most turmoils of early marriage and late divorce, not in the Ronda gorge or the Choptank safe-house did Fenn feel so agitated, frightened, torn. Come on, heart: crack! The reality of Susan; of her life and his, coursing away; of this river, that red and black buoy, the herring gull perched atop it, this moment in the history of the universe between Big Bang and Last Shlup. The airless middle afternoon: ninety plus and humid, summer not even begun. The spin of our gorgeous, dreadful planet, bejeweled bomb. Rotation, revolution—and the monster!

He leaps up; doesn't even know why. Leaps up too fast and goes dizzy. Will this be it? He catches at the boom to steady himself; springs up again to stand on the starboard cockpit seat. What's he up to? He doesn't know. Susan either: she watches him through her own blur, of tears, and her own heart-tightenment. Has she unhinged the man?

The awning catches his wide-brimmed hat and knocks it forward to the cockpit sole. Is he going to jump overboard? Climb the mast and scream? He has sprung to the gunwale, to the cabin trunk. Sue sits up alarmed. Fenn's looking about him like a crazy man. Now something's caught his eye! He has scrambled to the opposite gunwale, her side; he snatches the boat hook from its clips inboard of the handrail on the cabin trunk. Susan's up on her knees; glances sternward. Has Chessie followed us?

Half overboard through the midship portside lifelines, Fenn spears down and out of sight along the freeboard. Susan hears, oh dear, a small quick shlup is it? Her bowels draw in. Joyous Fenn cries out.

And now her bronze-and-silver Triton, middle-aged Nereus, guileless Odysseus, grins and drips back herward through the rigging and awning guys. Upon his head, leaking tidewater down his face, through his hair and beard, down his chest and back—a black beret.

## SOPPING, SEASLIMED BOINA!

He claps it with one hand tight to his pate and steps over her into the cockpit, walking on his other hat; he sits opposite her with the butt of the boat hook like a scepter on the sole. Chester River water trickles into his eyes; he snorts and proudly knuckles them.

Sue's incredulous. That's your new one! You just dropped it in and picked it up! Fenn shakes his head; can't speak. You found your old one at Key Island the day we lost it, and hid it away till now! Fenn shakes his head; beams with tearful joy. Somebody else's, then; some Sunday sailor's. Key I.'s a million miles down the Bay, and your hat sank while we were trying to rescue it!

Sitting and dripping like a surfaced sea god, Fenwick croaks Fetch up the Dom Perignon.*

Susan considers—irrelevant miracle!—then shrugs and does as bid. Pressing the cold green bottle-bottom to the front of her shorts, she grasps the cork fast, twists the bottle expertly, releases the gas without a pop, and pours two small paper-cupsful. We drift sluggishly downtide still, past that red and black buoy now, toward shoal water. She sets the bottle in the galley sink with a rubber stopper against spillage; fetches up the two cups. Fenn starts the diesel. When he takes a cup from her, standing before him, she lifts the seaslick hat momentarily from his head to examine its lining. The old one's was worn through; this one's has rotted away altogether, along with most of the inner headband. Fenwick, sitting, draws her to him with his champagne-hand; with the other he has shifted into forward and

---

*The same we were to have drunk and didn't when we closed our circuit at Wye I.

advanced the throttle; now he puts the tiller over. He kisses Susan's belly once, presses with his brow the undersides of her breasts, says Put it back.

On your head or in the river?

He looks up happily from her navel. She puts the boina back on his head. We've gathered way and turned, are heading back toward old Red and Black. Sue sits, cup in hand; waits; watches.

To Aristotle on Coincidence, Fenn proposes. What does he know?

We drink, Fenwick more heartily than Susan, to impermissible coincidence, implausible possibility. Glum Susan guesses Chessie didn't need a hat and scarf both. So where are we going?

Maybe Portugal. Drink up.

We've turned not Lisbonward but northeast, upriver, against the tide which sweeps now strongly past the buoys, leaning them seaward. Those western clouds are stacked and threatening. Fenwick opens the throttle to cruising speed. The past half-hour has quite laid us out.

What to this time?

To the crotch of the Y, Fenn says. The hub of the wheel. The place where three roads meet.

Sue hesitates. His eyes are on hers; his cup is at his lips.


### CACAWAY!


I'll drink to old Cacaway, she says and does, a proper gulp. For all her dejection, she is bemused and stirred; he's steering right north now up the river in that brined beret, so full of some kind of inspired confidence he seems a stranger. But a formidable stranger: Aeneas shed of his disguising cloud and refulgently himself; Odysseus sans swineherd drag and set to bend the bow. She empties and goes to refill her cup, saying Well, here's to ongoing nostalgia trips.

Nope, says Fenn. Check the forecast while you're down there, would you?

She does, and finds it serious. A heavy-weather alert is in effect; squall front with thunderstorms, hail, winds gusting to sixty-plus knots, possibly tornadoes—the works. Expected to reach the Baltimore area by 5 P.M. Boaters on the Bay urged to seek shelter promptly.

No problem, Fenwick says. We can run into Grays Inn Creek if things blow up early.

So it's not a nostalgia trip? she asks. Back where Fenwick and Susan started?

It is not. The scales have fallen from my eyes.

It's the salt water from your hat. Did you hear what I was saying before you found it?

I heard, I heard. But I wasn't thinking straight before, Suse. I told you dreams are dumb. Right, left, back!

Sue guesses she's still got her scales on. Fenn explains that at a place where three roads meet, there are four choices. Your Y has three legs, but four possibilities.

## *SHE'S LISTENING.*

Something happened just now, starting with Love Point and our sea-monster. No: starting with our storm in Part I or losing my hat; I don't know. This whole ride up the Bay, storm to storm, boina to boina, island to island! But today especially.

You're not making sense yet, Fenwick.

He grins, undaunted. Listen to what I'm going to say now. A while ago, when you told me I was a capital-A Et cetera. . . . I don't know. That sea-monster was important. There's a power I didn't know about, and now I think I've got it. Maybe I had it all along; that doesn't matter. You gave it to me by naming it. In fact, it's not mine: it's ours. And something else's. I don't know.

This is the voice of the Enlightenment? But Susan's listening.

Not enlightenment: illumination. It's our power and our voice, and what it's for is our story. Hoo! Everything's coming so clear! After we saw our friend Chessie back there, and you said what you said, and we came to that red and black buoy, I felt as if I could have shut my eyes and reached down into the water and fished out my boina!

Susan asks dryly is he sure that this sort of thing is what writers do. Fenwick replies without the least hesitation It's what writers do because we did it; and we did it because it was the thing for us as a writer to do. Susan observes that that wasn't mentioned in any writing course *she* ever took or taught. Rewrite the syllabus, then, says Fenn: we're plotting our own course now.

Mm *hm*. Where does Cacaway fit in?

At the beginning and the end. We'll work it out. Don't worry.

Sue remarks that the sky's sure getting ugly over there. Fenn says That doesn't matter. Dugald! he suddenly exclaims. Carmen and Miriam! All of us! Even Do-Me-True and the boys and the fucking *dog!* Orrin and Julie. *Marilyn Marsh!*

Even her, huh.

Chessie! Fenn cries. Key Island!

Susan says he'll explain it to her once we're parked and the motor's off. Fenwick draws her to his side; she likes that. Suse, he says: remember Homer's line about Wars are fought so that poets will have something to sing about?

Yup.

Well, I understand it! That proposition is rigorously correct!

Sue says he's losing her. We don't believe that Harry Truman created the Central Intelligence Agency for the sake of this story, do we?

## OUR STORY!

Fenn opens the throttle; it's hard to talk now over the diesel. Everything's getting clearer!

Behind Eastern Neck Island and across the Bay a terrific

wall of cumulonimbi turns blacker by the minute and advances usward. Well ahead at twenty degrees magnetic we can see the entrance of Langford Creek, almost as wide as the river itself bearing off northeast toward Chestertown. Considering that sky and that storm alert, Susan wonders whether we oughtn't to run into that aforementioned nearer creek right now. Fenwick estimates an hour to Cacaway Island, invisible in the hazy distance where Langford forks. She shrugs her mental shoulders: as we were prepared to do in the Patuxent pages past, in the worst case we can simply run under the lee of the river bank to port and ride out the blow on our trusty plow. Anyhow, her thoughts are back somewhere between Chessie and that red and black buoy.

No use trying to talk over this racket. Although Fenn's reflexes are still skiperly—he glances often at the lowering sky, the engine tachometer and temperature gauge, the eel pots and can buoys and landmarks, the compass, and Chart 12272, Chester River, on which little Cacaway sits in the yoke of Langford Creek: its confluence, given the almost ebbed tide; its fork, given our upstream course—his main attention is clearly elsewhere too. Sue sees his mind going, going. Now he frowns; now he nods and smiles; now he snaps his fingers, sucks in his breath, claps the cushion, grins at her. She rolls her eyes, shakes her head, but remains impressed. He is bursting to talk to her!

She de-rigs and stows the awning against the blow, then refills our cups with more Dom Perignon. She even thinks to put a fresh (cheaper) bottle on ice, for his sake. However genuine this illumination of her husband's—the general nature of which is beginning to come clear—it has yet to address the matters that have cast her down.

Now at last we see the lookout tower which, lined up with a white triangular marker on the beach of Quaker Neck, on the creek's east shore, is the range for sailing up Langford to Cacaway. A breeze commences from the west—first breath of what's to come—but to raise sail now would be pointless and imprudent. We chug on in the cooling air. The few other boats in sight are making for shelter too; they will be mostly Delawarians and Pennsylvanians whose weekend is over anyhow, headed back to their nearby marina slips.

There's Cacaway! Only we who know it could tell from here that it is an island and not merely the wooded tip of Broad Neck, between the East and West forks of Langford Creek. Susan scans with the binoculars. Remarkably even for a weekend's end, we have the anchorage to ourselves. Stirred now by the prospect of this place, so fundamental to our story, following upon Fenwick's peculiar transformation, she slips into her boat-shoes and a short-sleeved orange sweatshirt, hands Fenn his shoes and shorts and shirt, breaks out our foul-weather tops just in case, shortens up the dinghy painter—we've left the Chester now; we're in Langford proper!—and goes forward to unlash the anchor from its roller chock and draw out through the deck-pipe a generous coil of rode.

Minute by minute the breeze increases, northwest now. Though the trees are moving and a flag on somebody's lawn-pole stands straight out, the wave action so far is slight, there being but a short fetch from that quarter except down Langford's West Fork, of which we catch just a glimpse before slipping into the lee of Cacaway. Nothing like the rough chop that tumbled Sue's canoe and pitched her into Fenwick's life, not to mention what blammed and blooeyed us at the threshold of the Bay. But that sky over there has put on its green and black rampage dress; we hear thunder over the wide-open diesel; leaves begin to fly, the water blackens, *Pokey* starts whistling to himself. Moreover, on the little island, now we're close to it, we observe that since our last visit a number of major oaks and maples have been uprooted on the weather shore and fallen inland: evidence of with what force storm winds can roar down that fork. NOAA Baltimore reports that destructive "minitwisters" have touched down already west and southwest of the city; a tornado watch is in effect for several Eastern Shore counties including Kent, in whose waters we are. Our nerves buzz as we charge up behind the island at last, kill our headway, lower the plow.

The water's deep almost to the beach. While the banks are not high enough nor the anchorage snug enough from all sides to make Cacaway a hurricane hole like Mackall on the Patuxent (to the south-southwest, where we came from, there's no land in sight), we can ride out anything here short of an actual life-threatening storm. We set the anchor in good hard sand at what we estimate to be more than a falling-tree's-length from shore, at just about the spot where Susan and Miriam, with Orrin's help, brought their swamped canoe ashore eight summers since. For added insurance—those NOAA bulletins, like the sky, get heavier all the time—we set the spare anchor as well: that hefty Danforth with the help of which we kedged back to go forward in Redhouse Cove. A hundred feet of scope on each, in ten to twelve feet of water, forty-five degrees apart: we are secure indeed now from anything except a bona-fide tornado, against which the only possible further precaution would be to abandon *Pokey* and seek shelter in somebody's basement. There are in fact a few houses not far off on the West Fork—that one with the flagpole, for instance, whose owners have now sensibly struck their colors. But we're not of a mind to take that last resort.

Still wearing his wet boina—are we really to believe it's his?—Fenwick shuts off the engine. We satisfy ourselves that everything is battened down—awning secured, spray-dodger in place—and decide not to open the second bottle of champagne until the brunt of the storm has passed. There remains a splash apiece of the old. In the triple excitement of being after all back where we began, of preparing for a blow (we even put our life-vests on, welcome insulation against the cooling wind), and, for Fenn especially, of his extraordinary illumination, as yet unarticulated, at the Kent Narrows red and black buoy, we settle down in the cockpit to watch the world go bang.

Rather, Susan does. No settling down for the inspired, the

vision-ridden! Fenwick perches across from her, kisses her mouth, takes one of her hands in both of his, says I know what you're feeling, Suse. But something really is different now.

She raises her eyebrows, turns in her lips: resigned but ungrudging acceptance. What?

Fenn puts her knuckles to his cheek. It isn't just as if scales have fallen from his eyes: it's more as if some inauthentic self—layers of false or unworthy selves—got peeled off back there like clothes by skinnydippers. It's as if he had been disguised from his own best self, he tells her, or as if he'd only now heard and understood what he's been talking about for years. Just as he often wonders, with her, how it is he ever lived with anyone else—What were those years for? Who was he?—and yet knows there's an answer, so he wonders what he was doing in the Company, and farting around with free-lance journalism before that, and teaching before that? What was it for? What has even his life with Susan been for? What are we *about*?

Susan smiles uncertainly. You tell me.

### HE'S GOING TO.

I see now what we're about. It's the story!

Oh.

Listen: I'm not being sentimental. I'm not even being personal. . . .

You're not?

I'm not. We don't want some tacky roman à clef or half-assed autobiographical romance.

Half an ass—

Our story needn't be about us. You and I may not even be in it.

I like that, Fenn. We're not for public consumption.

Yet it's our story; it will be our story. What's more—he hopes Susan can take this the way he means it; he knows what the past few days and weeks have been for her—this story, our story, it's our house and our child. . . .

Susan quickly looks down, at our hands, on his knee now.

We'll have made it, says determined Fenn, and we'll live in it. We'll even live by it. It doesn't have to be *about* us—children aren't about their parents. But our love will be in it, and our friendship too. This boat ride will be in it, somehow. It'll be about things coming around to where they started and then going on a little farther in a different way. It should have ancestry in it and offspring; Once upon a time to Happily ever after.

The man begins to lose his calm again. Count! Gus! Tears leak into his beard; his voice croaks out.

Nature too is letting go: the wild line of the storm has crossed the Bay and is sweeping toward us over the peninsula. The air temperature plunges; trees whistle and go silver. Not just stray leaves but twigs and small branches fly, even dirt from corn and soybean fields nearby; *Pokey* horses on his twin halters. Fat rain comes hammering; the boat bucks; thunder cracks not far up the fork. We retreat below and haul the cushions in after us.

Fenwick is scarcely paying attention. He hasn't touched his last champagne. Upset Susan finds herself saying Well, my friend, that's a two-edged trope you're playing with there. Stories can abort, too. Plenty are stillborn; most that aren't die young. And of the few that survive, most do just barely.

Dauntless Fenn replies Think how it is with sperm and eggs! Yet here we sit. . . .

For better or worse, Sue says alarmed, because now the storm blasts all around us, equal of any we've seen. Hail pounds down as in Mackall Cove; visibility's zero through the ports; our heads ring; we can scarcely see the end of the cockpit. In the screaming wind we hear limbs splitting, if not whole trees coming down; though we're no more than fifty yards from shore, *Pokey* rolls and pitches as if at sea. Should we drag both anchors, we'll never know it till we fetch up on the leeward beach. Things bang around inside the cabin.

Yet Fenwick is not done. So far from registering concern

and checking the hand-bearing compass from time to time, he seems scarcely to be noticing the storm. It's clear as a bell! he announces over the racket. You and I aren't going to have any human children, only the kind Carmen was talking about, and soon enough not even those. I'll get myself vasectomized; a dozen years from now you'll be done ovulating. . . .

Fenn! Susan's tears are instant.

He catches up her hand. One day soon we'll have some proper kind of roof over our heads: maybe Wye I., maybe right here. That's not important. The story's our house, Suse. That's the thing that's both of us and neither of us. He says it: Drew and Lexie! Everything's so clear!

Not to hurting Susan, it isn't. What does "staying right here" mean, anyhow? Does she go to Swarthmore and he to Delaware? Does he want her to stay on at Washington College while he writes this famous story?

While *we* write it, Fenn declares, impervious. It's our story at both ends. He doesn't know about that, what she just asked, and the reason he doesn't know is that it doesn't matter in the same way any more. That's all clear to him now, too: we didn't make the decisions we'd hoped to make on this sabbatical sail because the questions we were trying to decide were the wrong ones. No, excuse him: they're the right questions, but we had the wrong handle on them. Key Farm, Delaware, Swarthmore—as far as Fenn's concerned, as soon as this storm passes we can leave *Pokey* anchored right where he is and go look for something to rent or buy ashore, as near Cacaway as possible.

Once more he assures her that he hasn't lost his mind or forgot about her or us; that he's simply been shown some real priorities. Only let his heart behave for a couple of years. . . . You, Suse! he finds himself nearly shouting, and must seize her hand again, kiss her forearm. You're the key to it. Hey: now I understand Key Island! *Blam! Blooey!* I understand it all!

Explain, frets Susan. Oh!

It is a tremendous flash and crash; some tree surely has been split not very far away. To Susan this whole episode feels like a catharsis in an automatic washer.

Not understand in the sense of how an island can be in the Bay but not on the charts or the LANDSAT photos.* Fenn understands what Key Island was *for,* in our story. Susan!

She sighs, still hurting. The worst of the wind and the lightning seems to be past. We see now that though our anchors haven't budged, our sturdy dinghy has actually been lifted out of the water, flipped over, swamped: it floats skeg-skyward just behind us, its painter cinched right around it. Twigs and leaves litter the cockpit and creek, and are stuck here and there under handrails and in *Pokey's* running rigging. Radio reports are coming in of buildings unroofed, doors and windows blown, wires and trees down all over the peninsula. And though the tornado-watch has been lifted, more weather's to come. Ordinarily we'd be excited; at least interested—and a little concerned for Chief and Virgie and Key Farm. But Fenn's imagination is still popping. Twins! he says suddenly, apropos of what? And a moment later We *should* stay here, Suse: right at the fork; right at the hub.

We should?

Maybe not literally. He takes her around, on her settee. I'd like us to spend a couple days right here right now for sure, if you'll stay with it, so we can begin to sort things out. Then I hope we'll get on down to Wye I. for the summer and get to work.

She shrugs, smiles.

He goes on, more calmly. Today was what this whole sabbatical was about.

---

*A splendid one of Chesapeake Bay will appear in the October 1980 issue of *National Geographic* (Vol. 158, No. 4). We shall examine it in vain for an island where we reckon ourselves to have been, off the mouth of York River: a small wooded island near or on York Spit, with a lighted breakwater and one snug cove. But precious Cacaway's not to be found in that LANDSAT photo, either.

That was some illumination you had back there at that red and black buoy.

Fenn swears she'll understand what he means as soon as he does. It is not a matter of answers, or even a philosophical position: just a perspective. Our perspective, for our story. Susan declares it would be nice all the same to know whether she's going to Swarthmore or back to Washington College or Fells Point or what, if she's to play muse to his bard, Véra to his Vladimir.*

No no no, her husband protests. It's not my story about us; it's our story about the whole thing, Big Bang to Black Hole.

You'll explain it to me later. I'm pooped.

Fenn declares We'll explain it to us. Oh, look: no doubt it's Swarthmore and Delaware; Swarthmore certainly. Your career is important; you're too fine a teacher to waste; we need the money. Maybe he'll try Delaware, maybe not; he might do the lecture circuit; we'll work that out. We must swing with the tides and winds, take what comes; so must our story, once we've done our best, as Drew and Lexie would have had to. We will live in reasonable care for Fenwick's heart, up to a point; we will do our work and savor our pleasures and each other, while we may. For the world we'll do our little and hope the best. It's all so simple! Nothing has us really by the throat. Chessie! Fenn sees where Chessie fits in! Oh god, we're so lucky!

*Pokey* settles down. The sky's still dark. Sue moves her face into Fenwick's shoulder and says Living with a visionary is going to be strange.

No it won't.

Oh.

He squeezes her, pats her happily. This euphoria of his

---

*Her reference is to the devoted marriage of the late Russian-American V. Nabokov (1899–1977), one of Susan's literary enthusiasms, and his remarkable wife Véra Evseevna Slonim, Jewish like herself.

will pass, surely, but the perspective won't; that's the key. He wonders whether there *is* ever anything for sale around here, where we can swim till October. Just the right mix.* It all fits!

Susan asks would he hold her for a while. Fenwick says Oh, Susan, will I ever. NOAA tells us we're in for rain and scattered thundershowers through tomorrow. Let 'er blow, says Fenn: there's no hurry at all. He will check the anchors and salvage the dinghy presently. What's for dinner?

Ma gave us fresh rockfish. I'll build a spinach salad while you broil it.

Susan, Susan: our life is delicious. Rockfish and champagne! Want to go swimming?

You're out of your mind.

Make love before or after? Both? During?

Sue hopes aloud she'll like this new friend of hers as much as she liked the old one. Fenn says she will: it isn't him that's new; it's us. Where's our full moon? Where's our geese and oysters? Everything's just starting! Let's open the new champagne and toast our story.

Well. We come out of our life-vests. Fenn opens the second bottle with a spray of foam—it's not chilled enough—and a shameless pop that blows the cork through the companionway, over the transom, into the creek. Now, he says: tell me something new about Arthur Gordon Pym.

Susan begs his pardon?

Fenwick thinks he's got F. S. Key and E. A. Poe sorted out, at least enough to get us started. They fit; they fit! But Poe's queer story still nags at him. It was a voyage, sure, but so was Odysseus's and Ishmael's. Here you go, darling Susan:

---

*Fenwick means, literally, enough freshwater flow to keep the medusa sea nettle from the creek; enough salt for the pleasures of oysters, crabs, tides.

### TO OUR STORY.

We drink, keeping our eyes upon each other. The wind has dropped; the desultory rain continues; thunder and lightning knock about in the offing. The tide will have turned now, chasing the invisible moon. Before dark, Fenn must go overboard to unfoul, right, and bail the dinghy— but we're near the solstice; there's time. The man desires the woman immensely. It is true that just now many things seem to him wonderful: our strong and graceful vessel, the fruit of centuries, even millennia, of human nautical experience, design, technology; this champagne (an okay California brut), splendid collaboration of green nature and human savvy; the Caribbean despite its history, the Chesapeake despite its; the Romantic fury of such a storm as this, if one be not among its victims. That anything should live, grow, evolve, reflect, respond to beauty, reproduce its kind . . . or make further beauty of another kind. Oh, wonderful.

These last considerations bring him to the brink of sentimentality. That this excellent female animal his friend, this finely nerved and tempered woman, should not join her lively Seckler chromosomes to his sturdy Turners; know the pleasures and discomforts of pregnancy and birth, the trials and rewards of parenthood. . . . He craves those for her; wishes he craved them again for himself; finds he firmly doesn't, after all. His desire is overborne by sympathy.

Tears in Susan's eyes again: she's thinking thoughts not unlike his, but from a different perspective. A baby. Two! Actual individual daughters and sons, Fenn's and hers, to delight in, worry about, care for; to nurture in fineness and strength of character, shield from remarkable America's ubiquitous silliness and arrogant vulgarity; to warm and/or break her heart, but anyhow season and mature it. What is art, Susan wants to know, what are learning and civilization, where they must substitute for parenthood instead of complementing it? The answer is that for Fenn, for whom

they *are* the complement, they are enough; for Sue—given
the magnitude of her love—they are far better than nothing.
Her heart, too, fills, less unequivocally but no less lovingly
than his.

He has drawn her onto his lap, on the starboard settee
berth. Under her bottom we feel his penis engorge in his
dungaree shorts. Sue removes the wet, sea-smelling boina
and kisses his brown bald head. He's nuzzling the front of
her sweatshirt; presently his hands and mouth will be under
there and everywhere; hers will be busy too; there'll be sex
and supper, storms and sleep; with luck there'll be some
years of loving work and play—and then the end, the end,
unspeakable. Meanwhile Fenwick's asking her seriously to
talk, how can she do that, even as his hand goes beneath her
shirt to soothe the small of her back. Tell him something
new about the voyage of Edgar Poe's Arthur Pym, he
lovingly recommends her; he has the feeling that whatever
Susan says just now will, you know, fit.

The cabin is storm-darkened, cozy with the putter of light
and rain. Her cheek on his pate, Sue watches through the
companionway the diorama of gray water, gray sky, and
gray-green trees swing past our transom as *Pokey* rides back
and forth on his rodes. Years ago, on our first visit as lovers
to this island, she had felt as excited and unsure as young
Nausicaa might have, had she eloped with briny middle-
aged Odysseus. Now, as his familiar hand calmly takes her
breast, she feels like a confident Scheherazade, hundreds of
nights after that first, upon the lap of her long-since-
conquered king.

She kisses his crown lightly; breathes; begins. In the
Nineteenth century, lots of people believed that at each of
the earth's poles there was a great abyss. These twin abysses
continuously swallowed up the ocean and continuously
disgorged it somewhere along the Equator, maybe at the
sources of the Amazon and the Nile, just as matter swallowed up in a Black Hole might reappear from a White Hole
somewhere else in the universe.

Mm hm.

We feel her nipples rise. Well. Pym's log of his voyage breaks off on March Twenty-two, Eighteen Twenty-eight, the vernal equinox, just as his canoe approaches the South Polar abyss. He's seen those queer caves in the shape of hieroglyphs on the island of Tsalal, and he's lost his mother ship *Jane Guy* and all but one of his shipmates, and now as his little boat sweeps along through the cataract toward the chasm he sees a giant white shrouded human figure—and his narrative breaks off.

### FENN'S LISTENING.

People have taken that figure to be everything from Jesus Christ to a giant penguin to the author himself, but never mind that. The interesting thing is that what we've been reading is supposedly Pym's own account, written back in New York after he somehow survived the voyage. Poe's conceit is that Pym sent him the journal in Richmond to edit and publish as fiction in the *Southern Literary Messenger*.

Okay.

So Pym's written account breaks off just as he's about to be vacuum-aspirated—

What?

Never mind. Just as he and Dirk Peters and the canoe are about to be swallowed up, the story breaks off without our ever learning how Pym survived and got back to New York City to write it. Then Poe comes in as anonymous editor— neither Pym nor Poe, in effect—to explain that Mister Pym was unable to conclude the narrative because of his quote late sudden and distressing death unquote, in New York City, presumably, the circumstances of which we're supposed to know from the newspapers. In other words, Pym somehow survived being flushed down the hole—maybe he popped up again in Uganda and floated down the Nile to the Mediterranean and back to the U.S.A.—but we'll never

learn how he managed it, because he gets killed or something back home in Eighteen Thirty-eight just when he
brings the log of his voyage up to the abyss ten years before.

Go on, Suse.

Okay. The anonymous editor—really Poe the author—in
his afterword to the journal, merely tisks his tongue over
that circumstance and goes on to speculate, not about what
we're interested in—which is how in the world Pym ever got
home to write the story and whatever happened to Dirk
Peters and the canoe—but about the resemblance between
those funny-shaped caves in Tsalal and certain Ethiopian
hieroglyphs. Are you listening?

I really am. Also.

Well, the point of my story* is that the point of Poe's story
is that the point of Pym's story is this: "It is not that the end
of the voyage interrupts the writing, but that the interruption of the writing ends the voyage." Would you make love
to me now?

Susan. Do you realize . . .

Sure I do. The interruption of our voyage begins our
writing.

Oh my! Where's my pencil?

Under here. Which comes first?

They both come first! How could either come before the
other, except as one twin happens to get delivered earlier?
The doing and the telling, our writing and our loving—
they're twins. That's our story.

Twins. It closes Susan's eyes to repeat that word. But
presently she opens them, tearless now, breathes another
breath, and says If that's going to be our story, then let's
begin it at the end and end at the beginning, so we can go on
forever. Begin with our living happily ever after.

---

*A point made by Professor John T. Irwin of The Johns Hopkins
University in his book *American Hieroglyphics: the Symbol of the Egyptian
Hieroglyphics in the American Renaissance* (New Haven and London: Yale
University Press, 1980), which memorious Susan goes on now to quote
verbatim.

Fenwick says he doesn't quite get it and then cries I get it! Oh Susan!

Yet we both know that not even a story is *ever* after. Here come more storms toward Cacaway, and we've yet to retrieve that dinghy. No matter, there's light left. Happily after, Susan prompts, unfastening. Come on. Right readily her grateful mate complies; we commence as we would conclude, that they lived

> Happily after, to the end
> Of Fenwick and Susie. . . .*

---

*Susan.
 Fenn.